PRAISE FOR *MASKED PREY*

"Addictive . . . Sandford always delivers rousing action scenes, but this time he's especially good on character, too. . . . There's enough violence to satisfy bloodthirsty tastes, enough information on neofascism to give us a chill, and enough sly humor to make American teenagers and their would-be killers sound as if English were their second language."

—*The New York Times Book Review*

"This entry in the phenomenally popular Prey series will engage longtime fans with its intricate plot and have new readers backtracking through the entire series. Thoroughly involving and very timely." —*Booklist*

PRAISE FOR *NEON PREY*

"[Sandford is] his usual entertaining self in this hardcore adventure. . . . Davenport is an inspired creation."

—*The New York Times Book Review*

"The Prey novels are wildly entertaining with their clever plotting, mordant humor, and smart-ass dialogue. This one doesn't break the pattern." —*Booklist*

PRAISE FOR *TWISTED PREY*

"[Lucas Davenport] is a hero for these perilous times."

—*The New York Times Book Review*

"Thoroughly entertaining . . . A deadly cat-and-mouse game that will keep the reader turning the pages up to the exciting climax." —*Publishers Weekly* (starred review)

"One of the best in an always-strong series. Given the current geopolitical reality, it's timely, too, and the conclusion is a rockin' 'didn't see that coming' beauty."
—*Booklist*

PRAISE FOR *GOLDEN PREY*

"Sandford is among the finer writers in the genre. In *Golden Prey*, Davenport is now a U.S. Marshal scrambling across the South and Southwest, as unfamiliar with the customs as he is with the terrain. The jarring ride gets hair-raising [and] the whole trip comes to a brakes-to-the-floor screeching stop with one sly little twisting slide that will leave you grinning."
—*The Post and Courier*

"Sandford's trademark blend of rough humor and deadly action keeps the pages turning until the smile-inducing wrap-up, which reveals the fates of a number of his quirky, memorable characters." —*Publishers Weekly*

"With *Golden Prey*, Sandford successfully breathes new life into his most famous series, creating a page-turning thriller that will grab your attention and hold on until the very end. Taking Lucas Davenport away from his long-time job and dropping him in new territory was a brilliant

MASKED PREY

JOHN SANDFORD

G. P. PUTNAM'S SONS
New York

PUTNAM
— EST. 1838 —

G. P. PUTNAM'S SONS
Publishers Since 1838
An imprint of Penguin Random House LLC
penguinrandomhouse.com

Copyright © 2020 by John Sandford
Excerpt from *Ocean Prey* copyright © 2021 by John Sandford

The Library of Congress has catalogued the G. P. Putnam's Sons hardcover edition, as follows:

Names: Sandford, John, author.
Title: Masked prey / John Sandford.
Description: New York : G. P. Putnam's Sons, [2020] |
Series: A Lucas Davenport novel
Identifiers: LCCN 2020008499 (print) | LCCN 2020008500 (ebook) |
ISBN 9780525539520 (hardcover) | ISBN 9780525539537 (ebook)
Subjects: LCSH: Davenport, Lucas (Fictitious character)—Fiction. |
Political fiction. | GSAFD: Suspense fiction. | Mystery fiction.
Classification: LCC PS3569.A516 M37 2020 (print) |
LCC PS3569.A516 (ebook) | DDC 813/.54—dc23LC record available at
https://lccn.loc.gov/2020008499
LC ebook record available at https://lccn.loc.gov/2020008500

First G. P. Putnam's Sons hardcover edition / April 2020
First G. P. Putnam's Sons premium edition / March 2021
G. P. Putnam's Sons premium edition ISBN: 9780525539544

Printed in the United States of America
10 9 8 7 6 5 4 3 2 1

For our good friend,
Cynthia Klahr Johnson

CHAPTER

ONE

Audrey Coil and Blake Winston had been sexting each other for weeks.

Winston's penis, of which Coil had seen perhaps seven or eight iPhone views in a variety of penile moods, was not clearly different than the penises of a dozen other classmates that Coil had seen, circulated through the smartphones operated by girls in their final year at The Claridge School—a school with a capital-T in "The," so it wasn't *some* Claridge School, it was *The* Claridge School, of Reston, Virginia.

And Coil suspected that images of her breasts wouldn't exactly be breaking news among selected males of The Claridge School's senior class. She was correct in that. Neither Coil nor Winston was a virgin, having dispensed with that handicap in the fifth form, known in less snotty schools as eleventh grade. They hadn't yet fully engaged with each other, but were edging toward it . . . though, not yet.

All of that was neither here nor there. Right now, Coil's main preoccupation wasn't with Winston's junk, but with his totally erect Nikon Z6 camera.

THERE WERE LED light panels to her left and right, dimmed by photo umbrellas that would kill any harsh shadows. A smaller light sat directly behind her, braced on a toilet seat, providing a rim light that gave a soft glow to her auburn hair. The camera sat on a tripod in the bathroom doorway, with Winston behind it.

Winston, who was seventeen, would someday inherit a bazillion dollars; his father ran a hedge fund with offices in Birmingham, Alabama, and Manhattan. In addition, Winston was good-looking, with dark eyes and dark hair, a square chin, and a pale, flawless complexion. He was further distinguished by the fact that he was already operating a profitable after-school business in video production.

At the moment, they were jammed into Coil's bathroom on the second floor of the Coil house in Arlington, Virginia, across the Potomac from Washington, DC.

Coil was dressed in a pale blue translucent chemise that revealed a slice of boob but—carefully—no nipple, because of the Puritan constraints of Instagram. Coil carried the fleshy pink face and body of a post-pubescent party chick, a tease and a promise, a girl that former President Bill Clinton would have instantly accepted as an intern. The daughter of U.S. Senator Roberta J. "Bob" Coil of Georgia, she was another budding entrepreneur and ran her own blog, which was spread across a number of social media outlets. The blog was called Young'nHot'nDC.

She had four paying sponsors: Macon Cosmo, a line of girly cosmetics out of Macon, Georgia; Sandy Silks, an Atlanta lingerie manufacturer marketing to richie-rich teens and college-age women; LA Psyche, a maker of dance-influenced tops and bottoms for young women, based in Paris (Texas); and Anshiser Aerospace, a defense company that simply wanted to encourage young entrepreneurs with *no thought* about influencing her mother, a ranking member of the Senate Armed Services Committee.

Coil turned away from a lighted makeup mirror, looked into the camera lens, smiled, and said, "Honest to God, I wouldn't bullshit you girls: this line from Macon *blows* everything else out of the water. Why? Because the colors are *gorgeous* and smooth and best of all, they *stay put* no matter what you do to them." She stuck out a long pink tongue, nearly touched her nose with it, then drew it back over her full upper lip, gave the lens a toothy smile, and asked, "Get it?"

"DONE," WINSTON SAID. "We got it."

"About time," Coil said. That had been the fourth take for two minutes of video.

They went into her bedroom and Coil put on her

glasses—she never wore them in public—sat cross-legged on her bed, and reviewed the video on Winston's Mac-Book Pro. Coil, eyes narrowed in thought, said finally, "Y-e-a-a-a-ah, I think that's got it."

"If they don't get the point from that, they won't get it at all," Winston said. He was standing behind her, looking down at the screen. "The big question is, you're showing quite a bit of titty. Is it gonna pass with Senator Mom?"

"She doesn't care what I show as long as I don't do it in blackface," Coil said. "And how come you say *titty*? Everybody else says tits or boobs. *Titty* sounds like an old man."

Winston deepened his Southern accent: "That's what you say when you're from Alabama."

"Oh, yeah," Coil said. "That whole sweet-home thing."

"Mmm. Listen, I need to clean the video up, put a credit on it," Winston said. "I'll email the file to you tonight."

Coil nodded, then frowned and said, "I've been meaning to ask you something. The other day you and Danny were talking about that photo-matching app. I was wondering if my stuff is getting around the 'net. You know, outside my own blog. Could you . . ."

"Yeah, take about twelve seconds," Winston said. He sat next to her, took the laptop, grabbed a bunch of frames from the photo shoot that showed Coil's head from different angles, including four that were almost head-on, but with varying expressions. He went to a website called Da'Guerre, dragged the photos into an open window, and pressed Return.

He handed the laptop back to Coil as it busied itself with whatever computers do. Winston stood and eased up behind Coil, who leaned the back of her head against his crotch and started slowly rubbing. In one minute, which was about two minutes too soon for Winston, the computer produced a hundred photos of young women who looked an awful lot like Coil, including six that *were* Coil.

"Are they all mine?" Winston asked. He leaned over her shoulder and touched the screen with a fingernail. "Wait. Not this one . . . I think that's the yearbook photo from last year. Didn't you put that up on the blog?"

"Yes—when I was bitching about how bad they make you look in yearbooks . . . but what's this?" Coil asked. She reached out at the screen, pointing at one of the photos. "That's me with Molly. We're walking out of school. Where did that come from?"

"We shot that for the blog post about the see-through yoga pants, remember? You guys were talking about seeing some fat chick's ass crack in the yoga class. It was only up for a day or two."

"Yeah, but . . . what's this link . . ."

They followed the link out to a blog called 1919, a primitive piece of work that featured candid photos of what looked like kids walking along different streets, or standing outside what appeared to be schools. A single column of type ran down the left side of the screen, which they ignored for the moment.

Winston said, "What the hell?"

"Yeah, what the hell? How'd that get over here?"

"Who are these other people?" Winston asked.

Coil tapped a different photo and said, "I know that kid. That little kid, that's Senator Cherry's daughter, that's Mrs. Cherry with her. And this one . . ."

She tapped another photo. "I don't know that kid's name, but his dad is a political big shot. Maybe in the House. I talked to him at the congressional baseball game, he was sitting with the families."

"Did you blow him?" A continuing joke; he always asked, she always temporized, as if it were a possibility.

"Not yet," she said.

"Here we go . . . here's their names . . ." Winston pointed at an awkwardly placed block of type.

THEN THEY HEARD, from down below, a garage door rolling up. Coil looked up from the screen and said, "Shit! That's Mom. Open the door a crack."

She pulled off the chemise and Winston took a few seconds to appreciate her breasts as he was opening the bedroom door. They disappeared as she pulled a black T-shirt over her head, tucked it into her jeans, and said, "Go on over and start taking down the lights. Don't take them all down until she comes in. Let her see you doing it, packing up. Try to do something about your hard-on."

She checked herself for propriety. Then, when they heard a door open at the other end of the house, she shouted, "Mom! Blake and I are in my bedroom."

Senator Coil, a tall, thin, over-caffeinated woman in a blue suit, stuck her head in the bedroom door a moment later. She looked at Winston and then at her daughter, suspicion in her eyes and tone: "What's going on here?"

"Doing a lipstick ad for the blog. We needed to shoot into my makeup mirror. But! We found something really weird . . ."

The elder Coil may have had more questions about the photo shoot, and more specifically about the rapidly wilting remnants of Winston's erection, if she'd noticed that, but she shut up when Audrey Coil began pointing out the photos on the 1919 blog.

"What the heck . . . and look at this," Audrey Coil said.

The senator tapped the computer screen, the column of type. "These people . . . these people are . . . oh, no."

AS THE SENATOR from Georgia and her daughter were looking at the photographs, Randy Stokes rolled his broken-ass 2002 Pontiac Firebird into the graveled parking lot of Chuck's Wagon, a crappy country music grill outside of Warrenton, Virginia, an hour's drive west of Arlington.

Stokes had had his problems—beer, wine, bourbon,

weed, crack, methamphetamine, oxycodone, and a short but violent teenage romance with paint thinner—none of which he would have had if the country hadn't been overwhelmed with greedy, grasping blacks, Hispanics, Arabs, and a whole range of Asians who kept him from his rightful due as a white man. Except for them, he believed, he might have become a lawyer, or a golf pro.

Lately he'd been clean, back working construction; clean except for the beer and Old Crow Bourbon, $7.99 a bottle. Even the Old Crow had adopted the foreign, and therefore un-American, 750-milliliter bottle, which was probably invented by the French or some other faggots over there, instead of the traditional American fifth, which actually contained three-tenths of an ounce more whiskey than the 750-milliliter bottle, but at the same price, SO WE'RE BEING SCREWED by this foreign intrusion.

In his opinion.

He'd been told his opinions were stupid, often by people who were bigger, stronger, meaner, and smarter than he was, but this was still America, and he had a right to his opinions, didn't he?

STOKES WAS A SHORT THIN MAN, with short thinning brown hair that he cut himself with a home-barbering set that he'd found at a garage sale for six dollars. It did a good enough job, he thought, but he only had one attachment head for the electric clipper, so his hair was exactly the same length all over his head, all the time. That gave him the aspect of a hedgehog when he took off his coiled-snake "Don't Tread On Me" ball cap, which he rarely did.

Other than that, he looked pretty normal, with brown eyes, a short button nose, and a small rosebud mouth that guarded the gray teeth left behind from his adventure with methamphetamine.

Before getting out of his car, Stokes collected the pile of Diet Pepsi bottles and Hostess Fruit Pie boxes from the floor of the passenger side, crushed them against his chest so he'd only have to make one trip, and deposited them in the trash can outside the Chuck's Wagon main door. Inside, in the dim light, he spotted Elias Dunn, sitting alone at the bar with a bottle of Budweiser, looking up at the Fox News program on the overhead TV.

"Hey, El," he said, as he slid onto a stool two down from the other man. He didn't sit right next to him because that'd seem a little queer.

Dunn looked over at him—was that a flash of disdain?—and said, "Stokes."

Stokes looked around. There were ten other people in the place, he and Dunn at the short bar, a dozen tables and booths, served by one slow-moving waitress. Chuck's Wagon smelled of microwave everything: barbeque, pasta, pizza, pot pies, anything that could be stored frozen and nuked.

Stokes and Dunn had met on a construction job. Dunn was a civil engineer, and had been leading a survey crew staking out the streets and drainage for a new subdivision over toward Gainesville. Stokes had been a shovel operator—the kind of shovel that had a wooden handle—and had peppered Dunn with questions about his thirteen-thousand-dollar surveyor's total station.

Stokes, it seemed, was an enthusiastic rifleman and was fascinated by the total station, which was an optically-linked computer on a tripod. With a scope and a laser range finder, the instruments had replaced the old sur-veyor transits. They could tell you that you were, say, four hundred and twenty-four yards, two feet, nine and three-eighths inches from your target and could tell you exactly how much higher or lower you were than your target.

After talking for a few minutes out on the job site, Dunn had concluded that even if Stokes could pull a trigger, the operation of a total station was beyond his intellectual reach.

NOW STOKES WAVED at the bartender and said, "PBR," and the bartender said, "No offense, Randy, but you got the cash?"

"I do," Stokes said. He pulled a wad of sweaty one-dollar bills from his pocket and laid them on the bar, where they slowly uncurled. "That's eighteen dollars right there."

The bartender walked down the bar to get the beer, and Stokes said to Dunn, "I was over to my sister's place last night and she's got a computer and she showed me that, uh, computer place you were talking about. The one you wrote on the napkin."

Dunn looked back over at him, ran his tongue across the front of his teeth a couple of times, and said, "So, did you read it?" He was vaguely surprised that Stokes hadn't lost the napkin.

"One of the articles on it. I didn't understand it all and then my sister shoved the napkin in the garbage, by mistake, and got ketchup and shit all over it. But she'd printed the article so I could read it in bed, and she said we could type part of it back in and search for it. We did that, but the computer went to a whole different place. The article was there, and a whole bunch of other articles, but the biggest thing was pictures of kids walking on the street. Seemed weird to me."

Dunn, who'd only been about nine percent interested in anything Stokes might have to say, because Stokes was a dumbass, found his interest temporarily jacked up to thirty-five percent.

"A different website?"

"Yup. Called itself, uh . . . 19? No. 1919. With a whole bunch of articles. Including that one you gave me. And the pictures of kids."

"Porn?"

"No, no, not porn, just kids walking along," Stokes said. "Some were pretty little, some looked like they were maybe in high school."

"With the article I sent you to?" Dunn asked.

"Yup."

"You know what the website was?"

"Yup. My sister wrote it down." Stokes reached in his hip pocket, found a wadded-up piece of computer paper, and spread it on the bar.

Stokes had spent some time in a previous visit to Chuck's Wagon bending Dunn's ear about his rights as a natural-born white man and a faithful follower of country music, as well as about how his custom-assembled .223 rifle could give you a half-minute of angle all day long.

Dunn had given him the URL of a skinhead site that combined the three—the white man stuff, country music, and guns, and where you could also buy a bumper sticker that riffed on the Bureau of Alcohol, Tobacco, Firearms and Explosives: "Alcohol, Tobacco and Firearms—Sounds Like Heaven to Me."

Dunn didn't recognize the name of the website that was written on the crumpled sheet of paper, in purple ink and a woman's handwriting. In fact, there was no website name at all, only a jumble of letters, numbers, and symbols that looked like a super-secure password. He took the paper and said, "Thanks. I'll look into it," and when the bartender came back with the PBR, Dunn said, "I'll get this one," and pushed a ten-dollar bill across the bar.

Stokes said, "Well, thank you, big guy. That's real nice. I'll get the next one."

Dunn tipped up his beer, finishing it, and said, "Actually, I have to get home. Got an early job."

"Well, don't fall in no holes," Stokes said.

Dunn was an excellent civil engineer and didn't fall in no holes and didn't appreciate hole-falling humor.

He nodded at Stokes, a tight nod—everything about him was tight, *really tight*, screwed-down tight, so fuckin' tight he squeaked when he walked—and he marched out of the bar in his high-topped Doc Martens 1460s, and, from Stokes's perspective, disappeared into the afternoon.

The bartender, who was looking up at the titsy chick reading the news on the Fox channel, glanced after him as he went through the door, and muttered to himself, "Asshole."

DUNN DROVE HOME, to a neatly kept, two story house on the edge of Warrenton, for which he'd paid seven hundred thousand dollars. He lived alone, his wife having departed six years earlier, leaving him with a red-striped cat, which, like his wife, eventually disappeared and was not missed. He did miss the eight hundred thousand in savings she'd taken with her, but he did all right, putting twenty percent of his income into savings every year, toward an early retirement.

With his tight black combat boots, his tight jeans, his tapered work shirts, his workout body, and blond hair cut in a white sidewall, Dunn looked like a comic-book Nazi. He wasn't a comic-book anything and he definitely was not a Nazi—Nazis were more dumb guys like Stokes who went marching around and saluting and carrying shields and baseball bats and generally behaving like fools.

Dunn wasn't a Nazi, but he *was* a fascist.

He went to political lectures in the evenings, when they caught his interest, and there was always something going on in DC; and he knew a few people and placed some money where he thought it might do political good, used for intelligent publications aimed at influential people. *Very* carefully placed the money: being known as a fascist would not help business.

After his wife left, Dunn had moved out of the master bedroom and into a smaller one, converting the master into an office and library. When he got home from Chuck's Wagon and his talk with Stokes, he went to his computer and typed in the URL address Stokes's sister had written on the paper. The website popped up: 1919 in large type, and in much smaller type, beneath that, the words, "Thy Honor Is Thy Loyalty."

Dunn immediately recognized the motto as one used by the Nazi SS. At first he ignored the photos on the page and instead flipped through the articles that ran on the website. He recognized several of them from his quiet lurking on neo-Nazi and white supremacist sites.

At first, he didn't understand. There was a space to post responses, but no way to directly address the owners of the site. The articles were routine and all over the place, some from Nazi or KKK fruitcakes, others that might charitably be regarded merely as ultra-conservative. It was one of the worst websites he'd ever seen.

He then turned to the photographs, and they mystified him. Pictures of the children of prominent politicians, but nothing to explain why they were there.

Still mystified, he went to his bedroom, stripped off

his clothes, pulled on a clean black latex bodysuit and a pair of ankle socks and walked down to his garage.

The garage had three stalls. He kept his Ford F-150 in one and a Ford Mustang in the middle. His ex-wife, when she was living there, had occupied the third stall with her Lexus, but when she'd left, he'd put up a studs-and-Sheetrock wall separating his two stalls from the third, painted the walls white, and built himself a home gym.

The gym was based around a Peloton bike for cardiovascular exercise, racks of free weights for strength workouts, and a wall of mirrors. He rode the bike five days a week for forty minutes or an hour. For the weight work, he'd divided his body's muscle groups in half, and worked each zone three days a week, on alternate days.

He did the bike first, pulling on the biking shoes, putting on the earphones and heart monitor, mounting the bike, bringing up a workout program, then following one of the tight-bodied women on the video screen, who pushed him up hills and more hills, standing, sitting, blowing off five hundred calories, cranking until his leg muscles were screaming at him.

Thinking about that 1919 website.

When he got off the bike, his body pouring sweat, he walked back into the house and drank a protein drink, moved around until the lactic acid had burned off in his legs.

When he was feeling loose and supple again, he went back to the gym, rolled out a yoga mat, set the alarm on his iPhone, sat and closed his eyes and meditated for exactly twenty minutes. When the alarm went off, he rolled onto his stomach, used the iPhone as a timer, and did a "plank" for three minutes, building core strength. That done, he rolled up the mat and went to the free weights.

Thinking about that website.

The workout took an hour. When he finished, he pulled off the bodysuit and the Nike weightlifting shoes, and checked himself in the mirror, nude, top to toe, looking for any extraneous fat. And, truth be told, he liked looking at himself. He posed, flashing his six-pack and biceps. He was pumped, his muscles inflated and burning again: strong, pale, perfectly cut.

If his ex-wife could see him now, he thought, she'd flop down on her back and spread her legs. Bitch.

He did poses for ten minutes, then walked back through the house to his bedroom, stepped into the attached bath, looked at himself in the mirror for a moment, then masturbated into the sink, watching his own crystalline blue eyes the whole time.

All done, he showered, dried himself, dressed again.

Feeling perfect.

Thinking about the website.

THEN—IN A FLASH—he understood.

The website was a message in a bottle, thrown out to whoever might find it, and might be willing to act on it.

He'd been looking for something like this, he realized. He'd been looking for a long time, without realizing it. Right there, in that cryptic setting, was a whole action plan and an invitation to anyone who could understand it.

He leaned back in his desk chair, staring at the ceiling.

This was it.

He was going in.

CHAPTER

TWO

Lucas Davenport took a waking breath and rolled over to look at the nightstand clock: 6:55. He dimly remembered setting the alarm for seven o'clock, so he had five minutes. If he turned it off, he might sleep for three hours, so he didn't.

Weather, his wife, was still asleep beside him, which meant that it was the weekend, the only days she slept in. He rolled away from her toward the clock side of the bed, winced from the dull ache in his chest and settled in for the last four minutes, eyes half open, looking up at the ceiling. Trying to nail the exact day of the week: Sunday? Sunday.

On Sunday, he had to get on an airplane. Everything was coming into focus.

Lucas had been shot the previous spring. With September half gone, he was still feeling after-effects;

which, he supposed, was better than the alternative. He was working hard to get back in shape, running, lifting, punching a heavy bag. Everybody said how good he looked.

When he checked himself in the mirror, though, in his own eyes he looked gray, and too thin. Not wiry, but something over toward emaciated. His cheekbones had been blunt, and were now knife-edged; the crow's feet at his eyes were like cuts; his watch was too loose at his wrist. He'd lost chunks of the hockey defenseman muscle he'd carried since college and getting it back, at his age, two years past fifty, was tough.

He wanted the weight. The morning scale said he was at 192, and for a cop who enjoyed the occasional fight, two hundred pounds was a good starting point.

Now something was happening in Washington, DC. Whatever it was, it wasn't good, and at the moment he wasn't in top form. Or maybe, his wife suggested, his body was fine, but his brain was still screwed up.

LUCAS HAD BEEN barbequing steaks in his backyard the night before for a couple of cop friends and their wives, when Elmer Henderson had called. Henderson was a U.S. senator from Minnesota, a former governor, a onetime vice-presidential candidate (he lost), and one of the richest men in the state.

Henderson had a ten-thousand-square-foot cabin on his own private six-hundred-acre lake, staff of six, up in the Northwoods, when he needed something simpler and more primitive than his life in the Twin Cities and Washington, DC. He had a dozen plaid shirts and numerous pairs of carefully ironed and faded jeans for the cabin life, along with several pairs of buffalo-hide loafers. Lucas had once spent a weekend at the cabin and he'd peeked in Henderson's main closet—because he was a cop, and therefore somewhat curious, or snoopy, take your pick. Henderson's Jockey shorts, Lucas believed, after a surreptitious inspection, were both ironed *and* starched.

Henderson also had a smaller, more discreet cabin in Wisconsin, which he called "The Hideout," where he and the other Big Cigars from the Twin Cities cut their political deals. Lucas had been there, as well . . . cutting a deal.

LUCAS WAS RICH HIMSELF, but not rich like the people who'd inherited wealth. He didn't assume its presence, because he'd made his money during a time when he wasn't working as a cop. He'd been run out of the Minneapolis Police Department after he'd beaten a pimp who'd church-keyed one of his sources. The beating had neither cured the pimp of his inclinations, nor the woman of her facial scars, but had made a point that had resonated on Minneapolis streets, at least for a while.

While he was in college, and later, working was a cop, he'd had a sideline as a developer of role-playing games. None of them got as big as *Dungeons & Dragons*, but they'd sold well enough to buy him a used Porsche 911.

Then computers came along and the in-person role-playing games began to die. That occurred as he was being pushed out of the Minneapolis Police Department. With the new 9-1-1 systems then coming online, it occurred to him that American police departments could use role-playing games for their 9-1-1 systems, giving their personnel practice in responding to emergencies before they had to handle the real thing.

He wrote the simulations, found a college computer freak who could do the programming, and the resulting Davenport Simulations, which he'd sold at exactly the right time, had made him wealthy.

But not rich like Henderson.

As F. Scott Fitzgerald didn't say, but perhaps should have, "The *very* rich are different than you and me." And as Ernest Hemingway didn't say, but probably would have liked to have said, "Yes, they have more money."

If the exchange had actually occurred, Lucas thought, Fitzgerald would have had the better of it. In his experience, many of the very rich never really touched the sides or the bottom of the world, of life, but were cocooned from it, even when they wound up dead with needles in their arms.

Henderson was a prime example of the privileges of inherited wealth. Still, he and Lucas were friends on some level, and Henderson had twice been in a position to give Lucas something that he wanted but couldn't get on his own: the authority to hunt.

After Lucas lost his job with Minneapolis, and after he made his money, he'd gotten, with Henderson's support, a political appointment as an agent with the Minnesota Bureau of Criminal Apprehension and a new badge. When the time ran out on that appointment, Henderson and another U.S. senator, Porter Smalls, had ushered him into a job as a deputy U.S. Marshal.

And they'd seen to it that he had the freedom to hunt, as long as he performed the occasional political task.

"I'LL SEND A PLANE," Henderson told Lucas, because of course he would. Sending a plane didn't mean much more to him than giving a cop cab fare. "In fact, I already sent it, if nobody's screwed up, or my wife didn't sneak off to Manhattan. You need to be here tomorrow morning."

"Tomorrow's Sunday," Lucas said.

"I'll talk to the bishop and tell him you're excused," Henderson said.

"Ah, Jesus, you know I got shot, I'm still in recovery mode . . ."

"I know all about that," Henderson said. "You weren't hurt so bad you didn't run off to Nevada and kill somebody."

"I didn't kill anybody," Lucas grumbled.

"Okay—you managed the killing. Well done, in my opinion. The world has enough cannibals," Henderson said. "Anyway, you're all healed up. My office, tomorrow, one o'clock. That should allow you to sleep in until eight tomorrow morning. Or seven. Whatever."

"Eight? Listen, Elmer, I never . . ." But Henderson was gone. Here was the rich man's assumption: make a call and the guy shows up on time, with a necktie and polished shoes.

WHEN THEIR GUESTS HAD DEPARTED, and the kids were soundly asleep, and the dishes washed, Lucas and Weather had had one of the snarly disagreements common to long-lasting marriages, and they had gone to bed a little angry with each other. The trouble came down to Henderson's request and Lucas's occasional political missions. The argument started there, compounded by Weather's unease with the increasing levels of violence in Lucas's job, and had moved to a more general political dispute.

Weather, a surgeon, was an unabashed liberal. Because they had much more money than they really needed, Weather had freed herself from the usual routine of plastic and micro surgeries. She no longer looked for clients, but spent much of her time going from one hospital to the next, doing necessary surgical repairs on indigent cases.

There was more work of that kind than she could handle and she was constantly exposed to a population that was unable to care for itself—including people literally driven into bankruptcy by medical costs, who'd had to choose between eating and medical care.

The American medical system was broken, she thought, and needed to be fixed. She'd gone to a convention of the American Society of Plastic Surgeons in Los Angeles, and had been traumatized by the sight of thousands of street people, including small children, living under bridges and viaducts.

"Worse than anything we had in the Great Depression," she said.

Lucas was not so liberal. He believed that no matter how much money or time you spent on the poor, there'd always be people at the bottom unable to care for themselves, and that was simply a fact to be lived with. Also, some people really *needed* to be shot, and, if only wounded, shot again.

"Your mistake," he'd told Weather, after one beer too many, and to his regret, "is that you characterize everything as a problem. A problem is something that can be solved. Some things aren't problems—they're situations. A situation can't be solved, it just is. Medical care is a bottomless hole. We could spend every nickel everyone makes in the country on medical care, and it still wouldn't be enough. If a guy thinks he's dying and somebody else is paying for all his care, why shouldn't he ask for the very best for the very longest time possible, right into the grave? And they do. We can't afford that, sweetheart."

"We can afford a lot more than we do. You can't possibly think . . ."

And so on. Snarling, just a bit.

SO THEY'D GONE TO BED GRUMPY. Lucas had packed that night, woke, groaning, at 6:55, and lay thinking about getting shot, and about the problems of the street people, until the alarm was ten seconds from erupting. He reached out and clicked it off, rolled over, and put his arm around Weather. "Love you, babe."

Weather muttered into her pillow, "Thank you. Let me know when you're out of the bathroom."

"You still pissed off at me?"

"No. I got over it at three o'clock when I realized I was completely right."

"God bless you, Weather. You're a good person."

LUCAS GOT CLEANED UP, dressed himself in a blue, lightweight wool suit from Figueroa & Prince, a tailor in Washington, with just a bit of extra room on the left-side hip to accommodate his gun. Black oxfords from George Cleverley, a Brioni shirt in pale blue stripes, and an Hermès tie completed the ensemble. He checked himself in a three-way mirror and thought that the soft colors of the suit, shirt, and tie did nothing but emphasize his grayness, putting colored threads on a scarecrow.

Weather, out of the bathroom and dressed in a T-shirt and underpants, turned him around and said, "You look great."

"Not gray?"

"Lucas . . . you don't have all the weight back yet, but you look good. Really good. Maybe a year or two younger, even . . ."

Weather rousted the kids from bed and they all had cereal together.

The kids ignored them, mostly, when Weather pushed him on the Washington job: "I think you're dealing with the devil here. Yes, Henderson, he might not actually be the devil himself, but they're Facebook friends. Lucas, he could make you do something crooked."

"No, he couldn't."

"Yes, he could," Weather insisted. "You wouldn't realize it at the time. It's like the old boiling frog story . . ."

"I know that story," Lucas said.

Weather went on anyway. "You put a frog in a pot in cool water and slowly heat it up until it's boiling," she said. "The frog never feels the change in temperature and winds up boiling to death. That's what happens with politicians like Henderson. Or Porter Smalls, for that matter. You get in the pot with them and when you try to get out, you find out you've got a dozen felonies around your neck."

Their son Sam asked, "Can I get a frog?"

In the end, Lucas kissed each of them and was out

the door at 7:40, at the fixed-base operator at 7:55, where the jet was ready to roll.

LUCAS HATED TO FLY; was frightened of it. He knew all the numbers, how much less likely you were to die in a plane crash than an auto accident or even on a train, but it made no difference. It made no difference because he was not in control of the plane. A friend who was also a shrink had explained that to him, and he'd thought, *kiss my ass*, but hadn't said it aloud because the shrink was also a nun he'd known since childhood.

In any case, after two hours and fifty minutes of abject fear, the plane had landed safely and he was climbing into a taxicab at National, across the Potomac from the capital.

"Watergate Hotel."

The cabbie looked over his shoulder, checked his suit, shirt, and tie: "You a big shot?"

"No. I'm a flunky."

"Huh. You don't have that flunky look," the cabbie said.

"I do carry a gun," Lucas said.

"That's disturbing. I don't have much cash."

"Yeah, well, I'm a U.S. Marshal."

"Okay, then. Say, how about them Nationals?" the cabbie asked, as they pulled into traffic.

"I don't want to hear about it," Lucas said. "You make a living by beating up on teams like the Marlins. That's like beating up on a troop of Girl Scouts."

"Okay, so you don't want to talk."

"I don't mind talking, but let's talk about something interesting. How's the President doing?"

"Ah, man . . ." Then he went on for a while, at two hundred words a minute, sputtering through the capital traffic.

SENATOR HENDERSON'S OFFICE had called the Watergate and had emphasized that an early check-in was no problem, and the hotel had agreed that it really wasn't any kind of a problem at all. A desk clerk with a tennis player's tan and perfect white teeth told Lucas that a car was waiting in the hotel parking garage and should he summon it?

"I'll call," Lucas said, and headed up to his room.

He unpacked, hung another suit and two sport coats in the closet, with five shirts, washed his face and hands, and called for the car, which turned out to be a Music Express limo—and he thought, as he climbed into the backseat, there'd be no government record of this pickup. The driver took him through a Starbucks on E Street, where Lucas got a blueberry muffin, a hot chocolate, and a *Washington Post*. A quick look at the *Post* suggested nothing that Henderson might want to talk to him about.

LUCAS HAD THE DRIVER drop him three blocks from the Senate Office Building and tipped him twenty bucks for his wait and the ride. The driver and limo would hover during the meeting and pick him up afterward.

The day was warm with an icy-bright-blue sky overhead, a good September midday in Washington, DC, heading toward a high in the low 80s. As he walked along Constitution Avenue, still sipping on the hot chocolate, the *Post* rolled and tucked under his arm, a couple of women smiled at him; or perhaps at his suit. Anyway, he smiled back. Joggers were out in force, and young women pushing strollers and boys with dogs.

One of the nannies tracked him with her eyes as they passed, and nodded.

Maybe, he thought, he wasn't looking *that* bad.

THE RUSSELL SENATE Office Building did look bad, like America's largest old post office, the aging limestone façade now resembling poorly laid concrete block. Lucas checked through security, where he was met by one of Henderson's staffers, the security process eased by the fact that Lucas's .40-caliber Walther PPQ was back in the hotel safe.

The staffer, whose name Lucas thought was Jaydn, or possibly Jared or Jordon or Jeremy—he didn't quite catch it—and who was wearing jeans, a nubby white-cotton shirt open at the throat, and cordovan loafers (no socks), led him through the building to Henderson's office and then to the inner office, where Henderson was waiting with the other Minnesota senator, Porter Smalls, and an FBI agent named Jane Chase.

As Lucas was ushered in, Henderson looked at the aide and said, "Hey, Jasper, thanks—I'll catch you later."

In other words, "Don't let the door hit you in the ass." When Jasper was gone, they all shook hands and Lucas asked, "If Jane's here, why am I?"

"We'll explain that," Smalls said. "Jane's here to outline what the FBI has done so far and why they can't do much more."

"Why can't you do much more?" Lucas asked Chase, as they all settled into chairs.

"Because no crime has been committed," Chase said. "Not yet."

"And because word of what was going on would inevitably leak, even with Jane's thumb in the dike," Henderson added.

Henderson was a tall, slender, fair-complected man, with longish blond hair and blond eyebrows, who'd hoped that the vice presidency might be a stepping stone to the top job. He and the presidential candidate had lost their race, although they'd won the majority of the popular vote. He was a Democrat, and liberal even for that party.

Porter Smalls's stature reflected his name: he was short, five-seven or five-eight, thin, white-haired, and tough as a lugnut. He was a Republican and extremely conservative, though he and Henderson were longtime friends, going back to their wealthy childhoods in Minnesota. Lucas had worked with both of them.

Jane Chase was an FBI bureaucrat, an effective one.

She'd been shot in the leg the last time Lucas had been in DC. She was middle-sized, outfitted in a navy pantsuit, carefully coifed and dressed, attractive but not cute—didn't want to get above yourself in the federal bureaucracy—and very smart.

Lucas: "Okay. What's going on?"

HENDERSON AND SMALLS looked at Chase, who said, "I trust nothing here is being recorded. Or noted. Even on paper."

"Absolutely not," Henderson said. "Say what you think."

Chase turned to Lucas: "Senator Roberta Coil—"

"Never heard of her," Lucas interjected.

"—of Georgia, has an ambitious seventeen-year-old daughter named Audrey who runs her own blog called Young'nHot'nDC. She has several sponsors who pay her to hustle their products—cosmetics, lingerie, yoga togs, fighter jets, and so on."

"Fighter jets?" Somehow, fighter jets seemed out of place on the list of sponsors.

"Her mother's on the Senate Armed Services Committee," Henderson said.

"Ah."

Chase: "Anyway, Audrey has a friend named Blake Winston. Blake wants to be a movie director. He's also seventeen, they go to the same school, and Blake makes Audrey's blog videos. A few days ago, they were making a video and Audrey asked Blake if he knew how to track down faces on the internet, using a face-matching app. She wanted to know if word was getting around about her blog. He did know about such an app. He loaded several photos of Audrey into it, clicked Return, and up popped a website that calls itself 1919."

"Like the year after World War I," Smalls said.

"Yes, but that title only comes up when you get to the site. The actual name of the site is a series of letters and numbers, plus dot-com. A code that you'd have to know to find it, unless you found it like these kids did, going in sideways with the photo search. In other words, it was hidden, and they only found it by accident. When they clicked on the link, Audrey found a photo of herself walking out of her school and also spotted a couple of other photos of people she knew—a daughter of another senator and the son of a congressman."

Lucas: "Huh. Why 1919?"

"There was some accompanying text," Chase said. "Apparently 'nineteen' refers to the letter S, the nineteenth letter of the alphabet. In that case, 1919 would be . . ."

"SS," Lucas said. "That's not good. No offense, Porter."

Henderson snorted and Porter Smalls said, mildly, "Fuck you."

"To go on," Chase said. "It appears to be a publication of a heretofore-unknown neo-Nazi group. What's particularly disturbing is that they go to extraordinary lengths to conceal the origin of the photos and the text.

Also, the Nazi Schutzstaffel, as you probably know, was both paramilitary and military."

"I didn't know that," Lucas said. "History wasn't my strong suit."

"Yeah, your strong suit was a pair of hockey breezers," Smalls said.

Chase ventured an eye roll. "Both military and paramilitary. Armed, in any case, and dedicated to violence, as are most of the articles on the site. Our analysts say we can't do a word-match analysis on the articles, to find out who wrote them, because they were all cut-and-paste, taken from a variety of white supremacist websites. They were not written by any one person. Actually, and this can't go any farther than here, one of the articles was written by one of our agents attempting to penetrate a white supremacist organization."

Smalls said, "There you go. Taxpayer money well spent."

"No direct threats?" Lucas asked.

"No, other than the fact that each photo has a cut-line, identifying the kid and his or her parent and the school the kid goes to," Chase said. "The lack of threats is almost as disturbing as the Nazi connection. We've kept this very quiet inside the Bureau, but one of my associates has argued, convincingly, I think, that whoever is doing this is running a kind of distributed-cell organization. Nobody issues or takes orders, so you can't pin down a chain of command, but everybody is marching to the same drummer. It's possible that not even the organizer would know who his followers are.

All the readers would know is, 'Here are some targets, if you want to do something about them.' Then, if somebody attacks one of the kids, the organizer—who probably doesn't even know the attacker—might begin with extortion of the other parents."

Henderson: "They chum the water with these photos and when and if an attack occurs, it's hard, if not impossible, to pin down the original responsibility. You might get the body, the shooter, but you don't get the brain."

"Have you checked the ISPs?" Lucas asked.

Chase was already shaking her head. "Of course. Nothing there. The internet service provider is in Sweden, one of the confidential sites. A month or so after the website was set up, the photos were all posted at once and came in from a Starbucks. There were some video cameras in the neighborhood, but not right at Starbucks. Our analysts have spent hours looking at the local videos, trying to spot somebody who might be our guy. No luck so far."

"License tags?"

"Yes, there was one camera that did a good job on tags, but we came up dry on that, too. We did all the routine. We continue to think about it and do more work. Explore new possibilities. Some senators decided . . . perhaps we needed something a little more off the wall. Like you. Whoever did this is apparently internet savvy and security aware, so the regular routine, however intense it is, may not turn them up."

"What happened to the website? Is it still up?"

"Yes, it is. As I said, the site doesn't come up as 1919-dot-com, or anything like it. You could never find it just by looking. It doesn't have much traffic and we're hoping that the people running it will post more photos—give us an idea of who's running it, where the photos are coming from. The parents wanted it taken down, of course, but reluctantly agreed to let us leave it up, at least for now. If we don't leave it up, it could be redone under another password-like URL and we might never find it again. We contacted the ISP, and after some back-and-forth, the Swedish government whispered into the owner's ear and we were informed unofficially that the site was paid for, in advance for two years, with a Western Union check. The check was bought here in Washington at a bodega that caters to immigrant Hispanics. No cameras. No ID possible."

Lucas said, "Maybe there'll be no attack. Maybe the whole idea is to intimidate. Have there been any demands for any particular kind of action?"

Smalls: "No. Maybe I should say, 'Not yet.' Or 'We don't know.' With the Senate divided so closely, shifting one or two votes could change the way the world works. You might never know that a vote was the result of extortion. Most senators would never admit to caving in."

"Are the kids protected?"

"They are now. Not 24/7, but the Secret Service has assigned agents to watch them in and out of school, and to run checks on the environments around them, the places they come and go," Chase said. "They're not covered like the President, but closely enough that a shooter would probably be detected unless he was very sophisticated. We're looking at license plates coming and going around the schools, to see if anything pops."

"What do you want from me?" Lucas asked.

Chase said, "You've developed a reputation in both the House and Senate as somebody who can take care of business quietly and effectively. I already know too much about that, from last year, and I really don't want to know any more. If your, mmm, investigation is successful, the Bureau would be ready to listen to what you have to say. If, hopefully, what you say points to an actionable crime. There's no crime in shooting photos of people in public: anyone can do it."

Henderson: "As background, one of the kids in the photos is the son of Burton Cherry from Colorado. He knew about you and that you were tight with Porter and myself. He got with the other people whose kids were on the website and they asked Porter and me to call you."

Smalls: "They don't like the FBI's basic attitude: no crime, nothing to see here."

Chase turned to Smalls: "That's not our attitude, Senator. We understand the situation, but we're handcuffed by the law and also by the fact that, realistically, we know there are leaks, even in the Bureau. We've worked with Lucas before, to our mutual advantage, and appreciate his discretion."

Lucas said, "I'll look at it. I need to see what the FBI has done."

Chase took a thumb drive from her jacket pocket and tossed it to him. "There's a program on there, encrypted, called Sesame. Easy to use. Open it, and you'll see all the photos and docs we've got, all of our reports. About as thick as three Bibles. Please don't export the stuff to anywhere else. When I get back to the Bureau, I'll send the key to your cell phone. Do you have a password vault on your phone?"

"Yes."

"Copy the key to your vault, then erase the message," Chase said. "You'll need the key every time you open the files unless you export them. Don't do that."

"I'll have to interview this girl . . . and her boyfriend, the photographer," Lucas said.

"Not a problem. They know you're coming," Chase said. "They don't know much, though. We did replicate their facial-recognition search, with better software, and turned up the same result."

"How many people, kids . . ."

"There are six children on the website, ranging in age from elementary school to college. Nobody older, although a lot of senators have older children. We think that's basically because all of these kids are going to school in the Washington area, so the photographer is probably from the area. The Starbucks, where the website was loaded, is right across the river, in a shopping center across I-395 from the Pentagon," Chase said. "All the kids, but one, are children of senators, all the senators but one are Democrats. One kid is the son of a

New Jersey member of the House, also a Democrat. A very senior member of the House. I could give you more details, but you'll get them all when you read the file. Names, ages, addresses, along with a commentary from our analysts."

"None of the kids were aware of the photo, or the contact?"

"No, they weren't. None of them felt a thing. Oh: most of the photos were apparently taken surreptitiously, but Audrey Coil's was lifted off her website—a photo that showed her outside her school with a friend."

LUCAS ASKED CHASE, "If I have questions, I should call you?"

"Yes. Nobody else. Although your friend, Deputy Director Mallard, has been read into this situation."

"You're friends with Mallard now?" Lucas asked.

"The deputy director and I have developed an excellent working relationship," Chase said. "He seems to have taken an interest in my career."

"Fascinating," Lucas said.

Chase blinked at him, then turned away.

Henderson leaned forward and rapped on his desk with his knuckles: "Lucas, we need to shut this down before somebody gets hurt. If somebody does get hurt . . . a kid . . . the shit will hit the fan."

"If somebody does get hurt, do you think we could blame the FBI?" Lucas asked.

Chase showed a tight smile. The last time they'd worked together, Lucas had seen signs that she had a sense of humor, even if it was a *Washington* sense of humor: "If that were going to happen, Lucas, do you think *you'd* be here?" she asked.

CHAPTER
THREE

There was more talk, which came down to a long series
of warnings about not involving the two senators or the
FBI in anything questionable. Lucas said he'd try not to
do that, which led to more warnings and pleadings.

"Then I'm like that *Mission: Impossible* thing, where
the secretary will disavow any knowledge of me?"

"So fast your head will spin off—although it'd probably be a deputy assistant undersecretary in charge of
cover-ups," Henderson said. "You're not nearly important enough to be disavowed by an actual secretary."

Lucas and Chase left at the same time, with Lucas
promising to provide regular updates to Henderson and
Smalls. When they were alone, leaving the building,
Chase said, "Don't get too detailed when you're updat-
ing the senators. Both of them are close to the local

media. If we nail these people, there'll be some credit to be given. Time on the CNN and Fox talk shows."

"Which might otherwise go to the FBI?"

"I didn't say that," she said. "I'd prefer that nobody got any credit at all. We don't need to plant this extortion idea in anybody else's head."

"Got it," Lucas said.

Chase had planned to get an Uber back to the Hoover Building, but Lucas still had the limo on call and offered her a ride: "If you know where we could get a sandwich around here, I'd like to talk for a few more minutes."

She knew a salad place that was open on Sunday, three or four blocks away, and they walked there and got salads and Diet Cokes and sat next to the window to eat. Lucas said, "I'll look at the files for the details, but tell me what you *feel* about them."

"There's a load of information there. Most of it is useless," she said, efficiently slicing through an asparagus spear. She popped the asparagus into her mouth, chewed, swallowed, and continued: "This whole situation has an odd feeling about it. There's something going on that we haven't been able to figure out, but it's not as straightforward as it looks. That's what I feel about it."

"Anybody I should pay attention to, in particular?"

"A Nazi named Charles Lang. Charlie Lang. He denies being a Nazi, but he is. He calls himself, and I quote, 'an expert on later forms of National Socialism.'

He inherited the Nazi gene and a lot of money from his father and grandfather, who also carried the gene. His grandfather made a fortune in aviation investments before and during World War II—he spent a lot of time in Germany during the Hitler years, knew the man himself—and was associated with Charles Lindbergh back in the 1930s and '40s. Charlie's pretty slick, well dressed, has a degree from Georgetown in international relations. Gets interviewed from time to time by the cable news outfits, has had some TV training. He claims his extremist contacts are part of his scholarly research, but it goes deeper than that. Read the paper, you'll see."

"Is he involved in this website?"

"Probably not. When we went to him, our agents said he appeared to be genuinely surprised by the site. Maybe a little sexually excited. He's been stirring around, trying to make contact with 1919. Putting the word out."

"You've been watching him?"

"No, but we've been interviewing everybody we think might possibly know something about 1919. A couple of people said they've been contacted by Lang. So he's out there, looking. Whether he's found anything, we don't know."

"I'll talk to him," Lucas said.

CHASE KNEW THAT Lucas had been shot the previous spring, and she'd been shot herself a year earlier while on a case with Lucas. "You're a dangerous guy to hang around with. We're the only two cops I know who've been shot."

Like Lucas, she hadn't entirely recovered. The wound had torn up connective tissue in the hamstring at the back of her thigh, and the scar tissue lacked the flexibility of the original muscle. She didn't limp, but it still hurt if she jogged too far and when she went skiing.

Lucas had been shot three times in his career: "I specialized in violent crime. That was my main interest. The one that came closest to killing me was a little girl who nailed me in the throat with a piece-of-crap street .22 . . ."

He'd been shot in a remote area of the Wisconsin Northwoods, in the throat, and almost drowned in his own blood, but a surgeon who'd been nearby sliced open his trachea with a pocketknife to free up an airway.

"You probably still owe him, then," Chase said. "And always will."

"Actually, it was a *her*, and she's gotten paid back with interest," Lucas said. "I married her and she's been in sexual heaven ever since."

"More than I needed to know," Chase said. She frowned. "Maybe I should call her and ask what that's like."

They talked some more about 1919 and watched people come and go and Lucas called the limo and dropped her at the Hoover Building. As she got out of the car, she said: "Talk to me, Lucas. Daily, if anything

is happening. When do you think you'll be out working?"

"I'll call this girl and her boyfriend today, see if I
can talk to them this afternoon. I'll want to read your
stuff on Lang before I talk to him. He seems to be the
best bet for a way into it."

"You take care," she said. "And *talk* to me."

LUCAS GAVE THE DRIVER the address of a Hertz
dealer where he'd reserved a car. They had to backtrack
a bit through Washington, but Lucas gave the driver
another twenty dollars and left Hertz in a black Cadillac CTS, a long German-looking sedan with a lot of
technology he'd never use.

At the Watergate, he left the car in the garage and
went up to his room. His phone dinged as he stepped
inside, and when he opened it, he found the code for
the FBI files Chase had given him. He plugged the
thumb drive into his laptop, opened the only app on
the drive, and was prompted for the code. He entered
it, the files popped up as Chase had promised, simple
PDFs in the shell of the encryption app. He put the
code into his phone's password vault and erased Chase's
message.

There were a lot of files, but the shell had a search
function and he dropped in the names of Audrey Coil,
Blake Winston, and Charles Lang. That gave him contact information for all three, which he noted in a fresh
pocket-sized Moleskine notebook.

He read for two hours, encountered quite a few facts and, as Chase had suggested, most of them were useless. Some of it was FBI clip-and-paste investigation files of neo-Nazi, white supremacist, anti-immigration, Klan, prison-based, biker-based, and states' rights hate groups, along with a few pro-Israeli and Islamic radical groups. Most of them had few members; some of them, only one, and so didn't even qualify as a "group." Even some of the single-member organizations produced publications, so could be involved in a website.

There was nothing substantial on the 1919 group, though there was considerable speculation. The lead agent looking at the group suggested that there might be only one person behind it, or perhaps two or three—". . . unless the group is tightly controlled with heavy security, which would suggest that they may be unusually dangerous."

Lucas skimmed a dozen files, decided the daylight hours would be better spent talking to Coil and Winston. He could always read in the middle of the night.

COIL AND WINSTON lived within a few miles of each other in Virginia. Lucas was somewhat familiar with McLean, where Winston lived, from the case he'd worked the year before. Coil lived on the north side of Arlington, the big Virginia city directly across the Potomac from Washington. Both were expecting calls from him.

The call to Coil went to the personal phone of Senator Roberta Coil, who picked up on the third ring and said, simply, "Yes?"

Lucas introduced himself, said he'd spoken to Henderson and Smalls, and asked if her daughter would be available for an interview that evening. "She is, of course, Marshal. She really doesn't have much to say about it. I'm sure you've read the FBI interview, but I understand you'd like to get a feel for the various personalities yourself."

"I would," Lucas said.

"We're home now. I have a small party beginning at seven o'clock, if we could get it done before then."

"I'm at the Watergate. I could probably be there in an hour or so," Lucas said.

"We will wait for you."

The connection for Winston also went to a parent, his mother, whose name was Mary Ellen, and who said her son was out with friends, making a movie. "I'll call him. I can have him here whenever you say."

And he called Lang, again on a personal phone. Like Coil, he answered with a "Yes?" He would be available Monday morning, at his home in Potomac, Maryland. "I hope the FBI people haven't confused you. You won't actually be interviewing a Nazi, a white supremacist, an alt-right person. I'm a scholar who studies those groups."

"I understand," Lucas said. A little suck-up, then: "I'm pleased that you're willing to share information with us."

"Always happy to help the government," Lang said. Lucas coughed, and took down his address.

FROM THE WATERGATE garage to the Coil home in Arlington was a fifteen-minute drive, out of the monuments of the District into a leafy, routine-looking fifties or sixties suburban neighborhood now showing its age.

Lucas had worked with a half dozen senators in his time as a marshal and had come to believe that the Senate was a club for the uber-wealthy. Roberta Coil was apparently not one of those. She lived in a nice-enough, but not elaborate mid-century red-brick house set on a bank in north Arlington, with a tuck-under garage and a curling set of flagstone steps leading up to the front door.

The FBI's background material on her daughter, Audrey, said that Senator Coil and Audrey lived in Arlington, while the senator's husband, the owner of a grass-development company, stayed at home in Tifton, Georgia. The file noted that the grass involved was for lawns and golf courses, not for smoking.

Lucas parked in the street and climbed the bank to the house and was about to ring the bell when the door popped open. Senator Coil was a tall woman, with an angular face and dark hair. She wore a black dress suitable for a party, and careful, almost bland makeup. She smiled and said, "Marshal Davenport? I'm Bob. Come in. Audrey's in her room, I'll call her."

The house smelled like bakery and Lucas could hear somebody banging around a stove in the kitchen, which was down a hallway off a large and sparsely furnished living room—a room designed for people to stand in, at a party, rather than to lounge in. Coil climbed some stairs and disappeared down a hallway, calling for her daughter.

Lucas perched on a narrow couch, looked around; there were built-in bookshelves and the books themselves, biographies, histories, and the more serious kind of political tomes, appeared to be little used, as if they'd come with the shelves.

"HERE WE ARE."

Coil reappeared, trailed by a pretty teenager in a loose silky blouse and fashionable denim boy-shorts with a string of oversized buttons on the fly. Like her mother, Audrey Coil was carefully made-up, except for her lipstick, which was bloody red and deliberately overdone, the fake-cheap/hot-sexy but too-expensive-for-you Hollywood look.

Lucas stood up to shake hands with Audrey, nodded at a right-angled couch, and when the women were sitting, sat down again. Looking at Audrey, he asked, "I've read the FBI reports, so this should be short. Did you ever have any hint of this 1919 website before you found it with your friend?"

Then something happened.

Audrey said, "No! I was amazed!"

At the moment he asked the question, Lucas saw something lizard-like flicker in her eyes. She hadn't expected precisely that question and she'd come up with an answer that was at least partially false.

Lucas thought, *Uh-oh.* That's what he thought. But he didn't know what was behind the flicker.

"You're sure? I mean, young people go through dozens of websites and I imagine with your business, you go through more than the average . . . person." He bit off "girl," "woman," and "teenager" and opted for the most neutral noise he could make.

Audrey shook her head: "I'd remember it. These people are Nazis and they have nothing to do with fashion. That's my crew: fashionistas. I'm strictly focused on girls. Nazis? No. I don't even do boys."

"I understand the photo was taken by a friend of yours . . . Blake, uh . . . ?"

She nodded. "Blake Winston. He does photos and video for my blog. You'll talk to him, right?"

"Soon as I leave here," Lucas said.

"Okay. Well, Blake knows everything about photography. He took my picture for a blog entry, we picked that up, right away. We couldn't figure out what it was doing on that crazy website, Nazis and all that. Then, the other pictures, he says they were all taken with a telephoto lens. He can tell, something to do with what's in focus, and what isn't. He can explain it. But, they're taken from a long way away. He also thinks that even then, they have to blow them up quite a bit. That's why they look so crappy."

"I'll talk to him about all that," Lucas said. "You don't think there's any possibility that Blake—"

"Oh, no." She was shaking her head. "No, no, no. For one thing, he hates Nazis and all that white nationalist stuff. He's really a nice guy, for being as rich as he is."

"He's rich?"

"His father is, anyway," Audrey said. "He runs a fund. His father does. A hedge fund."

Lucas smiled at her: young as she was, she sounded like she knew what she was talking about, that she knew about funds. He turned to Roberta Coil: "Nobody's contacted you about this?"

"No. I know what you're thinking, that came up with the FBI agents. Nobody's tried to blackmail me into changing a vote," she said. "If you looked at all my votes since this website was created, you'd see they were all party line and my vote wasn't critical in changing anything."

"All right."

"And that worries me," Roberta Coil added. "They *should* have contacted me. If they don't contact me, and if they haven't contacted the other parents, what does that mean? Does that mean it's *not* an extortion racket? Does that mean the kids are simply up there as targets?"

"Jeez, Mom, thanks a lot," Audrey said. "That totally makes me feel better."

Lucas looked back at Audrey. "Since you found the photo, you haven't felt like somebody was watching you?"

"No. Nothing."

"There was another girl in the photo with you," Lucas said, going with "girl" since Audrey used the word. "Is there any possibility that she was the targeted one?"

The senator shook her head: "That was Molly McWilliams. Her father owns a liquor distributorship here in northern Virginia. They're quite well-off, but not political. All the kids on 1919 are children of politicians, so it seems unlikely that Molly would be the target."

Lucas asked how a predator might locate Audrey and be able to pick her out from all the other students at her school.

Audrey brushed back a hank of auburn hair: "It's easy. You go to mom's website and it lists my dad's name and mine—I'm the only child. Then you look me up on the internet and you find my blog and there I am. All kinds of pictures. I write about school, and parties, and I get kids to give me iPhone snapshots of who's looking hot, and so on."

Lucas asked, "Does all this . . . scare you?"

"Scares the heck out of me," the senator said.

"It's a little scary," Audrey said, glancing over at her mother, who nodded. "I now get dropped off by a Secret Service man and go in the back way at school. I only go three days a week—I do assignments at home the other two, which really helps with the blog, you know. I've got more time to work on it."

"Do you miss school?" Lucas asked.

"Yeah, I do, all my friends. I still see them three

times a week, though," Audrey said. "To tell the truth, I'd rather work than go to school, but I know school's necessary."

"She does well in school," Roberta Coil said, smiling. "She's gotten about three B's in four years, everything else is A's. And it's a tough school."

"That's great," Lucas said. To Audrey: "Have you responded in any way to the 1919 site?"

Another flicker in the eyes, but Audrey shook her head: "No. I'd be scared to. Have you looked at it?"

"I got here a couple of hours ago—I haven't had time."

"There aren't many replies, but they're all from guys with fake names. One of them is 'Lizard Shooter.' Who calls himself Lizard Shooter? And there's never any replies from the blogger. The people replying ask questions and so on, but there's never an answer. Blake did a Google search and he says there has been some talk about 1919 on a couple of Nazi websites and there are links . . . that's about it."

"Do you know what websites?"

"I don't, but Blake knows."

THEY TALKED FOR a while longer, touching on the discovery of the website, but the Coils had no real information about the site itself. Lucas gave them his Marshals Service email address and asked Audrey to send him a link to her website, which she said she'd do immediately.

"I gotta get these guys off my back," she said, miming a shiver. "They're cramping my style. You ever try to talk fashion to a Secret Service agent?"

WHEN LUCAS GOT up to leave, Senator Coil asked him to wait a minute, went to the kitchen and came back with two warm oatmeal-raisin cookies in a plastic baggie.

"Smells good," he said.

"They taste even better. Georgia cookin'," she said.

"Bye," Audrey said, and she scrambled up the stairs and out of sight. Roberta Coil looked after her, then touched Lucas's arm and said, "She's a good kid. She's being brave about this, but I'm really not. Do you think I should hide her? I could send her back home."

Lucas said, "I can't make that call for you. We don't know that there's any threat at all. But we don't know that there isn't. With Secret Service coverage, she should be okay. Those guys are good. But, we're dealing with crazy people with guns and . . . you really don't know."

"Why do crazy people have guns?" Coil asked.

"You'd know the answer to that better than I would, Senator," Lucas said.

AS LUCAS DROVE to Blake Winston's house—he ate the cookies on the way, and they were excellent—it occurred to him that not only had he discussed fashion with a (former) Secret Service agent, a woman named Alice Green, but that Roberta Coil might even know her.

Green was running for a Virginia seat in the U.S. House of Representatives, had won the Democratic primary, and was leading her Republican opponent with less than two months to go to the election. Green was a clotheshorse, as was Lucas, and they'd spent a few pleasant hours on a campaign bus with Elmer Henderson, reading fashion magazines and exchanging ideas.

On the drive from Arlington to McLean, Lucas passed through a number of housing zones, arriving in the million-dollar-plus zone a few minutes after leaving the Coils'. The size and apparent values continued to climb the farther north he got and the closer to the Potomac. Following his phone's navigation app down a narrow tarmac lane, he eventually came to a sprawling ultra-modern white stone-and-glass house set in a forest that appeared to go on down to the river.

When he pulled up to the house, the front door opened and a young woman walked barefoot down a stone walkway to the driveway. Lucas got out of the car and she stuck out a hand to shake and said, "I'm Anne-Marie, I'm Mrs. Winston's assistant. They're waiting for you in the tennis room."

Anne-Marie had an attractive accent that might have been German or Dutch; and she looked German or Dutch, pretty, with short blond hair and square shoulders; she might have been a competitive swimmer. She led Lucas through a wide stone entry, down a stone-and-plank hallway past an oval living room designed for entertaining, with a huge black concert-grand piano in one corner.

They passed a couple of closed doors and finally stepped out into a semicircular room that Lucas would have called a family room, except the shelves showed off tennis trophies and the oversized windows looked out over a tennis court, which was built lower than the house so the room functioned as a gallery.

Blake and Mary Ellen Winston were sitting on a long flat couch positioned both to look over the court and to half-face another long flat couch. Anne-Marie said, "Marshal Davenport," and turned away and left them.

Mary Ellen was a tall athletic woman with carefully colored and coifed dark hair around an oval face. She wore a high-collared white dress shirt and navy slacks, with coral-colored linen slippers that matched her lipstick. She got up and gave Lucas a tennis-callused hand to squeeze, then backed up and sat next to her son. Blake looked a little like himself, Lucas thought, when he was seventeen. Lucas hadn't had the accoutrements, like the multimillion-dollar house, but there was a distinct resemblance.

Mary Ellen said so, to her son, with a smile: "The marshal looks more like you than your dad does."

The kid said, "Nah. He looks meaner."

"That's something you develop on your own," Lucas said, as he sat down. "If you're gonna be a movie-maker, you're gonna need a mean streak. If you don't have one, you should get started on it."

Blake, serious, lifted his eyebrows and asked, "Why is that?"

Lucas said, "Think about your basic hundred-million-dollar action movie. You've got to cast a lot of ugly people being stupid. Or fat ugly people. Have you ever thought about holding the auditions for those roles, about choosing the actors? How mean that must be?"

Blake put a finger to his lips and said, "No, really. I never thought about that."

LUCAS: "HOW DID you find the 1919 website?"

Blake explained about the face-matching software, originally developed, he thought, to detect unauthorized uses of copyrighted photographs.

"You'd have designers looking for photos for the website they were designing, and if they didn't have a big budget, they'd steal the photos. Sometimes, for pretty big companies. Pro photographers started asking for software that would help track their photos . . . online photographs are basically enormously long strings of pixels that are unique—no two photos are exactly alike on the pixel level. You put in your string and the software looks for a matching string. Eventually, it got sophisticated enough to match faces."

"Audrey wanted to match her face?"

Blake nodded. "Yeah. She wanted to see if her face was getting to be known. It's not, much, there are only about a zillion girly websites doing what she's doing, though she's actually got some decent sponsors. Anyway, we found some headshots of her. One of them, a shot I took, was on the Nazi site. They lifted it off her blog."

"Audrey said you had some ideas about the cameras used in the other photos."

"Not the cameras so much as the lenses. The way the images are compressed, and the thin depth of field . . . you know about depth of field?"

"Yes, some."

"Well, the combination of compression and thin depth of field tell you the pictures were taken with a telephoto lens. The same one, I think. All outdoors, in good light, but from long distances. To get those close-up headshots, they had to crop the photos quite a bit, then blow up what was left. That's why they look a little grainy. If I had to guess, I'd say a decent one-inch camera with a long zoom lens. There are a lot of those around. Uh, you know about metadata?"

"Yes. Information attached to photographs, usually including camera settings and a time-and-date stamp."

"It was stripped off the photos. I looked," Blake said.

"Then the photographer is fairly sophisticated?"

He shrugged: "Everything you'd need to know, you could learn in an hour. So, no, he's not necessarily sophisticated. He'd have to know about the metadata to get rid of it, but if he knew, then stripping it off is easy."

"You know a lot about photography," Lucas said.

"Blake had his own darkroom for film cameras, when he was twelve," Mary Ellen said. "He and his dad built it in our basement, in Birmingham."

"Dad said if I was serious about it, I should start with film," Blake said. "I moved to digital pretty quick, but . . . film is good. Knowing about it."

"How did you and Audrey start working together?"

Blake threw a quick glance at his mother and Lucas suspected he wouldn't be getting the full story.

"We're friends, from school," he said. "She dated a friend of mine for a while. Then she started doing her website with, you know, selfies that she took with her iPhone. She even made phone videos of herself, really bad videos. Later she tried a real camera, a point-and-shoot that wasn't much better. She's smart, and she knew she had to step up her game. She knew I was into photography and video and we did a couple of shoots. She got some sponsors and started throwing a few bucks my way. Now we've got a thing going."

Blake said that he didn't know anything especially interesting about the 1919 site, except that the people who had put it up didn't know much about creating a website: "It's crude. There are fifth-graders who could have done it better. They took crappy photos and slapped them on a preformatted form, along with the texts. The texts were ripped off from right-wing websites. They didn't even bother to change the fonts on the texts they took—they cut and pasted them, so they all look different, which is not a good look, technically speaking."

Mary Ellen said, "Blake told me something that you

might be interested in, but he didn't want me to tell you. I've decided to tell you anyway."

Blake: "Aw, jeez." He flopped back on the couch. "Audrey will kill me."

"We won't tell Audrey," Lucas said. To Mary Ellen: "What am I not supposed to know?"

"Blake said that Audrey got excited when they figured out what was going on, and the FBI came around and questioned them. She thought it'd make a great blog entry, pull in a lot of new traffic. The FBI agents asked her not to do that, but . . ."

"She might do it anyway," Blake said. "Don't tell her I said so."

"That could cause some trouble," Lucas said.

"Yeah, trouble," Blake said. "Trouble is another word for 'going viral.' That's living the dream. That's going on Fox News."

"If you have any influence . . ."

"I don't know if I have that much. You really don't want to be standing between Audrey and a TV camera," Blake said. "I say that, even though she's a friend of mine."

"All right," Lucas said.

Blake: "One more thing. It's sorta funny. Funny strange, not funny ha-ha."

"Yeah?"

"When the FBI agents were here, they told me some of what they'd found out. Not a lot, but I asked questions and they answered some of them. They told me they hadn't been able to break down the website because it was paid for anonymously and it's run out of Sweden."

"Is that unusual?"

"No, that's not unusual, if you know what you're doing and you want to stay hidden. But this is a really shitty website . . ."

"Thanks for the 'shitty,' Blake," his mother said.

"Well, that's what it is," Blake said. "Shitty. Way too bad for somebody who knows enough about what he's doing to get an anonymous check to Sweden and hire a Swedish ISP to carry the site. You know why he went to Sweden? Because they have strict privacy laws. You'd have to know that, to go there for your ISP. Also, you can get good, free anonymous website formatting software that will let you put together a functional website in a couple of hours, with decent design. But this site looks like it was put together by complete retards."

Mary Ellen: "Blake!"

"Sorry, but that's what it looks like," the kid said. "So, is it an experienced computer guy putting together a retarded website? It looks almost deliberately bad. How is it that somebody who knows enough to go to Sweden, knows how to get the money to them without giving himself up . . . doesn't know how to make a decent website?"

"An interesting question," Lucas said. "What do you think about that?"

He frowned. "I dunno. I smell a rat. Something's not right." He raked over his bottom lip with his lower teeth, then glanced up at Lucas, and said, "You know, I thought maybe the FBI put the website up, spoofing the Nazis. Getting the crazies to try to get in touch. Then, when everybody freaked out, the FBI figures it screwed up and tries to bury it. Now they can't admit that they're behind it."

"Oh, boy," Lucas said. He shook his head and said, "You're a smart kid. Nobody's said anything like that to me, or even hinted at it . . . but now I'm gonna have to think about it. It would explain some things."

Blake said he'd done a Google search for 1919, but there were 492 million results—"Really, 492 million"—so that didn't help. He'd done a follow-up search on the ISP name, the code, and had come up with three neo-Nazi sites that mentioned the ISP, but only in the last few days. There were no older references to it.

Lucas took down the ISPs for the three sites and would look at them later.

As Lucas was leaving, with Anne-Marie waiting to take him out, he handed Blake his card. "If you identify that rat you've smelled or something else occurs to you . . . call me."

LUCAS CALLED WEATHER to tell her about his first day in Washington, then spent the evening reading through the files that detailed the FBI investigation, focusing on those involving Charles Lang. Lang had attracted attention not only for his writings on neo-Nazism, but also because of his contacts, and what some said was his support of the groups.

His support was classified only as "possible" and "likely," not a sure thing, by agents who'd looked at his bank withdrawals. Lang had, in three separate documented cases, made serial withdrawals of $9,500 from a savings account, which had then been replenished from an investment account. In one case he'd withdrawn a total of $66,500 over five weeks. In the two other cases, he'd withdrawn $38,000 over two four-week periods. That was interesting because cash withdrawals over $10,000 had to be reported to the government and serial withdrawals of $9,500 suggested that Lang was evading that reporting requirement.

Where the $66,500 went, the FBI didn't know.

Of the two $38,000 withdrawals, an undercover agent working inside a group called Pillars of Liberty noted that shortly after the final withdrawals by Lang, Pillars had experienced a financial resurgence and had sent money to other neo-Nazi organizations to support publications and political actions.

A secret look at emails between the head of Pillars and the neo-Nazi organizations suggested that $38,000 would be a good guess as the amount of money involved. The connection was there, the investigators thought, but would be hard to prove.

Complicating the situation was that Lang had confided to a friend, who was also an FBI-recruited informant, that he'd lost some significant amounts of cash at a place called the Horseshoe Casino in Baltimore, Maryland; and that he'd used cash because he didn't want anyone to trace his credit cards to a casino.

The confession had suggested to the feds that Lang was onto their informant, and was using her to provide himself with an alibi.

Lang, Lucas thought, might not be as dumb as the average Nazi.

CHAPTER

FOUR

Elias Dunn understood that "fascist" wasn't a hot brand anymore, but in his research he'd found that it had been a wildly popular political philosophy in much of Europe in the 1930s, as well as in parts of South America and even in Japan, and that it was rising again in Eastern Europe.

Roughly equivalent philosophies had been popular in the U.S. as well, although they'd never gotten to the point where they achieved major elective status. They might have, if it hadn't been for that moron Adolf Hitler.

And for good reason.

There were lots of different flavors of fascism, but they all tried to deal with what Dunn had identified, through extensive reading, as the major failing of America: the nation had lost its founding values and had fallen into a fatal decadence.

The light was going out. The country was being invaded by people of inferior cultures and inferior races. The real, vital, white America was being submerged.

TO GET BACK would require a strong leader, a strong intelligent leadership group below him, and a strictly ordered society below that, with each group fixed in an honorable place. From top to bottom, from president to even some dumbass like Randy Stokes, there would be honorable work with decent, livable wages.

Most of all, there would be Order.

Although it was clear that blacks were an inferior race, and that Hispanics were certainly blighted, even those who claimed some European blood, there'd be honorable places for them in the American culture. They'd be separate, not equal, but would have their own secure place.

Eventually, he believed, they would, like his wife and cat . . . disappear.

Jews, of course, were a different problem. They were the Other, intelligent parasites who lived off the work of the superior races, running the banks, the media, all those middleman jobs that chipped a few greasy percentage points off the hard work of others. And, of course, their real allegiance lay elsewhere, far from America.

How to get to that new, clean, vibrant, and ordered America? Not through democracy, that was clear. Democracy had always been a danger, and even the Founding Fathers had recognized that. If everyone had an equal vote, what do you do when blacks and Hispanics became the majority, as they were sure to do, if allowed to breed as they wished?

Dunn believed in the Fourteen Words; believed with his entire being.

After Stokes got him to the 1919 website, and he'd realized the importance of the site, he'd spent several days thinking about it. As an engineer, he'd worked meticulously through several scenarios, just as he would with a housing site development, including a scenario in which the 1919 site was a fraud. That simply didn't compute. The site had been carefully crafted to send a particular message and he'd received it.

To make this omelet, Dunn had always understood, some eggs, even good eggs, would have to be broken.

One of those eggs, if not an especially good one, was Randy Stokes.

APROPOS OMELETS, he was making one, pushing cooked portions of the three eggs into the center of the hot pan over the steaming butter, tilting the pan this way and that until the eggs were thoroughly cooked, the size and shape of a large pancake. He dumped some pre-chopped ham, cheddar cheese, and onion onto half the frying egg, flipped the other half up on top to make a sandwich, let it heat for an extra moment, then flipped it onto a plate.

He carried the omelet and a bottle of Miller High

Life to the dining room, where he could look out over his back lawn as he ate.

ONE PROBLEM WITH meaningful political action, he knew, was that the federal government was all over it. Dunn didn't believe in the ZOG—the myth of a Zionist Occupied Government— but there was something ZOG-like about the way the government was passed back and forth, with much shouting and the expenditure of billions of dollars, between parties with barely discernible differences.

But to step back: the FBI was all over the people who might demand real change. Open your mouth too strongly, and the next time your lawnmower threw a rock into a neighbor's yard, you'd be looking at a federal felony.

The only way you could best the feds at that game was to be truly harmless; to be a hobby Nazi.

Or to keep your secret.

The far right referred to people like Dunn as lone wolves. He liked the mental image that conjured up, the wolf, and that's the way he wanted to remain. Let the alpha wolves and the betas get snarled up in alt-right politics, and their sex and power dreams. He'd remain alone.

But that message in the bottle . . . that 1919 website.

There could be only one reason for the message. Somebody, some serious group, was looking for political leverage and wanted an anonymous sympathizer to deliver it. The group's basic philosophy would be an amalgam of all those political causes reflected in the texts attached to the website. In other words, something in the direction of fascism, even if they didn't call it that. And they wouldn't call it that—they'd call it "Americanism" or "The Restoration" or something similar. He'd know it when it came about.

If somebody—a lone wolf—acted on their behalf, gave that group the leverage, gave them the ability to call up a senator or a Supreme Court justice and demand a vote, a nudge in the right direction . . .

That would be a step toward a renewed America.

DUNN HAD NO THEORETICAL PROBLEM with the idea of violence. Violence was built into fascism, had a purifying quality. But just because you were okay with the concept of violence, didn't mean you were okay with getting caught committing it. That kind of thing was for the skinheads of the world, the doofuses who showed up for the riot with a shield and baseball bat and a funny-looking flag.

If you were going to use violence, if it became necessary, you had to be logical about it. You had to think it out. You had to plan. You had to cut your liabilities. *You had to engineer it.*

General George Patton had expressed it best: "No dumb bastard ever won a war by going out and dying for his country. He won it by making some other dumb bastard die for *his* country."

Randy Stokes was a threat that would have to be cleared away before Dunn could take action. Stokes had put Dunn onto the 1919 website. If Stokes had left any hint of his identity on the website, and the FBI showed up at his door, he'd give up Dunn in a New York minute.

WHEN DUNN FINISHED DINNER, he watched his backyard for a while—sometimes deer appeared from the neighboring woods, to graze on a bed of hostas that he'd laid out at the back of his yard. Hostas were the hot fudge sundaes of the deer world, and Dunn liked to watch them ghosting through the trees, and then delicately stepping out on the yard to browse. The deer were worth any number of hostas.

No deer appeared this night and he washed and dried the omelet pan, the spatula, his fork and plate, cleaned up around the sink, put the beer bottle in the garbage and got another one from the refrigerator.

Up in his office, he composed a letter on his computer using Microsoft Word. He labored over it, getting everything just right, about 1919 and his beliefs concerning the website. He printed three copies on Boise Cascade computer paper—the most common decent paper he could find. He would never touch this particular sheet of paper with his bare hands, because he knew all about DNA. He put the letters in three self-sealing envelopes addressed to three other men he considered serious possibilities for acting in the cause.

With gloved hands, he applied self-sticking "Forever" stamps on the envelopes, put them in an unused brown business envelope and carried the package down to the front door and placed it on the floor. No DNA from mucus or skin or hair contact; no fingerprints; no return address. He would mail them the next day from Gainesville.

The men who got them would have to make up their own minds about what to do.

They'd have to decide whether they really wanted to go in.

If they finally wanted to act.

DUNN HAD THREE GUNS. The first was a Ruger SR9C, a compact 9mm semi-automatic pistol, his "house" gun. While small, the Ruger had an extended magazine that gave him the full seventeen rounds. The second was a Ruger 10/22, a .22-caliber carbine-style semi-automatic rifle with open sights, useful for killing small game, like rabbits and squirrels. The third was a scoped bolt-action Winchester Model 70 in .308, good for deer and other large game.

He wasn't highly skilled with any of them. He'd go to a local shooting range a couple of times a year to practice with the pistol, and occasionally to a three-hundred-twenty-acre tract of wooded land he owned in West Virginia, to shoot the rifles. He'd bought the land as a possible refuge when Barack Obama was elected president.

He'd also bought a thousand rounds of ammunition for the .308 and another two thousand rounds for the .22. Things hadn't collapsed, as he'd feared they would, under Obama. Since he hadn't needed to shift to a survival status, he'd considered selling the land, but hadn't gotten around to it. The tract had a small cabin on it and two ten-acre ponds with panfish. In the back of his mind, he retained the idea that he still might need it someday.

He'd bought all three of his guns under the loose Virginia laws, which allowed unregistered transfers at gun shows. Again, in the back of his mind, he thought it wise to keep his weapons purchases as private as possible, given the growing power of the deep state.

HE THOUGHT ABOUT SHOOTING Randy Stokes and that sister of his who'd given him the website password. Imagined it, almost as a video, and re-ran it through his mind, over and over. At times, it seemed too crazy. Shooting, killing two people that you didn't even care about? One that you didn't even know?

He considered other possibilities, including doing nothing about the Stokeses. If he took out one of the targets on the 1919 site, and if the FBI came around, he might admit talking to Randy Stokes but denying everything else. If he were careful enough . . .

There were lots of reasons that wouldn't work: there was simply too much surveillance to claim that he wasn't somewhere a camera said he was. If Randy had told his sister about Dunn, which was perfectly possible, and if the Stokeses got suspicious and gave him up, and then if the FBI started searching videos for his specific face, they'd find him. There were cameras everywhere. But if the Stokeses weren't around to give him up, if the FBI didn't know what face they were looking for . . .

HE RECOGNIZED THE RISK in killing the Stokeses, but trusted his planning skills. One step at a time. Details.

And, of course, planning the killings, and then doing them, would be useful gauges of his physical and emotional capacity for murder. He wasn't a crazy man. Not at all. Maybe, when it came to actually pulling a trigger, he'd find he couldn't do it. Maybe he would falter—he saw that possibility in himself. That was something to be tested.

AS A CIVIL ENGINEER, he occasionally did property searches to make sure that he wouldn't be digging up somebody's sewer line or fiber-optic cable. The day after Stokes had told him about the 1919 site, Dunn had gone to the Fauquier County courthouse. Stokes had mentioned that he'd been a renter, but had eventually been kicked out of his apartment and was temporarily living with his sister, Rachel, who owned an acreage around the town of The Plains.

He found a Rachel Stokes on a six-acre property in a rural area three miles north of The Plains, a small town not far from Warrenton. He cruised the place—an old flat-roofed cracker box with two pillars holding up a porch roof, all of it badly in need of paint. Another house sat a couple of hundred yards away, but the weather was still warm, verging on hot, and everybody would be using air conditioners, which made effective silencers.

He'd read that, anyway, or maybe had seen it on a TV show.

After spotting the Stokes property, he'd gone back to his job site, talked briefly to the general contractor's foreman, and then he and his crew continued laying out a series of cul-de-sacs. After a long discussion of drainage issues in the afternoon, he left an hour early, went home to shower and get his guts up for killing Randy and Rachel Stokes.

He wouldn't do it without regret. Randy would be a loss to no one, but Rachel might be a perfectly decent woman caught in a moment of political necessity. He'd always liked that name: Rachel, even though it sounded Jewish to his ear.

THE FOLLOWING DAY WAS A SATURDAY, and he began moving from planning to action. He began by renting a car; he didn't want his car anywhere near the Stokeses' house. He cruised the house twice on Saturday, but never saw Randy Stokes's car parked there. No matter: he wasn't quite ready to kill. He noted that the road was most often empty.

On Sunday, he cruised the house twice more. Still no sign of Stokes's car, and that began to worry him. Had Stokes taken off for parts unknown? At home Sunday night, he prepped the Ruger 9mm, making sure that it was mechanically perfect, that all possible prints and DNA were scrubbed off the cartridges. When he was satisfied, he smelled somewhat of gun oil, but . . . so what?

On Monday, he went to work, as usual. Stokes was there, leaning on his shovel. Dunn stayed away from him.

At home that afternoon, Dunn put on a long-sleeved overshirt, worn unbuttoned at the front, which would conceal the pistol tucked into the small of his back, under his belt, but would be loose enough to provide easy access to the gun. For the trip over to the Stokes place, he put the Ruger, in a fabric holster, under the front seat of his car.

When he was set, he checked the time: ten minutes after five. Way too early. Stokes was a regular, in the way only an addict can be regular, at Chuck's Wagon. He'd be there as soon as he got off work, and would stay as long as he had money, or until the bartender cut him off. That might be as late as eight o'clock.

A Walmart Supercenter and a Home Depot both had busy parking lots not far from Chuck's Wagon, and after checking them out, he found a spot in the Home

Depot lot from which he could see the bar's driveway. He drove over to the bar to make sure that Stokes was there: and he was.

Encouraged by the way his plan was working, in his head, anyway, he drove back to the Home Depot and parked. And waited. Longer than he'd hoped. People came and went from the Home Depot, and as far as he could tell, nobody paid him any attention. Six o'clock. Six-thirty. He began to get cold feet. Killing two people? What was he thinking? He almost left then, headed back home to think about it some more.

He might have, if he hadn't seen Stokes's car pulling out of the parking lot . . .

HE FELL IN BEHIND STOKES, who drove too slow, the speed that experienced drunks drive when they know they've had a few too many. They threaded through Warrenton, then out Highway 17 to the turnoff at Old Tavern, across I-66, through The Plains and then out of town on Hopewell Road and finally to Rachel Stokes's house, where Stokes pulled into the driveway.

As he did, Dunn honked his horn twice, then pulled into the driveway and half-climbed out of the rental car, tucking the gun in behind his belt, pulling the shirt over it. Stokes was out of his car, squinting into Dunn's headlights.

Dunn called, "Randy—it's Elias Dunn. I thought that was you. This where you live?"

Stokes called back, "Hey, El. Yeah. What are you doing out here?"

"Got a client over by that Antioch Church. Anyway, I saw you, thought I'd honk."

Then, what Dunn had hoped for: "Hey, whyn't you come in, have a beer? I'll introduce you to my sister."

"Well . . . I gotta get over . . . well, maybe one beer. That can't hurt. It's been a long day."

THE EXTERIOR OF THE HOUSE was in bad shape, but the interior was surprisingly habitable, neatly kept, homey, in a latter-day-hippie way. Bead curtains and fabric art. Rachel Stokes was apparently a quilter or a quilt collector, with a variety of quilts on the walls of the living room, all neatly displayed, hanging off one-inch dowel rods.

Rachel was in the back of the house, in the kitchen, when they walked through the front door, and Stokes called out to her, and asked, "You decent? I got a friend here . . ."

Rachel came out to look, wiping her hands on a dish towel, and seemed a little surprised when she saw a neat, well-groomed friend. She was dark-haired and short, early thirties, Dunn thought, a few pounds too heavy but pleasant-looking, with warm brown eyes. "I'm Rachel," she said.

Dunn nodded and said, "Pleased to meet you, ma'am. I saw Randy turning in here, just stopped to say hello. I'm an engineer, we've worked on a couple of jobs together."

"An engineer? What kind?"

"Civil engineer, ma'am. I lay out roads and the curbs and the lots and drainage and so on. Randy and I are working on that new subdivision over by Gainesville."

Stokes said, "I asked him to come on in for a beer."

Dunn: "You know, I . . ."

"Oh, have a beer," Rachel said. "I don't drink and there are only two cans left, so that'll be one less for Randy. I think he's probably already had a couple more than he needed. And stop calling me ma'am. You sound like a cowboy in an old western movie."

"Come on, Rachel," Stokes said. "I'm, like, totally sober."

"Whatever, I doubt one more or less is gonna hurt," she said.

That's when he should have shot them, Dunn thought later. Rachel went to the refrigerator to get the beers, and Dunn slipped his hand under the gun stock at his back, and to distract them, he asked, "Did you make those quilts?"

"That's what I do," Rachel said, from the kitchen. She came back out with two cans of Miller. "I'm Bear Wallow Quilts. That's my business. Actually, I ought to talk to you about it. I've got this idea for quilts based on landscapes. You know, like you see from the air, all the different sizes of the fields and the way the woods ramble around, and the creeks follow the land . . ."

Dunn blinked and his hand slid off the gun stock. An aerial image of the landscape around Warrenton flicked through his mind, and he was struck by the beauty of it, interpreted as a quilt. "Boy . . ." He looked down at his feet, then back up. "That really would be something else. They are a quilt, aren't they?"

Rachel picked up on that, and they talked around it at the kitchen table, and it was perhaps the most pleasant half hour Dunn had experienced in the past decade. He finished his beer, still feeling the cold press of the pistol at his back, but said goodbye, especially to Rachel, and left.

Out in the car, he figured he'd screwed up. They needed to go, and he'd been unable to do it. He had to harden his heart, he thought. Had to harden his heart.

HE THOUGHT ABOUT that the entire next day; and he hardened his heart as he worked, laying out the subdivision that was being carved out of the red dirt of a former farm. He sometimes used an independent surveyor, but on this job, did the surveying himself, working with a rodman and two assistants. They were all taciturn men who'd worked together on other projects and moved quickly and efficiently with almost no chatter; they even ate lunch separately.

At the end of the workday, he drove around the subdivision until he spotted Stokes, leaning on his shovel at the end of a new culvert. He got out of his truck and walked over to Stokes and said, "Listen, what time are you getting home?"

"Couple beers, probably about seven. Why?"

"I found some old color aerial photographs at my house. I thought I might drop them off for your sister to look at. There are some interesting quilt ideas in there."

Stokes shrugged. "Sure. You could drop them off anytime, though."

Dunn shook his head: "I think it'd be better if you were there. I mean, she doesn't really know me. Semi-strange man, and all."

"Okay. Come by at seven-thirty. I'll be there. I think Rachel kind of liked your looks, if you know what I mean."

"She seemed like a real nice girl," Dunn said.

"She is a nice girl," Stokes said.

BETWEEN THE END OF THE WORKDAY and seven o'clock, Dunn did nothing but shut down all of his softer thoughts about Randy and Rachel Stokes. They had to go. They knew about him—as they were sitting around the kitchen table the night before, Rachel had asked about the weird website he'd sent her brother to, and he'd managed to laugh it off. "Something a guy told me about, and the way Randy talks, I figured it was up his alley."

She'd bought that. Maybe. And maybe not. If a question ever came up, they'd remember.

RANDY STOKES GOT to Rachel's house just as Dunn was leaving home. Randy said to Rachel, "Dunn's coming over. Mostly to see you, I guess. He said he found some aerial pictures you'd like for your quilts. Or maybe he just wanted to talk to you some more."

"Oh, for God's sakes, Randy, he's *your* friend. He's just being nice."

"He was never that nice to me in the past," Stokes said. "I kinda had the idea that he thought I was a dumb shit."

"Whatever," Rachel said. "By the way, the mortgage payment is up. You were supposed to give me a few dollars while you're living here . . ."

They talked about that for a while, and Randy put her off and then went to heat up a frozen beef pot pie in the microwave. With Randy otherwise occupied, Rachel took a moment to wash her face, check herself in the mirror, add just a hint of makeup and a touch of lipstick. A hint of perfume, but only a hint, she didn't want to come off like a floozy. Her blouse was all right, she thought, she wished her jeans weren't quite so tight, she really had to get back on her diet . . .

DUNN THOUGHT: SHOOT RACHEL FIRST, she'd never suffer. She'd never even see it coming, if he shot her from behind; she'd go from everything to nothing in a split second. Then Randy Stokes. More dangerous that way, shooting Rachel first, Stokes had that muscle from his shovel work, he could be in your face in a hurry. But he didn't want Rachel to suffer.

Dunn got to Rachel Stokes's house a few minutes early, saw Randy's car parked in the side yard, a light in the back, where the kitchen was. He took a few long breaths, got out of the car, touched the pistol tucked in his belt, the sight pressing against his coccyx like the devil's pitchfork. He reached over to the passenger seat and grabbed a four-foot-long plastic tube, the kind used to protect building plans or artwork, and walked up to the door.

Rachel met him there, smiling, backed into the front room, said, "Hi, El, come on in. Randy said you had some photos?"

Dunn said, "Uh, yeah," lifted the tube with his left hand while his right went under his shirt, grabbed the pistol, clicked the safety off . . .

Randy Stokes came into the room carrying a bowl and a spoon and said, "Hey, El . . ."

Dunn yanked on the pistol stock, but the sight hung up in the fabric of his Jockey briefs and in his haste he'd already slipped his finger into the trigger guard and when he yanked on the gun, his finger yanked on the trigger and he fired a shot between the cheeks of his butt and into the floor, and the noise was terrific and Rachel's mouth dropped open and her eyes widened and then the pistol was up and Dunn shot her in the face and she went down.

Stokes threw the bowl past Dunn's head and turned

to run and Dunn shot him twice in the back, then stepped over Rachel's body and put the pistol close to the back of Stokes's head and fired another shot.

When he turned back, he found, to his real horror, that his slug had hit Rachel in the jaw and had come out the back of her head, and she was still alive and aware, looking up at him in fear and trying to back-crawl away, like doing a backstroke, and she gurgled something and he stepped closer and said, "I'm sorry, I'm sorry" and shot at her head and missed, though he was only four feet away. He put the pistol right at her forehead then, and her eyes tried a final plea and then went calm, accepting, and he pulled the trigger again, and then she was gone.

He'd dropped the plastic art tube, and he picked it up and turned away from the bodies. Dunn had no idea of how many times he'd fired the gun, but it seemed like a lot. And he hurt. His butt hurt, and he reached back to feel it, and his hand came away bloody. He stumbled toward the door, and out, to his truck, and he climbed into the driver's seat, and then thought, *DNA*.

He fumbled in the backseat pocket and found an LED flashlight, climbed back out of the truck and looked for blood on the ground. He found nothing. The blood seemed restricted to his underwear and an orange-sized spot on the seat of his pants.

His buttocks were on fire; but a hand check seemed to indicate that he had only creased the skin on both cheeks, and had never actually poked a bullet hole in himself.

He didn't want to revisit the horror inside the house, so he got back into his truck and drove home.

He was all right, he thought. He needed some bandages, he needed some antiseptic, but he was all right. His blood-spotted clothing would go into a wood-burning fireplace, and the ashes scattered in the woods.

He was all right: except for nightmares that would last for the rest of his life.

After a nine o'clock breakfast Monday morning, as Elias Dunn was working toward the murders of Randy and Rachel Stokes, Lucas drove to Potomac, Maryland, where Charles Lang lived in a newer but traditionally styled stone-and-timber house, off Bentcross Drive, set among mature oaks and a screen of lower pines.

Two granite pillars flanked the driveway entrance, and the long blacktopped driveway led to a detached garage eighty or a hundred feet from the house itself. The house side of the driveway was edged with a knee-high granite wall. The wall looked nice, but it occurred to Lucas, who'd seen a similar driveway at the home of a powerful intelligence officer in Mexico, that it also worked as a security feature: you couldn't get a car or truck close to the house—or a car or truck bomb.

Lucas parked at the garage and walked through a

four-foot-wide slot in the granite wall, up to the house. Before he had a chance to ring the doorbell, the door opened and a tall slender man, with a neat Vandyke beard, perhaps thirty-five, opened the door and asked, "Marshal Davenport?"

Lucas nodded and said, "Yes."

"I'm Charles's assistant. He's in the den."

Another assistant, Lucas thought—it must be a Washington thing.

The assistant backed up and Lucas followed him inside. Once past the entry, he found himself in an expansive living room decorated with eighteenth-century British hunting prints and paintings, mounted on pale blue plaster walls; a six-foot grand piano sat in a corner, half the size of the piano at the Winstons' house. There was no sheet music in sight, but a crystal vase sat on the piano top, filled with yellow and pink bell-shaped flowers; the room smelled of funeral.

As they went through, Lucas asked, "What's your name?"

The man said, "Stephen." And after a pause, "Gibson."

"Have you been with Mr. Lang for a while?"

"Thirteen years," Gibson said. He was prematurely balding with close-cropped hair, and wore beige trousers, a yellow shirt open at the throat, a blue linen sport coat, and brown loafers. A pair of narrow silver-rimmed glasses hung from his neck. "About twelve years longer than I expected to, when I graduated from the university. I assist Charles with his research, in addition to . . . ordinary business chores."

They walked through a smaller room, whose function Lucas couldn't quite identify—maybe a more intimate meeting room, with a sideboard for drinks, and a faint odor of nicotine—to the den, another large room lined with books. There were three photos in a cluster in a niche between bookcases: a young Lang shaking hands with Ronald Reagan, a middle-aged Lang shaking with George W. Bush, and a near-elderly Lang shoulder-to-shoulder with Donald Trump.

Lang himself sat behind a walnut desk that had the look of an Early American antique: not elegant, but formidable. Another crystal vase of flowers sat on a credenza behind the desk.

He looked up from a manuscript when Gibson led Lucas into the room, and stood up to shake hands. Lang was a middle-sized man, fleshy, bald with a few strands of steel-gray hair layered over the top of his pate, a narrow nose, extra pink at the tip, and watery green eyes. His hand was soft as warm butter. He was wearing a gray suit coat and trousers, a white dress shirt, and a yellow bow tie.

"Marshal Davenport," he said, showing small pearly teeth as he smiled through his greeting. "I'm pleased to meet you. I won't apologize for it, but I asked Stephen to background you, and you seem to have had at least two extremely successful careers."

"We'll have to see how successful the current one is," Lucas said. He took a blue-leather visitor's chair in front of Lang's desk, as Lang sat down again.

Gibson said, "Charles, I need to finish with that email. Would either of you like a drink before I do that? Orange juice? Lemonade?"

Lucas said, "No, thanks. I just ate breakfast."

Lang said, "Not yet, but bring me a lemonade when you finish with the mail." Gibson left, and Lang turned back to Lucas.

Lucas said, "You know why I asked to see you—I've been told that you're one of the leading experts on these alt-right groups, white supremacists, neo-Nazis, and so on. We're looking particularly at a group called 1919."

"1919. Extraordinarily interesting. Came out of nowhere. You're aware of the 88 meme . . ."

"The letter 'H' is the eighth letter of the alphabet so '88' is code for 'HH' which is code for 'Heil Hitler,'" Lucas said. "1919 is SS, as in the Nazi SS."

"Exactly right." Lang had never stopped smiling, his eyes bright. "I've researched these groups for years, but I'd never encountered 1919 before, but now, it seems obvious. Not the existence of the group, but the existence of the name."

"You wouldn't know who might have invented it, where it might have come from . . ."

"No, no, not a clue. I've spoken to some of my contacts in the field and they're asking around. I've put out word that I would like to speak to the 1919 folks."

"That might be a little risky?" Lucas made it a question.

"Oh . . . some of them aren't harmless, you know,

but they generally seem to appreciate my attention," Lang said. "The biggest problem most of these groups face is misunderstanding—"

"I would think their biggest problem, if you'll excuse the language, is that they're racist assholes and they're widely hated," Lucas said.

Lang's smile faded a bit. "Let me finish my thought, if you would, Marshal. The biggest problems most of these groups face is misunderstanding. Most are extremely conservative in the traditional sense of that word, but most have no particular liking for Adolf Hitler or the German National Socialists. Yet, when they go public with their beliefs, the media immediately brands them as 'Nazis.' Now, you used the word 'racist.' Perfectly good word, until recently. Look at what's been happening with the Democratic Party in the struggle between the so-called Progressives and the so-called moderates. All of these people are liberal by normal standards, but they accuse one another of being racist at the slightest deviation from the Progressive party line. And heaven help the poor Republicans—they're all racists, every last man jack of them. Once accused, once labeled, there's barely any way to escape. The same is true with these—I hate the term 'alt-right,' but everybody uses it—these alt-right groups. The media won't allow them to be alt-right without being Nazis."

"But 1919 *is* SS," Lucas said.

Lang's wide smile returned. "Yes, it is. It makes them almost unique. Very interesting. *Very* interesting. From my perspective, of course. As a scholar."

"Of course," Lucas said. "Listen, I need to ask, if I were to go looking for them, where would I start? It seems like they'd be pretty far off on the extreme right end of things. The clippings on the website include everything from old Klan people to, you know, actual saluting goose-stepping neo-Nazis."

"The most extreme of these people would be unlikely to talk with a marshal. You're the enemy," Lang said.

"So you wouldn't be able to make an introduction."

Lang's chair was on a swivel, and he'd been swiveling from side to side as they talked, and now he slowly turned all the way around, his lips pursed, looking at the ceiling. It had the feel of a well-rehearsed act, Lucas thought.

When Lang came back around, he said, "That might not be quite right. However, before we get to that, I would like to ask . . . why do you think this group is alt-right? 1919?"

"The files they posted . . ."

"Are all alt-right, or extreme right, or crazy right— the KKK and so on. But if some child should get shot, those very groups are the most likely to be attacked by the federal government. Why would they invite that? It seems to me just as likely that the posts were put up by some left-wing group, who might be able to make the same phone call to a senator that the alt-right people might make, without the risk of being attacked by the government."

"You're the first person to suggest that," Lucas said.

"I wouldn't doubt it, since there seems to be a hunger by the liberal deep state to eradicate the alt-right," Lang said. "Now, you want to know about who might organize something like that. Let me suggest that you check the American National Militia. They're certainly not Nazis. They're more like what I would classify as anarchists—extreme libertarians. They don't want a powerful fascist government, they don't want any government at all—and they may very well have committed violent acts. I don't know that for sure, that's what I hear. The actual leader of the group is unknown to me, or to anyone other than a few members. He's supposedly called Old John. There was some controversy over in Kentucky about a group of men doing firearms training—sniper training—and practicing guerilla tactics at a camp in a forested area, and they were said to be members of the ANM. There were quite a number of them, so it is a substantial group."

"What violent acts? What'd you hear?" Lucas asked.

Lang leaned forward and put his forearms on his desk. "A number of things. There was a developer in Erie, Pennsylvania, who asked the city council to use its power of eminent domain to condemn a series of older condominiums that took up a prime city block, so that he could build one of those mixed-use business and condominium projects. Replace something old and ugly with something new and expensive. Brew pub, fern bars, that sort of thing. Starbucks. The council was going along with it when the developer got plugged between the eyes in what looked like a road-rage incident. There was a rumor among certain extremist groups on the left that he was killed to stop the eminent domain process. And that happened. The old condominiums are there to this day."

"People think the ANM did it?"

"That was the rumor on the alt-left, if I can call them that. Then there were two shootings in Michigan. Do you know what tax deed states are?"

"Mmm . . . not exactly," Lucas said.

"Okay. In a tax deed state, if you're late with your taxes, the county can sell the deed to your house, usually to an investor. There are a number of companies who buy the deeds, and quite a few individuals. The real victims are usually people who are too poor or too dumb to pay the taxes they owe, and don't understand the process. So, somebody has a little farm acreage worth, say, a hundred thousand dollars, and owes five thousand dollars in taxes. If he doesn't pay, or make payment arrangements, the county auctions off the farm. The minimum bid is the amount of the taxes plus processing fees. If the winning bid is twenty-five thousand, the county takes its cut, gives the rest of the money to the homeowner, and the deed to the investor."

"Then they kick out the original owners?"

"That can happen," Lang said. "When an investor buys your deed, there's usually a redemption period, in which the original owner can pay off the amount the investor paid for the deed, plus a hefty interest and service charge. Bottom line, your five-thousand-dollar tax bill could cost you eight thousand dollars to pay off, if you can afford to pay it at all.

"Anyway," Lang continued, "an individual investor in Michigan bought a tax deed in Westmoreland County. The sale was held by the sheriff and he signed the papers in the sheriff's office at the courthouse, stepped out on the front steps, and was killed with a single rifle shot. They never identified the shooter or even where he shot from. The bullet was recovered, a .30-caliber slug, and because of the weight of the slug, the police believe it was probably fired from a .300 Winchester Magnum, which I am told is a favorite sniper rifle."

"And people thought the ANM . . ."

"Then, three or four months later, the president of one of the investing companies was shot at his front door after his company won another Michigan auction. Another long-range sniper action, another .30-caliber. They did find the sniper nest the second time—and there was a note that said something like, 'Buy a tax deed and die!' That put at least a temporary chill on tax deed sales. There was a rumor that the ANM was involved in both shootings."

"Huh."

"Then there was a murder in Ohio," Lang said. "A man was accused of rape, got three hung juries despite a lot of evidence—DNA evidence—because he'd been a local football star. Girl committed suicide after the last hung jury. A couple of days later, the alleged rapist was killed by a sniper. Once again, a heavy .30-caliber slug. There were more rumors."

"But no substantial investigation?"

"The police didn't have much to work with. And I don't think anyone looked at it too closely, the rape thing. For several reasons, like, not many people really cared about the rapist, plus, there was no evidence about who did it and if you did find some evidence . . . the killer might come for you."

"Can you put me in touch with the ANM contact man?"

"Actually, it's a woman. She may or may not be willing to talk with you. Before I agree to reach out on your behalf, there'd be a condition," Lang said.

"That would be?"

"If she reaches out to you, and you interview her, you consider sharing the substance of the interview with me," Lang said. "You tell me what you find out about the group."

"I'd consider it, but I might not be able to do that," Lucas said. "This is a federal investigation, not scholarly research."

"I'm not asking for a promise, only a consideration." Lang's tongue flicked out, wetting his lower lip. "I've been curious about the ANM for a while."

"Is there any other group? Or contact?" Lucas asked.

"Actually, there is. I can give you that one right now, Richard Greene of the Greene Mountain Boys. Greene with an 'e' at the end. There are only a few dozen

members in the group, they're alt-right, and I've sometimes thought that Richard is more interested in publicity than in actually doing anything. He's . . . and I'll
apologize for the language, as you did earlier . . . a
bullshitter. But. Because of the publicity, he knows a lot
of people. Being media-aware, he collects rumors and
tracks everything alt-right. He would be the most likely
person to have heard something."

"How would I reach him?" Lucas asked.

"He lives outside Annapolis . . . I have a phone
number . . ." Lang reached for an old-style Rolodex.

LUCAS TOOK DOWN a phone number for Greene, but
Lang wouldn't tell him how he planned to reach the
ANM contact, other than to say he'd call some people
he knew and ask that somebody call him back. The
word might or might not get to the right person. If it
did, he'd pass along Lucas's phone number.

"You can't count on it, but it's a possibility," Lang
said. "They have responded to occasional inquiries in the
past. I've never met the woman myself. I would like to."

Gibson returned with an iced lemonade for Lang,
and then took a seat in a chair at the side of the room.
Lucas sniffed; he didn't normally have allergies, but the
flowers were getting to him and when Lang went past
with the lemonade, he thought he smelled alcohol. He
asked about alt-right groups with a reputation for criminal activity, especially violence, but Lang shook his
head.

"There's *always* some of that. Most of these groups are populated by younger men who feel repressed, ignored, slighted, pushed aside for wealthy or politically connected groups. They're a political version of a motorcycle gang. In fact, some of them *are* motorcycle gangs."

"Politically connected? Do you mean, like, teachers' unions? Or Jews?"

Lang's smile lost some wattage, but then he blinked and brightened and said, "They would both be considered problems . . . by these people."

"But not by you?"

"I'm not a racist, Marshal, but I am a realist. Jews control the banks and the media; that's a fact. And how far do you have to look to see the damage being done to this country by the media and the banks?" Lang asked. "The teachers' unions . . . well, teachers live their privileged socialist lives and they look around, and ask why shouldn't everyone live their privileged socialist lives? Good salaries, excellent pensions, long vacations. The average workingman in this country works 260 days a year; the average teacher, 170 to 180. What's not to like about that life? They don't seem to understand that somebody actually has to provide the money for their lives, for the pensions that are absolutely ruining the states, and bought in return for funding left-wing politicians like Obama . . ."

Lang went on for a while, his face going bright pink, and in a shaft of sunlight coming through the slats of half-drawn wooden shades, Lucas could see small drops of spit flying across the desk toward his lap. He shifted away, as much as he could without getting up. He'd touched a button and Lang apparently was having trouble reining in the rant.

He eventually trailed off, having disposed of Jews, teachers, Hispanics, and Arabs—"Maybe nice people as individuals, but they don't share our culture and they don't want to have anything to do with it; they want our money and nothing else"—as well as mentally ill street people and "welfare queens," a phrase Lucas hadn't heard since the '90s.

When he stopped to take a breath, Lucas broke in with, "I have to say I don't totally agree with you on all of that, but I think I understand your point of view. I guess I've lived something of a socialist life myself—except for a couple of years with a software start-up, I've worked for governments most of my life."

"Then you know what I'm talking about," Lang snapped, pointing a yellow pencil at Lucas's chest. He leaned back, took a breath, got a grip, and smiled again. "Anyway, that's really . . . for another discussion. I will try to help you hook up with the 1919 organization. I do want to speak to them myself, though. They have kept themselves, whoever they are, very carefully secret. I find that intriguing."

GIBSON, WHO'D SAT QUIETLY through the rant, showed Lucas out of the house. At the door, he said, quietly, "Charles is doing important work. When he's gone, which I hope won't be for many, many years, people will look back and wonder why they didn't listen to him in his prime."

"It's a thought," Lucas said.

His phone buzzed in his pocket, and he took it out as he was walking down the walkway to the car. Jane Chase. He poked Accept and asked, "Did something happen?"

"No, I wanted to find out if you'd come up with anything new," she said.

"Jesus, it's not even noon."

"You're a fast worker."

"Let me get in my car," Lucas said.

He got in the Cadillac, started it, punched up the air-conditioning, went back to the phone, and said, "I'm at Charles Lang's place. He's a fuckin' Looney Tunes. So's his assistant. You got anything on a guy named Stephen Gibson? He's worked for Lang for thirteen years?"

"I haven't heard the name, but I'll look. Is Charlie going to help out?"

"He's already put out the word for a 1919 contact. I'm not holding my breath on that. He's going to try to hook me up with a group called the American National Militia, ANM, and the Greene Mountain Boys."

"I've heard of those. The Greene Mountain Boys are not harmless—they've participated in a couple of marches that got ugly. They weren't the instigators, but they were out there swinging signs. The ANM is something different. We've heard about them, tried to get inside, but no luck so far. They're pretty picky about their membership. They don't let anyone in that they don't know about, a lot of times through family connections. Their leader is supposedly called Old John. No last name. We've heard that the movie *Fight Club* is a cult film with them—that's where they want to go."

"Love that movie," Lucas said. "But I guess you could take it the wrong way."

"No kidding. Anyway, if Charlie hooks you up with the ANM, tell me. We'll want to cover you."

"We'll see," Lucas said. "I'm not an FBI agent . . ."

"Lucas . . ."

"Lang said there are rumors in the alt-left that the ANM has killed some people," Lucas said. "He has three or four examples, if you could get me what's available on those killings."

He told her about the Erie, Pennsylvania, developer, the two Michigan shootings, and the execution shooting of the alleged rapist in Ohio. Chase said she was familiar with the rapist killing, from news stories, but the FBI hadn't been involved in the case. She hadn't heard of the Pennsylvania or Michigan shootings.

"Why do you think the ANM might be involved with 1919?" Chase asked.

"Lang suggested it. That they could have created a fake site to hang the blame on the alt-right, while they take advantage of it. They are apparently willing to shoot, if the rumors are true. And they're at least somewhat media-aware—they have a PR woman. Lang's going to try to get me in touch with her."

"Keep me up on that."

"We'll see," he said again. "Another thing: I hate to say this, but there's something not quite right about Audrey Coil and her story about finding 1919. I don't know what to do about that."

"What's wrong with her story?"

"I don't know, but something is. She was lying to me about something, but I can't think what it might be."

"Audrey and I had a little talk away from her mother, and—keep this under your hat—there's been a little sexting going on there," Chase said. "With her friend Blake and probably some other boys at the school. But she knows a lot about the workings of the internet and she's been careful not to let any really identifying stuff . . . get out there. Bare breasts, maybe some below-the-waist stuff, but not anything that you could say, 'That's Audrey Coil.' At least, not unless you'd visited the neighborhood in person. She told me that she was completely aware of the problems sexting could cause downstream in her life, and was careful. I believed her."

Lucas said, "Huh."

"That was a skeptical-sounding 'Huh,'" Chase said.

"No, that could be it. I'm an older male, talking to her with her mother present. There may have been subjects she really wanted to avoid."

LUCAS DROVE BACK toward the Watergate; on the way, he phoned Richard Greene, but got no answer. After six rings, Greene's phone kicked over to an automated answering service, and Lucas left a message.

———

WITH NOTHING MUCH TO DO BUT WAIT, he went to his room, took off his suit and put on jeans, and started picking through the FBI files again. Jane Chase called and said she was forwarding a brief file on Gibson and longer files on the Greene Mountain Boys and the American National Militia. Lucas opened the files on his computer, using the encryption code Chase had given him.

Gibson, it seemed, was more than a paper-pushing assistant and researcher. He held a Maryland private investigator's license and concealed carry permit, had taken a three-month "executive protection" bodyguard course, including tactical driving, was an ongoing student at a martial arts studio that specialized in Krav Maga, and had completed a Maryland state police–approved handgun training course. Concealed carry permits were tough to get in Maryland, which suggested that either Gibson or Lang had a connection, or had demonstrated a clear threat to one of them.

The Greene Mountain Boys—a wordplay on the "Green Mountain Boys," a fractious group of Vermont militia during the American Revolutionary era—were the creation of Richard Greene, a right-wing podcaster and shoe store operator in Annapolis, Maryland. Greene had served as a Navy officer, reaching the rank of lieutenant, before leaving to run the shoe store, which he'd taken over from his parents. His podcasts had a couple of thousand followers and when he called out the troops to participate in a political action, twenty or thirty would turn up to march.

He had finished the Greene file, and had started thumbing through the file on the American National Militia, when Greene called back. "Charlie Lang got in touch and said you'd be calling me," Greene said. "I get a lot of junk calls so I didn't pick up when you called earlier—I looked up your message after I talked to Charlie. He told me what you're doing."

Lucas said he'd like to talk face-to-face and Greene agreed to meet him halfway between Washington and Annapolis that afternoon, at a Panera Bread restaurant. "How will I know you?"

"I'll know you, if your podcast picture is recent," Lucas said, looking at his computer screen.

"Yeah, it is," Greene said. "See you there, Marshal."

Lucas set the ANM file aside to listen to a couple of Greene podcasts, not quite broadcast-quality rants about America going into the toilet because of the Usual Suspects. When Lucas finished listening, he wasn't sure whether Greene was a true believer, or a con artist jumping on the bandwagon most likely to get him attention.

Lucas went back to reading the file on the ANM, which apparently had the goal of eliminating most government above the county level, although they would make provisions for a small military, and for some infrastructure coordination on things like highways.

The feds had little information on the group and had been unable to pinpoint its actual leader, who operated mostly through the more obscure reaches of the internet. He wasn't entirely faceless, though: he apparently had shown up, from time to time, at meetings of ANM cells. The cell leaders knew his face, but not his real name. Cameras were forbidden at all cell meetings, and members were required to leave cell phones in their cars; personal sidearms were permitted.

There were no connections between cells. Even if a cell was penetrated by a government operator, he or she could discover only the names of the local cell members, usually less than a dozen people. All connections were through internet "dead drops," which were used only once. After a dead drop was used, "Old John" or somebody else in the leadership group would issue a cell leader the location of the next dead drop. Since Old John picked the cell leaders, apparently on the basis of personal connections, getting an undercover agent chosen as a cell leader was virtually impossible.

It was all fairly sophisticated and Lucas was fascinated. He had a growing feeling, as he read, that the group might actually be dangerous—not that it might someday overthrow the government, but in the sense that it might kill somebody or even some large number of people. There was an intelligence working there. The overall goals might be absurd, but the organizational work and tactics were intriguing.

ON HIS WAY out of the Watergate to meet Greene, Lucas ran into a plainclothes security man for the hotel, an ex-cop named Jeff Toomes, who he'd met during his last stay at the Watergate, during which there'd been a firefight outside Lucas's hotel room.

"That was a hell of a thing," Toomes said as they shook hands. "Man, the shit got thick after the shooting upstairs. We had the FBI, the Secret Service, the DC cops up our ass for freakin' weeks. Then I read about marshals involved in those shootings over in Virginia, and I figured that was you."

"Yeah, I was there," Lucas said. He lied a little: "We never did get the shooter, though."

The shooter was dead, though not at the hands of the cops.

"Can't win them all, brother," Toomes said. "Listen, if you need anything . . ."

THEY TALKED FOR ANOTHER MINUTE OR SO, then Lucas left, heading for Maryland and his meeting with Greene. Ten minutes later, he got a call from an unknown number, but with a 202 Washington area code.

"Davenport."

"Lucas? This is Jeff Toomes, again, from the Watergate. I got your number through the reservation system."

"Yeah, what's up?"

"Maybe nothing, maybe something," Toomes said. "I'd been walking around the garage for ten minutes or so when I ran into you. A couple cars came and went, but nothing unusual. I was in the stairwell when you drove out and I heard a car engine crank right as you were leaving, but I hadn't seen anybody going to their car. I stuck my head back out and there was a car leaving, moving fast. A dark blue Toyota RAV4. I got a feeling about it. Like he'd been waiting in his car for you to leave and he was hurrying to catch up."

"Huh. You get a tag number?"

"That's the other thing. I didn't, because there was something on his tag. Mud? Maybe mud, but I couldn't read the number, which worried me a little. That bullshit mud-on-the-plates thing. Maryland plates, though."

"Hey. If it turns out to be something, I'll send you a dollar," Lucas said.

Toomes laughed. "Four more and I can get a cup of coffee. You take care, man."

LUCAS LOOKED IN HIS REARVIEW MIRROR, but didn't immediately see anything that looked like a dark blue RAV4. He checked repeatedly on his way to the meeting, never saw a RAV4, as far as he knew. But who really saw any difference between a RAV4 and about a million other mid-size SUVs? Dark compact SUVs were like cockroaches scurrying along the highway.

Still, he called Jane Chase, told her what Toomes had said, and asked, "Could you check Lang and Gibson, see what vehicles they have registered to them? I don't know who else could have picked me up."

"With a hotel security guard, could be a figment of his imagination," Chase said.

"The guy's an ex-cop and not stupid."

Chase said she'd check, and Lucas relaxed in his Cadillac and dialed up some tunes.

GREENE WAS WAITING IN A BACK booth at the Panera Bread finishing a grilled cheese sandwich when Lucas got there. Lucas got a lemonade and slid into the booth across from him. Greene was a heavyset man with skin-flaking sunburnt forearms and a fleshy nose set in a weathered face. He had white patches around his eyes, as if he wore dark glasses while recreating in the sun—fishing or golf, or something like that. Sailing, maybe, since he was ex-Navy. His face and forearms had an oily sheen, possibly sunscreen.

He was wearing a short-sleeved Ralph Lauren golf shirt, had a gold bracelet on one wrist, a gold Rolex on the other, what looked like a Navy ring on one ring finger, and a pinky ring on the other hand, with a cracked green stone that might or might not have been an emerald. He appeared to be in his forties.

He said, "Marshal. You're not gonna eat?"

"Had a late breakfast," Lucas said. "Thanks for meeting me. We have a situation . . ."

"Lang told me. 1919. I hadn't heard of them until he mentioned the name and I called around—don't bother looking, I used a burner. Anyway, a couple of guys had heard rumors about the site, but nobody had actually seen it. I don't know how much credence you can put in a threat."

"We're uncertain about the reality of it, but we can't

take the chance," Lucas said. "How about taking a guess for me? Who'd do this? What about this American National Militia?"

Greene gave a quick shake of the head. "I don't think the ANM would be involved. They're not like us anyway, though sometimes I feel a . . . temptation to move toward their position. You know, strip the country down, go back to basics."

"Why don't you think they're involved?"

"Because . . . they're so quiet. Very secretive. You know, we're a little paranoid, over where I am, and we like to know about other political groups that might be out there and give us a hard time. Most of those black-flag dudes, they're the guys who travel around the country, the Antifa and those people . . . they're fools, but they can disrupt a peaceful demonstration. They'll fight you. The ANM? You hear things. Like they might have snipers who actually snipe. Charlie said he mentioned the shootings in Pennsylvania and Michigan and so on. So . . . I don't believe they'd be involved in a complicated conspiracy with websites and social media and all that. If they wanted to hit somebody, they'd just do it."

"Charlie suggested that they could be behind the site, but intended to hang the blame on the alt-right . . ."

"That could be, I guess," Greene said. "That would still leave them open to exposure, though, if you feds managed to trace the origins of the website. And it was sure to create a lot of investigative activity." Greene shook his head. "There's something off about the idea of that site. I can't tell you exactly what's wrong about it, but there's something. It's kind of . . . childish. Or, incredibly evil. One of the two. I think if the ANM was involved, there'd be no website. There'd be a dead kid and some secret phone calls."

"I'll think about that," Lucas said. "In the meantime . . . who might do something like this website?"

"I was hoping to pick *your* brain about that," Greene said. "I know you guys have files on everybody. Mine must be an inch thick."

"I can't talk about the investigation, but I'll tell you, Richard: one of those bigwigs' kids get killed and the feds will be all over you guys," Lucas said. "All over you. You're ex-Navy, so I suspect you know what could happen if the government really decides to kick some ass. If the hammer comes down."

"Why do you think I'm talking to you?" Greene asked. "I need the brownie points. My people aren't nuts—well, some of them might be, but it's usually manageable. I don't want anyone to know I was talking to a federal marshal, but if I find out anything, and I do have some lines out, I'll call you."

"Do that," Lucas said. "Anything that might possibly be relevant. Anything."

LUCAS WAS IN HIS CAR again when Jane Chase came back and said that Charlie Lang had a BMW seven-series sedan and a BMW X5 SUV. Gibson had a BMW three-series sedan. "Good German cars, right outa Munich," she said. "Not a Japanese car in the bunch."

"Okay."

"And I hate to say this, but we've got a problem."

"Uh-oh."

"Yes. There's been a leak. Fox is asking about 1919. They've apparently been on the website . . . hang on a minute . . ."

She went away from the phone for a few seconds and Lucas could hear somebody talking fast in the background. Chase came back and said, "Okay, CNN is calling. They've been on the website, too. They've all got it."

The traffic back into DC was brutal and Lucas didn't get to the Watergate until almost six o'clock. When he got to his room, he turned on the television and switched back and forth between CNN and Fox; nobody was talking about 1919. Maybe, he thought, it was a false alarm, or maybe the FBI had made an appeal to the networks.

The day had been warm and he'd been running around since early morning. He decided to get dinner in the hotel restaurant and then sit with his notes and figure out what his next step might be.

Back in his room after a Santa Fe salad, he hit the shower, and when he got out, CNN's talking head was shouting about breaking news, and sure enough:

"CNN has learned exclusively that an apparent alt-right website has been publishing photographs of the children of prominent national politicians in what seems to be an implicit threat. The FBI has asked that we not reveal the name of the website, but we have reviewed the site and find it rife with alt-right articles in addition to the photographs. We have asked Barney Grier, an expert on the alt-right, to tell us what he thinks this site may mean. Barney?"

Lucas: "Ah, shit."

The camera switched to a man with an exceptionally bad black toupee to go with a ruggedly squared-off nose and chin and deep-set eyes. A caption identified him as a former Navy SEAL officer.

"This is a startling development, something we've not seen before—the children are those of Democrats, according to our source. Given the history of violence from the right-wing extremist groups, this threat has to be taken seriously . . ."

Lucas turned to Fox, where a nearly hairless, soft-faced man was saying, ". . . most likely a provocation from some group like the Antifa organization, which has shown its willingness to use internet tools to spread fear. When you actually *examine* the articles on the website, you find that they come from a wide range of right-wing organizations, some of whom greatly disagree with others. In other words, this is a pastiche, a fabrication . . ."

Blah blah blah . . .

But, Lucas thought, the story was out there, and that complicated everything.

He went back to CNN and watched for a few more minutes. Despite the tone of excitement, they were already repeating themselves. He turned the TV off, put on underpants and a T-shirt, and lay on the bed to read notes and files.

At 8:30, his cell phone rang; the caller was "Unknown." He answered with "Yes," and a woman asked, "Is this Marshal Davenport?"

"Yes, it is, who is this?"

"I'm Marcia Miller, the public representative for the American National Militia," the woman said. "We understand you've been trying to get in touch."

"Yes, I have. Where are you located?"

"Here in Washington—my office is actually across the river in Virginia, but the DC metro anyway."

"Great. When could we meet?"

"Right now. I operate a small public relations firm and we normally keep regular nine-to-five business hours, but when I spoke with Charlie Lang, he suggested that your request might be somewhat urgent. I would be willing to meet with you tonight. I could come to your hotel."

"I could come to your place . . ."

"I don't think that's necessary. I'm only a short distance from the Watergate. I could be there in fifteen minutes." Miller said. "We could talk in the restaurant."

Lucas wanted to deal with her on her home ground, but couldn't immediately think of a credible excuse to avoid a meeting right then, in a restaurant virtually on the other side of his hotel door. "I'll see you in fifteen minutes, then. I'll be wearing a dark blue jacket and a checked shirt," Lucas said. As he got dressed, he tried to remember if he'd told Lang that he was staying at the Watergate. He wasn't sure.

Downstairs, in the restaurant, he got a beer and was halfway through it when Miller arrived. She was wearing a subdued women's business suit, gunmetal-gray jacket with matching pants, and an icy blue, high-collared blouse. She carried a black leather satchel that could accommodate a full-sized automatic, if she felt the need for one.

She spotted him, nodded as he raised his glass, and strode over. She was a middle-sized woman, auburn hair off her shoulders, a square nose and chin with blue eyes and freckles. She all but sweated competence and focus.

She slid into the booth across from Lucas and asked, "Do you have a badge?"

"I do," Lucas said. He showed her his ID case, with the marshal's badge and the plastic ID card. She took it and actually read the card, then handed it back.

"I should tell you a few things before we get started," she said, knitting her fingers together on the tabletop. "I can't help you in identifying my clients. I repeat that: it's not that I wouldn't, it's that I *can't*. I was recommended by somebody, I don't know who, to Old John. He interviewed me by telephone, hired me by telephone, and pays me in cash, which I carefully record so I can faithfully report it to the IRS. I get an envelope with two thousand dollars in it shortly after the first of each month, plus whatever expenses I've incurred, usually printing expenses. I have a series of ANM position papers that I

send to people I'm told to send them to. They're not recruiting documents, they're arguments."

"Two thousand dollars a month doesn't . . ." Lucas
shrugged.

"Sound like much? It isn't. That's because we don't do
much for them," Miller said. She waved at a waitress,
pointed at Lucas's glass, and mouthed, "I want one." The
waitress gave her a thumbs-up, and went to get a beer.

Turning back to Lucas, Miller said, "As I mentioned
on the phone, I run a small public relations group, ori-
ented toward conservative causes. I have five associates
and we represent thirty-two different groups— everything
from nonprofit conservative advocacy groups to small
businesses to alt-right organizations. We began by repre-
senting some lesser-known guns-rights groups and then
some smaller gun manufacturers, then other general
small businesses, and so on. A couple of the alt-right
groups, over-ground groups, got in touch, and we took
them on, and then Old John called. We have no information that the American National Militia is engaged in any
kind of illegal activity. If we learned that they were, we
would drop them immediately."

"You say you don't know who they are, but you
must be able to get in touch—I assume you're here with
Old John's permission."

"I was asked to meet you. I can get in touch much
of the time; other times, I can't. Somebody will send
me a Gmail address. It's good for exactly one outgoing
message, as far as I can tell. They always read the first
email, but I've never gotten a response to a second one

to that address. Then sometime later . . . sometimes days later . . . another address will pop up in my email. Going the other way, from them to me, isn't a problem, of course. They send what they call 'white papers' to my email. I take the papers to a printing company and then send the printed documents to congressional or other influential leaders at their office addresses. Whether or not anyone reads them, I have no idea."

"Do you have a contact address now?"

She shook her head: "No. I used the one I had to tell the ANM person at the other end of the line about Charlie Lang's call, about you. Charlie said that you're investigating this 1919 group. I gave the ANM the website address for 1919. ANM got back to me and told me to get in touch with you and to tell you that they are not 1919 and have no idea who might be behind the website."

Her beer arrived and when the waitress had gone, Miller took a sip, said, "Good, it's been a long day," and then added, "I told them what Charlie said about the website—that it seemed to be an invitation for somebody to shoot a child, possibly as part of a vote extortion scheme."

"Did they react?"

"Yes. They said that was crazy."

"They're right about that. Now it's out in the media."

She wrinkled her nose. "Won't last long, as a story, unless something happens. With all the insane politics going on, the cable networks will have moved along in two days."

"I hope."

"So do I, or you might actually get an attack from a crazy person. Anyway, Old John or whoever is on the other end of the email said I should give you the white papers so you could see who they were." She reached down into her bag and pulled out a stack of computer paper, maybe twenty-five sheets, stapled in separate packs of three or four pages each. There was a simple "ANM" in large type at the top of the first page of each pack, with blocks of professionally laid-out type filling the pages. "They send us the material, we edit and format it and send it to the printer. I pay the printer, send the billing amount to the ANM when I get an email address, and they pay me."

Lucas took the paper, but said, "This is not going to help much. I don't care what their papers say—I need to talk to one of the leaders, preferably Old John, if he's a real person."

"He is," Miller said. "Or at least there's a person who calls himself that, and the three times I've spoken to him, it's the same voice. He sounds older and gruff."

"Then when you get an address, give him my number and tell him to call me. There's a reason that I need to talk with him."

"Which is?"

"I'll tell *him*," Lucas said. "He might not want you to know."

"Okay." She took two large gulps of beer, then pushed the glass away and slid out of the booth. "I don't know when they'll send me a new address. I don't even know *if* they will, since I've been talking with a federal marshal. If they do, I'll give them your phone number."

"Do that," Lucas said. "We don't need any kids killed by nutcases. They might help prevent that."

She nodded and walked away.

LUCAS FINISHED HIS BEER, paid for both of them, and carried the ANM material up to his room. He spent a half hour reading it—and it was more interesting that he'd expected. The ANM was apparently a radical libertarian organization, unlike the usual race-based whack jobs. They didn't like taxes and didn't think there should be any, or very few.

They didn't like a big military, they didn't like authority, they didn't like cops or social workers or any kind of welfare, in which they included Social Security, Medicare, Medicaid, and school lunch programs. They did like private property and self-reliance. They apparently didn't care about a lot of stuff. They didn't care about race, they didn't care about gay marriage, they didn't care about feminism, they didn't care about prostitution or gambling or drugs.

"We don't care what people inject in their arm. That's their business. If they overdose, it's not our business to take care of them—it's theirs."

They did like guns. Guns, the papers said, were a practical symbol of self-reliance. Their media list of recommended titles, contained in the shortest of the white papers, included both Henry David Thoreau and the movie *Fight Club*.

None of the papers were signed.

JANE CHASE CALLED AS LUCAS was about to turn out the lights and go to bed, and he filled her in on the meeting with Miller. "We'll look her up," Chase said. "We should have done it before now, but I guess we didn't know about her. Should have."

"Don't disturb her," Lucas said. "If she's telling the truth, the thread that goes to the leadership is pretty thin. As far as we know, she could have some way of signaling that she's been approached . . . or might be monitored. I need her to get to Old John for me."

"What are you going to ask him?"

"It seems to me that he's got an interesting organization and they're sort of right-wing, in an unusual way. They're not really alt-right, the way TV talks about alt-right. If Charlie Lang is correct, I wouldn't be at all surprised if they have a lot of . . . intelligence . . . on these other right-wing groups. That would be their natural recruiting grounds, picking out certain people who might tend to agree with them more than they would the crazier alt-rights. If they sent feelers out to all their cells . . . if they really have cells, like Charlie thinks they do . . . then they might come up with something."

"All right, but, Lucas—no midnight meetings with Old John down in Whiskey Holler. Talk to me."

"I will. I gotta have somebody calling me, because right now, I'm fresh out of things to do."

SOMEBODY CALLED AT NINE O'CLOCK the next morning, about the time Lucas was thinking of getting out of bed. A man's voice: "I'm a member of the ANM. I understand you would like to talk with one of us. I won't talk on the telephone because of your surveillance techniques. In fact, I'm about to throw this phone into a trash basket. If you do want to talk, walk out under the front canopy of your hotel at exactly ten o'clock, turn right toward the Washington Monument, and start walking. Don't cross Virginia, stay on the Watergate side of the street. You might have to walk quite a way, so wear good shoes. We checked the internet and we know what you look like. Come alone. If you're not alone, we won't talk. If you don't like these terms, don't come."

Click.

That was clear enough, Lucas thought.

He got cleaned up, decided on jeans, a golf shirt, and a sport coat, with trail-runners, along with his Walther PPQ. He thought about calling Jane Chase. FBI surveillance teams were good, but the caller warned him about a long walk and the only reason for that would be counter-surveillance. There was a lot of security on a weekday in downtown DC, so he wasn't concerned about being shot or kidnapped.

Still: Ten minutes before he left the room, he sat

down and wrote a note to Jane Chase, explaining what he was doing and about the ANM contact. He sealed the note in an envelope with her name on it and left it on the hotel room desk. If he got shot or disappeared, she'd find it soon enough.

At ten o'clock, he walked out from under the canopy into the bright sunlight, took a right, and started walking toward the Washington Monument.

And he walked. And walked. He didn't try to hurry, but ambled along, for twenty-five minutes, when he could see what appeared to be the end of the street. The Washington Monument was obscured by overhanging trees, but when he could see it, he knew it wasn't far away, and there was a sprawling park around it. That's where he'd be picked up, he decided.

He crossed the last small street before he'd come to a much larger one, and started past the small triangular green space on the other side. He passed a bronze statue where a man stood reading the legend beneath it, and as he passed, the man turned and said, "Marshal Davenport."

Lucas looked back.

The man was as tall as Lucas, thin, but not hungry looking, maybe a runner, perhaps thirty-five years old; brown hair sprinkled with white, conservatively cut. He had a tanned oval face, brown eyes, narrow nose and lips. He had an ex-military or ex-LEO feel. He was dressed almost as Lucas was, running shoes and jeans, but with a black T-shirt under the sport coat, instead of a golf shirt.

"You're my guy?" Lucas asked.

"Yes. I am," the man said. "If you arrest me, I won't resist, but I won't say a word except 'lawyer' and by-and-by, you'll be in desperate legal trouble for arresting me, since you have no cause. You also won't get any help from us. Agreed?"

"I'm not here to arrest you or even hassle you," Lucas said. "I followed your instructions. You aren't Old John, I take it?"

"No, I'm not. We were fairly sure you would follow the instructions, but not positive," the man said, mildly enough. "You are being followed, though. Doesn't look like federal people, to us."

"Blue RAV4?"

"He *was* in a blue RAV4, but he ditched it after a while—found a lucky parking place—and now he's on foot," the man said. "He's on Virginia, a block or two behind us."

"Goddamnit. I'd really like to know who it is," Lucas said. "He was back there yesterday. I think he's trying to figure out who I'm meeting."

"We've taken a couple of pictures of him. We'll send them to your phone. An email address would be useful, too."

Lucas took out his ID case, extracted a business card with his official email address, and handed it across. The man dropped it in his jacket pocket.

Lucas: "Now . . . I wanted to talk to you because Charlie Lang thinks you're a large well-organized group with good contacts among the alt-right. We need to track down this 1919 group as quickly as we can. If a kid gets hit, the FBI will tear up everybody in sight and that includes you. We need you to put out feelers to all your cells: anything will help."

"I don't think we have that many people in the District, or around it," the man said. "I'll talk to my friends and see what they want to do. See what they *can* do. We'll get back to you by telephone, the number we called this morning."

"You don't know how many members you have? What's your position with the ANM?" Lucas asked.

The man smiled. "I'm a trusted member. We don't have officers, as such. Even Old John is more of a coordinator than an officer —he can't order people around, because, well, that's the kind of thing we're against."

"You can't really promise me anything? Make any commitments?"

"No. I'll get in touch with Old John if I can and he'll trickle the information around, and maybe something will trickle back up. That's all I can tell you."

"You know, from the outside, you *sound* like this 1919 group," Lucas said. "They don't identify themselves, they don't ask for anything specific, they apparently are trying to recruit people they don't know and who don't know them . . . and from the looks of the website, they're fond of guns and we know you guys are."

The guy rolled up his hands in a "what can I say?" gesture. "They want to shoot kids, they're nuts. Our basic philosophy is that the country is going to hell in a handbasket. We don't want to overthrow it, we just want to survive the coming catastrophe. We want to help create a sustainable form of social organization, where people re-learn how to take care of themselves."

"I saw that in your papers," Lucas said. "On the other hand, there've been some shootings . . . like in Michigan and Ohio and Pennsylvania, that some alt-right people think you were involved in. If you're willing to pull a trigger, then . . . where are you going to stop?"

"I don't know anything about that," the man said.

"If you can't give me any information or commit to anything, then . . . why are we talking? And why you?"

"We're talking because apparently the PR lady wasn't enough for you, you wanted to go face-to-face with a member. Here I am. We also wanted to get a look at you—we've got some pictures now. From what we've read on the internet, you've been involved in some killings yourself."

"As a cop."

"Some people would say as a tool of the deep state. I don't necessarily say that, since I've had some . . . relationships . . . with the deep state myself. But, some people would say that—about you. You work for people who pull the levers, but don't come out in the open to do it."

"And you're here . . . why? You personally?"

"I was chosen to make contact because my particular friends, my group, is here in the District, and includes people with operational intelligence backgrounds with the U.S. government. They could spot somebody tracking you. I specifically was chosen to meet you because I'm very fast and can run like hell, if necessary."

He smiled at that, as a phone buzzed in his pocket. He answered, listened for a moment, then clicked off and said, "The guy who's following you is trying to sneak up on us. He's about a half block down Virginia. I'd rather he not see my face."

Lucas looked down the street and the man said, "I gotta go."

He waved a hand and a car crossed the street and pulled up next to them, a blue LED "Uber" sign in the window. He nodded at Lucas and said, "We'll call, one way or the other," and climbed into the Uber. The car pulled into a stream of traffic and was gone.

It had been, Lucas thought, as he looked after the Uber, well done. He'd hoped to get some hint of where the man was from, or where he was going, or who he might work with, or, with any luck, something with a bit of DNA on it. He'd gotten only a sliver of that: the guy might be a government employee, somebody with intelligence contacts, he was a sprinter, and Lucas had a good description. Maybe the FBI could work with that, and maybe not.

A teenaged couple were walking past. Stoners, Lucas thought. The boy looked at the bronze statue, then at Lucas, and asked, "Who the fuck was General José Artigas?" He pronounced the general's first name as "Josie."

Lucas shook his head. "Who the fuck knows?"

———

HE WAS LOOKING FOR A CAB—he was apparently one of the few people on earth who didn't have the Uber app—when his phone dinged with an incoming message. He checked it, and found himself looking at a photo of Lang's assistant, Stephen Gibson, walking away from a blue RAV4. A second photo showed the RAV4's back license plate, still with a smear of mud, but he could make out the tag numbers. Probably a rental, he thought.

It also told him more about the ANM. They could call for help from people who could do effective surveillance, and not be seen, even when taking photos of someone who was, or should have been, wary.

Lucas waved at a taxi. The driver waved back and sped on.

HE WOUND UP WALKING BACK to the Watergate and called Jane Chase on the way, to tell her about the meeting. "Damnit, Lucas . . ."

"I didn't want to scare the guy away. When he was telling me the conditions for the meeting, I figured he'd spot you. Anyway, I'm good, and I know Gibson is following me, but I'm not exactly sure why. I'll call Lang and ask him."

"Tell me more about the guy you met. The ANM guy. If we have enough detail, we might be able to put a finger on him."

Lucas gave her what he knew: the man had been an inch over six feet, a few pounds either side of one-eighty, blue eyes, brown hair with a touch of white, athletic, a runner, maybe ex-military or a cop, possible connections in the intelligence community, well-spoken, likely a college grad.

"That gives us a chance," Chase said. "Why don't you come around later in the day . . . two o'clock . . . I'll have my assistant put together a video show."

"All right, I'll see you then. Did the media coverage kick out anything?"

"Not so far. The media doesn't seem to have reporters anymore, they just have commentators. What we're seeing is mostly hot air. Our guys who work the alt-right say there's some talk about the 1919 site, and apparently it was mirrored on a couple of alt-right websites before it got taken down, so the web page is still out there."

WHEN LUCAS AND CHASE were finished talking, he called Charles Lang, and asked, "Why is Gibson following me? I assume you assigned him to do it."

Lang tried bluster: "Stephen isn't following you. That's ridiculous. What makes you think . . ."

"I've got a photograph of him, Charles. Standing right next to the RAV4. I suspect that's a rental car, right? In case I spotted it?"

Silence. Then, "We wanted to see who you spoke to. We *are* a research team and you wouldn't commit to keeping us informed."

"Well, tell him to fuck off. If I see him around anymore, I'll find a way to put him in jail. Interfering with a government investigation or something. Maybe you could go with him. It'd be a new cultural experience for you."

"I'll pull him back. I apologize, but I find this whole episode rather fascinating and I couldn't help myself."

"Well, help yourself. Make him go away."

BACK AT THE WATERGATE at eleven o'clock, Lucas decided he didn't want to read any more of the FBI files, which left him nothing to do, except go shopping. He got the Cadillac and drove over to N Street, to Figueroa & Prince, a custom tailor shop where he'd spent a few thousand dollars on previous trips.

His sales clerk was named Ted, who brightened when he saw Lucas coming through the door. "Lucas! I was thinking of you only yesterday. You won't believe what we got in from Italy. It's the finest piece of wool I've seen this year and just right for Saint Paul in the winter."

Lucas spent two hours in the shop—it *was* a fine piece of wool, an absolutely perfect shade of blue to chime with his eyes—and after picking out three neckties and three shirts that would go with it, he was in the back of the store, being measured by Jim the Tailor, who said, "For you, we'll have it in three weeks. Your measurements have changed, though. You've lost weight. Will you get it back or are you slimming down?"

"I'll get it back: best go with the old measurements."

"So it wasn't a diet?"

"No, I got shot last spring."

"See, don't do that . . ."

ANOTHER TAILOR CAME THROUGH, nodded at Lucas, and asked, "You on a case?"

"Yeah, I'm trying to chase down some right-wingers. No big deal."

"That 1919 thing? The SS?"

Lucas nodded. "That's the one. You saw it on TV?"

"Yeah, the girl is on CNN. She's a cutie."

Lucas: "What girl?"

"You know, the high school kid who uncovered the whole thing. She's on right now."

"Oh, boy." Lucas stepped off the box he was standing on, and asked, "Where's your TV?"

"Back in the fabric room."

Lucas followed the tailors back, where a small television sat on a shelf among bolts of fabric. A card table and four metal folding chairs were crowded into an aisle between racks of cloth, apparently used for lunch breaks. On the TV, Audrey Coil was shown comfortably ensconced in a guest chair on the CNN news set, while the talking head was saying, "It takes a brave girl . . ."

Lucas stopped listening and called Chase. "Are you watching CNN?"

"Oh, no. Somebody got shot?"

"Not yet. I may go over and shoot Audrey Coil as soon as she gets off the set. She's up there now, spilling her guts."

"Oh . . ."

"Go ahead and say it," Lucas said.

"That little bitch, I'll wring her neck."

SEVEN

Chase's assistant, a young man named Donald, met Lucas in the Hoover Building at two o'clock and took him to a conference room that had a seventy-plus-inch television screen hung from one wall. The screen was connected to a chunky black laptop computer.

"Ms. Chase is trying to get on top of the Audrey Coil situation," Donald said. He was a pale man with reddish hair, dressed in a blue suit, white shirt, and burgundy necktie, the suit precisely the wrong shade of blue; altogether, his outfit had the grace you'd expect from a one-man band in a vaudeville show. Lucas decided he would have a personal conversation with Donald before he left. "I don't know what's happening there. Based on what you gave us, I doubt we'll find your man from the ANM, because there are so many possibilities, but we can try. A runner, possibly a com-

petitive runner at some point, white, thin, tall, perhaps a current or former government worker, possibly
ex-military who may have expressed political sentiments
and has contacts in the intelligence community. We included your height and weight estimates with hair and
eye color."

"That's about all I got," Lucas said.

Donald plugged a thumb drive into the computer,
handed Lucas a remote control, and said, "What will happen now is that you can click between pages. There are
forty headshots per page, and almost two hundred pages.
That's eight thousand headshots. You will get through
them surprisingly quickly . . . a few seconds per page, most
of the time. Probably less than an hour to get through all
of them, if you don't spot him. If you see a possible, note
down the number on the headshot and the page."

He handed Lucas a legal pad and a pen.

One of the chairs was a worn leather recliner and
Lucas took it. Donald brought the computer up, opened
the thumb drive, and Lucas clicked the first page. The
photos came in ranks of eight, five ranks per page. He
could scan a page and reject it with barely a blink. Donald said, after a moment, "If you find something, you
have my number. Call when you're finished."

LUCAS FOUND HIS MAN, David Thomas Aline, on the
twelfth page. He scrambled to the door, which had
barely closed, and caught Donald before he turned a
corner in the hall: "Hey! I got him."

"You're joking," Donald called back.

"No. I got him."

Donald came back, took down Aline's name and an index number, and said, "I can't believe it worked."

"Neither can I. I spent a good part of my life looking at mug shots and hardly ever found anyone. Let's look the guy up." Lucas paused, and then said, "Donald. About your suit . . ."

DAVID THOMAS ALINE WAS EX-ARMY, a former captain who'd served for six years after graduation from West Point. He'd been a middle-distance runner at West Point and had spent four of his six years in the Army as a logistics officer at an air base in Kuwait. When he left the Army, he'd joined Bechtel Corp. as a logistics manager.

"Odd job for somebody who doesn't like the government," Donald said. "Bechtel's a major government contractor."

They were sitting in Chase's office, paging through a computer printout of everything the FBI had on Aline.

Lucas said "Mmm," because he hadn't thought about it.

Chase showed up as they were reviewing Aline's file. She was slightly disheveled—wrinkles in her usually perfect suit, a hank of hair out of place. "That little . . . person . . . really screwed us. What are you doing here?"

"Lucas found the ANM guy. We have a file on him," Donald said.

"You're joking."

"That's what Donald said, but I wasn't." Lucas took her through the sequence of events and filled her in on Aline. "What we need to do now is find out who he's been talking to . . . who he's been getting phone calls from."

"That could be tough if he's got a burner phone," Chase said. "Which he probably does, if he's security-conscious."

"If there's any way you could call him a national security threat, we could black-bag him," Lucas suggested.

"Nope, that won't work," Chase said, shaking her head. "He's basically a political operator working for a conservative political group. If we went for a warrant, the judge would laugh us out of the courthouse."

Donald said, "Stingray."

They both looked at him and he added, "Or a tower dump, if we know where he's at in the evenings. When the PR lady talked to Lucas, she probably connected with Old John right away, or at least somebody high up in the ANM. They had to do some organization to make the approach to Lucas so quickly. They had to talk to Aline, and he had to get in touch with whoever photographed Gibson, the people looking for surveillance."

Chase said to Lucas, "If he's at home in the evenings, we can dump the nearest cell phone tower. There'll be thousands of calls, but most of them will go to homeowners and we can get the associated addresses, which will leave a certain number of burners, but not a huge number. We'd look for a cluster of calls from a burner. It's all computer-sorting . . ."

"You don't need a warrant?"

"No. We can issue a subpoena on our own to the cell companies, get a dump," Chase said.

"Or we could track him with a Stingray unit," Donald said. "The Stingray'll force all the nearby calls through the unit, so we can see who he's calling. We can't actually intercept the call, though."

"Let me talk to some people," Chase said. "We'll explore the possibilities."

"What happened with Audrey Coil?" Lucas asked.

"What you saw," Chase said. "Her mother's a little angry with her, but not too, because she'll undoubtedly get a few invitations herself, from Fox or CNN or MS-NBC, to talk about this. Audrey was insufferably cute, by the way. Insufferably sincere."

"She won't be cute if somebody shoots her in the face," Lucas said.

They all thought about that, then Chase asked, "What's next up? You got anything else going?"

"Not a thing," Lucas said. "I've got nothing to work with. None of the alt-right people have given me anything useful. I could go interview the other kids who were photographed, and their parents, but you guys have already done that and I've read the transcripts. If nothing comes out of the Aline thing, I might as well go home."

"Please don't," Chase said. "Let me get something going on Aline. Take the rest of the day off. Take tomorrow off. We could have something by the day after."

INSTEAD OF TAKING THE DAY OFF, Lucas went back to the Watergate and called Charles Lang. Gibson answered and said Lang was shopping.

"I don't need to talk to Charles," Lucas said. "You'll do fine, since you're the researcher. Charles told me that the ANM had a training camp in Kentucky. I need to know where it was. Exactly."

"We never looked into it," Gibson said. "We didn't want to . . . expose ourselves . . . to them."

"Well, look now," Lucas said. "You were snooping on me and that pisses me off, and it might even be a crime; and you do research, so do some research and call me back."

WITH THAT UNDERWAY, Lucas changed into jeans and walked a mile or so to Dupont Circle, to a bookstore he'd visited the last time he was in DC. He spent a pleasant hour browsing, got a sandwich at the café, talked to Weather for ten minutes, and was strolling back to the Watergate with a Martha Grimes novel under his arm, when Charles Lang called back.

"Well, you scared Stephen, thank you very much. He gets upset when people snap at him."

"Life in the big city," Lucas said. "Did you find out where that training camp was?"

"I've emailed you what we found, along with a map and a satellite photo of the area. It's in Kentucky, as I said, not far south of Cincinnati, Ohio. It's a farm owned by a person named Milton Faye."

Back at the hotel, Lucas booked a Delta flight to Cincinnati the next morning, leaving a little after nine o'clock, and another one back, in the evening, and reserved a Jeep at Hertz. He checked his email, found the incoming file from Lang. The place he was looking for was outside a Kentucky hamlet called Piner, and from the looks of things, was in the hills.

"Take a day off, my ass," he muttered to himself, as he settled back with the Martha Grimes novel.

THE NEXT MORNING, after another fear-inflected but absolutely smooth flight to Cincinnati—the airport was actually across the Ohio River in Kentucky, where Lucas got a couple of bagels with cream cheese at a Bruegger's— he picked up the Jeep and headed south. The town of Piner turned out to be a crossroads with a couple of dozen homes, a red-brick school, a red-brick church, and a convenience store where Lucas stopped for a Diet Coke and to check that he was on the right road.

He was. He headed south out of Piner, through heavily wooded hills and small farms, turned east on a narrower road and eventually found a mailbox that said

"Faye" at the end of a gravel-and-dirt driveway that disappeared up a hill into heavy timber.

He went on by, eventually intersected with a larger highway, where he pulled over and checked his cell phone: he had three bars and called Chase.

"Nothing yet," she said, when she picked up.

"I'm in Kentucky, checking out the farm where ANM supposedly did weapons training," Lucas said. "It's remote and spooky, but there's good cell service."

"Jesus, Lucas . . ."

"Could you check on a guy named Milton Faye, see if he has a cell phone? If he does, could you watch who he calls?"

"I can do that, but are you going to get shot?"

"Not if I can help it."

"Why don't I call in the state cops to go with you?"

"No. I don't want to make a deal about this. If I show up with a bunch of cops, I don't think he'll call anyone. He'll hunker down. I want him to think that the only thing I've got going for me is an old newspaper clipping."

"I don't know . . ."

"Call me when you're set up."

"Might take more than an hour," she said.

WHEN SHE CALLED BACK, an hour and a half later, Lucas was wandering through a Flying J Travel Center in the town of Walton, off I-75. He took his phone outside to the parking lot and asked, "What do you got?"

"Milton Faye and Barbara Faye have AT&T phones, plus Milton may have gotten sneaky and acquired a second phone from RurCon, which is an MNVO, which actually buys time through AT&T . . ."

"It's a what?"

"MNVO—Mobile Network Virtual Operator. Since it buys time through AT&T, we only have to talk to one company to look for connections and we're all set to do that. Our phone guy faxed a subpoena to AT&T a half hour ago and they've acknowledged it, so we're all set. I bet if Mr. Faye calls Old John, he'll do it on the Rur Con phone. Sneaky-like."

"Whatever. I'm going over there," Lucas said.

"Lucas . . ."

"Watch the phones."

LUCAS CRUISED THE FAYE place a second time. He couldn't see a house or any other structure up the hill; there was a small cornfield that ran along the road, and an old rust-covered hay rake in one corner of the field, probably dumped there a few decades earlier.

He turned around, got out of the car, pulled his shirt out to cover the cross-drawn PPQ on his left hip, got back in the car, called Chase and said, "I'm going up there now."

"We're all set. Call when you leave."

Lucas turned up the driveway past the "No Trespassing" sign. The Faye house, a metal barn, and a trailer home on blocks, were four hundred yards up the rutted driveway, where the hill flattened out into a long narrow crest. The house looked like it came out of a '60s low-income suburb, a faded baby-blue ranch-style with asbestos shingle roof. A well-waxed black Ford F-150 was parked in the yard; a bumper sticker read, "I support U.S. Truckers."

As Lucas parked, a heavyset bearded man stepped out on the stoop at the front door; he was dressed in crusty jeans and a flannel shirt, though the temperatures must have been in the upper seventies. An oversized black-and-tan Rottweiler came out behind the man, walked around him and down the three steps. He might have come all the way to Lucas, but the man spoke a single word, which Lucas couldn't quite hear, and the dog stopped.

The dog would have looked more dangerous than the man, had the man not been carrying a shotgun. He didn't point it, it just dangled from one hand, but it was there.

"Guess you didn't see the 'No Trespassing' sign," the man said.

Lucas wrinkled his nose—dog poop, he thought—and said, "I did, but I'm a U.S. Marshal working on a case and I came to see you, if you're Mr. Faye."

"I'm Faye. See me about what?"

"About a militia training camp here on your property a couple of years ago," Lucas said. "I found an article about it in the Cincinnati paper."

"Didn't talk to the paper," Faye said. "Told their reporter to get off my property."

"You didn't talk to them, but they identified you," Lucas said.

"Nothing illegal about a training camp," Faye said. "A bunch of guys came up to do some self-defense shooting."

"I didn't say there was anything illegal, unless it was done as part of a conspiracy—say, to shoot somebody," Lucas said. "I need to talk to someone high up in the militia. I talked to one man who wasn't, and he couldn't give me the help I need. That's why I'm here."

"Can't help you with that." Faye switched the shotgun to his other hand, still dangling. "Gentleman come up here and said he knew I had a shooting range on the property. He asked if he could rent it for a few days for some friends of his to do firearms training. He give me nine hundred dollars in advance and some guys came up for four days—they stayed up in Cincinnati or somewhere, came down during the day—and that was about it. They shot up some ammo, got back in their cars, and went home."

"Who arranged it? What was the guy's name?"

"Ed," Faye said. "Never did catch no last name."

"Were all the guys from around here?"

"Listen, Marshal, I didn't spend a lot of time talking to them," Faye said. "Showed them the range, let them be."

"You didn't see their license plates?"

"Nope, guess I didn't think to do that. And I got to tell you, I'm getting tired of being talked to on my own property."

Lucas ignored that. "What kind of weapons were they using?"

"Rifles, some pistols, too, I guess. I could hear that difference, you know, rifles going *bang bang*, pistols going *pop pop*. That's about all I got to say. Don't know no more."

"Mind if I look at the range?"

"I do mind. If you want to look, come back with a search warrant," Faye said. "I done nothing wrong and I like my privacy. Now, I'm going inside to call my attorney. C'mon, Butch."

The Rottweiler followed him inside and the door closed.

Lucas looked around, saw nothing that might give him reason to stay, got in the Jeep, turned around and headed back down the driveway. At the bottom of the hill, he called Chase and said, "I'm out."

"I'll call you back," she said.

Three or four minutes later, she did: "He made a call to Cincinnati. They're still on the phone."

"You got a name and address?"

"Yes. One John Henry Oxford. I'll text the address to you. I'm going out to the NCIS, right now, to see if we've got anything on him."

"Call me."

His phone beeped a moment later and he pulled over, found a text with John Oxford's address, put it into his cell phone navigation app and continued north, following the app's vocal instructions.

Kentucky looked not unlike Minnesota, as long

as he was looking at the foliage piled up along the Interstate. As he got closer to Cincinnati, that changed,
and the landscape began to look older, more eastern;
more wrought iron, more like New Jersey, somehow,
than the Midwest. He passed a tall cylindrical building
and began picking up the buildings of downtown
Cincinnati—again, they looked more eastern than midwestern, more like Philadelphia than Chicago—and he
crossed a muddy brown Ohio River on the lower deck
of an interstate, stayed to the right, and took I-71 into
Cincinnati.

CHASE CALLED BACK: "Interesting stuff. Oxford has
one arrest, for disorderly conduct as a member of the
Weatherman faction of the Students for a Democratic
Society, during some riots called the Days of Rage in
1969. I never heard of them before this, but I read the
Wiki article on it. Days of Rage was a violent anti-
government and anti-cop demonstration. Lot of people
were hurt. After that, nothing."

"So he was political when he was a kid, and then,
what? Went underground?"

"Maybe he did politically, but not personally. He
worked for the post office from 1970 to 2010, a letter
carrier the whole time. Forty years. He's been retired
ever since. One interesting thing. Before he was with
the Weatherman, he was in the Army, a draftee, for two
years."

He'd been sent to Korea as a clerk, Chase said, and

was eventually promoted to Specialist E-4, equivalent to a corporal.

"Anyway, he had a bit of trouble and his company commander tried to give him what's called an Article 15, which is like a traffic ticket for a minor infraction. But in the Army, you don't have to accept an Article 15. He refused to take it and demanded a summary court-martial, which is a big risk, because with an Article 15 you might pay a small fine, but a court-martial can send you to jail."

Chase said Oxford had been accused of negligence during a routine practice drill intended to put a fast-reaction squad in front of possible North Korean commandos. He claimed that he was in no way negligent, that his apparent negligence was in fact negligence on the part of the company commander, who had supposedly organized the fast-reaction squad.

When all was said and done, he was found not guilty by the military court and all charges were dismissed.

"I FIND THAT INTERESTING because he refused the easy way out and was willing to take on his own commanding officer. He's a rigid guy. Even when he was young. He knows his rights and he won't bend. Then he comes back home, goes to college at Wayne State, apparently gets radicalized by an anti-government group. And then . . . fades into the background."

"I wonder how long he's been doing the ANM

thing?" Lucas asked. "Is this a retirement hobby or has he been at it longer than that?"

"Well, you saw what we have on them. They've been around at least since the early 2000s and maybe back into the nineties."

"Huh. Then he could be anything. He could have an army of his own."

"He could," Chase said. "We've got an office in Cincinnati. I could scramble a couple of people to go to his house with you."

"Let me think about that," Lucas said. "I need a relatively friendly talk rather than an angry confrontation. Get him demanding a lawyer and we're screwed."

"Have him shoot you and *you're* screwed."

"I don't see that happening," Lucas said.

"Tell you what. I'll line up a couple of agents, have them nearby when you go in," Chase said. "Then, if there's trouble, you hide behind the couch and we come crashing through the back door with guns blazing."

"The thing most people don't know about couches, is that they're really good cover," Lucas said. "In movie shootouts, you see people hide behind them all the time. Got those big bulletproof steel plates inside them."

"Call me when you're close," Chase said. "Try not to get any davenports shot."

"Wait. Was that a pun?"

But she was gone.

LUCAS TOOK A BAD off-ramp, got tangled up in some side streets that his phone nav didn't seem to recognize, finally got reorganized and back on I-71 heading northeast into the suburbs. He got off I-71 and onto a back highway called Wilmington Road.

He called Chase, said he was about there; she said two agents had already spotted Oxford's house and were parked a few hundred yards away. "Turn your phone on, call them, then stick your phone in your shirt pocket and leave it on. I'm texting you the number."

"Okay."

There were a variety of houses and businesses along the road, some older, some newer, some close together, some with expansive lawns and fields around them, mailboxes sitting on posts along the roadway. When the numbers on the mailboxes started getting close to Oxford's, he pulled off the highway, called the feds, said he was going into Oxford's house, and they said they'd be listening.

John Oxford lived on a low hill, in a broad two-story white house with an open front porch and a well-kept, sweeping lawn that ran down to the highway. A middle-aged woman wearing jeans, a long-sleeved blue shirt, and a straw hat was driving an orange riding lawnmower across the lawn, and when Lucas turned up the gravel driveway, she lifted a gloved hand in greeting and kept cutting.

Lucas went to the top of the hill and found a parking pad to the left side of the house, with a three-car garage in back. He parked and walked around to the front door. A screen door was closed, but the interior door stood open, and he could hear a television playing inside. Lucas pushed the doorbell. A dog started barking and a hulking old man with a gray beard, using an aluminum cane, came trudging toward the door, followed by a sleek gray dog the size of a German shepherd.

The old man stepped up to the door, peered through the screen, and said, "Well, goddamnit anyway, You're that marshal. Davenport. I've seen the pictures of you."

Lucas nodded, and asked, "How are you, John?"

"Not as good as I was one minute ago, in there watching the TV." The screen door was held shut with a simple hook and he unhooked it and pushed it open and said, "You better come in."

Lucas followed him into what, in an old farm house, would have been called the parlor, a small side room with a couch and two overstuffed chairs; Oxford pointed at one of the chairs with his cane and dropped onto the couch. The dog lay down by his feet and closed its eyes. The screen-covered window was open. The lawnmower continued to drone up and down the yard, and Lucas could smell the fresh-cut grass.

"You have a hip problem?" Lucas asked.

"I have an *age* problem, as you'll find out in twenty-five years or so. Hip joints are okay, but there are a couple pieces going bad in my lower spine. Not much to be done about it."

"Sorry about that," Lucas said.

"I'm not going to tell you a hell of a lot about the militia except there's nothing illegal about it," John said. "Bunch of friends out politicking."

"From what I've seen, there's more to it than that," Lucas said.

John frowned and said, "Let me see. You were down at Milton's place, but you wouldn't have gone there if you already knew about me. Milton didn't tell you anything, so you must have tracked his phone call to my phone. Some of the boys said we should all have those cheap phones—burners?—but I thought they were an unnecessary expense. Guess I was wrong about that."

"Well, you know . . . technology. It's hard to keep track of," Lucas said. "Anyway, I didn't come here to arrest you. Not yet anyway."

Oxford grunted and said, "Not yet."

"The government doesn't have much information about your group. You've covered it up pretty well. But there are rumors about you and the rumors somewhat fit what we know about that website that I asked your Washington guy about."

"What do the rumors say?"

"That you might not be afraid to use guns."

"That's horseshit," Oxford said. "We might shoot in self-defense, we might train for that, but we're not cold-blooded assassins. That's all we were training for out at Milton's place, self-defense. We were making a point about self-reliance."

"I heard there was some sniper training going on."

"I didn't go out there, so I don't know," Oxford said. "Even sniping can be self-defense."

"Depending on how you define self-defense," Lucas said.

"Probably about the same as you do," Oxford said.

"Or maybe a bit broader? People who hurt other people, maybe deserve to get hit?"

Oxford grunted again, and said, "We don't think that somebody's going to pass a law we don't like, up in Washington, so we oughta kill a kid. That's crazy."

Lucas noticed that he'd evaded the question. "But you do have relationships with right-wing groups that might be a little crazy. Nazis, KKK, all that."

Oxford lifted his chin and scratched his neck for a moment, then said, "We have not much to do with them. A little maybe, mostly by accident. Here's the thing, Davenport: a group calls for a political protest on some point where we agree. We notify our folks, and if some of our members want to go, that's up to them. Then the Nazis and the KKK show up, and we all get thrown into the same pot. You know, you get a rally over on the left side, say, pro-choice, or maybe gun control. The Communists and the anarchists and the socialists and the mainstream Democrats, they all show up, but the media doesn't call them all Communists. That's what they do to us. The fuckin' Nazis, I hate those guys. The KKK, the same."

Lucas looked at him for a couple of beats, and Oxford looked back, and finally Lucas said, "Suppose I buy all that, everything you said. I'm not sure I do, but maybe. My job is to find the people who put up that website and find out what the hell they intend. It sure looks like a threat of the worst kind. There are people in Washington, with the FBI, who see your group as their best candidate. It would be a good thing for you to put the order out on your networks that your people, whoever they are, help to locate that 1919 group and give me a name and address."

Oxford continued to stare for a moment, then said, "Two things here. We've outlawed, in our group, the word 'orders.' We don't give them and we don't take them. We do what we call 'asks.' We can ask an individual or group to help out, but I can't order anything. The second thing is, we're not cops. We're not going to investigate for you."

"I'm not talking about being cops. I'm talking about self-defense," Lucas said. "A senator's kid gets killed and you're gonna get torn up, because nobody'll want to take a chance that you *might* be innocent."

"That sounds about like our government," Oxford said. He said in a new voice, quoting, *"Another horse, fiery red, went out. And it was granted to the one who sat on it to take peace from the earth, and that people should kill one another; and there was given to him a great sword."*

"Who said that?" Lucas asked.

Oxford sighed and said, "Never mind. All right. I'll put out an ask, heavy-like. I hate doing it, but I will. One of the things I hate about you guys, you government people, is that you put an innocent man in a box and make him do things he doesn't want to do, isn't required to do either legally or morally. It's like the sixties with the draft. Government fights an immoral, unnecessary war in Vietnam, that all the politicians knew was wrong and unwinnable, fifty-eight thousand boys get killed, and what happens if you don't want to go? You get your ass slammed in prison and your life ruined. I hate it. I hate every goddamned inch of it."

"So hate it," Lucas said. "But do your 'ask' anyway."

The old man stroked his beard, once, and said, "Shit." And, a moment later, "Goddamnit, I'll send out your ask."

"Thank you."

"You better be on your way," Oxford said. "If Marty finishes her mowing and comes in here and finds out who you are, she'll tear a strip off your back."

But the lawnmower was still going, so Lucas said, "I read the papers from your PR lady. You don't seem nuts, but how the hell do you think the world would run without governments?"

Oxford shrugged. "We don't. We do think the government should be a lot smaller. Maybe . . . ten percent of what it is. We've got two million people in the military, counting the reserves. You really think we need two million soldiers? When we've got missiles and hydrogen bombs? Who's going to invade us? We've got all those soldiers because we're poking our noses into other people's business. Let them take care of themselves. There are almost a million cops. You think we need a million cops? There are one-point-three-million lawyers, all sucking on the government tit in one way or another. You think we oughta need one-point-three-million lawyers to get through our lives? We have no problem with a government that builds roads and bridges and sewers and water plants and such. But two million soldiers and a million cops? More than a million lawyers? And listen—I could go on a while. Don't get me started on how all our tax money gets pissed away."

Lucas: "From our point of view, us deep-state people, it looks like it might help your cause if you had some leverage over the people who run the government, who pass the bills that do all the things you don't like. Leverage you could get from a site like 1919, if a kid gets shot."

"Bullshit. How in the hell would we keep track of that?" Oxford asked. "We'd need a hundred over-ground people in Washington to figure out what's going on in Congress and who's voting for what, and when. We're not that kind of group. What we are, is, we've got an idea and we're pushing it. We're growing, slow but steady. We've got more people with us than anybody knows. Smart people, too. Not crazy."

"All right, but you've still got those alt-right contacts," Lucas said. "John: call me."

They talked for a few more minutes, and John pushed Lucas into admitting that he thought that government was often overbearing and wasteful, and that maybe there were too many cops and soldiers and lawyers.

"See," John said, "You've got some potential to think for yourself. Maybe already been doing it."

Outside, the lawnmower shut down and Lucas said, "I guess I better run."

"Guess you better." Oxford pushed himself up from the chair and followed Lucas to the door. He said, "You'll soon enough find out what you've done here and it really gets me down, as a personal thing. Really bums me out, as us old hippies used to say."

Lucas stopped and turned: "What have I done?"

"You'll find out."

CHAPTER

EIGHT

Elias Dunn had been so shocked by his murder of Rachel and Randy Stokes that he called in sick the next day and the day after that and spent most of his time lying facedown on his bed with a killer headache crawling up the back of his head, a headache that neither Advil nor Aleve could touch.

He couldn't eat, couldn't hold anything down. He lived on tap water. It all had been too close, too personal, much more bloody than he'd expected. He hadn't done it efficiently—he'd even shot himself.

That shot had traveled between his buttocks, cutting a shallow groove in each of them. He'd bled through his clothes and onto the car seat, but the seat was made of some kind of leather-like plastic and was easily cleaned.

The wounds were not easy to treat, because he

couldn't see them well. Even in his floor-to-ceiling dressing mirror, he had to bend over and peer at them between his legs, which was not only painful, but humiliating. He washed the two wounds with soap and water, then slathered them with disinfectant ointment, covered them with stickless gauze from a first aid kit, and then, because he didn't have enough actual medical tape in the first aid kit, used duct tape to cover the layers of gauze.

The first night and the following day he couldn't leave the house because he couldn't drive with the headache. When he stood upright, or sat upright in his truck, clusters of bright blue specks flickered in front of his eyes like neon gnats. He called his survey crew, told them he was sick, told them he'd pay them full wages each day until he was back on the job, and he'd call them the night before they should come back to work.

The second night, he managed to get out to a Walgreens, where he bought a heavy-duty first aid kit including some disinfectant ointment that incorporated a painkiller. He rewashed and re-covered the wound, following instructions he found on the internet, and the pain eased a bit.

He woke on the next morning with a lingering ache at the back of his skull, but no gnats in front of his eyes. He crawled out of bed, nearly fell, staggered to the kitchen and ate a whole box of raisin bran with one-percent milk. He managed to keep that down and walked unsteadily to his computer and out to the Fauquier Now website, which covered Fauquier County and Warrenton. He poked around there, found nothing about any murders.

Nobody had found them yet?

He could hardly believe it, but that was apparently the case. He was tempted to search for the Stokeses by name, but decided that might be a security breach. He'd wait to hear.

HE SHUT DOWN THE COMPUTER and went back to his bed and flopped facedown. He didn't sleep—at least, he didn't think he did—but when he went back to bed, it had been morning, and when he got up, it was nearly three o'clock in the afternoon. The hours in between had been taken up with dreams not only of reruns of the shootings of Rachel and Randy Stokes, but also imagined videos of gunned-down children, police sirens, screaming politicians.

Eventually the reruns of the Stokeses' shootings had faded and the imagined images of screaming politicians and urgent media coverage had come to the fore. When he got up, his bare feet hit the floor and he sat there for a moment, imagining CNN and Fox and MSNBC covering those future shootings.

He wasn't a man given to a lot of self-analysis, but he recognized something he hadn't felt before: he was now more important than he'd ever been, or ever imagined he'd be. He was now a man who could change the nation.

He walked up to the bathroom and stared at himself in the mirror. He looked bad, without a doubt, three days of whiskers, his hair in disarray, his face sallow, gaunt. He cleaned up, taped a piece of plastic bag over his buttocks to keep the water off, then stood in a hot shower for fifteen minutes. He needed to work out, or jog, but was afraid that either one would break open the wounds.

But the shower helped: he was better.

On the phone to the job foreman: "Bill? This is El . . ."

"Man, how you feeling?" Bill sounded like he actually cared.

"Better. Whatever it was put me on the toilet every ten minutes for three days, but I went out and ran this afternoon. No after-effects, far as I can tell. I think I got a bad salad. Not coughing or anything. Where're we at?"

"You were running far enough ahead of us that we're okay, but if you could work tomorrow, that'd be a good thing."

"We'll be there at dawn, we'll work right down to dark and not charge you an extra nickel."

"You're a good man, El. I'll see you out there."

DUNN HAD NEVER gotten much in the way of email, and what he had, he caught up with, and then walked out and got his snail mail, his butt still throbbing as he walked. He found a couple of bills—he did bills every Saturday morning, so he was always current—and a first-class letter with his name and address printed on a laser printer. He carried the mail inside, opened the letter, and to his astonishment, found a copy of the letter he'd sent out to the three men he thought might use them.

The appearance of the letter fogged up his brain for a minute or so, until he realized what had happened. One of the original recipients of his letter hadn't known where it had come from, but he had thought that Dunn might be somebody to send it to. Anonymously. Dunn didn't know which man had passed it back, but he assumed that man might also have passed it to more people.

Maybe he wouldn't have to shoot again.

Maybe somebody else would do it. If enough people saw that letter. He walked around with the letter in his hand, and then went to the bathroom, burned it, dropped the ashes in the toilet and flushed them. He sat at the kitchen table, looking out at the tree line along the backyard, and thought about it: and was surprised by the feeling of disappointment.

Somebody else was going to be important?

Wasn't that a good thing? Setting himself up with alibis while the dirty work was done by someone else? Nobody would ever discover that he was the instigator of the whole thing.

His butt was bothering him and he got the idea that he had to keep moving it. He checked the wound, making sure it was thoroughly moisturized and heavily padded and taped, then went out in the backyard and walked around.

The next-door neighbor waved and Dunn lifted a hand. The next-door neighbor was a golfer and a fan of

every major sport he could think of, even including soccer. That's all he thought about: the guy knew so many
sports numbers for so many teams that even Dunn was
impressed. Would that guy, the sports guy, ever think
that the man standing in the next yard was planning to
kill the children of U.S. senators? Dunn smiled to himself: the idea was ridiculous.

And the spark of secret power bit him again, the
feeling of importance.

As Dunn had methodically built his political stance,
he'd read everything he could find about the rise of fascism in Europe, South America, and Japan. Though he
despised the stupidities of Hitler and his cronies, how
they'd corrupted a political ideal with their moral de-
pravities, he'd nevertheless read the standard works on
Nazism, Italian and Spanish fascism, and World War II.
As he walked in the backyard, pretending to inspect the
turf, he recalled a historian's theory that Good Ger-
mans had been able to kill men, women, and even small
children by dehumanizing them.

That, he thought, was why he was so stricken by his
murder of the Stokeses: he'd actually *humanized* them.
He'd enjoyed Rachel's company the night before the
murders, had felt an attraction to her. Thought she
might be attracted to *him*. Was that an error that could
be corrected?

Yes, it was, he thought.

He could not allow himself to focus on his targets as
humans. He not only had to harden his heart, he had to
re-think his whole approach to his . . . symbols. They

were meat, of no particular value. Ciphers. They simply weren't important when they were walking around, but they'd be important in death. Not human. Not human. Not human.

THAT NIGHT, he got his laptop and went out to a laundromat—another security move—that was open until eleven o'clock and had free Wi-Fi. He signed on and began researching the children identified on the 1919 site.

ALL BUT ONE OF THE CHILDREN, it seemed, went to private schools. The exception was a tenth-grader at a high school the size of a small city. Nothing he could find gave him a home address for her. Dunn crossed her off his list of possibles—how would you ever find her?

After an hour of research, one kid seemed to stand out. The son of Senator Ross McGovern of Arkansas, Thomas McGovern was a fifth-grader at the Stillwater School, a day school in Tysons Corner.

The school wasn't large—fewer than four hundred children—and was built on a former par-three golf course that had gone broke during the '09 crash. Though it had extensive grounds, it was surrounded by a thoroughly urban landscape, including a hospital with a parking structure that according to Google Earth was one hundred and sixty yards from the back wall of the school. The parking structure overlooked the playing fields—a baseball or softball diamond, two basketball courts, two tennis courts, a soccer field, a track.

The boy, Dunn thought, should be out on those fields a couple of times a day, at least until it got cold.

But a hundred and sixty yards was a fairly long shot. And he wasn't sure how much of the playing field you could see from the parking ramp—there was a line of trees along the school fence, and while he thought the parking structure was high enough to look over them, he wasn't sure. He needed to do some scouting and he needed to do some shooting.

By ten o'clock, the clothes he'd brought to the laundromat had been in the dryer for two hours. He retrieved and folded them, packed up his laptop, and headed home.

The next day, a Friday, he spent on the job, working until six o'clock, pushing the crew hard. After work, he drove to Tysons Corner, to look at the hospital parking structure. He hadn't realized it from looking at the satellite photos, but the hospital was on a low rise looking down on the school's playing field, which effectively boosted the height of the parking structure.

As he drove by, he saw one car entering, and one car leaving. Both stopped at parking gates, which would be a problem if he had to get out in a hurry. If he shot from the parking structure, the investigating cops would know the exact time when he pulled the trigger, from witness testimony. They would know soon enough that the shot came from the hospital, and would therefore know within a minute or so of when the car would be leaving the structure. And if there were cameras . . . and there probably were . . .

He couldn't use his own car and even a rental would be dicey—renting a car involved showing a driver's license and he suspected the rental agencies took secret videos of the renters, shot across the rental desk.

Dunn was a fan of military thriller fiction and movies, black ops stuff, and while the operators always seemed to know where to get a gun or a fake ID, or how to start a stolen car by rubbing a couple of wires together, Dunn didn't know any of that.

It seemed simple enough in a movie: you'd go to a sleazy neighborhood where some vaguely Middle Eastern–looking guy would sell you everything you needed to go underground. He didn't know any Middle Eastern–looking guys. He didn't know enough about car electronics to steal one. Another problem— he didn't know when the kid would appear on the playing fields. Could he sit in a car for an hour or two without attracting attention?

The parking structure was looking like a bad idea. He drove around the neighborhood, and four blocks behind the hospital found a possibility. An old cemetery, not more than a hundred yards long and fifty across, sat at the crest of a hill behind a neglected picket fence. The grass inside had been mown, but not recently, and was ankle-high in most places, even higher in scattered clumps of sumac. There were a few large granite tombstones, but most of the stones were small flat arches of what looked like once-white limestone, tilted this way and that, many so weathered that the inscriptions were barely legible. A dozen mature trees were spotted across the cemetery, and there were clumps of saplings, self-seeded volunteers.

On the hospital side of the cemetery, the hillside fell away sharply toward the back of the hospital. A weed-choked track ran along the bottom of the slope, and on the other side of it were an electrical substation and a mechanical yard, probably related to the hospital, with what looked like backup generators and a couple of large tanks, possibly for diesel. The hospital parking ramp rose on the other side of that, probably two hundred and fifty or three hundred yards away.

Dunn parked on the street a block away from the cemetery, walked along the rough track between the cemetery and the electric substation, until he thought he was about at the middle of the graveyard, then climbed the embankment. The picket fence on the back side of the cemetery was more than neglected—it had crumbled and fallen in several places.

Once on top of the ridge, Dunn looked down at the school's playing fields, which were clearly visible, but a long way out. How far? Four hundred and fifty yards? More? Even with his surveyor's eye, he wasn't sure.

He looked around, found a handy tombstone, and sprawled beside it. He was six feet back from the bluff, and a rifle, he thought, would set up perfectly for a shot at the school. A senile cottonwood tree stood twenty yards down to his left; he moved over to it. The trunk was big enough that he'd be invisible from the street that ran along the front of the cemetery, and the slope below was sharp enough, and the hospital far enough away, that he couldn't be seen from below, either.

But it was an extremely long shot; with a moving target, almost impossible for a man of his limited skills. The target would have to be motionless.

He spent a few minutes walking around the cemetery, zeroed in on a crumbling wooden shed, which probably once held yard tools. The shed was sitting on patio-style concrete blocks, each three inches thick, two blocks to each stack. He knelt and looked at them, and on one side of the shed found a loose block. He used his pocketknife to pry at it, careful not to make any obvious scratches. When it was loose, he pulled it out, and peered under the shed, then stuck his arm under. There was enough space, he thought, to hide a rifle.

He put the block back in place.

HE LEFT THE CEMETERY in the dark and walked back to his car. At home, he loaded Google Earth, which had a fairly accurate measuring tool, called up a satellite image of the school, and measured the distance from the cemetery cottonwood to the back of the school. Four hundred and ninety-six yards.

He thought about that and a question popped into his head. Was it necessary to actually kill the kid? Or only hit him? And maybe, not even hit him, if the bullet hit close enough to frighten him. It now occurred to Dunn that the important thing was that the right people knew that the kid had been shot at.

Better if he was actually hit, because then there'd be no doubt, but a close miss might be good enough. He thought about it that night, in bed, and decided that he needed to find out exactly how bad a shot he was.

And the next day was Saturday, the job site closed down.

HIS WEST VIRGINIA CABIN was deep in the woods and more than rustic: it was primitive, and for that reason, had never been broken into, although somebody had peppered the outhouse with a .22.

The cabin itself was a prefabricated metal shed with four windows and one door, which was locked with a heavy padlock, and all of it set on a concrete slab. Inside was an old wooden table with two metal folding chairs, a waist-high shelf that served as a kitchen counter, and a wide wooden rack that would keep an air mattress off the floor. There were fluorescent lights hung overhead with a plug-in cord that dropped to the floor at one side of the shed.

All of that could be seen through the windows, which was why nobody had ever tried to break in: there was nothing to steal and breaking in would be a pain in the ass.

When he went to the cabin, Dunn brought from home a Honda generator, a compact microwave, five gallons of gas, twenty gallons of water, an air mattress that was double-bed wide and five inches thick, and quite comfortable when inflated, and a sleeping bag. The generator would sit outside, with a single cord running through a hole in the side of the cabin to a multi-socket extension, where he'd plug in the lights and the microwave. He did have cell phone service.

Primitive, but snug.

ON THIS SATURDAY, he took along his total station, the tripod that supported it, and the reflector that bounced the distance-measuring laser beam back to the instrument.

Dunn had bought the land a couple of years after it had been clear-cut, and was therefore cheap—it no longer had harvestable timber and wouldn't for a couple of decades, and was useless for agriculture, too rough and, in places, too swampy. A few hundred yards from the cabin, a narrow creek wound across the property and he thought if he shot a line along the creek he might find a place where he could set up a five-hundred-yard shot.

He spent an hour finding the spot, lasing various possibilities with the total station, until he found a place on a hillside not quite as high as the cemetery in Tysons Corner, shooting to a creek bank over a patch of cattails. He stapled a target to a tree trunk and carried his .308 back to the spot on the hillside. A rotting log made a convenient rifle rest. The rifle mounted a 5-25 variable-power scope; he went with 25 power and began shooting.

He fired six times, taking his time, then carried the rifle down to the target, and found that he'd missed the entire eighteen-by-twelve-inch target all six times. He couldn't even find a place in the creek bank where the shots might have hit.

He had to think about that for a while. He wasn't *that* bad a shot. Maybe the scope had gotten bumped. He marched back toward the spot where he'd started shooting, but only a rough-paced hundred yards back. He found a place to shoot, braced the gun against a tree trunk, and fired three shots. Back at the target, he found a half-moon hole at the bottom far-right edge of the paper. He was shooting low and right.

He gave the scope four clicks of left windage and eight clicks of elevation, went back to his hundred-yard spot and fired three more shots. At the target, he found all three shots on the paper, but all over the face of it.

"It's not the gun," he said aloud. It was his shooting.

He marked the three shots with a Sharpie pen and went back to the five-hundred-yard stand. He'd have to hold very high at that range, but he didn't know exactly how high. He started by holding one paper-height—eighteen inches over the center of the target—fired a shot, held about twelve inches over, fired another, held on the top of the paper, six inches above the bull, and fired a third. He tried to do it all correctly, as was taught in the rifle magazines: good hold, steady trigger pull, breath held with the squeeze . . .

At the target, he found no new bullet holes at all. This would get tedious. He walked the five hundred yards back, fired a single shot, holding what he estimated was two feet over the target. No hole. Held about three feet over. No hole. He stapled another target face with the bull four feet over the primary target, to use as an aiming mark. No bullet hole. Maybe he'd overcorrected to the left, he thought. He gave the scope two clicks to the right. Nothing.

"It's not the gun," he said again. He thought he might be unconsciously flinching, yanking the trigger in anticipation of the recoil. At five hundred yards, with good gun support, plenty of time to shoot and no stress, he couldn't hit a target as big as a grown man's chest.

He needed analysis, and it occurred to him that he had a handy little computer in his pocket. He took out his phone and went out on the internet. After browsing for a while, he found a simple .308 ballistics chart and was astonished to find that he should be holding a full *six feet* over the primary target.

He restapled the aiming marker at six feet, and fired three more rounds at five hundred yards. This time, he found two holes on the extreme right side of the target, one five inches above the other; the third, he thought, was probably farther right.

He corrected the scope to shoot farther to the left, fired three more shots, and finally placed all three on the target, but not neatly grouped. His shoulder was getting sore from the repeated recoil, and he walked to the cabin to gather his gear and return home. On the walk back, another thought struck. While it wasn't *entirely* the rifle, some of it might be. And, he reminded himself, he didn't necessarily have to kill the kid, just hit him or come close.

At the cabin, he sat in his truck and went back to his iPhone. If he were to shoot a fairly high-powered .223 round, from a good rifle made for target shooting, he might be able to tighten his groups, and the much-reduced recoil might help prevent any tendency to flinch.

He was disappointed to find that he might reduce bullet drop only by six inches to a foot. That was better, though, and he might find the rifle more congenial to shoot. He deleted the app and shut down the phone.

He did know where he could get an anonymous high-quality .223, if he had the balls to go get it.

And if the cops hadn't been there first.

DUNN GOT TO THE PLAINS at seven o'clock, with the sun right on the horizon. He first cruised the Stokeses' house without slowing down. There were no signs of a police presence—no crime scene tape, no cop cars, nothing. He continued over to Warrenton, in the growing darkness, stopped at a Safeway, bought groceries for the next few days and a box of throwaway latex gloves.

At his house, he stowed the groceries, thought hard about it, and at nine o'clock, in full darkness, he cruised the Stokes place again. Again: no sign of life. He continued on for five miles, pulled off the road for a moment, got the lug wrench out of the back of his truck and put it on the floor behind the passenger seat.

The next trip back, he turned into the drive, continued past Randy's parked car and around to the back of the house, out of sight, but still on gravel; his heart thumping like a drum.

He put on the gloves and got out and listened—nothing but crickets. He went to the back door, listened again, tried the doorknob: locked. He pressed against the door's glass window with the wedge-end of the lug wrench. When it broke, almost silently, he reached through and unlocked the door, taking care not to cut himself.

Inside, he was hit by the stench. He hadn't thought about it, but the nights had grown cool, almost cold, and the heat would be on in the house, and the bodies had been there for four days, and were decomposing. He had a penlight, and he turned it on, careful not to shine it at a window.

He was in the kitchen. He couldn't see Rachel's body but Randy was lying halfway through the arched doorway between the kitchen and the front room. There was a closed door to his left, and he opened it and looked through.

Rachel's bedroom. A single bed, with a quilted coverlet, more quilts on the wall. Randy, he thought, would keep his guns in his bedroom, as there wasn't a lot of space in the small house.

He swallowed, tried not to breathe through his nose, backed out of the bedroom and followed the pencil-beam of light out of the kitchen and into the front room, high-stepping over Randy's body, trying not to look at Rachel's, a dark oval lump on the floor.

On the other side of her body, there was another door. He stepped over her, pulled open the door, and found a narrow staircase. A second door was off to his right, and he pushed it open. A bathroom.

Must be up the stairs. He climbed them, slowly, trying not to touch anything. At the top, he found a tiny bedroom with another narrow single bed, unmade. Clothes were strewn on the floor with copies of porn magazines; Randy had displayed a lack of knowledge about the internet, and this proved it: where did you even get porn magazines anymore? A wastebasket, overflowing with empty beer cans, sat next to the bed, and a radio sat on the floor beside it.

No guns, no gun cases, no gun safe. Was there a basement?

He turned away, then his eye caught a shadow under the corner of the bed. He knelt, and found two gun cases lying flat, and a range bag. He pulled out the range bag and found it half full of ammunition.

As he was pulling out the first of the guns, he heard a high-pitched creak and then another.

Someone on the stairs. He clicked off the flashlight and held his breath: he thought about calling out, but choked it back. The room wasn't quite dark, with a bit of moonlight filtering through the single window. *Creak.*

A dark, human-sized shape moved into the doorway, and Dunn, who'd been on his hands and knees,
rolled into a crouch, lifted the penlight, and shined it at
the shape.

Rachel Stokes was there, missing much of her head,
her eyes gone, her mouth a gaping hole. She didn't
speak, she reached toward him and hissed. Dunn fell
backwards, tried to scoot away from her as she rushed
toward him.

"No! No! No!"

And he saw the light from his flash was penetrating
her, and when she stepped in front of the window, and
looked back at him, the moonlight came through her
eye sockets and mouth, and then . . .

She faded away, hissing.

Dunn never cursed, or swore. Now, "Jesus. Jesus
Christ. Jesus God . . ."

He got to his knees and to his feet, stepped into the
doorway, shined his light down the stairs, to the open
door at the bottom. She'd be waiting there, he thought.
He looked back at the window, thought about climbing
out . . .

And finally caught himself. Not a ghost. A freak-
out. That was it: he'd freaked out. He had to leave, the
death stench of the bodies now suffocating, the stink
buried in his nostrils. He managed to gather up the two
guns and the ammo bag, and slowly, his hair again
prickling all over his body, got down the stairs.

He looked at the body this time; she was looking up
at him, as she had when he shot her that last time. He

stepped over her, then ran toward the door to the kitchen, vaulted Randy's body, dropped the ammo bag and a box of shells broke loose and scattered on the floor. He picked up a couple of them and then heard a hiss behind him, and his hair stood up. He grabbed the bag and the guns and ran out the back door to his truck. He threw the guns into the backseat, looked at the house—the door was standing open—and he hurried back to it, pulled it mostly shut, got in the truck, roared out of the driveway and away.

Halfway back to Warrenton, he almost lost control on a curve, and saw that he'd gone into it at more than ninety miles an hour. If a cop stopped him, guns in the back . . . .

He forced himself to brake, bring his speed down to forty-five, and into town.

He didn't try to sleep that night. He sat watching a series of mindless old movies, because when he didn't have a screen in front of him, he would see the moldering face of Rachel, rot and hanging flesh, coming for him in the dark.

Stepping back:

Lucas flew back to Washington on Tuesday afternoon. From the Cincinnati airport, he called Chase one last time, told her everything he'd gotten from John Oxford, and said, "I think we're on the wrong scent with the ANM. They may be odd, but their general . . . attitude . . . strikes me as inconsistent for the kind of group we're looking for."

"Oxford could have been lying to you," Chase said.

"Remember, he wasn't expecting me to show up. He was talking off the top of his head. If he'd been lying, I would have picked it up," Lucas said. "He seemed more intent on growing a political philosophy than trying some kind of judo to get legislation passed or killed. I'm not saying that they might not have been involved in some killings, but they'd be individual actions, given the kind of group they are. For this 1919 thing, we're looking for a smaller, crazier group. A few people, maybe. Not somebody trying to grow a political organization."

"Okay, as long as he puts out one of these so-called *asks*," Chase said. "When will you get back?"

"I'll be at the Watergate by seven-thirty or so. What's happening with your Aline investigation? You got anything more?"

"It's slow because we don't want to tip him off," Chase said. "Everything we've got so far seems innocuous. He carries a security clearance because of his military service and his current job and he had to go through a couple of background investigations to get it. He told an interviewer that he considered himself a libertarian but mostly voted Republican, didn't like the Tea Party, and so on."

"No mention of the ANM."

"No. But then, he wasn't asked. He was asked if he belonged to any groups that were on the State Department's terrorist list, or advocated the overthrow of the United States government, and he said no. We're looking at some of his financial records now, tax records, to see if anything's going on there, but so far, everything looks clean."

ON THE FLIGHT BACK, only half of Lucas's mind was looking for signs that the plane was breaking up and that he was about to die. With the other half, he thought about the whole presumed plan of the 1919 creators. Were they really looking for a killing? Or was something else going on?

If the plot were carried out, if somebody took a shot at a senator's child . . . how would the blackmailers get in touch with a senator they wished to influence? If phone books still existed, senators wouldn't have been listed. He assumed that their private phone numbers would be highly guarded, or every political junkie in the country would be calling. What would 1919 do, phone a senatorial aide and ask that the threat be relayed? That obviously wouldn't work—word of the threat would inevitably get out, making it impossible for the senator to comply. And no aide would give out the senator's private number.

Was it possible, he wondered, that the threat came from somebody who already had access to the senator's private phone number? An insider? The big danger, he thought, was that some crazy would think that 1919 had it all worked out and would shoot a kid.

WHEN THE PLANE UNEXPECTEDLY failed to crash at National, Lucas drove back to the Watergate, took a shower, got dinner, called Weather to chat, thumbed apathetically through the pile of FBI reports that he hadn't yet read, and went to bed at one o'clock.

At six the next morning, his phone rang and he groaned, picked up the phone, saw "Unknown" on the screen, and answered, "Davenport."

"This is the ANM guy," a man said. "Do you have a pencil and paper?"

"Give me a second," Lucas said. He had recognized the voice as belonging to Thomas Aline. He found his notebook and pen. "Go ahead."

"To begin with, and please write this down . . . go fuck yourself."

"What?"

"John Oxford put out a letter saying that he'd been compromised," Aline said. "He and his cell are now out of the ANM. There won't be any more contact between ANM members and John or any of his cell members. They're out. Done. He spent his life organizing it and now he's gone. So go fuck yourself."

"I didn't make him do—"

"Yeah, you did. Now. In accordance with an ask from John, before he removed himself from the organization, I have seven groups for you, and six leaders' names. Patriotus, looks like fake Latin, but combines 'patriot' and 'US.' Roland Carr is the leader, maybe a dozen members. Forlorn Hope, Mark Stapler is the leader, maybe fifty to a hundred members, we're not sure. White Fist, Toby Boone is the leader there. They're organized and they're dangerous, you gotta be careful if you go after them. Controlled Burn, we don't know the leader or the numbers, but they're basically a gang of parolees who got out of the federal penitentiary at Marion. Mostly career criminals but there's an underlying political thing going on. We also have Lethal Edge, which combines white power ideas with knives and swords, Dominick Caruso is the leader, Italian name but old Southern background . . ."

"What?"

"I know, but two of their members were charged with killing a black guy with a rapier," Aline said.

"Jesus. Who else?"

"The *White Gazette*, which is an underground on-line newspaper, compiled by a man named Jackson Wheatley and issued weekly, he's a growing influence on the alt-right because it's pretty well done. He apparently has a group of people working with him, but we don't know who. And Pillars of Liberty, leader is Leopold Brooks, whose members follow and picket and harass members of Congress. And they're good with cameras— they try for shots that make liberal politicians look bad, scratching their asses, picking their noses, and so on. Your problem seems to be over in that direction."

Lucas said, "Huh," and remembered that Pillars of Liberty was one of the groups that might have been funded by Charles Lang.

ALINE GAVE LUCAS a list of addresses for the six known leaders, four in Virginia, one in Delaware, and one in Maryland. "You have to go to your fed files for the other one."

"Is it a coincidence that they're all so close to DC?" Lucas asked.

"No. We mostly considered groups that would be active around the capital and have a history of violence or some other possible relationship to the 1919 website. Controlled Burn and White Fist are both prison-related groups, white gangs with a history of violence and extremist right-wing views. Forlorn Hope is weird, they're gun guys, they're believers in the ZOG, but they're also involved with some of these anti-female groups, these incel groups, the involuntary celibates. . . ."

"*What?*"

"Yeah, I know," Aline said. "Some of the junk they publish is completely off the wall. They do like guns and have argued that rape is not necessarily a crime, but in some cases, is a natural right."

"Have they raped anybody? For real?"

"Rumor says yes. We don't know of any actual cases. Anyway, they're nuts and supposedly heavily armed. Gotta be careful there. Patriotus, not so much guns, but they have talked about ways to force Congress to vote their platform, which involves shipping blacks back to Africa, Hispanics back across the border, and gays to prison camps where they'd be reoriented to heterosexuality. They could have come up with something like 1919—it fits some of their ideas. They might be the leading contender for putting up the website, but if somebody gets shot, the shooter would probably be a lone wolf. Lone wolves are admired, but not usually part of a group. Some of us think 1919 is an advertisement for a guy like that. Timothy McVeigh, the guy who did the Oklahoma City bombing, was a classic lone wolf and much admired by these guys."

"That's encouraging," Lucas said. "That they have a role model."

"You wanted nuts, they're nuts. I'm going now. No point in trying to track this phone, it's a very old untraceable burner and I'm throwing it out the car window," Aline said. "Oh, and don't forget. Go fuck yourself."

LUCAS WENT BACK TO BED; woke again at eight o'clock and called Jane Chase and told her what Aline had given him and that Old John supposedly was no longer a member of ANM.

"If it's true, that's a tough group," Chase said. "I'll have our HVE guys look at the names you got from Aline and I'll tell everybody to lay low on Aline. If Old John is gone, Aline could be a key to finding out who else is involved with ANM."

"What's, uh, HVE?"

"Homegrown Violent Extremists," Chase said. "The new flavor of the day. I'll get back to you on the other groups."

"And soon? If you don't give me something to do pretty quick, I'll have to go bowling."

"Not a fate worse than death, dude. But don't do that. Go eat breakfast, I'll have some preliminary stuff on its way before you get through your Wheaties, so you can keep working."

LUCAS TECHNICALLY WORKED for a Marshals Service bureaucrat named Russell Forte, who had an office across the Potomac in Virginia. Lucas called and told him about the ANM and about the extremist groups named by Aline.

"If I'm going to be sticking my nose into those hornets' nests," Lucas said, "I'll need some backup. Marshal backup. The FBI seems okay to me, but what I really need is . . ."

"Bob and Rae," Forte said.

"You think that's possible? On short notice?"

"I'll check and get back to you. You want them on a plane today?"

"If they want in," Lucas said. "I don't think I'll need them for more than a week, at the outside. If something hasn't happened by then, then probably nothing will."

BOB MATEES AND RAE GIVENS were members of the Marshals Service Special Operations Group (SOG) based at the group's headquarters in Louisiana. They specialized in finding and arresting hard-core fugitives, kicking doors and taking names.

Rae called Lucas a half hour after he talked to Forte, as he was getting dressed. "Is it something interesting?" she asked.

"Yeah. It's also somewhat classified at the moment, but basically, we'll be talking to some prison gang members and some other heavily armed fruitcakes. It's no harm, no foul—if they talk, we walk away. We're not there to arrest anyone, at this point."

"That's no fun," she said.

"Could get to be fun, though. You want in, or not?" Lucas asked.

"Oh, yeah. We want in, because we know you. Sooner or later, there'll be our kind of trouble," Rae said. "We're going through a training sequence with some new guys, but there are other people here who can pick up the slack. Bob is already headed back to his house to load up his gear and kiss his sweetie goodbye."

"And you'll be doing the same?"

"We'll talk about that when we get there," she said.

Lucas: "Oh-oh."

"Yeah, but it was inevitable. Sandro's already there in DC and I ain't going with." Rae had been involved with an FBI agent named Sandro Tremanty.

"Maybe you could have lunch . . ."

"Nope. I've still got feelings for him, but we're done. He's basically political, and he'll be a big shot. Having a tall black gunslinger chick hanging around won't help him with that. He sorta wanted both, the politics and the gunslinger, but I had the feeling that if he was forced to pick, he'd go with DC. So, I let him go."

"I'm sorry, Rae."

"I'll get over it. And I'll see you tonight, if Forte keeps his promise on the plane tickets. He's thinking two o'clock out of News Orleans. If that works, we should be there in time for you to buy us dinner."

"Bring your guns."

"We don't leave home without 'em."

WHEN HE HAD FINISHED DRESSING, Lucas called Charlie Lang and said, "I need whatever you have on Patriotus, Forlorn Hope, White Fist, Controlled Burn, Lethal Edge, and on the *White Gazette*." He omitted Pillars of Liberty from the list, because if Lang was their major source of funding, he'd warn them.

"I've heard of all those groups, but we wouldn't have much in our files—with the exception of White Fist and the *White Gazette*, they're all small and insignificant," Lang said, in his oily voice. "That said, that's a good list—they're exactly what you're looking for. I'll have Stephen pull together what we do have in our files and send it to you. And, I'll have him make some calls. We have some sources who would know those people."

"Excellent. I need it soon."

"Of course you do. Now, do you have anything for me?"

Lucas thought for a moment, then said, "I talked to Old John."

"No! You found him!"

"I've been told, by another ANM source, that John told the other members of ANM that he'd been compromised and his cell has now pulled out of ANM. No other cells will remain in touch with him. He's out."

"Fascinating," Lang said. "If you could give me his real name . . ."

"I can't do that. I could call him and ask if he'd call you. I have no problem doing that, and I think he might be interested in talking about his ideas . . . in a general way."

"I will wait by my phone."

LUCAS WENT DOWN to the restaurant for breakfast, and when he'd returned to his room and brought up his laptop, he found another group of encrypted files from Jane Chase. He opened them and found a note from her, along with files on each of the groups named by Aline.

In the note, Chase said that Controlled Burn, a prison-linked group, had been run by a man named Sawyer Loan, who was currently locked up in a hospital in Chattanooga, Tennessee. He and another member of the group had gone into a Chattanooga liquor store with guns and got all shot up themselves. Loan was hit four times, and his partner, Daniel McCutcheon, had been killed.

In her note, she said that McCutcheon had been shot seven times, three times while he was already lying on the floor, wounded, because the liquor store employees "wanted to make a point," which they had. Loan, she said, probably wouldn't stand trial in Tennessee, since he was out on parole and liquor store holdups were not an approved parolee activity. He'd be going back to a federal prison for at least another six years.

She added that Loan had not been so much a leader, as a phone number for the other members of the group. The Virginia state police believed his replacement was his girlfriend, Tabitha Calvin, who lived in a place called Goochland, Virginia.

Lucas looked up Goochland on Google Maps, and found it to be a bit more than a hundred miles and a couple of hours by car from Washington.

HE LOOKED THROUGH THE OTHER FILES. All six of the other groups, and their leaders, were closer than Goochland, and seemed to be bigger threats. Goochland, on the other hand, was out a ways, but he could be there and back before Bob and Rae got to Washington. If the Virginia state police were correct, he only had to deal with a girlfriend.

He checked his watch: 9:30. If he hurried, he could be in Goochland by noon, back before five. He hurried.

GETTING OUT OF WASHINGTON was a hassle, twenty minutes to the Potomac after he got stuck behind a moving van that was jammed up in a corner, but once on I-95, he began to roll. The landscape was like neither Minnesota nor the Cincinnati area—it was green, but if it wasn't industrial or commercial, it was forested, with relatively few farms visible from the highway. The route took him almost into Richmond, then swerved west on I-64, and from there cross-country into Goochland.

Goochland was an odd small town, because it *was* small, but it also apparently was the county seat. Lucas hadn't done any research on the place, having simply poked Tabitha Calvin's address into his phone's navigation app.

Once in town, he spotted a clutch of red-brick buildings with cop cars in the parking lot. He slowed and turned in and found he was at the Goochland County Sheriff's Office. A deputy was walking out to his car and Lucas grabbed him, showed him his ID. The deputy frowned at the Cadillac, and said, "Marshals are living high on the hog, huh?"

"I'm paying for it myself," Lucas lied. "I got shot a few months back and I need the cushion of a big car."

"Yeah? C'mon, I'll introduce you to the sheriff, he's having lunch," the deputy said. "Where'd you get shot?"

"Los Angeles."

"No, I mean, where on your body?"

Lucas tapped his chest: "Right here. .223 full metal jacket, thank God. A hollow point, I'd of been dead."

"Kind of dumb, using a full metal jacket," the deputy said, holding the door into the sheriff's department.

"I'm told they were using them in case they had to fight cops with bulletproof vests," Lucas said, over his shoulder. "FMJs are the redneck equivalent of armor-piercing bullets."

"Didn't think of that," the deputy said. "Bet it hurt."

"It did."

THE SHERIFF WAS A BEANPOLE, a tall, slender, friendly man, thick glasses giving a yellow cast to his blue eyes. His name was Preston Uwell and he was eating an egg-salad sandwich at his desk. He pointed at a visitor's chair and said, "Tell me all about it."

Lucas told him most of it, and Uwell said, "We all knew that Sawyer Loan was a bad one. He grew up here, went to school here, I'm told he was an evil little bastard when he was twelve years old. He was one of those boys who believed that power came out of the barrel of a gun and proved it on some cats. When we heard about Chattanooga, everybody who knew him said, 'Yup.' Though I gotta say, they must have a mean species of liquor store clerk down in Tennessee."

Lucas nodded. "I myself would pick a different state if I was going to hold up a liquor store. Maybe . . . Oregon."

"You got that right," Uwell said. "So you're here to see Tabby Calvin?"

"Yeah. I've got her address."

"Well, I'll tell you Lucas, Sawyer was a bad one, but Tabby's probably worse. Had a kid, she was beating that girl when the girl was two years old, finally put her in the hospital, like to die. Tabby got sent down the road to the women's prison for two years, where she refined her mean streak. The girl was taken away and put in a foster home, probably the first real home she ever had. Tabby never even asked to see her again. If you're going to talk to her, I'll send a deputy or two along."

"Does she work in town?" Lucas asked.

"She seems to have a private source of income," Uwell said, with a thin, skeptical grin. "She spends some money, got a nice truck, but as far as anyone knows, she doesn't do a lick of work. Not family money, either—her parents live over by Cumberland, don't have a pot to piss in or a window to throw it out of."

"Okay. Well, if you could give me a guy or two, only should take ten or fifteen minutes, unless she downloads everything she knows about these guys."

"Controlled Burn, huh? Nice. Can't say I ever heard of them, though."

"They don't advertise much," Lucas said. "At least, not in the circles we travel in."

THE SHERIFF SENT an investigator named Larry McCoy and a patrol deputy, Eric Cousins, to show Lucas to Tabitha Calvin's place, which they said was a mobile home, one of a dozen or so mobile homes on a Goochland side street. Lucas followed the two cop cars out of the parking lot, over a couple of blocks, and down a shallow hill where the mobile homes were lined up, not unlike, he thought, a bunch of cartridges in a clip.

McCoy pulled his car up at the next place down from Calvin's home, and Cousins pulled up in front of it, next to a white Ford F-150 with oversized wheels. Lucas was last in line, but couldn't park at the house up from Calvin's because a truck was already there, so he stopped a couple of homes farther back, parked, and walked down to Calvin's.

Cousins was already out of his car, McCoy was

walking up as Lucas got there, and the door at Calvin's mobile home popped open and a tall, rawboned woman with a face like a chunk of granite stuck her head out and shouted, "You get out of here. I'm not talking to your kind."

McCoy said, "Hey, Tabby, we got a U.S. Marshal here who needs to chat with you about some friends of Sawyer. You need to talk to him."

"Fuck you, you're the same fuckers who shot Sawyer. Get the fuck out of here."

Lucas called, "We only want to talk. We understand there was a group called Controlled Burn that Sawyer . . ."

"Fuck you!" She slammed the door.

There was an open window near the door, and Lucas called, "It'd be a lot easier to just come out and talk, Tabby. We're not here to arrest you, we just . . ."

BOOM! SHOTGUN!

Lucas didn't know who she was shooting at, but glass sprayed over the yard and he and McCoy and Cousins scattered, down behind cars, and the door of the trailer kicked open and Calvin barreled out, a pump shotgun in her hand pointing at the sky.

Lucas had his Walther out, but he was down on his hands and knees behind a neighbor's car when Calvin triggered another shot, this time straight up into the sky, and Lucas heard a pistol shot that smacked off the windshield of Calvin's truck and she screamed, "Larry, you asshole," and she pumped and fired another shot, leveled this time, and then she was in her truck, cranking it, and was off, straight down the street.

McCoy and Cousins were both up and unhurt, and shouting at each other. Lucas was closest to the patrolman's car and Cousins popped the passenger side door and Lucas piled inside, and Cousins hit the siren and began shouting into his radio as they spun out of the parking area, McCoy a few yards in front of them.

The street looked like it was a dead end, but actually was a loop, and they followed the white Ford up to the main street and then left. They went through town at sixty, then eighty, then a hundred miles an hour, Lucas registering a bank, a school, a church, a residential subdivision, and then they were out in the countryside, flying low.

When Cousins, crouched over the steering wheel, had stopped shouting into his radio, Lucas asked, "Where's she going?"

"Beats me," he shouted, amped from the chase. "There's nothing out here but trees."

A FEW MILES OUT OF TOWN, close behind Calvin's Ford, they saw another light bar flashing well up ahead, but coming toward them. "That's Roy," Cousins said.

Instead of slowing, Calvin sped up and Lucas feared that she was going to take the approaching cop head-on, a crazy suicide run, but then a side road broke to their right, and she hammered on the brakes and slewed sideways into the new road, straightened out, and headed up the hill.

They all followed, with a third cop car now behind Cousins, McCoy still right behind the Ford, and they went up the hill and around a couple of curves and then the Ford braked suddenly, turned, rolled down through the roadside ditch and up onto what looked like a timber road and Cousins said, "Oh, shit," as McCoy followed.

The cop car was no damn good on the rough track, banging around like a marble in a pinball machine and the Ford was getting away. Two hundred yards back into the woods, though, the track ended in a circle and the Ford skidded to a stop and Calvin was out and running into the woods, the shotgun still in her hand.

The three Goochland cops gathered behind the Ford, and McCoy said, "We gotta keep her in sight."

They could still see her, fifty yards away, crashing through the undergrowth. To the cop who'd just joined them, he said, "Roy, you stay here and coordinate. Get the guys up here, see if Bill King is on the road, get him in here and any other troopers that might be around. Let's go."

"She's fired three times," Lucas said, as they jogged toward the tree line. "Unless she took some extra shells, she's probably only got two left."

"So *one* of us will get out alive," McCoy said.

LUCAS, MCCOY, AND COUSINS went after Calvin, spreading out behind her, twenty-five yards apart, like a net, so she'd have to keep moving forward and couldn't reverse field and get around them. There was nothing subtle about either the runner or the chase: they were crashing through waist-high brush, clambering over rotting logs, occasionally falling. They saw Calvin fall into a deeper hole, where a tree's root ball had pulled out in a storm, but she was back up with the shotgun.

Another fifty yards and they were closing on her, and she pointed the shotgun back over her shoulder without looking and pulled the trigger, and the shot went into the overhead, knocking leaves down around them. McCoy shouted, "That's four," and as he did, she fired another shot over her shoulder and Cousins shouted, "Five!"

Up ahead, Calvin threw the shotgun away and bulled through a patch of red berries. Lucas was in the center and stepped in an animal hole just inside the berry patch and fell down, the brambles scratching at his face and hands. He was up and running again, pain lancing down into his foot.

They were narrowing the net as they got close to her and a dead branch tore at Lucas's sport coat, and then Calvin stumbled and fell. Lucas was right on top of her when she got back to her feet and she turned and had a two-inch-thick rotten dead branch in her hand and whipped it across his eyes and it broke but he went down again and then McCoy and Cousins were all over Calvin.

She was a big woman and fought them, cursing, with flailing fists, and Cousins gave her a solid punch in the cheekbone and when she went down, Lucas scrambled to his feet and dropped one knee on her head as the other two cops bent her arms behind her and put on the cuffs.

McCoy bent close and said, "We gotcha, Tabby. Now you can either walk out of here, or we'll drag your ass back through that berry patch."

"You motherfuckers," she sputtered.

McCoy looked at Lucas: "What happened to you? Your face is bleeding."

"She hit me with a branch." Lucas put a hand to one eye; his cheekbone was throbbing from the impact.

McCoy and Cousins hauled Calvin to her feet, and she spat at Cousins, who dodged, then leaned into her and said, "You do that again, I'll bite your fuckin' nose off."

They marched her out of the trees to the cars and called off other incoming cops, and Cousins drove her back to the sheriff's office. Lucas rode back to the Cadillac with McCoy, got cleaned up in a restroom at the sheriff's department. He'd have a black eye where he'd been hit with the branch and had bloody scratches across his face and neck. He patted the scratches with paper towels until all but two stopped oozing, and the sheriff, Uwell, came in with a first aid kit that had Band-Aids.

"Your jacket's ripped," the sheriff said, as he handed the kit to Lucas. "Not gonna fix that."

"This was supposed to be easy," Lucas said. He smeared some disinfectant ointment on the bleeding scratches and stuck on the Band-Aids.

He looked at his jacket—a four-inch rip across the fabric behind one pocket. The sheriff was right: it wasn't fixable. His shoes were okay, but his left ankle hurt; he sat on a toilet to check it and thought it might be swollen.

"We'll get you some ice for that," the sheriff said.

"Wonder what the hell that was all about? What was she doing?" Lucas asked.

"She panicked. We got a guy down at her trailer, turns out she had about a thousand yellow pill bottles sitting on her kitchen table and she was packaging up a few pounds of oxycodone tabs," Uwell said. "Biggest dope bust we had here in a while."

"Ah. Where is she?"

"Gotta a couple of our gals with her, getting her cleaned up. We're waiting for her lawyer to show up."

"Everybody else okay?"

"Everybody's scratched up from that briar patch, and McCoy banged up his bad knee again, but that happens about once a month. In return, we got ourselves a nice combat shotgun and a truck, unless the federal court takes it away from us."

"I don't think they will," Lucas said. "Cops getting shot at, high-speed chase, big drug bust—that doesn't seem like an excessive fine to me."

"And the county could use the truck," Uwell said.

"She won't need it. She's going back to the women's prison. Lucky for us, it's just down the road, nice and convenient."

CALVIN'S LAWYER WAS AT LUNCH in some other town and Lucas hung around, dabbing at his face, rotating a series of Blue Ice packs on his ankle, until she showed up at two o'clock. An earnest young bespectacled woman, she spent twenty minutes reading the reports by McCoy and Cousins on what had happened before and during the chase, and questioned Lucas about his involvement, then spent a half hour with Calvin.

When she came out of the interview room, she said, "We're not going to talk to anyone right now, except the marshal. Marshal, my client is willing to cooperate to a certain extent, but we will expect you to testify at trial, if there is a trial, about our willingness to cooperate."

Lucas agreed that he could do that, within the Marshals Service guidelines, and they discussed those for a moment, then Lucas and the lawyer went into the interview room and Lucas said to Calvin, "All I wanted to do this morning was to have a chat. We could have done that on your porch in fifteen minutes."

"Why the fuck didn't you say that?" Calvin snarled. Then she started to cry and said, "They gonna take my truck."

"Didn't have a chance to talk to you—and when you started shooting, you know . . ."

Calvin wiped the tears off her face and asked, "What do you want?"

"I want to know about Sawyer and about this group, Controlled Burn."

"Ah, that's just some guys Sawyer knows. There ain't nothing to it."

"I'm interested in their political beliefs—"

That made Calvin laugh, a bark-like sound that she cut off after a single bark: "Politics? I mean, they're . . . I mean, they don't even vote, far as I know. Sawyer doesn't, nor me neither. Voting's just another fuckin' scam. Don't never do no good."

"But they, the Controlled Burn guys, they don't like the government, right?" Lucas asked.

"Who does?" Calvin asked. "Nothing to do about it, though. I mean, Dick Willey got busted for fightin' that judge over in Lynchburg and I guess some things got said at the trial about the government pissing on people like us and Controlled Burn gonna get them, but nobody really thought it amounted to anything. I mean, some people came to Dick's trial and they made some speeches outside the courthouse, but it all frittered away. Dick's up to Marion now."

"You don't think the members, these people in Controlled Burn—"

"Controlled Burn is a bunch of guys that know each other," Calvin said. "Half of them couldn't tell you who the president is. After Dick Willey got busted, you know, there was talk about going up against the government, but it was all a lot of horseshit. Those guys get all shot up holding up a fuckin' liquor store. How are they gonna overthrow the government? They may be dumb, most of them, but they know that much."

They talked for a while longer, but Lucas eventually believed her: Controlled Burn was a group of holdup men who knew one another through a variety of different prisons, and whose anti-government stance derived from a single "fight" with a federal judge.

When he was done talking with Calvin, he stepped outside the interview room, thanked Calvin's attorney and gave her a card, and then went to his iPad and looked up the Dick Willey–judge fight.

Turned out that Willey had been convicted of an assault on a U.S. Postal Service letter carrier, who, Willey said, had been delivering more than mail to Willey's girlfriend. Out on bail while awaiting sentencing, he had ambushed and nearly beaten to death the federal judge who presided over his trial.

The news stories covering the subsequent trial and conviction, for assaulting the judge, were unclear about how the second trial attracted protests, although it appeared that the judge may have had an undisclosed blood relationship with the letter carrier. The protesters were Willey's relatives and a few friends.

Nothing there, Lucas thought. A bunch of criminals in a prison-linked gang got their name in the papers for assault on a judge, but it appeared the assault was based on a personal grievance, not on politics.

Lucas had a black eye, cuts on his face and hands, a sprained ankle, a torn Canali sport coat, all bundled up in a waste of time. When he limped into the Watergate lobby a little before seven o'clock, black eye, scratches, sprained ankle, and ripped jacket, he found Deputy Marshals Bob Matees and Rae Givens checking through the front desk, Bob carrying a gear bag, which Lucas knew was full of guns and other pieces of miscellaneous gear that the two marshals had found useful from time to time.

Lucas gave Rae a hug as Bob gawked at him: "What the hell happened to you? You look like you fell out of an ugly tree and hit all the branches on the way down."

"Something like that," Lucas said. "That's about what I did. Thanks for caring."

"And it left him a little cranky," Rae said to Bob.

Bob was a wide man, but not tall; as a senior at the University of Oklahoma, he'd finished third in the heavyweight class of the NCAA wrestling national championships. He was looking exceptionally well dressed, to Lucas's eye, possibly because he'd consulted Lucas on the clothing purchases. Lucas reached out and tapped his tie and said, "I'm proud of you."

Rae was tall, at six feet, a black woman with close-cropped hair, dressed in dark gray slacks and a dark gray long-sleeved blouse, with bits of gold jewelry here and there. Though slender, she had muscles like steel cables and weighed a hundred and forty pounds. Bob said she could reliably bench press over two hundred. She had a fondness for full-auto M4 rifles, although she wasn't allowed to carry one as often as she wished.

"I am a little cranky," Lucas admitted. "Right now,

all I want to do is get upstairs and stand in a shower for twenty minutes and get some ice on my ankle. I've got nothing for you tonight, but tomorrow we're going to run over to Delaware. You get a Service truck?"

"We did," Bob said. "A Tahoe, seventy-two thousand miles and it smells funny and the tranny sorta grinds, but, what the hell."

"Why don't we grab a bite in a half hour or so," Rae suggested. "Talk about what we're doing."

Lucas nodded. "Sounds good." As he walked away, he half turned, and said, "Good to see you guys. Glad to have you here."

"Glad to be here," Rae said.

CHAPTER
TEN

Lucas, Bob, and Rae got a snack in the hotel restaurant, caught up with one another. They talked for an hour; Rae wouldn't discuss her recent heartbreak and Bob said that his relationship with a local gym teacher might be developing into something serious. "Girl is smart and nice-looking and she could throw a cow over a barbed-wire fence. I'm saying she's in shape."

"And cow-throwing is a much-needed skill set," Rae said.

"You know what I'm saying," Bob said.

"I know exactly where you're coming from," Rae said. To Lucas: "Andi's got the best ass in Louisiana. That even includes my ass, which ain't exactly chopped liver."

AFTER EATING, they rendezvoused in Lucas's room, so Lucas could lay out the problem. He told them about the initial threat and what he'd done so far, about his request that Charlie Lang and Stephen Gibson do some research for him, and how he'd gotten all beaten up that afternoon.

"That's one lucky lady," Rae said, when he finished. "Shootin' at cops, and still alive. If I'd been there, I'd have killed her."

"Yeah, I expect you would have," Lucas said. "She might be the least of my problems here. I'm looking at six more groups. One of them is another prison-linked gang, and to tell the truth, after what Tabby Calvin said, this White Fist group might be the same deal as Controlled Burn. I mean, think about it: how many geniuses have you met in prison gangs?"

"Not many," Bob said. "They mostly couldn't figure out how to sign up for welfare, much less overthrow the government. That's not exactly in their thought processes, most of them being complete dumbasses."

"Exactly. Then, there's this Forlorn Hope group," Lucas said. "Whole different thing. I'm told that they like guns, they're probably dangerous, and the scary thing is, they are definitely crazy. They're pro-rape, for Christ's sakes."

"You don't hear that every day," Rae said.

"No, you don't. The impression I got from the ANM guy is that they hate everybody, and they see themselves as people with nothing to lose. They're dead-enders. Might as well die now because there's nothing to live for. Can't even get laid."

"What about the other groups?" Bob asked. "Lotsa guns?"

"Some of them could be armed, not all of them. The ANM guy thought Patriotus might be the most likely to set up the 1919 website. They're anti-black, anti-immigrant, anti-whatever you got. They do work the politics, though. They leaflet, they march, they propagandize, they call their congressmen."

Rae said, "Since we're mostly worried about shooters, let's go see this Forlorn group first thing."

"One thing that bothers me," Bob said, "is that we're not really getting at what the 1919 site is set up for. They want *somebody else* to do the shooting. Even if it turns out Forlorn Hope or one of the others set up the website, that doesn't get at the potential shooter."

"That worries me," Lucas agreed. "If it's a lone wolf, somebody out there nursing his paranoia, how in the hell do we stop that? We do have some Secret Service coverage—a few people assigned to get the kids to school. They've scouted out places where a potential hit might start and are covering them."

"That's good," Rae said.

"Gotta think about all of this," Bob said. "They've taken down the website, right?"

"Yeah, but if you want to read it, I made a copy before it was taken down," Lucas said.

"Send it to us—maybe we'll come up with some ideas."

"I will. And I'll send you the files on all these groups. Read through them, see if anything strikes you. I'm not seeing much."

———

AND THE NEXT MORNING, Rae asked Lucas, over waffles, "Did you actually *read* the stuff about Forlorn Hope?"

"Yeah, I think so, I sort of skimmed some of it," Lucas said. "What about it?"

"This Mark Stapler guy, the leader. He lives in the back of a coffeehouse and the front of the place is like a clubhouse for the Forlorn. We might be walking into a whole bunch of assholes who like guns and don't like us."

"You want to pussy out?" Bob asked.

Rae gave him the heavy stink-eye: "You know what I think about that word."

"I was using it in the non-vaginal sense," Bob said. "A synonym for fraidy-cat."

"Oh. Okay, then. No, I'm not trying to pussy out, I'm just pointing out that the files say they like guns and there may be a whole bunch of them."

"Not so likely early in the morning," Lucas said.

"I looked the place up and it opens up at six a.m.," Rae said.

"But how likely is it that they have club meetings at six in the morning?" Lucas asked.

"Not likely, but maybe more likely at eleven o'clock, which is about when we'll get there, at the pace we're moving."

"Then drink your coffee and let's go," Lucas said.

———

THE WOKE CAFÉ WAS IN DOVER, Delaware, a few blocks from the Dover International Speedway, according to a Google map on Lucas's iPad. Bob said the speedway featured NASCAR races a couple of times a year, but neither Rae nor Lucas knew anything about NASCAR so they didn't care about that.

The café was two and a half hours from Washington, and they took the Marshals Service Chevy Tahoe, Rae driving fast through traffic, through Annapolis and across the bridge to the Delaware farm country on the other side. Lucas rode shotgun, Bob sprawled in the backseat reading the *Washington Post*, the *Wall Street Journal*, and the *New York Times*, which they'd picked up before leaving the hotel.

"*Woke* means aware of societal injustice, usually referring to racism, but in this case, maybe sexual discrimination against men who are involuntarily celibate," Rae said.

Lucas said, "Hum. Might also mean you wake up when you drink their coffee."

"Could be a pun," Bob said. "They're outraged by the unfairness of being incels, and they also wake you up with the coffee."

"You gotta look at it from their perspective. There is something corrosive in the inability to get laid," Rae continued.

From the backseat, Bob flapped a newspaper page and said, "Rae, you ever look around on the streets?

You ever look at some of the guys who actually *have* women? Remember Elliott Horton, for Christ's sakes?"

"Who's Elliott Horton?" Lucas asked.

"The biggest goddamned loser criminal peckerwood you can possibly imagine, on the run for counterfeiting. When I say counterfeiting, I mean running off twenty-dollar bills on a Xerox color copier and them cutting them apart with scissors," Bob said. "Anyway, when we caught up with him, he was living in an unpainted concrete box on the banks of the Tombigbee, and his face looked like one of those old pictures of a witch, complete with a wart on his chin, and he had about one tooth, and he had *two* women. My theory is, show me a guy who doesn't have a woman, and you're looking at a guy who's got some other problem than not having a woman. Probably a large problem. Psychosis—something that actually repels women."

"You gotta admit, though, Horton's women only sorta loosely fit the definition of women," Rae said over her shoulder to Bob. "They weren't exactly Stacys."

Lucas: "Stacys?"

"Yeah, that's incel talk," Rae said. "The good-looking guys are Chads and they get all the good-looking women; the good-looking desirable women are Stacys. We should have given you a test on those FBI files."

"I didn't pay too much attention to that part," Lucas said. "The incel part."

Bob: "The problem the incels have, is not that they can't get *some* woman, it's that they can't get a Stacy. In my opinion. They grow up thinking they're gonna be nailing supermodels who'll be doing everything they see on their favorite porn channel, and when that doesn't happen . . . they're victims. And they're pissed."

"And they got guns," Rae said. "At least some of them."

Bob: "We got two mass killers supposedly involved with the whole incel thing. We take them seriously, Lucas. We don't do that 'Hum' shit, like you just did."

"Okay," Lucas said. He looked out at the countryside: it looked so *normal*. Where did all the flakes come from? How did you get whole collections of them, and in one place?

LUCAS HAD NEVER been in any part of Delaware. He knew Dover was the state capital, but driving through town to the Woke Café, the place seemed poorer than he'd expected, since state capitals were usually stuffed with well-paid bureaucrats. Maybe, he thought, Delaware didn't well-pay its bureaucrats. Rae said, looking out the windows, "Lots of black folks around. I didn't see that coming."

The Woke Café was a half mile north of the speedway, in a low rambling brown stuccoed building set back from the Dupont Highway. There were three cars and five pickups in the graveled parking lot out front, and two more in the back, which they spotted as Rae drove a loop around the place.

"How do you want to do it?" Rae asked.

Lucas thought for a moment, then said, "The guy, Mark Stapler, supposedly lives in the back. Maybe we knock on the back door? Maybe Rae knocks on the back door?"

"She's pretty much your basic Stacy," Bob said from the back seat. "Probably let her in. Once she's got her foot in the door . . ."

"Vests?" Lucas asked.

"It's warm," Bob said. "Wouldn't be able to cover it up without looking a little weird."

Rae shook her head: "No vests. That's hostile. Let's go in and talk—we're not here to bust anybody."

"Here to bust their balls," Bob said.

Lucas: "Let's try to keep the conversation away from the condition of their balls. They're incels, remember?"

LUCAS AND BOB STOOD back and to the sides when Rae pushed the doorbell button on the back door. No reason to think anyone would come out shooting; not that it made any difference, because there was no answer, or any sign of occupancy, even when she leaned on the button.

"Do it the other way, then," Lucas said, and they trooped around to the front. Inside the café, with Rae leading, they found a dozen people, all male, all white, drinking coffee, spread around five tables and three barstools, with a dozen more tables, all empty, stretching toward the back of the café. A newspaper rack sat to one side, with a few used magazines; three were gun magazines. The patrons all checked out Rae, Bob, and Lucas, and didn't go back to talking.

A man in a white chef's apron was standing behind a counter in front of a standard stainless steel coffee bar; a glass case off to one side held pastries, and a stack of *Wall Street Journals* sat on the counter next to the cash register.

The man behind the counter was short and not so much chubby as out of shape. He had a long sharp nose and expansive, feathery white hair sticking out from under an all-black logo-free trucker's hat. "Can I help you?"

"We're with the U.S. Marshals Service," Rae said. "We're looking to interview a Mr. Mark Stapler."

"I'm Mark," the man said. He appeared to be in his mid-twenties. "What did I do?"

"We don't think you did anything," Rae said. "We're doing research on a whole bunch of organizations in the Washington area, trying to make some important connections. We understand you're the, uh, president of a group called Forlorn Hope?"

"That's correct, but we haven't broken any laws, we haven't done anything that would interest you guys," Stapler said.

Another man stood up from one of the tables. As Lucas turned to him, he said, "I'm in Hope, and so is Jason here." He nodded toward a man still seated, who raised his hand. "What's going on?"

The man who'd stood up stepped over to the bar.

He was wearing a long-sleeved plaid shirt despite the warm day and the shirt was worn loose. When he bumped the back of a barstool, there was a distinct *clank*. Bob asked, "Sir, are you carrying a concealed weapon?"

The man said, "Yup, and I have a license for it."

"Please keep your hand away from it," Bob said.

"What is this?" Stapler demanded.

"We need to talk to you about an ongoing investigation," Lucas told him. "It would be best if we did it in the back, you know, for privacy reasons."

Two of the men sitting at a table to one side stood up and one said, "We're leaving, if that's okay."

Rae said, "Sure," and they left.

"You're messing up my business," Stapler said. He was getting red in the face.

"Let's go talk, no reason there should be a problem," Rae said.

"Who's going to watch the counter?"

"You've got two guys here from your group, they could keep an eye on it for a few minutes," Lucas said. "They can call you if somebody comes in."

Stapler looked at the other two men standing by the bar, and said to the man with the gun, "Ron, could you watch it? We'll go in the back. I'll make it quick as I can."

A LONG NARROW ROOM full of coffee-making supplies, a desk, and file cabinets sat behind the café's main room; Stapler led them through a second door into his living quarters, a two-room apartment with a couple of decrepit couches and a monster TV in the main room, with an unmade bed visible to the side. The walls held several antique guns, flintlocks and caplocks, mounted on pegs. The mounted head of a deer looked down from over the bathroom door.

Stapler didn't sit down. He stood, with fists on his hips, facing Bob, Rae, and Lucas, and said, "So tell me."

Lucas: "What do you know about a group called 1919?"

"Nothing. Well, nothing but what I seen on Fox. That redheaded chick talking it up."

"You haven't heard anything about it from your organization's members? No speculation about who might be behind it?"

"Nope. Not a thing," he said. "Just a minute."

He went back to the door that led to the café, opened it, and called, "Ron? Come here a minute, will you? Jason, could you watch the counter?"

The man with the gun stepped through the door and said to Stapler, "Nobody coming in right now." He was a bulky man, something not right about his left eye, which was watery and a bit inflamed.

Stapler nodded: "Okay. The marshals want to know if the members have heard about 1919. I told them I seen it on Fox."

Before he could reply, Bob asked the bulky man, "What's your last name?"

"Linstad." To Stapler, he said, "A couple guys were

talking about it last night, after that Fox show. Nobody ever heard of them before. They had pictures of kids belonging to politicians . . . like some kind of threat, I guess."

Stapler said to Lucas, "That's what I heard, too. You done some research on us, I'd guess, so you know what we're about. You would think we would have heard something . . . but we haven't heard anything."

"How come you come to us?" Linstad asked.

"Because you're somewhat . . . out there . . . in your politics, and you seem to like guns."

"We do like guns, for self-defense," Stapler said. "Nothing illegal about that."

"How about that whole rape thing?" Rae asked. "About how, sometimes it might be a reasonable activity?"

"That's all theory," Stapler said, flapping one hand dismissively. To Linstad, he said, "Go back out front, watch the register and send Jason back here. Let's see what he has to say."

Linstad went, and a moment later, Jason came through the door. "What's up?"

Rae explained, and Jason said, "Doesn't have anything to do with us. I saw that girl on TV, that's about it."

Lucas pressed them: they didn't move. They knew nothing about 1919.

Stapler said, "You know who you oughta talk to, is that Stacy chick on TV."

Lucas: "That Stacy . . ."

Stapler waved again. "Whatever her real name is.

She's been all over the media. You guys are running around trying to find 1919 and you wanna know what? The only one making anything off the whole 1919 thing is her. I'm in the coffee shop all day with that TV going on the wall and she's all over it."

"She does this thing with her mouth," Jason said, running his tongue around his upper and lower lips. "Like she's dying to give us all blow jobs. Course, she won't be giving them to the likes of *us*."

"Easy," Rae said. "She's a teenager."

"Name only," Stapler said. "She's coming on like she's hot to trot and then she's all, 'I'm a victim fighting back,' and she gets those teary eyes. Bullshit. I bet she's pulling down more money than I'll make in ten years running this place."

Another man came through from the front, a hulk, a lard-can head, shoulders a yard wide in a plaid shirt, all of it set above hips barely a foot across, with spindly legs dangling below. He had a voice like a bass guitar: "What the hell? Ron told me you was back here."

Stapler said, "Hey, Darrell . . . U.S. Marshals asking about 1919."

"What? The year?"

"The group, the website."

Darrell, who was wearing a photographer's vest, said, "Never heard of it. Are they like us?"

"No . . ."

Bob asked, "Sir, are you carrying a firearm?"

"Sure, isn't everybody? I'm all licensed."

LUCAS FOUND HIMSELF CONVINCED. Forlorn Hope was a bunch of sad sacks with guns. He wouldn't be totally surprised if one of the men went off some day and shot up a store or a newspaper or a school, or was busted for rape, but they probably knew nothing about 1919.

Rae pushed a few more questions out—why the "Woke Café" she asked, and Stapler said that woke people were aware of the various kinds of tyrannies inflicted on individuals by the American culture, including the tyrannies inflicted by women on helpless men.

"I'm not suggesting you do this," Rae said, "but . . . you know, you want sex, you go to certain parts of town . . ."

"Hookers?" Darrell blurted. "We could go to hookers. Some do. But that's not what we're looking out for. We want women who want us. We're entitled to women who want us. Everyone's entitled to somebody who wants them."

"Okay," Rae said. "I don't see how you solve that problem."

Darrell was getting angrier. "You think I like being like this? You think any woman gonna want me like this? You think—"

"Whoa, Darrell, save it for the meetings," Stapler said.

"Fuck it," Darrell said, and he disappeared back into the café.

Lucas called it off: "Mr. Stapler, I'm sorry we had to bother you, but you see our problem, I hope. If you hear anything at all, please call me; we'd be grateful."

He left his card. If his card had had a GPS transmitter on it, he wouldn't have been surprised if it landed in the nearest dumpster about two minutes after they left the café.

AT THE TRUCK, Rae said, "Five perfectly good hours we'll never get back."

"You think they're clear?" Lucas asked.

"If they had a website, it'd probably be as dumb as 1919, I gotta give you that. But, I didn't get a guilty vibe from them; nothing there," Rae said. "I kinda feel sorry for them. But, you know, as a woman, they were distinctly creepy."

"I didn't feel anything," Bob said. "Though, I gotta say, I'd like to hear that rape theory. That's gotta be some interesting theory, right there. Some guy out there is like the Isaac Newton of rape? I bet . . ."

"Shut up," Rae said.

Lucas said to Bob, "Why don't you ride up front?"

"Well, you're the big boss. Why would you want to ride in the back of the bus?"

"Careful," Rae said.

"Because I want to think," Lucas said. "I can think better in the back when I don't have Rae to talk to."

"What are you thinking about?" Rae asked.

"About what Stapler said."

Lucas sat in the back and thought. Bob and Rae chatted about the landscape, about boats they saw from the bridge going back into Annapolis, about the traffic and weather and tourism possibilities within walking distance of the Watergate that they hadn't seen on their previous trip to Washington, and when they got back to the hotel, Bob turned and asked Lucas, "Where'd all that heavy thinking get you?"

"Not where I wanted to go," Lucas said. "I need to go see a rich kid."

LUCAS WENT UP TO HIS ROOM, washed his face, and called Mary Ellen Winston. "I need to talk with Blake. Is he around?"

"He will be," she said. "Is something wrong?"

"Something worries me. I would best explain it face-to-face. When will he be home?"

"He usually gets home around four, unless he stops with friends . . . you don't think he's done something?"

"No, I don't. Actually, I need his help," Lucas said.

"I'll call him and tell him to come home."

"Great. Listen, ask him not to say anything to any of his friends. *Any* of them. Not even Audrey."

"I'll tell him."

LUCAS GOT A QUICK sandwich and a Diet Coke, collected the Cadillac, and went back across the Potomac to McLean and the Winston home. Mary Ellen Winston's assistant was nowhere to be seen and Mary Ellen came to the door herself, said, "Blake's on the way, he should be here . . . here he is."

Blake Winston rolled into the driveway in a black-and-white Mini Cooper. He left it in front of the garage doors and climbed out, hustling, looking concerned. "What happened?" he asked.

Lucas said, "Why don't we go sit?"

THEY WENT BACK TO THE ROOM overlooking the tennis court and Lucas took a long look at Blake Winston and finally said, "I want to ask if you could do something for me, something really tough, that you might not like, at all, but could be a huge help."

The Winstons looked at each other and then Mary Ellen said, "I imagine that would depend on what it is."

Lucas rubbed his hands up his face, thinking about how to begin. "Okay," he said. "We've been investigating extremist groups that we thought might be connected to 1919. We've talked to some strange people, but we haven't come up with anything. One of those people said to me today, that the only person who seemed to be getting anything out of this is Audrey Coil. She has been booked into several different TV shows."

"She's booked on more of them tomorrow," Blake Winston said. "This has gone total Hollywood."

Mary Ellen Winston, no dummy, jumped out in front of Lucas. She asked her son, "Blake . . . is it possible that Audrey invented the 1919 site? That's what Marshal Davenport is trying to lead up to, I expect."

Lucas nodded. "Yes, that's right. I can't find anyone else who might profit from this website, who might have a reason to put it up. Audrey is smart, everyone agrees on that. She knows a lot about websites. Her photograph on the site is the only one that wasn't taken specifically for the site —and If she took the other photographs, she obviously couldn't take her own. So I've been thinking . . . Could she have anticipated this kind of public reaction? Could she have done this to drive attention to *her* website, to get herself on television?"

Blake Winston's mouth dropped open. "Holy shit."

Mary Ellen: "Blake . . ."

Blake ignored his mother: "Holy shit, you think? I mean, she *is* way smart. I know a lot about cameras and all, but she knows *everything* about social media. Way more than I do."

Lucas said, "If you're still shooting videos for her . . ."

"I'm doing one Monday afternoon, after school. We're shooting in the gym with some jock-o. I know for sure that Audrey's going out of town for the weekend, so I can't do it any sooner than that."

"You'll have access to her computer? You told me that she has a laptop that you use when you're filming."

"When we're filming at her house. When we're on a location, like Monday, I usually bring mine," Blake Winston said. "I could ask her to bring hers, tell her that mine has a problem. They're the same machine,

MacBook Pros. You want me to search hers, see if something comes up?"

"That's what I would ask," Lucas said. "Figure out a bunch of search terms. I'm sure you're better at that kind of thing than I am."

"There's something of a betrayal involved here," Mary Ellen Winston said. "A betrayal of a friend."

Lucas nodded and said to Blake, "Yes, there is. That's why . . . mmm . . . I'd understand if you said no. I can't go and get her computer—I have no grounds for a search warrant. You don't need grounds, because you're not a cop, and you'd be using her computer with her permission."

Mary Ellen Winston said, "That still doesn't address the ethical problem."

"I think it does," Lucas said, turning to her. "We have a lot of people struggling with what seems to be a terrible threat. Scared kids, Secret Service agents trying to protect them. If she created this problem, a fake problem, to sell lipstick, then . . . and frankly, if she actually inspired some crazy idiot to shoot a kid . . ."

Mary Ellen said to her son, "It's your call, Blake."

Blake grinned: "I got no problem with it. If there's nothing there, we don't tell her I looked, right?"

Lucas said, "Right. If you do find something, I'll try to keep you out of it. Make up some excuse to confront Audrey. Maybe nothing would *ever* go public. We'd wrap it up and go home."

"Audrey wouldn't be punished?" Mary Ellen asked.

"She's a juvenile . . . so it could all be handled quietly," Lucas said. "Nobody would want to make a big deal out of it."

Blake delivered another blindingly white grin: "I'll call you. Hot damn, this is like spy stuff. Gives me a little woody."

"Blake!"

LUCAS WENT BACK TO THE WATERGATE, annoyed that Blake Winston couldn't get at Audrey Coil's computer over the weekend—Coil was doing something with a group of teenagers who were all the sons and daughters of politicians, and it involved an overnight stay at Camp David.

So he had to wait. Over the next two days, Lucas, Bob, and Rae tracked down the leaders of Lethal Edge and Pillars of Liberty, and the editor of the *White Gazette*. None of the probes revealed anything relevant to the 1919 investigation. Each man seemed stranger than the next and the three marshals marveled at the number of guns that seemed to float by.

"Everybody's got a gun," Rae said. "Most of them got *lots* of guns. That Brooks guy looked like a librarian and he had a Kimber .45 in his jacket pocket. You could kill a wild pig with that thing. A mountain lion."

"How many guns you got?" Bob asked. "Fifteen?"

"No. Not fifteen. Besides, I'm a law enforcement officer. I need the familiarization," Rae said.

"So do I, but I get by with five guns," Bob said. "Not counting the job guns, of course."

"Lucas: How many personal guns?" Rae asked.

"Several," Lucas said. "I don't want to talk about it. It's too depressing."

THERE WAS ONLY ONE moment of tension over the weekend, but the tension wasn't between the marshals and the subjects, but between the *White Gazette*'s publisher, Jackson Wheatley, and his wife, Constance.

The Wheatleys had apparently been fighting when the marshals arrived at their house in the suburban Maryland town of University Park. Constance Wheatley answered the knock on the door, a tall, dignified, fiftyish white-haired woman carrying a little too much weight. She looked at the badges, turned away from the door and screamed, "Okay, shithead, this is it! Now we got marshals breaking down our door. I want a divorce! I'm going to Nancy's and I want a divorce. You'll hear from my lawyer on Monday and I'm taking the Benz."

Jackson Wheatley came steaming out of a hallway, a short, stocky red-faced man in a white shirt and green slacks, wearing white socks with sandals, who shouted, "You're not taking any of my cars, you cunt! You try to take one of those cars and I'll . . ."

He saw the marshals on the other side of the screen door and his voice trailed off, but then Constance came out of the kitchen, where she'd gone after turning away from the door, and she had a claw hammer in her hands. "What are you going to do, mister? What? Call me a cunt, I'll stick this hammer so deep in your brains all the squirrels will get out."

And she went after him with the hammer, Jackson Wheatley shouting at the marshals, "You're witnesses, you're witnesses," and he ran around a sofa and then behind a leather easy chair and grabbed a hardbacked copy of *Good Poems: American Places* by Garrison Keillor, off a built-in bookshelf, and fumbled it open. A pistol fell on the floor and then Bob, Rae, and Lucas were all inside, and Jackson Wheatley stooped to pick up the diminutive gun and Bob kicked it and Lucas stepped behind Jackson Wheatley and scooped it up, while Rae faced off with Constance and said, "If you swing that hammer at me, you'll get badly injured."

Wheatley stopped with the hammer in the air and Rae said, "We might even shoot you."

Wheatley pointed a finger at her husband and said, "That sonofabitch is keeping me here by force so he can satisfy his perverted appetites."

Jackson shouted, "What? You haven't fucked me in ten years! I called you a cunt? I apologize: I don't think you got one." He shouted at Lucas, "You saw that, she tried to kill me with a hammer . . ."

Bob held up a hand. "I have a solution for this. Everybody be quiet for one moment while I go outside. I promise, this will settle things down."

He went out the door and Lucas, with the small gun in his hand, said to Jackson Wheatley, "This gun is a piece of junk. What century did it come from?"

"That was my father's personal sidearm . . ."

"Your father was an animal," Constance Wheatley shouted. "A criminal. Your mother should have cut his nuts off before they had you, but she didn't have the brains to do it! Now you got the marshals coming to get you. Well, good riddance." To Lucas: "Take this racist asshole away. Put him in prison!"

Bob came back: "Okay, folks, I called nine-one-one. The cops will be here in a couple of minutes, they'll be talking to both of you."

Constance Wheatley took a step back, then asked, "What are you talking about? I didn't do anything." She dropped the hammer on the floor, as if they might not notice.

Lucas looked at the Keillor book. The center had been cut out, the edges of the pages glued together so the gun could be concealed in the hollowed-out portion. With the covers closed, it looked intact.

"That was a damned good book," Lucas said. "Put together by one of my neighbors. You guys ruined it."

"I thought it overreached itself," Jackson Wheatley said.

The cops arrived three minutes later, and after a brief seminar on domestic violence, Lucas, Bob, and Rae went on their way.

"And another useless few hours dribble into history," Rae said, as they got in the Tahoe.

"She looked so dignified when she opened the door," Bob marveled.

"But they had a gun," Lucas said. "Like everybody else."

Dunn was at work with his crew before the sun poked over the horizon on Monday, hustled all morning, pushed the crew through lunch, and quit at one o'clock, a full day's work done. By three he was at his cabin and by five o'clock had satisfied himself that one of Stokes's rifles, a Colt LE6920 in .223 with a variable power scope, would do the job.

The smaller rifle was more comfortable to shoot than his .308, with a much crisper trigger, and also had a snap-down bipod as a shooting support. Altogether, he was significantly more accurate with it. By the end of the shooting session, he was keeping all of his shots on the twelve-by-eighteen-inch paper, many grouping around the bull. He kept in mind that he didn't actually have to kill the kid, he only had to hit him or come close.

Stokes's second rifle, also a .223, had a more radical,

skeletonized look, but didn't have a scope, and Dunn didn't want to learn how to mount one, or take the time to do it.

When he finished with the shooting, he sat in the cabin and cleaned the rifle, scrubbing out the bore, putting a light coat of lubricant on the mechanical parts, then wiping those down. As he worked, he continually flashed on the plan, and on his place in history, even if that place, with good luck, turned out to be anonymous.

Probably wouldn't be admired. He would be shooting a kid. The effect, though, would be critical: the planners of 1919 would change history, dragging the nation away from catastrophe . . .

Maybe, he thought, he could leave a will that disclosed his part in the program. Or a letter locked in a safe, so that his name would be known.

THAT NIGHT, LATE, he drove to the cemetery overlooking the Stillwater School, parked a half block away. He snuck down the narrow road at the bottom of the cemetery slope, climbed the slope when he thought he was about halfway down the length of the graveyard. At the crest of the slope, he sat and listened, then walked as quietly as he could through the weeds to the old tool shed. He found the loose supporting brick, pulled it free, and pushed the rifle through the hole. He listened again, heard only a distant rumble of cars, and slid the block back in place.

He sat and listened for a few minutes more, heard

not much but the usual trucks and airplanes, and then snuck back out to his car. He picked up a dog walker in his headlights, three or four blocks away from the cemetery. Not a problem. The man paid no attention to Dunn and his truck, but it made him think: *dog walkers.* People also walked dogs in the morning. He'd seen them on his way to work. The old cemetery would be a nice spot to take a dog . . .

The next morning, before going to work, he cruised the cemetery, saw no dog walkers. The school's schedule, available online, showed classes beginning at 8:30, with a fifth-grade recess at ten o'clock. Lunch was at 12:30, with a fifth-grade gym class at two o'clock. Watching from the top of the hill, but well away from the cemetery, he found a hefty percentage of the arriving kids didn't go directly into the school, but walked around to the playing areas and hung out there until a preliminary bell rang at 8:25.

Would Thomas McGovern be one of them? He had no idea. He'd prefer to shoot early, a time with heavier traffic to get lost in; and decided that checking the pre-bell time slot would be worthwhile.

HE SPENT A SLEEPLESS NIGHT, getting his guts up and playing and replaying in his mind the shot he might be making the next morning. He was out of bed at six, as the sun was coming up, dressed himself in field pants and a tan barn coat. He got a Canon digital camera and his camera bag out of a cupboard, put a 35mm lens on the camera, tucked two zoom lenses in the bag, along with a pair of Swarovski 8x25 binoculars.

By 7:30, he was ambling down the street at the top of the cemetery, hands in his jacket pockets, camera bag hanging off one shoulder. It occurred to him then that a dog would have been an excellent decoy and possible alibi . . . but he didn't have a dog.

As he came up to the graveyard, he checked around—there were houses across the street, but no activity. In the two-block walk, he'd been passed by only one car. With one last check, he stepped through the cemetery gate and immediately moved back behind a screen of brushy trees, toward the slope overlooking the hospital and the cemetery.

He walked quickly to his shooting position next to the cottonwood, and sat down in the grass, but without the rifle. Glanced at his iPhone: 7:40. The morning was cool and damp, with dew glittering in the grass; he was wearing a wool sweater under the barn jacket and was warm enough, but he could feel the stress building in his chest. He got the Canon out of his camera bag, perched the bag atop a ground-level limestone grave marker that said, in eroded letters, "George Janson, 1864–1929."

He put the camera atop the bag, turned it on, framed a few shots, made them, switched lenses to the 70-200 zoom, made a few more shots, went back to the first lens, then used the binoculars to scan the school grounds. There was only one kid on the playing area, and he was too tall to be McGovern.

He put the binoculars on the camera bag, then half stood, and looked back toward the street. He'd heard a couple of more cars pass by, but hadn't yet seen an actual human being on foot.

Three more kids showed up on the playground, two girls and a boy. A few cars trickled into the hospital parking ramp below him.

The first kid was still shooting baskets, the other three were standing in a huddle, looking at cell phones. With a last look around, Dunn duckwalked thirty yards to the empty tool shed, pulled the concrete block loose, reached through the hole under the shed, caught the end of the gun case, and dragged it out. He removed the rifle and the magazine tucked in next to it, and duckwalked and crawled back to the shooting site. He propped the rifle on the camera bag and scanned the playground. A dozen kids now. The binoculars were excellent, the sharpest available. He couldn't quite make out faces, though. He could see hair color and complexion and height and dress. Should be good enough: nobody he could see looked like the photo of McGovern.

Below him, a white pickup turned into the parking ramp, disappeared inside.

The kids were now walking into the playing grounds in a steady stream, and four or five were shooting around with the basketball; most of the rest were looking at cell phones or talking, and Dunn thought that one particular huddle of girls might be passing a cigarette.

"ON THE GROUND! GET DOWN ON THE GROUND! LET ME SEE YOUR HANDS. LET ME SEE YOUR HANDS!"

DUNN FLINCHED AND DUCKED behind the camera bag, looked over his shoulder, toward the street, saw nothing. Men were shouting, had to be cops . . . but they weren't shouting at him. He'd seen no sign of police cars.

More shouting and a car's engine howled in the parking structure and brakes squealed and more men were shouting, and looking down toward the open walls of the structure, Dunn saw five or six men in suits pointing guns at somebody that he couldn't see, on the far side of the ramp.

And he thought: *It's somebody else. My God, somebody else was there to take a shot and the police had staked out the parking ramp.* And he, Dunn, was right there, above them, with a rifle, and nobody was looking at him, nobody was coming.

He pulled the rifle off the camera bag and low-crawled over to the tool shed, hurriedly pushed the gun back in its case and shoved it as far as he could beneath the shed. Then he crawled back to the camera bag, put the binoculars in the bottom of the bag with the lenses on top of them, crawled toward the street, and when he was eight or ten yards out, peeked from behind the screen of trees.

Nobody.

The screaming from the parking ramp had stopped. He slung the bag over his shoulder, walked out of the cemetery and over through the neighborhood to his truck. He sat in the truck, shaking, and not from the cool weather.

So close.

He wondered if the other man was one of the two people he'd sent the letter to—or if he was the man who'd sent a letter to Dunn. No way to know, unless there was media coverage. He caught his breath, started the truck, and drove away from the cemetery into the brightening day.

So close.

HALFWAY BACK TO THE JOB SITE, he stopped at a convenience store where he'd once seen two wall-mounted pay phones. They were still there and he called WUSA in Washington, a CBS affiliate, and told the woman who answered the phone that there'd been a gunman arrested at the hospital above the playing field where the son of Senator Ross McGovern went to school.

He was curious about the failed shooter. Was it somebody he knew? The media should tell him. He went to work. By the time he got home at the end of the day, the story was everywhere.

THE MAN WAS IDENTIFIED at a press conference at Arlington police headquarters that included representatives of the FBI and Secret Service, who spent several minutes patting one another on the back for the great cooperation between their agencies, as if anybody really gave a shit.

Dunn had never heard of the guy, but everything about him seemed familiar. He was a lone wolf. He had, in the past, some contact with extremist groups, but apparently found them lacking in discipline and focus.

The press conference had been recorded before the news program, and a reporter, cued by the anchorwoman, said, "A source in the Arlington Police Department has told us exclusively that William Christopher Walton was found to be carrying a letter that suggested he might wish to take action based on the 1919 website which originally published photos of the children of prominent national politicians . . ."

He went on for a while, but Dunn thought: *my letter.*

His letter had been turned into a chain letter, completely out of his control. If the feds managed to trace that letter back to a sender, if somebody hadn't been as careful as Dunn had been, then it was possible that Dunn's name might come up.

He stood up, holding an empty beer bottle, and watched as the anchorwoman repeated what everybody had already said three times. He was in danger, no question of it.

But.

It hadn't really occurred to him earlier: the cemetery was a perfect perch from which to shoot a kid at the Stillwater School. *And nobody had come to look, because he was too far away, and the hospital seemed to be a* perfect *shooting platform, and much closer.*

He could, he thought, go back.

The cops might or might not continue staking out the place, but given the media uproar, any other potential shooters would be scared away.

That's what the cops would think. And Thomas McGovern's parents.

TWELVE

Jane Chase got Lucas up at 8:30 and said, in a preternaturally calm voice, "There's been an arrest outside a school where Senator McGovern's kid goes. No shooting, but the guy who was arrested had a high-end scoped .223 and was apparently planning to use it. He set up a spotting scope inside his car and had it focused on the school's playground."

"Who's got him?" Lucas asked, as he got out of bed.

"He was arrested by a joint Secret Service, FBI, and Arlington police team, and we're holding him at the federal building in Arlington."

"Is there anything for me to do?" Lucas asked.

"You could find the people who set up the fuckin' site." She sounded angry.

"Working on it, without a lot of help," Lucas snapped back. "So far, nothing's panned out but one crappy drug bust. We're talking to Patriotus today, if we can run down the leader, this Roland Carr guy. That could be something."

"Make something happen, Lucas, goddamnit," she said. "That's what you're here for."

"I'd be happy to hear a specific suggestion," Lucas said, still in a prickly voice. "Why don't you get one of your HVE people to tell me exactly where Carr might be found. That would help."

"I'm going over to the federal building. Maybe there'll be something. I'll check on the Patriotus guy," she said. Then: "I'm actually running down a hallway. Sorry about the attitude . . . there's a lot of stress right now. I'll call you back."

LUCAS CALLED BOB, who was working out with Rae: "You guys get ready to move," Lucas said. He told Bob about the arrest, and Bob said, "Waterboard the motherfucker."

LUCAS WAS IN THE SHOWER when his phone rang again. He'd put it on the bathroom sink and he stepped out, dried his hand, and picked it up. Not Chase.

"Davenport."

"Davenport! This is Charles Lang! Somebody's murdered Stephen! He's dead! Shot in the head! There's a lot of blood, I just, I just . . ."

"Where are you, Charlie?" Lucas asked.

"I'm at home. When Stephen didn't come down from his apartment—he lives over the garage—I went looking for him. He's in the garage, on the floor. He has a bullet hole in his forehead and there's this red . . . halo . . . around his head, it smells bad, like . . . I dunno."

"Where are you in the house?"

"In the den, I ran to get my phone . . ."

"Have you called the police?"

"No, I called you . . ."

"Okay. Don't go back to the garage. Sit down in the den. Don't do anything. The cops will be there in five minutes. Tell them the FBI and the Marshals Service will be working the case and are on the way. Just sit there, okay? Sit there."

"I'm afraid there might be somebody here in the house. What if he's still here, the killer?"

"Do you have a safe room? A room where you would feel secure?"

"I could lock the dressing room. It's got a solid door."

"Go there. Right now," Lucas said. "Stay on the phone talking until the door is shut. I'll be listening."

"I'm going now, I'm running."

TEN SECONDS LATER, Lang said, sounding out of breath, "I'm in the dressing room. The door is locked."

"Stay there. The cops will be coming . . ."

"I've got a pistol in my dresser."

"No! Leave it there. You don't want to be handling a gun, especially if a couple of patrolmen show up and a man's been shot. Sit there, Charlie, do nothing, and we'll be coming."

He called Bob: "Where the fuck are you?"

"In my room. About to take a shower. What?"

"One of the men we're looking at got murdered. We're on the way. Call Rae, tell her ten minutes in the garage. No. Seven minutes."

"Got it."

LUCAS CALLED CHASE: "What? I'm not there yet," she said.

"Charlie Lang just called me. Somebody murdered Stephen Gibson at Lang's house. We're going. We need some FBI backup and I need you to call the cops. He lives in Potomac."

"Oh, shit! Shit! I'm on my way. I'll turn around and head that way. Give me his address . . ."

Lucas clicked on his phone's navigation app and read Lang's address for Chase. He heard her giving orders to somebody, probably a driver, and he said, "I'll see you there. I gotta run."

Jeans, shirt, jacket, gun, cross-trainers. Running.

THEY TOOK THE TAHOE, which had lights and a siren, with Lucas driving, because he more or less knew the way. He briefed Bob and Rae on his interview with

Lang and told them about his last conversation with Gibson, in which he ordered him to find the ANM training camp. He didn't know what kind of research Gibson had done, but now he was dead.

"We've got a guy we can go after, a Thomas Aline. Jane might not like it, because they want to use him as a wedge to find out more about ANM, but, he might be a wedge we need to use now."

The lights and siren on the Tahoe helped, but it still took twenty minutes to get to Potomac. At Lang's house, two Montgomery County patrol cars were parked outside along with a well-used and unmarked sedan that looked like nothing more than a cop car.

They didn't need much ID; the Tahoe's lights were still flashing as they turned the corner a block from Lang's house. A uniformed cop pointed at the curb, they parked, and a plainclothes cop came out of the house to look at them.

"Marshals Service?" The cop was tall, burly, weathered like an addicted golfer—and he dressed like one, in no-wrinkle slacks and a golf shirt, except for the sport coat that covered his gun.

"We were working with Charles Lang and Stephen Gibson on the 1919 investigation," Lucas told him. "Lang called me, I called the FBI." A dark SUV, lights flashing, turned the corner, and they all turned to look. "That's probably them. Her name is Jane Chase and she has some clout. She called you."

"Anybody else coming?" the cop asked. "CIA, NSA, NC-double A?"

"Could happen," Lucas said. "Secret Service, maybe ATF."

"You're shittin' me . . ."

"Not really. The Secret Service and FBI and some local cops busted a guy this morning who was apparently planning to shoot a senator's son at his grade school."

"Oh, boy." The cop glanced back at Lang's house. "This is tied in?"

"Could be. We don't know. I got a bad feeling about it."

The cop's name was Andy Jackson—"Not the President." Chase came up, trailed by her assistant, and shook his hand.

"You want to go in?" Jackson asked. "Not much to see except a dead body, shot once in the forehead, apparently after getting out of his car. The car door is still open, but the garage door is down. It looks like he went to meet somebody at the exit door and was shot where he stood. Probably a .38 or .40-something caliber handgun, judging from the hole. The slug went through his head and into the wall and out the back—the wall's Sheetrock, and didn't slow it down much. We're probably not going to find the slug without jumping through our butts. I'd like to finish with the crime scene stuff before we trample all over it . . ."

"Finish with the crime scene," Chase said. "What does Lang have to say? Can we talk to him?"

"Sure. He's in the main house, Gibson has an apartment over the garage." Jackson pointed at the garage and Chase turned to look. "Far enough away that Lang says he never heard a thing. Neighbors didn't hear anything, either, the ones we've been able to find."

"What do you think about Lang?" Lucas asked.

"Don't tell him I said so, not yet, but he looks okay to me. Shook up, bad. Of course, you could be shook up if you killed somebody, but I don't think he did. No complicated alibi. He said Gibson went out last night, after work, said he was going to meet some people on a research project. He was talking to some members of a group called White Fist. Lang's not sure of the time, but he watched a news program until 10:30 or so, and spent some time in the bathroom, washing his face and brushing his teeth and putting on his pajamas, so he thinks he was in bed around eleven. He saw headlights on his curtains before he went to sleep, and that's the last thing he knew until he got up this morning."

"He's sure it was Gibson? The headlights?"

"He assumed it was, but he didn't look. Not to say that there might not have been somebody in the car with him. But it looks to me like somebody might have either followed him here, or been waiting for him here, and met Gibson at the door."

Chase: "Was Gibson involved with anyone?"

"Lang says no. He said Gibson had a girlfriend a couple of years back, for a short time, but he hadn't seen her for a while. We'll check to see what she has to say: we've got a name. We haven't had time to talk to Lang much—I've been here for . . ." He looked at his watch. ". . . about fifteen minutes."

"LET'S TALK TO LANG," Chase said.

On the walk to the main house, Jackson asked, "You think it had to do with Gibson's research? On these alt-right people?"

"That's an obvious possibility," Chase said, "depending on who exactly he was looking at, and how he was going about it."

"As soon as your crime scene people are done, we need to get up in his apartment and look for a notebook or a laptop or anything else he might have taken notes on," Lucas said. "We need to check his phone calls, see if there are GPS links that the phone company can help us with."

"We can do all that," Jackson said. "There is a laptop up there for sure, and quite a few legal pads."

"We'd like to be there when you look," Chase said. "If there's a link going out to a shooter group—this White Fist sounds interesting—we need to know which one it was."

"So do we," Jackson said.

LANG WAS SITTING on a purple couch in the living room, a vase of yesterday's yellow flowers wilting on the piano behind him.

When he saw Lucas, he started to get to his feet, but Lucas put up a hand and he settled back down, his face nearly as purple as the couch.

"Are you okay?" Lucas asked. "I mean, physically? You don't look good."

"I'm completely undone," Lang said. His mouth hung open. Then, "What am I going to do? Stephen is dead."

"Do you know who he was talking to the last few days? Where his research was going?"

"I think it must be the ANM who did this," Lang said. "Stephen found that gun training site for you."

"Okay, we'll look at that for sure," Lucas said. "Who else was he looking into? Any groups with a history? Patriotus?"

"He did talk to Patriotus, to Roland Carr. That seems unlikely to me, that Roland would be involved with a killing. They're more . . . verbal."

"Like the Greene Mountain Boys?"

"More like that."

"What about Forlorn Hope or White Fist?" Lucas asked.

Lang nodded: "He talked to White Fist day before yesterday. He went to their headquarters and talked to Toby Boone. And he went back last night, I think. I told him to be careful—after his first trip there, he said a man who was there with Toby was 'scary.' I think . . . an ex-convict."

Jackson: "Scary?"

"That's the word he used," Lang said.

Lucas said to Jackson, "White Fist is prison-based. They're on our list. The three of us . . ." He nodded at Bob and Rae ". . . were going to look them up. We can still do that. You could send an investigator along, if you want."

"Maybe a SWAT team," Jackson said.

"Bob and Rae are SOG," Lucas said.

"Then you won't need our SWAT—I'd like to come along, if I can get a break here." Lang told them that Gibson had been asking about the 1919 website when he approached White Fist and two other groups, one called River Klan and the other called Bellum. River Klan and Bellum were both small, no more than a dozen or so members each, and both were focused on states' rights issues, Lang said. Both had been present at a violent demonstration in Charlottesville, Virginia, in 2017.

"'Bellum' is Latin," Lang said. "It means, 'civil war.'"

"Terrific," said Rae.

CHASE'S PHONE RANG and she walked away to answer it.

Lang asked, "What happens now? What about Stephen's . . . body?"

Jackson explained the crime scene routine and the body's removal to a medical examiner, and gave him a timeline. There was a chance that they'd be finished in the garage and the apartment by the end of the day, but they might want to look at it again, depending on the preliminary findings, so it would be sealed for an indefinite time. Gibson's car would be taken to a secure parking lot where the crime scene techs could scour the interior for DNA.

"We'll need to interview you about Gibson's lifestyle," Jackson said. "We can best do that at the station . . ."

"Do I need a lawyer?" Lang asked.

Jackson shrugged: "That's up to you. If you haven't done anything . . ."

Chase came back, had overheard the last comment, and said to Lang, "As a law enforcement official, I hate to say this, but you'd be better off with an attorney present when you're interviewed. It's best to have somebody on your side with you, even if you're totally innocent."

"Thanks," Jackson said.

Chase shrugged: "Hey, I'm an attorney."

She turned to Lucas: "The man they arrested this morning is named William Christopher Walton. They're sure that's his real name because they found his fingerprints, taken when he joined the Army twelve years ago. He was discharged after four months as being psychologically unsuitable for military duty. He has no priors of any kind, that we can find. They're entering his house now, he apparently lives with his mother. They did find a rather unusual letter in his pocket, which refers him to the 1919 site, explains what it means, and suggests that he might want to take action. The letter is smudgy, apparently a Xerox copy of an original. It was still in an envelope addressed to him. Walton's asked for a lawyer—or as he put it, a white lawyer—so we're not getting anything from him."

"Lone wolf," Lang said. "How are you going to stop that?"

Lucas said to Jackson, "Give us some booties. We need to look at the body and up in the apartment. We really can't wait all day." And he asked Lang, "How did Gibson take notes? Did he take them on a laptop, or in notebooks, or a recorder?"

"He had a recorder, a very expensive one. Digital. A lot of the time, though, it wasn't possible to take notes. He had a lavalier microphone that he could put inside his shirt, with a wire to the recorder, but he rarely tried to do that. Getting caught would be . . . disastrous, in some cases. Like with White Fist, you wouldn't want to risk it. What he usually did—he had a very good memory—he'd interview people and then drive around a block and get his recorder out and talk into it. That's what he probably did yesterday. I doubt that he would have transcribed anything, getting home when he did. He was an early-to-rise fellow. If he needed to transcribe anything, he would have waited until this morning."

"We need to listen to that recorder," Lucas said to Jackson.

"And look at his computer," Chase said. To Lang: "Do you know if it's password-protected?"

"Of course it is, but I happen to know the password," Lang said. "I'll have to write it down for you.

It's complicated, it's one of those super-strong ones you can get generated on the internet."

"Please do that," Chase said.

Lang said, "I will. Oh, I do want to call my attorney." He nodded at Chase and said, "Thank you for that, young lady."

They got the password from Lang and as they walked away to the apartment, Chase muttered, "Nazi nincompoop."

"About that password," Lucas said.

"I've got it . . ."

"Looks quite a bit like the password to the 1919 site."

Chase stopped in her tracks, looked at the slip of paper in her hand. "Now that's a thought." She looked back at Lang's house. "Charles Lang is exactly the kind of person who'd love to have some power over a senator."

LUCAS, CHASE, BOB, and Rae followed Jackson out to the garage, where a crime scene technician was pulling on a pair of Tyvek overalls. Somebody had run up the garage overhead door, and even standing back, they could see Gibson's body on its side, with a puddle of blood around his head. He had the sudden-shot, ragdoll look, collapse and complete relaxation, his tongue partway out of his mouth, his eyelids half open, reddish streaks under the skin of his face, where gravity was pulling blood down through his flesh.

Lucas took a step closer, squatted, as the crime scene guy said, "Not too close," and looked at the bullet hole in Gibson's face. No sign of a fight, no abrasions on his hands that Lucas could see. He'd simply been shot.

Lucas said, "There's no powder penetration in the skin around the bullet hole. The shooter might have used something to muffle the shot, a towel or something."

The crime scene guy squatted next to Lucas and said, "Look, there on his chest. See that white stuff? Looks like little specks of fabric. I think you're probably right. We'll bag it."

"Huh."

"And right there, by his hip, by his other hand . . ."

Lucas could see a black cord. He and the crime scene guy both edged around to the other side of the body, and they could see a thin plastic box under Gibson's hip, like a cell phone, but too thick to be a phone.

"His recorder," Lucas said. "We gotta pull that out of there. Right now."

"That could be a problem," the crime scene guy said. "We could lose some evidence."

LUCAS CALLED JACKSON OVER, pointed out the plastic box, and after a brief argument with the crime scene guy, Jackson agreed they should pull the recorder, but should give the tech time to process the area right around it.

"Let's go look at the apartment, then," Lucas said.

Chase, who'd been watching from the driveway, said, "We've got a crime scene team on the way. They'll help process the apartment. Since the murder happened here, we'll mostly be talking about looking at his records, at his notebooks and computer and recordings and all that."

The apartment, connected to the garage area by an interior stairs, was fairly large and an extremely efficient work space. What normally would have been a living room was more like a working library, with a long center table covered with notebooks, papers, and magazines; the walls were lined with overflowing bookcases, one section filled with military thriller fiction, but most of it was packed with nonfiction war and political histories. An odd-shaped musical instrument case sat against a wall, next to a music stand; somebody later told Lucas that the case contained a rare and expensive oud.

A small functional kitchen showed unwashed dishes on a breakfast bar, the remnants of a microwave taco dinner. The bedroom showed a queen-sized bed with a night table holding several more books and magazines, with a reading light hanging over a central stack of pillows.

Lucas stepped around the place, looking without touching, then said to Chase, "There's nothing really for me, here. This is for your crime scene team. Let's go see about that recorder."

THE COUNTY CRIME scene tech had pulled the recorder from under Gibson's thigh and had bagged it.

"There appear to be several recordings," the tech said. "I assume you want the last folder. The folder appears to have three segments . . ."

"Play it," Jackson said.

The recording consisted of dictated notes of an interview with the leader of the group called Bellum, a Lawrence Gray, followed by dictated notes of an interview with the White Fist leader Toby Boone.

And at the end, they found a recording of Gibson's murder.

"COP, PLEASE, C'MON, please, man . . ." Gibson began crying. "I'm not talking to him, I'm not giving him anything, please, man, he came to us, we didn't go to him. You want to kill somebody, please please, man, kill Davenport, don't do this. Did Toby send you? I bet Toby doesn't know you're here, we're friends . . ."

A man's baritone voice:

"Toby knows I'm here. The problem is, you saw Linc, and Linc, well, we can't have any connections back to Linc, because Linc's gonna kill himself a senator's kid. If you'd gotten there two minutes later, we wouldn't have a problem. But . . ."

"Cop, please. I will not tell a soul. I will not tell Charles. I will not say a word to any . . ."

BAP.

CHASE JUMPED: "Good God!"

Rae: "I don't think he was present."

"Man had some balls," Bob said. "He knew what was coming and managed to record it and leave us some names."

"Was Cop a name or a profession?" Rae wondered.

"The way he used it, I think it was a name," Lucas said. "We got three people we've got to hit, and right now: Toby, Cop, and Linc."

Chase said, "I'm aware of Bob and Rae's skills, because I've seen them work, but they're not enough. I'm calling in one of our SWAT squads, or maybe two of them. I'll have HVE run Toby Boone, I know we've got stuff on him, but we need to run Cop and Linc to see if we can identify them. We need search warrants. This is gonna take a while."

"We need to have a presence . . ." Jackson said.

"Of course. You're invited, absolutely," Chase said.

"We really don't have a while," Lucas said. "The school day is already underway, we had one possible shooter this morning. If this Linc's waiting for school to get out . . . we could have another problem."

"When I said a while, I meant an hour," Chase said. "If Charlie sent Gibson to interview Toby Boone, and Gibson saw Cop and Linc there . . . then Charlie has an address for us."

Lang did have an address, on his old-fashioned Rolodex, in Frederick, Maryland, an hour outside of Washington.

CHAPTER

THIRTEEN

Rae drove the Tahoe down Rosemont Avenue in Frederick, Maryland, past Boone Precious Metals and Pawn, which FBI files on White Fist identified as the group's headquarters. The store was a converted two-story clapboard house remodeled with larger windows above a two-step stone porch, a red LED sign in the window blinked, successively, *Gold* and *Silver* and *Bought* and *Sold*. A ten-foot-tall orange Gumby, the kind inflated with a shop vac, was dancing outside the house with a banner that read, "Gold, Gold, Gold."

A detached garage sat behind the house, and, as with Charles Lang's place, had an apartment or storage area on the second floor above car parking spaces, with a window looking out at the street. The business building, garage, and a surrounding parking lot were set into a heavily treed lot, which made it impossible to see the back of the place—but also provided an approach for the FBI SWAT team.

"Count the doors," Rae said. "We know there's one on the side, probably gotta be one in the back, so that's three on the main house, probably two on that garage, if it really is a garage."

"Looks like a garage," Lucas said.

"Could be a meeting space," Rae said.

"Hadn't thought of that."

Bob was inspecting the place with imaged-stabilized Canon binoculars. "It has an air of being sorta old and fucked up, but I don't think it is. You look close and everything seems to be in good shape. Those garage doors aren't old wood, they're metal, and they don't look that old, and the windows are in good shape. The side door looks to be metal. There's that hip-high concrete foundation on three sides, nothing's going through that."

"I'll talk to Jane," Lucas said, as they passed on down the street. "The SWAT guys are on the way. They should know they may be cracking a bunker. They need to do some serious recon, maybe make a video."

"Sidewalks, but no pedestrians," Rae said. "That's one good thing."

"Lotsa cars," Bob said.

THEY MADE ONLY THE SINGLE PASS, then continued on to the Frederick city police headquarters, a red-brick building eight minutes through traffic from Boone Precious Metals and Pawn. On the way, Lucas called Chase, who said that a reconnaissance and a video were underway.

When they got to police headquarters, Chase was huddling with the police chief and two other ranking officers. Lucas, Bob, and Rae were ushered into the chief's office, and when Chase saw them she said, "Half an hour," and, to the cops, "U.S. Marshals SOG team."

"Where're your people?" Lucas asked Chase.

"They're on the way. They're staging here in the parking lot. It's not too visible and I'm told we're reasonably close to Boone's place."

"Eight minutes," Bob said.

Lucas told her about the layout and the bunker aspect—the concrete foundation—and she said they'd already looked at it from a satellite view, but couldn't tell from that what might be at the back of the buildings. "We've got one of our street guys from DC, he'll be going into those trees in the next few minutes with his camping stuff and a GoPro. There's a creek in back but a driveway comes in from the side of the buildings. We'll hit both front and back." She looked at her watch. "Doug should be there now. The street guy—he's convincing, if anybody sees him. He stinks to high heaven."

The Frederick police would not be involved in the raid and most wouldn't know about it, or the target, until a few seconds before it took place, when patrol cars would be given a general alert in case there were reports of gunfire from the area.

"Lot of traffic in there, residential single-family

homes across the street," the chief said to Chase. "You gotta be careful. I know for a fact that Toby Boone's got a handgun and what he calls hunting rifles in there, though they're ARs and AKs that supposedly belong to his brother. His brother doesn't have a felony record, so he can buy what he wants. With all those guns . . . I mean, I don't need any innocent citizens getting killed."

"Does his brother actually work there?" Lucas asked.

"I don't know the exact arrangement, but I think he does. When Toby was still on probation on his ag assault conviction, two of our investigators went in there looking for a couple of stolen guitars. One of our guys spotted the pistol and braced Boone about it, and he said it was his brother's weapon and his brother confirmed it and they had a sales receipt. We keep tabs on Toby because of this White Fist thing and because of his record. He went down on ag assault, but that wasn't a one-time thing."

Chase took a call, listened for a minute, then said, "Okay, get him out of there. I'll see you in the parking lot."

To Lucas, she said, "The SWAT team will be here in two minutes, our street guy has been making some movies of the target, those should be coming in any time now. Three trucks, eighteen guys. They're asking that you guys, you and Bob and Rae, stand down. We're all coordinated and they don't know you."

"Well, poop," Rae said.

Chase said, quickly, "As soon as the area is cleared,

though, we want the three of you in there. You've been talking to these people and our SWAT guys haven't been."

Bob said to Rae, "The good-guy trophy."

"All right with me," Lucas said. "The last time I went on a SWAT raid, some asshole shot me."

FIVE MINUTES LATER, the SWAT teams were in the parking lot, the agents getting their armor on, a few Frederick cops coming out to look as the news moved through the department. The team was hard to miss, manning three large gunmetal-gray vehicles that looked like products of a bad marriage between a tank and a rec-vee. A minute or so after the trucks arrived, a video came in from the street guy, shots of the two target buildings from all angles. As Rae had suggested, both had back doors not visible from the street.

The SWAT commander, an agent named Adam Carlucci, pointed out relevant considerations to the team members—location of the creek, the quality of the concealment and cover, distances from unloading points to entry points. Bob pointed out the newer metal doors and Carlucci took another look at the videos. "Gonna need the rams on the garage and the back doors," he concluded.

The team members were all heavily experienced, had been pre-briefed on the way up from Washington; the on-site briefing took six or seven minutes, then the team was loading and moving out.

Lucas could feel the intensity building in his chest: going into combat.

"What do you think?" Lucas asked, as Bob and Rae pulled on their bulletproof vests.

"They know what they're doing," Bob said.

"I gotta say, Jane doesn't skimp on the resources," Rae said. "She could start a war with those boys. When me and Bob go out, it's more like a poolroom fight . . . Hey, we got a vest for you. Put it on."

Lucas put on the vest as the last of the trucks disappeared from the parking lot, and Rae got behind the wheel of the Tahoe. They had been asked to wait at the police headquarters until they got a call from Chase, who was riding in one of the trucks. Because the trucks had to come in on the target from different directions, one of them would be stalling while the other two were running fast on a more circular route, aiming for a simultaneous arrival; Lucas wanted to arrive as the doors were going down.

"Fuck waiting," he said. "Get on that last truck's ass."

"Now you're talking," Rae said, and she cranked the Tahoe over.

"LOT OF CIVIL WAR SHIT AROUND HERE," Bob said, making nervous conversation from the backseat, as they rolled out of the parking lot. "We're closer to Gettysburg than we are to Washington. If we have time, I'd like to take the tour." He had two M4-style rifles in the backseat and checked them out one last time as they drove across town, seating a thirty-shot magazine in each.

"Probably won't have time," Lucas said. They were gaining on the slow FBI vehicle until they were, as Lucas recommended, right on its ass. Hearing Bob working with the rifles, he took out his Walther PPQ just to be doing something, and Rae glanced at him and said, "Don't go shooting your big toe."

"I was winning pistol competitions when you were in diapers," Lucas said.

Rae snorted. "Diapers? Didn't have no diapers in the Givenses' house. We used burlap bags."

"In Oklahoma, we used dirt," Bob said. "I'd poop, they'd take me outside and hose me down and throw a little dirt on me. Makes you a tough little baby, getting through winter. Icicles hanging off your little wiener."

"I got nothin'," Lucas said. "Though, I gotta say, it amazes me that the Givens family didn't have diapers, when your father was a pharmacist. Couldn't he steal some?"

"Fucker's been reading our files," Bob said to Rae.

"Shut up, everybody," Rae said. "We're coming up on it."

THEY CAME AROUND A LONG CURVE and the big dark FBI truck swerved into the parking area outside Boone Precious Metals and the SWAT guys came out like peas being shucked out of a pod. Four of them hit the front door of the main building while two of them set up facing the front door of the garage. The agents in the other two trucks would hit the doors at the back of the buildings, and were covering the side doors, and were not immediately visible.

Lucas, Bob, and Rae were twenty feet behind the SWAT agents, running up the steps and through the front door; as they did it, Lucas saw Chase clambering out of the lead vehicle.

Inside, three men, a woman, and a big gray dog were faced off against the SWAT team, the humans with their hands over their heads and the woman was chanting, "Don't shoot my dog, don't shoot my dog, I can lock him right there in the bathroom, right there," and the dog's teeth were bared and it rumbled a warning.

"Hold him, hold him tight," one of the agents said, and he eased behind the counter as the women held the dog—Lucas found out later that it was a Belgian Malinois, the kind often used as war dogs—and went to the bathroom door, looked inside, opened a medicine cabinet, then came back out and said, "Lock him in there."

The dog had to be half-dragged into the bathroom, but the woman got him inside and slammed the door and then locked it with a key: "She opens doors," she explained.

One of the men, middle-sized, stocky with curly blond hair, demanded "What the hell is this?"

Chase came in the door with a roll of paper: "Which one of you is Toby Boone?"

The blond man said, "That's me. I haven't even

been speeding. Is this about 1919? I got nothing to do with that shit."

She handed him the paper: "Search warrant for the premises, including the garage."

To the agent behind the counter, she said, "Cuff him."

The agents moved the other two men and the woman to a corner of the counter, and the agent behind the counter cuffed Boone, who said, "I want an attorney."

"You'll get one, though I feel sorry for the guy," Chase said, facing Boone across the counter. "Oh yeah, I almost forgot. You're under arrest for conspiracy to commit first-degree murder."

Boone gave himself away: he said nothing, didn't seem surprised.

Chase said, "Put him away," and the agent who'd cuffed him led him to the door. At the door, Boone turned and said to the other three prisoners, "Don't let the cops get at those coins. They'll steal them if they get half a chance." And he was gone, out of sight.

Chase said to the other SWAT team members, "Okay. Let's get the other three to where our people can talk to them, get your armor off, and let's tear this place apart."

LUCAS HAD NOTICED SEVERAL DARK sedans rolling into the parking lot, more agents climbing out. As Rae had said, Chase didn't skimp on resources. The SWAT team was basically made up of thugs with law degrees; the sedans would be the interrogators, he thought.

THE INTERIOR OF THE BUILDING, as far as Lucas had seen it, consisted of hanging racks between the windows, filled with electric guitars; side cases filled with used tools, '80s boom boxes, cheap amps, questionable-looking binoculars, and even a few non-precious film cameras and out-of-date digitals, all covered with dust; and a counter/case showing gold coins in narrow blue boxes.

Lucas stepped behind the counter, walked along it, saw the butt end of a pistol in a drawer and said to Chase, "Gun," and pointed at it, then took a door through to the back, where he found an expansive room with more tools and guitars with tags hanging on them, plus a space with a table and three chairs and a couch facing a television.

A hardwired telephone hung on the wall next to the door; useful for calls that you didn't want going through a cell tower or a Stingray, Lucas thought. He walked on by, but then noticed a sheet of scratch paper thumb-tacked to the wall beside the phone. He looked at it: a list of phone numbers. Carly's, Ross, Shirley, Tom B., Tom N., Cop, Andy . . .

Cop.

He went back to the front, where one of the SWAT team members still in armor, still with gun in hand, was watching the three employees. Chase was there, across the counter, on the phone again. Lucas nodded at the three employees and said, "Miz Chase will talk to you as soon as she gets off her phone. We'll try to get you out of here as quickly as we can. That list on the back wall, by the phone, can somebody tell me who Tom B. and Tom N. are?"

The three looked at one another, then one said, "I'm Tom Brenner. Tom N. is Tom Nader, he works evenings."

"What's Carly's?"

"Pizza place," the woman said. "We order in a lot."

"You call the cops a lot? I see a Cop on the list."

The talkative man shook his head and said, "That's Rusty Wannamaker, he's a part-timer, usually works evenings when Tom Nader can't."

The other man said, "I'm Ross Parker."

Chase had gotten off her phone and had heard the last part of the conversation, and asked, "Lucas, could you step outside a moment?" To the three captives, she smiled and said, "I'll be back in a minute. If you cooperate with our agents, no reason you can't be home in an hour. We were basically here for Toby Boone."

On the porch, she said to Lucas, "I heard that. Rusty Wannamaker. Can't be too many people with that name."

"Why don't you go ask what Tom Nader does as a day job and what Cop does. You're less threatening than I am."

She nodded and went back inside, while Lucas hung on the porch. Bob and Rae were having a gun fest with the SWAT team and Lucas let them talk. Chase came out a minute later and said, "Wannamaker is a UPS driver during the day."

"I'll get my guys and we'll take him," Lucas said.

"Careful. He's an assassin."

"Yeah, well, so are we," Lucas said.

"We would like him without bullet holes."

"We'll do what we can." Lucas turned and called, "Bob. Rae. Let's go make a movie."

WHEN LUCAS EXPLAINED THE SITUATION, Bob said, "UPS. Damn. I worked for them when I was in college, three a.m. to six. Then in the summer, they had me working the pre-load, too, three a.m. to nine. Wanna talk about a shit job?"

"He doesn't load, he's a driver," Lucas said.

"This time of day, he's out on delivery," Bob said. He was messing with his phone and said, "Okay, I've got a location. English Muffin Way."

"English what?"

"Hey, I didn't name the place," Bob said. "I've got it on my phone app. We go talk to his boss, figure out where Cop should be right now."

THE UPS DISTRIBUTION CENTER was in a warehouse district south of town, a beige structure built with nothing in mind other than function: a box that a decent-looking building should have come in. The delivery supervisor, whose name was Rick, was unhappy to see them, and even more unhappy when Lucas wouldn't tell them what Cop had done.

"We do need to see him right away," Lucas told him.

"I could call him . . ."

"No, no. He's not to know we're coming," Lucas said. "If word should get to him . . . and you're the only person we're talking to . . . then you could be looking at a very tough future. Very tough."

"You know, like federal prison," Rae said.

"Tell us about where he's at, and we'll find him," Lucas added.

"Well . . ." Rick looked at them nervously. "I can tell you exactly where he's at. Like, to the foot. All the trucks are monitored."

"Then when we get up in the right area, we could call you and you could give us an exact location?"

"To the foot."

Cop's car, Rick said, was in the parking lot, an older, dark gray Mustang, and locked.

COP WAS DRIVING AROUND a suburban development on the north side of town called Clover Hill, twenty minutes from the distribution center. They drove over, and when they were in the neighborhood, checked back with Rick, gave him their location, and he directed them to Claiborne Drive, where they spotted the brown UPS truck parked in front of a house.

Cop was either in the truck or in the house, because he wasn't outside, and then the truck pulled away, went around a corner. They hovered, watching, until he stopped again and then Lucas, who was driving, eased up behind the truck as Cop hopped out and started up the front walk to a house.

He was a tall, thin man, balding, appeared to be in shape. Bob and Rae hopped out of the Tahoe, ran around opposite ends of the UPS vehicle so they'd have Cop between them. Lucas ran around behind Bob and when Cop saw them coming, he simply stood and stared at the guns pointed at him.

"What?"

"You're under arrest," Rae said. "Get down on the ground, put your hands behind your back."

Cop dumped the box he was holding—something broke inside with a china-like crack—and dropped into a crouch and then suddenly bolted. He got about eight feet before Bob, who, despite his size, was quick, got him by the collar, threw him on the ground, and knelt on his back.

"Don't do that," Bob said.

"Motherfucker."

"Potty mouth." Bob bent Cop's arms behind his back, cuffed him, and then lifted him off the ground by his belt. Rae gave him the Miranda speech and they put him in the back of the Tahoe. Bob got Cop's work keys and they locked the UPS truck and called Rick and told him that Cop would no longer be working that day, and that the truck was locked.

———

LUCAS GOT ON THE PHONE TO CHASE, who asked, "You get him?"

"Yeah, got him."

"Bring him down, we'll transfer him," Chase said. "What's happening there?"

"The garage looks like a National Guard armory. Toby Boone had a pistol in his car, so we got him on that, regardless of whether or not we can make a murder charge stick. Ton of literature here. Crazy stuff, a mix of white supremacist and prison reform. Where are you? You should see this."

"Be there in ten minutes," Lucas said.

In the backseat, next to Bob, Cop said, "You didn't tell me why I was arrested."

"Murder," Rae said. "You can get the details from the FBI supervisor."

Cop looked away, his face turned to stone. He knew what they were talking about.

BACK AT THE TOBY BOONE PAWNSHOP, they turned Cop over to an FBI agent, who read him his rights again, and took him away.

Chase came over and said, "Good day, good day."

The garage she'd called an armory wasn't actually an armory, but to somebody unfamiliar with the gun world, as Chase admitted she was, it might have looked that way. More than two dozen long guns were locked against a wall with steel rods and heavy padlocks, some of everything: six AR-style black rifles were side-by-side with four AKs and scoped bolt-action rifles in a variety of calibers from .223 to .300 Winchester Magnum; four tactical shotguns and two high-end over-and-under shotguns were lined up next to the rifles, and no fewer than six Ruger 10/22 autoloading .22 caliber rifles.

Lucas had a 10/22 himself, at his cabin, for dispatching porcupines, because, as everybody knows, porcupines will eat the rubber on your boat's gas lines and anything with sweat salt on it, like canoe paddles. And if a SWAT team ever raided his house and cabin, they'd come up with . . . Lucas had to think about it . . . maybe ten guns, including rifles, pistols, and shotguns. He also had a couple of street guns hidden away, with a few other items he preferred that no one see—an electronic lock rake—but a SWAT team wouldn't find those.

BOB, RAE, AND LUCAS toured the garage, which was actually a gunsmith's workshop, including a sophisticated reloading bench in addition to all the weaponry. Chase was on the phone talking to somebody in Washington about what to do about the guns—Toby Boone's brother claimed that they all belonged to him, but it turned out the buildings belonged to Toby Boone, and not the brother, so . . .

"It's gonna take a platoon of lawyers to figure out

what to do," one of the SWAT guys told Lucas. "Hate to see it, but they might get to keep the guns."

"You ask anybody about all those Ruger 10/22s?"

"Yeah, they said they have a shooting club, go out to a range for training. Nothing illegal about that. Same with the ARs, AKs, and shotguns."

Chase was still going full speed on the radio and the phone. Bob and Rae went to talk guns'n stuff with the SWAT team, but Chase finally got off both the radio and the phone and drifted over and asked Lucas, "What do you think?"

He shrugged: "What did Toby Boone tell you?"

"He asked for an attorney, but I hit him with the 1919 thing and he said he'd heard of it, but it didn't have anything to do with them. He said it looked like something run by crazies. He said the Senate was run by people on their side, why would they want to shoot anybody? He said he didn't know anybody named Linc."

"If Cop was telling the truth in that recording, both he and Boone know a Linc who might be shooting a kid."

"And we'll be talking to them about that, as soon as we get back to Arlington and get them lawyers," Chase said. "That recording is almost enough to hang them— Cop for sure, we not only have Gibson calling him that, we have his voice, and we can match it. We'll be talking to Boone about the needle, if Linc winds up shooting somebody. That could catch his attention."

Lucas: "We've been talking about this, me'n Bob and Rae. We got unbelievably lucky with Gibson's digital recorder and busting Cop. We'll be even luckier if we find this Linc guy before he pulls a trigger. But we won't find any more of them this way. We won't get that lucky again."

"What then?"

"You've got to start planning some kind of media offensive—and FBI offensive," Lucas said. "Take down all the sites that mirrored 1919, file lawsuits, make explicit threats, talk about people getting the needle. Talk to Greene, the Greene Mountain Boys guy, about doing a blog post on the penalties you're talking about. Don't just take down likely extremist groups, take them all down. Roust them. Make threats. Make it look like the end of the world is coming down."

"What about you? Are you giving up?"

Lucas spread his hands: "If you wind up taking down everybody we know about, then what would we contribute?"

"Stay on a while longer. I tend to agree with you about a media blitz, but that's gonna take a few meetings," Chase said.

"We could stay a couple days anyway. We could do some sight-seeing if nothing specific comes up . . ."

"Do that. Or go look around Cop's house and see if you spot anything that might lead to this Linc guy—you've got a great eye," Chase said. "If you hadn't seen that phone list, and taken the time to read it, we might not have gotten to Cop as quickly as we did. We're really looking good. So stay. Buy me some luck."

"All right. I *would* like to take a look at Cop's place, the sooner the better. And we'll want to take a look at his car. We've got that spotted. We're gonna need warrants."

"I'll have those in an hour. Boone's married, we've already hit his house. I understand his wife is giving us a hard time. But, that is what it is; so far, nobody's called to tell me about any big discoveries there."

LUCAS'S PHONE BUZZED and he looked at the incoming call, but didn't recognize the number.

"Davenport," he said.

"Marshal Davenport?" Young male voice, heavy breathing. "This is Blake Winston."

"What's happening, Blake?" His eyes clicked over to Chase, who'd caught the name, and stepped closer. Lucas thumbed the speaker option so she could listen.

"You were right. I got into Audrey's computer and that 1919 site is in there, the pieces of it. Audrey put the site together."

"Where are you?"

"At home," Winston said. "I put all the pieces I found on a thumb drive for you. I have it here."

"Don't talk to anyone. I mean, *anyone*. We're coming," Lucas said. "I'm way up north, it'll take an hour."

"I'll go hit some tennis balls with my mom. I did tell her about it and she's royally pissed."

"Try to calm her down, Blake. I'm on my way."

———

LUCAS CLICKED OFF AND CHASE, eyes wide with horror, said, "No, no, no, no-no-no."

Lucas: "Oh, yeah. I had a funky feeling right from the first meeting with Audrey and her mother. I recruited Blake to spy on her."

"That's awful."

"What's awful is that she did it," Lucas said. "Anyway, I don't think you want to have heard what you just heard."

"Lucas . . ."

"This can't get out," Lucas said. "The Senate will go batshit, or at least half of it will. If something happens and you have to claim later that you didn't know about this, I'll back you up. I'll lie. I'll say nobody knew but me. 'Cause this is about to get desperately political. If it gets out, then everybody who knew about it, about a cover-up, which is what we're talking about, is going to carry a little stink."

"What about you?"

"I've got forty million dollars in my investment accounts," Lucas said. "If it turns into a huge deal, I could maybe lose my job, but so what? I'll take the chance, and if I lose, I've got a pillow to fall on. What do you have?"

She bit her lower lip and then said, "Probably be a county prosecutor, but it'd be a small county in a cold place."

"Exactly. So, you *know*, but you don't know. You might be able to direct some traffic that you wouldn't if you didn't know. Take the emphasis off uncovering 1919 and put it on finding any lone wolves who are rattling around. But that's only because you're really, really smart—not because you *know* who put the site up."

Chase stepped back: "You're right. About all of it. I *know*, but I don't know."

She walked away, glancing back only once.

FOURTEEN

Lucas pried Bob and Rae away from the SWATs, said, "I need the truck, but you guys can't come. What you need to do is, get a ride from Jane. She'll give you a warrant to search Cop's car down at the UPS center. Call me when you get it done."

Rae: "We can do that, but why?"

"Because this is about to get political and you don't want to know about it. You want to be able to look a Senate investigating committee in the eye and say, 'Davenport never told me about it.'"

Bob and Rae looked at each other, and Rae shrugged: "You usually know what you're talking about," she said. "But it sounds bad."

"It is bad."

Lucas called Chase, who was standing fifty feet

away, and fixed a ride for Bob, Rae, and their guns, first to the UPS center, then back to the Watergate. Then he headed south, the late-afternoon traffic beginning to congeal, but most of it was coming toward him, rather than with him. On the way, he called Senator Elmer Henderson on his private line.

Henderson picked up on the fifth ring and said, "I'm in a meeting—on a scale of one to ten . . ."

"Ten."

"Give me a second to get out in the hall," Henderson said. There were some shuffling sounds and a door closed, then Henderson said, "I assume you cracked it. Did you kill anyone?"

"I've cracked part of it. I'll know for sure in an hour or so."

"What is it?"

"We're talking on radios and I'm told it's child's play for somebody to listen in, if you've got the right child," Lucas said. "I'll want to see you in, say, two hours. But not with your Minnesota sidekick. Just you."

"Uh-oh."

"Yeah."

"I do have a certain level of trust in my sidekick," Henderson said, referring to Porter Smalls.

"Then you can tell him—or call him and I'll tell him, but I want to talk to you first."

"You're at the Watergate, right? What room?"

Lucas told him and Henderson said, "Two hours. See you then."

THE TRIP SOUTH, across the Potomac, was mostly on interstate highways, and traffic wasn't terrible; Lucas made it to the Winston house in exactly one hour. He was met at the door by an angry Mary Ellen Winston, who said, "I find this whole thing . . . despicable, including Blake's part in it. I've told him so."

"You've heard that the FBI arrested a sniper outside the school of a senator's child?" Lucas asked. "Depending on how this breaks out, your kid could be saving the lives of other children."

"Blake is betraying a friend—"

"To save lives," Lucas snapped. "Tell the truth, Mrs. Winston, I don't want to hear some bullshit about how this is an ethical complication. You ever look at somebody who's taken a bullet in the head? I have, and just this morning. That was bad enough: if it'd been a kid, I'd be having nightmares."

She froze up at the tone, then said, "Blake's in the tennis room."

LUCAS WALKED THROUGH THE HOUSE, with Mary Ellen Winston trailing him, and the place smelled improbably like fresh-baked bread and cinnamon; he thought it might be a spray of some kind, because he didn't see anybody baking and Winston didn't seem to be in the mood for anything so mellow.

Blake was looking as frozen as his mother, sitting on

a couch looking out over the tennis court, an Apple laptop on the table in front of him, the bright Apple logo glowing from the back of the machine. When Lucas walked into the room, he looked up and Mary Ellen said, "Blake, I've told you . . ."

"Get the fuck off my back," Blake Winston snapped.

"What!"

"Get the fuck off my back. We'll talk about this later when Dad gets here. Right now, I don't want to hear about it. Go read a *New Yorker* or something."

His mother turned and steamed out of the room. Lucas walked down the three steps into the tennis room and said, "I'm causing you trouble."

"You're not causing me anything—I'm causing it," Winston said. He seemed five years older than he had the last time they talked. "Mom makes complications where there aren't any. Or shouldn't be. That's what she does. Come look at this."

He took a thumb drive out of his shirt pocket, plugged it into a USB port on the side of the computer and said, "I won't bother you with the details. The 1919 site is down now, but I'd downloaded the whole site. I searched Audrey's computer hard drive and found the 1919 articles in her deleted files."

"Which weren't totally deleted?"

"No. They're still there on the hard drive until they're overwritten and they hadn't all been overwritten. I also found four of the photographs . . . the rest were gone."

"How do you know she didn't take the files off the

1919 site because she was interested in learning something about them?" Lucas asked. "I mean, you did." Winston waved him off. "Remember how the photos on the website didn't have any metadata? The metadata had been stripped off? Well, the metadata is still there on her photo files, which means she didn't get them off the site. The photos were all shot with a Sony RX100 Mark III, which is a nice little camera. I happen to know she has that exact model. The metadata has all the dates and stuff that the photos were shot."

Lucas sat silently for a moment, then said, "Let's see the photos."

Winston brought them up one at a time, showed Lucas the metadata, which included the time, date, and camera setting used to make them. They'd been done the past spring, before summer vacation.

When he'd looked at them all, Lucas said, "Okay. Give me the thumb drive."

Winston ejected it, pulled it from the USB port, and tossed it to Lucas. "It's gonna hurt if you tell her where this came from," Winston said. "The word will get around the school that I'm a narc."

"I'll cover you if I can, but she may suspect," Lucas said. "I'm willing to tell her some lies to cover up my sources."

"Try hard," Winston said. "What Mom's saying . . . that's what a lot of my friends would say, too. You say, 'Maybe a kid would get killed if you didn't turn her in,' but that's all theoretical. If a kid doesn't get killed, I'm gonna be the school dick."

"I understand," Lucas said.

"Do you?"

"Yes. I did murder investigations in Minnesota and I had a number of confidential sources," Lucas said. "If they were found out, they weren't the school dick. They were dead men walking."

Winston thought about that, then bobbed his head: "Okay."

Lucas stood, patted him on the shoulder, said, "Go easy on your mother," and left.

HE WAS BACK AT THE WATERGATE fifteen minutes before Henderson was due to arrive, so he took a quick shower and changed into a clean shirt. As he was getting dressed, he took a phone call from Rae.

"See," she said, "you really don't want to be one of those shitkickers who kills somebody, but then thinks, 'This is an expensive gun, I think I'll keep it.' And then, you get clever and hide it under your spare tire, where every moron who ever wore a Carhartt jacket hides his gun."

"What kind?"

"Smith M&P nine, the perfect size to make that hole in Gibson. Threaded barrel, and we found the suppressor stuck in the crack between the seat back and the seat, in the back of the car. About the only thing small enough to fit back there."

"Call Jane . . ."

"That's all done, the FBI guys have the gun and

suppressor. Nothing else of interest in there. We're leaving here now, heading back to the Watergate."

"Let's meet at nine tomorrow; I'm jammed up right now."

"See you then."

HENDERSON MESSAGED that he was running ten minutes late, so Lucas plugged Winston's thumb drive into his own MacBook, pulled up the files, and ran through them again. He was making notes on the metadata on the last photo when Henderson knocked.

Lucas let him in, and the senator, looking harried, yanked his necktie loose, took a chair, and asked, "I don't suppose there's a beer in that refrigerator?"

"As a matter of fact, there is."

Lucas got a beer, popped the top, and handed it over. Henderson took it, swallowed some beer, said, "You know the most amazing thing about my job? It's talking to famous people, people you see on TV all the time, pontificating, and realizing how many of them are grubbing around for money. Still looking for angles that will make them a few bucks. And they don't care what they have to do. Bend over the desk and take it in the ass? Sure, no problem, give me a hundred bucks."

"Maybe you're amazed because you never had to do that," Lucas said. "Being born with a gold brick up that ass."

"That's not it," Henderson said. "Sure, I chose the right parents and got born rich. But if I wasn't rich, I wouldn't grub. I know all kinds of good people who are willing to work hard but would refuse to grub around for money like some of these guys. I'm mean, it's embarrassing."

He hesitated in mid-rant, then said, "Anyway, that's not why I'm here. What happened? And why can't I tell Porter?"

"Because Porter's a Republican and Roberta Coil is a Southern Democrat who is holding on to her seat by her fingernails. I looked. She won her last election by fewer than nine thousand votes. And the Senate is delicately balanced right now."

Henderson leaned forward. "Jesus Christ, what are you about to tell me?"

Lucas said, "The 1919 website was invented by Audrey Coil, Senator Coil's daughter."

Now Henderson leaned back, nearly speechless, until he managed, "Oh, fuck me! Lucas, that can't be right!"

"Yeah, it is, I was afraid Porter . . ."

"Porter can't know about this," Henderson sputtered. "He would turn it into a political sledgehammer. In fact, nobody can know. If it gets in the media, Coil might have to resign from the Senate. We can't afford to lose her."

"That's what I was thinking."

"And you have proof? That the daughter did it?" Henderson demanded.

Lucas explained about Audrey Coil's laptop and about Blake Winston's investigation, and about the metadata.

"You trust this Winston kid?"

"Yes. He looked because I asked him to," Lucas said. "His mother was dead-set against it."

"Wait—so there are at least two other people who know about this? Winston, and his mother?"

"And his father will probably hear about it, if he hasn't already. I've warned them to keep their mouths shut, but, you know . . . freedom of speech. I don't know their political affiliation, but they're rich and have Southern roots."

"Goddamnit, that's not good," Henderson chugged half of the remaining beer, eyes closed.

Lucas didn't mention Jane Chase.

"WHAT DO YOU WANT TO DO?" Lucas asked.

Henderson got up, prowled around the room, hands in his jacket pockets, a scowl on his face. He looked out the window where he could see a curve in the Potomac, and down at Lucas's Walther sitting on the desk, in its holster. He picked up the gun, hefted it, put it back down.

Finally, he said, "We have to talk to Bob Coil. Like, right now. I'll call my office, get her personal cell phone. Maybe we can catch her on this side of the river."

"You want to talk to her without the daughter?"

"If we can. Because, we're gonna sit here and figure out how we can convince Bob Coil that Audrey did this and how she might get Audrey to admit it, so we know for sure," Henderson said. "Then the daughter gets shipped back to wherever they're from and where no media is likely to go chasing after her."

"The FBI may start a blitz, hitting alt-right groups. They'll use that would-be sniper they caught as an excuse," Lucas said. "They'll try to scare the shit out of the leadership, so maybe there won't be any more attempts and the whole thing will go away. If we can just make it go away for a while, drop out of the news . . ."

Henderson pulled at his lower lip. "If the FBI does that, we'll go to the media outlets, Porter and I, and tell them that their coverage is encouraging crazies to go after these kids. We'll tell them that if somebody gets shot, we'll start a bipartisan boycott of their advertisers. That'll cool off the news coverage. You're right—if it goes away for a while, we're probably good."

HENDERSON CALLED HIS OFFICE, got a number for Roberta Coil, called it, learned that Coil was in a staff conference. He asked her to come to the Watergate, told her it was urgent. She asked about that. "I was told not to discuss certain things on cell phones because they're actually radios, that other people listen to," Henderson told her, glancing over at Lucas.

He gave her Lucas's room number. When he hung up, he said, "She'll be here in an hour. Let's go downstairs and get something to eat. I could use something stronger than a beer."

They adjourned to the dining room, got hamburgers, and Henderson got a vodka tonic and then a second one while Lucas settled on a Diet Coke. They talked for a few minutes about wives and family, then Lucas yawned, and said, "I'm getting tight about talking with Coil. It's giving me the yawns."

"So am I. I don't know her well, but she has the reputation of a woman with sharp edges," Henderson said. "This will not make her happy."

"She gonna get me fired?"

"No, that won't happen. You've got way too much protection and from both parties. But if she quits, or is forced out, then you're right—Georgia has a Republican governor who'll appoint her replacement and we'll lose the seat."

"I get nervous when I'm tangled up with these political considerations," Lucas said. "It feels . . . corrupt."

"Yeah? Welcome to the big time."

AS THEY FINISHED EATING, a bearded guy, wearing an ill-fitting tweed sport coat and black jeans, came by and said, "Senator Henderson. How are you?"

"Dave. Trolling the Watergate, huh?" He said it with a smile. "Hoping for a repeat?"

"I wish. I'm told your Obamacare enhancement bill won't be going anywhere," the man said. "It's deader than Elvis."

"It's a work in progress. It may not go anywhere this session, but I've got commitments from several Republicans now and it'll rise out of the grave next year. It's gonna pass," Henderson said.

"Maybe," the man said. He didn't sound interested. He looked at Lucas. "Who are you?"

"A friend of the senator's from Minnesota," Lucas said. "Who are you?"

"Works for the *Post*," Henderson said, before the man could reply. "He wrote a story a couple of years ago that got turned into an HBO movie, so he's probably rich now."

"Right. My total take was about the same as your daily income," the man said. He took a step away and asked Lucas, "You sure you're from Minnesota?"

Lucas said, "Yah, you betcha."

"You're not here to soak the federal government for huge sums of money? You're not selling hammers for four hundred dollars each?"

"Go away, Dave," Henderson said. "Lucas is a school pal and there's no government business going on here. At all. We're talking about old high school girlfriends and whatever happened to them."

"Had to ask," the guy said, and he drifted away, eye-checking the other tables in the restaurant.

"HE'S SMARTER THAN HE SEEMS," Henderson said in a low voice. "Given what we're talking about here, I want to get under cover. I hope to hell he doesn't spot Coil coming in."

They went back up to Lucas's room, Henderson carrying a third vodka tonic in a plastic tumbler, switched through CNN, Fox, MSNBC, talked about how, exactly, they'd tell Coil about her daughter, and didn't quite jump when Coil knocked. Henderson answered the door, said, "Come in," and Lucas saw her face tighten when she spotted him sitting on the bed.

"What happened?"

"We have a problem," Henderson said. "You have a problem. Actually, everybody has a problem and we've got to figure out what to do about it."

When Coil was sitting down, Henderson said to Lucas, "Go ahead."

Lucas: "I can't tell you my sources for the information I'm going to give you. I cannot do that. We've learned, and this is beyond question, I've checked and double-checked . . . I'm afraid Audrey is the one who set up the 1919 website."

Coil gaped, turned to Henderson and demanded, "Is this a joke?"

Henderson: "This is no joke, I can assure you. The question is, what to do about it?"

She turned back to Lucas: "How do you know this?"

Lucas explained about the photos and the metadata. Coil asked how he'd gotten into Audrey's computer and he told her that it had been compromised by teenaged hackers interested in her website because of her provocative photos, and that he'd found the people who'd done it through sources at the FBI.

"They were talking about blackmailing you. They

put out a feeler to one of the more radical hacker guys, who happens to have a side job as an FBI informant," Lucas lied. "The information was routed to me and I dropped the hammer on them. Told them they were looking at twenty years in prison. Took their computers over to the FBI lab, found some sexting photos of underage girls, which in Virginia counts as child pornography. They are sealed up tight, they won't be talking to anyone, ever."

"Which is a good thing," Henderson said to Coil. "Makes you, you know, throw up in your mouth a little, letting those weasels go free, but that's where we're at. Anyway, we've cauterized that."

Henderson then went through all the problems Audrey had created, for Audrey, for Coil, for the Democratic Party as it involved the U.S. Senate. "This is a disaster waiting to happen," he concluded. "You've got to shut Audrey up. Get her off the air. Preferably, find some excuse to pull her out of school and send her back home, to finish school there. Or wherever, but someplace there aren't reporters every five feet."

Lucas said, "Your daughter's a minor, so any legal penalties wouldn't be as severe as they would be if she were eighteen. There might be some, but I don't know. I'm not a prosecutor and you're a person of some influence, and that could change what happens. At this point, very few people know about this—me, Senator Henderson, my sources, although my sources don't have the whole story."

"Could she go to jail?"

"I don't know. If somebody actually gets shot, I suppose that could be a possibility, but as I said, I'm not a prosecutor," Lucas said. "What we're doing here, Elmer and I, is trying to seal off possible leaks. From anyone, including Audrey."

Coil picked up her purse, which she'd dropped on the floor, and said to Lucas, "You're clearly convinced about this. I'm not. I'll go home and talk to Audrey, and I *will* get the truth out of her."

She turned to Henderson. "If somebody gets shot, what are the chances that it'll all come out?"

"Depends on whether we spring a leak. The likeliest way we'd do that, spring a leak, is if Audrey keeps talking and if somebody decides they'd like to get in on all the publicity. So Bob—get her out of here."

"I'll call you tonight," she said. She stood up.

"Dave McCall from the *Post* was wandering around the restaurant a while ago. Be nice if he didn't see you," Henderson said.

"I'll take care." She looked again at Lucas, said, "Come on. Let's go."

Lucas looked at Henderson and back to Coil. "I wasn't planning . . ."

"Bullshit. You're coming. Get your car."

Henderson said, "Go."

LUCAS FOLLOWED COIL across the river, trailing her right up to the house, parked in the driveway as she rolled her car into the garage. She waited until Lucas was inside before she dropped the garage door, saying not a word as she opened a side door that led to a stairway to the main floor.

Once there, they could hear music from the next floor up. "Sit down," Coil said, "I'll get her."

Lucas sat and Coil climbed the stairs, disappeared down a hall. Lucas heard a harsh exchange without being able to make out specific words, and Coil reappeared, trailed by Audrey, who saw Lucas, stopped at the head of the stairs, and asked, "What?"

"Get down here," the senator said.

Audrey Coil came slowly down the stairs, her eyes fixed on Lucas. Her mother pointed at a chair, and said, "Sit."

When Audrey was sitting, nervous, playing with the ends of her hair, Coil said, "Audrey: did you make up the 1919 website?"

"What? No! What are you . . ."

Coil said to Lucas, "Ah, God. She's lying. I've been able to tell when she's lying, ever since she was a small child. She's lying now."

"I am not," Audrey wailed. "I don't know where—"

"You don't protect your laptop from outside intrusion," Lucas said. "You leave it plugged in, turned on and running. Overnight sometimes. The photos you took with your RX100 camera are still on your hard drive."

Audrey stared at him for a minute, with something that looked like pure, unadulterated hate, sniffed, then started to cry: "All this wasn't supposed to happen. I thought it might get me on TV, but I never thought . . ."

"Ah, God," Coil said again. To Lucas: "All right. We know she did it. What's next?"

"Like Senator Henderson said . . . she's got to go away." Lucas turned to Audrey, who was sobbing, but trying to suppress it by pressing her knuckles to her teeth. "Audrey . . . who else have you told about this? Is there anyone else we have to shut up?"

"No . . ."

"How about Blake Winston?" Lucas asked, throwing a head fake. "He must've known."

"No, I didn't tell anyone . . ."

"How did you do this?" Roberta Coil asked. "I know why, but how?"

Audrey explained that she'd gotten the idea from a story on Ars Technica, a website that covered technology and computers, about how websites were used to create whole fictitious stories for political and monetary reasons. The techniques, she said, were simple enough.

"How did you avoid the cameras around that Starbucks, where you set up the website?" Lucas asked.

"Easy. I never went there," she said. "I walked in from the back and uploaded my stuff from the alley." Then she asked, "Are you saying there's somebody in my laptop?"

"Not anymore. When I found out about it, I shut it down," Lucas lied. "I also shut down the people who were doing it. The computer penetration—and they were going after a lot of people besides you—is illegal. If this blows up, they're going to prison. I made that very clear to them."

"Jeez, are they in *my* computer?" Roberta Coil asked.

Lucas shook his head. "They say not. But what do I know? I'd have it checked, if I were you."

ROBERTA COIL SNAPPED a couple of more questions at her daughter, her voice climbing in volume, until she was just shy of shouting: "I could lose my Senate seat. I wasn't planning to stop at the Senate, and now you've put everything at risk . . ."

Lucas said, "Senator Coil . . . I'm going to leave you two alone. You figure out the rest of this. Maybe talk to Senator Henderson some more. Let's all hope that there aren't any more crazies out there who took the website seriously."

BACK AT THE WATERGATE, Lucas called Weather, swore her to secrecy, and told her what had happened. She was properly appalled. They spent ten minutes speculating on possibilities, then a few more talking about the kids, and Weather told him about an intricate surgery she'd be doing in the morning.

When they'd rung off, Lucas mulled over the situation, thinking about how much trouble he might be in if the whole thing came out, realized there wasn't much he could do about it, and turned on the TV. He found an old movie, *The Little Drummer Girl*, and was halfway through it when Henderson called.

"Senator Coil told me about your little séance. She said that her husband, George, has been having a series of heart problems and that Audrey has asked that she be allowed to go home for a semester to be with her father. Coil has already spoken with the school head, and he's agreed to the semester in Tifton, without loss of place toward graduation. Audrey'll be down there for several months, at least."

"Are the heart problems real?" Lucas asked.

"Lucas, I mean, *for Christ's sakes . . .*"

"Okay."

Audrey would be on a plane to Atlanta in the morning, Henderson said, and any press inquiries would be deflected with the heart-problem excuse. Her blog would be temporarily suspended, since Young'nHot'nTifton probably wouldn't gather a crowd.

"Bob's catching a plane to Jerusalem. She hooked onto an Armed Services Committee junket to talk about fighter jets with the Israeli government. She'll be out of pocket for at least a week, which will also deflect media inquiries to her. If we can have this done in a week . . ."

"The problem is that we won't know when we're done," Lucas said. "All we can do is hope there's not another lone wolf out there, still believing in 1919."

"So we fall back on prayer. I was afraid we'd get there sooner or later."

FIFTEEN

Dunn arrived at the cemetery a few minutes after 7:30 in the evening, sunlight fading under the western horizon, his car parked on the other side of a residential block opposite the cemetery. His reasoning: if he should be discovered, and if there were a foot chase, he could run across the street and disappear into the trees and bushes around a half dozen different houses, before cutting over to the car.

He was a fan of Jason Bourne movies and he'd remembered that when Bourne wanted to drive cross-country and not be followed, he would slip up behind a random car and steal a fresh license plate. Dunn scouted a couple of shopping centers, the Shops at Stonewall and the Virginia Gateway, but could never get comfortable with lifting a plate: there were eyes everywhere, people coming and going, and sometimes unexpectedly, cars turning down the parking aisles, sweeping the aisles with their headlights . . .

And cameras. He spotted a couple, but thought there must be more that he didn't see.

He left both places with a chill down his spine and an unused screwdriver still uncomfortably large in his jacket pocket. That Bourne shit, he learned, was harder and riskier than it looked.

So his car carried its own plate, and if there were some survey of cars being done in the area, well then, he was cooked. He'd take that chance, simply because, he thought, no such surveys were being done.

He had his camera bag slung over his shoulder and now carried a tripod as well. He entered the park unseen, he thought, went to his shooting nest, settled into it. He'd dressed warmly, though it wasn't apparent: he was wearing silk long underwear under his long-sleeved shirt, and had a military casualty blanket strapped under his camera bag.

He set up the tripod, locked the camera onto it, took a couple of shots of the western sky, and settled in to watch.

Because if the cops were still there, at the parking structure, they'd be working in shifts, and one way or the other, he'd catch a shift change, suspicious arrivals and departures.

He hadn't planned to get bored, and he didn't. He dozed from time to time, but not so heavily that he didn't pick up cars arriving at, or leaving, the parking structure down the hill. Then, a few minutes before nine o'clock, he heard voices. He couldn't see anyone, but the voices were close, and muted; a little laughter, and a few moments later, the sweet funky smell of marijuana.

A couple of kids, he thought, were off to his left, near the edge of the cemetery, inside a screen of trees. He'd been sitting on the tarp, the silvery foil side up and folded over his legs. Now, with the kids not far away, he wrapped the blanket over himself, nothing poking out but his head. The outside of the blanket was done in a camo pattern and he was confident in his invisibility. Unless, of course, they literally tripped over him.

He stayed focused on the talk, and the occasional giggling, which he suspected meant there was something sexual going on; but who knew, really, or cared?

At 10:30 or so, there was a burst of louder conversation and then the sounds of the intruders moving through trees, and then a pale light that he recognized as the flashlight from a cell phone. The flashlight bobbed around, eighty or a hundred feet away, and then disappeared up the hill.

A half hour later, he heard somebody on the street, more talking. He risked a look, and there was enough ambient light to make out a couple and a dog, walking down the hill with a flashlight showing the way. They stopped at the edge of the cemetery for a moment, then moved on. Another moment and he picked up the scent of fresh dog shit.

Didn't bother to bag it. That annoyed him; that always annoyed him when he saw it.

Time dragged. He let it drag. Slept off and on, with no cars to disturb him. If there was still a shift of cops, he thought they'd be arriving perhaps two hours before the school opened. He set his cell phone alarm to vibrate, and dozed, sitting upright, but comfortable, his back against a gravestone.

At five, he woke, found a thin layer of dew covering the blanket. He began watching again, alert now: his time was coming. At 5:30, he saw a suspicious-looking car pull into the hospital parking structure—there appeared to be two men in it. Tracking its taillights, he watched though his binoculars as the car drove to the top floor of the parking ramp, although there were empty spots on the two floors below.

He was too far away to tell if the men got out of the car; he heard no car doors slam, but they might have closed them quietly.

Over the next hour, when the car didn't reappear, he decided that it was very possible that the occupants were FBI or Secret Service agents. He was not sure if they'd hear the shot from his .223—if they were inside a car, or if they were behind a hospital door, he thought they probably would not.

Just in case, he decided that he needed to be closer to the spot where he'd hidden the gun, so he could conceal it again after taking the shot. He crawled the fifty yards to the shed and lay down beside it. From that position, he didn't have as clear a view of the playground as he did from his tombstone lair, and the rifle's bipod wasn't high enough to give him a clear view over the grass and weeds. He tied his coat, blanket, and camera bag into a bundle, thick enough that he could get a steady gun rest that was high enough to see over the weeds and the edge of the slope. He couldn't see the parking ramp's top floor, but that wouldn't make any difference one way or the other. Once he took the shot, he had to re-hide the gun, and then move, fast, without looking like he was moving fast.

He was a full minute from his car, but unless he was unlucky, the feds, if they were there, wouldn't be aware of the shot for at least that long; and if they were aware of it, they wouldn't be aware of where it came from.

He settled into the new spot and checked his watch. Ten minutes to seven—forty minutes or an hour to wait. Now, if the kid only showed. After the previous attempt, maybe he wouldn't.

A FEW KIDS began straggling onto the playing field at 7:30. More came behind them, waiting for the first bell. He picked out a boy who seemed to be about McGovern's likely height and counted bricks on the wall behind them—three courses of bricks with concrete joints were about eight inches high. He counted eight three-brick courses up the school's brick wall above the boy's head and marked the height in his mind.

Then McGovern showed up.

At ten minutes to eight, the boy ambled around the corner of the school building with two other kids. He was wearing a ball cap, but his lower face looked right.

Had to be right. Quick white smile, that square jaw. He was wearing a black Patagonia jacket and a blue shirt over dark slacks.

Dunn was breathing harder now, struggled to control it, but the adrenaline was on him. He pulled on plastic kitchen gloves, got the gun from under the shed, unzipped the case, took the rifle out, fumbled the magazine but then got it seated, jacked a shell into the chamber, put the gun on top of his jacket. He used the binoculars to spot the kid again. He was still standing with two others and they were looking toward the hospital and the kid jerked a finger at it and laughed.

He was standing still.

Dunn went to the scope, found him. Thought about windage—but there was little or no wind at all, not even enough to stir the leaves on the trees. Without moving his eye from the scope's eyepiece, he fumbled the binoculars back into the camera case. He clicked the safety off, steadied the gun, holding five feet over the kid's head.

Said to himself, *Ready, set . . .*

He breathed out, and the gun seemingly fired of its own volition, a sharp *crack* and a light punch to his shoulder. Less than a half second later the kid folded up like a broken kite.

And Dunn was moving: gun and the case shoved under the shed, ten seconds gone, ten more seconds gone getting the concrete block perfectly back in place. He rolled up the rest of his gear, duckwalked into the scrubby trees, then got to his feet and jogged through the saplings toward the street. He stopped a few yards before he got there, then strolled casually out of the cemetery, up the hill and around the corner to his car.

He opened the driver's-side door, threw the camera case onto the passenger seat, started the car, and was gone.

He'd never looked back at the school, never looked to see if the kid was really down. He'd find out soon enough, he thought: now the problem was moving quickly and safely away, turning corners out toward the freeway, then getting back down south. If he hurried, he'd be at work in half an hour, building an alibi . . .

Calm, he thought. Needed to be still, calm, isolated during the day, to ask no questions about news.

But now he pounded the steering wheel with the palms of his hands. In his heart, he was thrilled.

CHAPTER

SIXTEEN

The phone rang at the wrong time and Lucas snapped awake, already feeling the dark vibration: "What?"

"Somebody shot a kid at the same goddamn place the guy got caught yesterday," Jane Chase shouted at him.

"What senator?"

"No senator—the senator's kid is hiding out. This was another kid, nothing to do with politics."

"He gonna die?"

Long pause. "He's dead."

LUCAS, BOB, AND RAE got to the school thirty minutes later. Bob and Rae had already been up, Lucas pulled on jeans and yesterday's shirt and ran out the hotel room door and down the stairs to the garage, where the other two were waiting for him.

Lucas talked to Chase again, but she was also on the way, from farther out, and hadn't yet gotten to the school when they arrived. Lucas called Elmer Henderson, who was on his way to his office, and told him. Henderson made loud and meaningless noises and then told Lucas he would call Porter Smalls.

When they got to the school they found the playground taped off, students leaving down a funnel of rifle-armed local cops, to be picked up by a line of cars driven by panicked parents. The cops didn't care about late-arriving marshals and directed Lucas to park a block away, in a dirt turnout next to a six-foot-wide creek.

When they got back to the school, nobody had time to talk. Lucas couldn't even discover who was in charge, if anyone was, and Lucas got on the phone to Chase again. She was still twenty minutes out. Lucas said, "Call somebody here. Tell them to talk to me, for Christ's sakes. They won't even talk to us."

"One minute," she said.

One minute later, an FBI agent hustled up and asked, "Who's Davenport?"

Lucas raised a hand and the agent said, "I'm temporarily the number-two guy here. I got people crawling out of my ass: what do you want?"

Lucas: "You got the shooter? Got any leads?"

"No and no."

"Where'd the shot come from?"

"Not the parking structure." He pointed. "That's where the Secret Service guys grabbed the shooter yesterday. They were up there again, but never even heard the shot. They didn't know anyone at the school had been shot until they were called and told about it."

"So you have no idea where the shot came from?"

The agent waved impatiently across a wide arc of low hills and shrugged. "The kid was hit in the chest with an exit wound through his spine right between his shoulder blades. We don't know how he was standing. He was in a circle of kids who were talking, moving around, changing positions. We'll figure it out when we find where the bullet hit, probably in the ground behind him, but you know what that's like. It's gonna take a while. We got metal detectors on it, and so far we've found three pennies and a dime."

"Hospital window?" Rae asked.

The agent looked toward the long row of windows on the hospital, as if nobody had even thought of it. "Can you get the windows open?" he asked.

Rae said, "I don't know, but there are a heck of a lot of places in a hospital where you could hide a gun. With all the crap that comes in and out of those places, day and night . . ."

"I'll ask," the agent said. He took a long look at Rae, creator of this new and difficult possibility, then said, "I gotta get back."

"Let's go look," Lucas said to Bob and Rae.

They drafted on the FBI agent's urgency, staying close in a convoy, and nobody asked who they were or tried to stop them. Behind the school, the body was covered with a black plastic tarp, the kind only used to cover dead bodies. There were agents all over the place, but nobody was looking at it, except the three of them and the body was like a black puddle in the grass and seemed isolated and lonely.

Bob said quietly, "Bullet didn't come from the hospital," he said. "The guy would have to be crazy."

"The guy *is* crazy," Lucas said.

"Yeah, but . . ." Bob scratched his head. He and Lucas were both looking past the hospital, at the top of a hill well behind the hospital.

"The hill," Lucas said. "Too far?"

"It'd be a hell of a shot," Bob said. "Must be at least four or five hundred yards. Maybe longer."

"Could explain why he shot the wrong kid," Lucas said.

"And these guys are gun nuts," Rae said. "Boone's place yesterday—that was like a shooting school. He might *be* a hell of a shot."

AT THAT MOMENT, a short blond woman in jeans and a raspberry blouse struggled round the corner of the school where she could see the black tarp and she screamed, "Jamie! Jamie!"

She was struggling because a female FBI agent had her by the arm, but the woman slashed at the agent with her fingernails and wrenched free and sprinted across the grassy swale between her and the tarp. An agent tried to get in her way but she eluded him and got to the tarp and snatched it away and Lucas could see the boy's face: he lay faceup, pale, rigid, sightless, eyes half-open, lips bloodless, and the woman shrieked and went to her knees, hands in the air, a long vibrating *aaiiiieeee* . . .

Lucas took a step toward her but Rae caught his arm and whispered, "No!" and then the female agent caught up with the woman and went to her knees as well and wrapped an arm around the woman's shoulders as the woman continued the echoing wail and some agents seemed unable to look away, and others seemed not to be able to look at all.

Lucas was caught by the sight of the kid's paper-white face. Rae asked, "Lucas . . . you okay?"

Lucas mumbled, "He looks like my boy. He looks like Sam."

Rae tugged at him: "Lucas, c'mon. C'mon."

Lucas turned away and said to Bob and Rae, "There's nothing here for us."

"And I can't look anymore," Rae said; tears were running down her face, and behind them, the mother's wail continued to vibrate around the schoolyard.

"Let's go look at that hill," Bob said.

THEY WALKED BACK TO THE TAHOE, drove out two blocks, took a right up the hill, drove past the hospital, farther up the hill, and another right, and yet farther up the hill to a cemetery that looked to be abandoned, spotted with a few healthy trees, some that were dying, and a rash of saplings among the knee-high weeds.

They got out of the car and walked across the cemetery, past the old crooked tombstones, their shoes wet from dew, to the edge of the hill looking down at the school.

"This is where I would have been," Bob said. Bob was sniper-qualified.

"Where?" Lucas asked.

They looked and Bob pointed farther up the slope. "Closer to those little trees. Good for exfiltration, plus you couldn't be seen from the street."

They walked that way, along the edge of the slope and, halfway to the trees, Bob put his hand out, slowing Lucas and Rae.

"Somebody was sitting here—see? Where the weeds are crushed down? There's no dew on them, so it was this morning."

"Let's get the feds up here," Lucas said. He took his phone from his pocket.

"C'mon, man," Rae said. "We're the feds, too. Don't be a fuckin' bureaucrat. This is ours. Give it ten minutes anyway."

Lucas didn't have to think about it. He stuck the phone back in his pocket and said, "It looks like he went that way, up toward that shed . . ."

"He was crawling," Bob said. To Rae: "Go run to the equipment bag, bring back some of those flags and some tape."

"Yes," she said, and she jogged off toward the truck. She was back in a minute, with a roll of yellow plastic tape and a bunch of playing-card-sized yellow plastic flags stuck on foot-long pieces of stiff wire. With Bob directing traffic, they laid the yellow tape along their own tracks through the weeds and pinned it with the flags. When they got to the shed, Bob pointed at a larger, round crushed spot in the tall grass next to an old cottonwood.

"He set up here."

He moved to the right, bending over the weeds. "There we go."

Lucas looked: a single brass .223 shell was nestled down in the grass.

They looked down the hill. The school seemed to be a long way away, maybe five or six football fields, though it was hard to tell exactly because of the change in elevation. The agents on the field looked about the size of ants, when seen by a person standing upright. "What he did was, he was up here more than once, he figured out the exact distance to the back wall of the school," Bob said. "Then he looked up some ballistics tables and probably fired some test shots out in the woods to confirm bullet drop at that exact distance. With a good steady setup here . . ."

Lucas looked back and could see another, thinner trail going through the screen of trees toward the street.

"He ran out there with the gun on his back?"

"Down his back, maybe," Bob said. "If you hung it on a loop and down your back, nobody would see the gun if they were looking at you from the front.

With a jacket over it, they might not even see it from the back."

"But he wouldn't have parked his car right at the curb, too many people would have noticed it. He'd park it up the block, where there are some other cars," Lucas said. "He walks up there with a rifle banging his butt?"

Bob said, "Could have."

LUCAS GOT ON HIS PHONE: "Jane? Where are you?"

"Coming up to the school. It's like a carnival. Where are you?"

"Can you see the hospital?"

"Yes . . . are you there?"

"No. We're on the hill behind the hospital. We found the shooter's nest up here. There's nobody here but us marshals."

"God . . . bless me. All right. I'm coming. I'll get our crime scene people moving that way . . . in a few minutes."

Lucas got off the phone and Rae said, "You guys look here, behind the shed. Look at the grass. He was messing around doing something here, you can see knee prints."

They looked, and Lucas made a wide step around the knee prints, squatted, and said, "That brick's been moved."

"He dumped the gun," Rae said. "The gun's under there."

"From your mouth to God's ears," Bob said.

THEY MOVED AWAY from all the trampled grass, marking their own movements with the tape. Two minutes later, Jane Chase pulled up in a red Mazda MX-5 convertible.

"Who knew?" Rae muttered. "I had her figured for a Prius. A brown one."

Chase was wearing jeans and a Barnard College sweatshirt; her hair was perfect. "Tell me," she said.

"Where's everybody?" Lucas asked.

"They're a few minutes behind me," she said. "I sorta wanted to . . . be here first. After you guys, of course."

"Naturally," Rae said.

"I mean, I didn't mean . . ." Chase said, momentarily flustered.

"Don't worry about it, boss lady," Rae said.

"Ignore her," Bob said to Chase. "She likes to stir the shit. Anyway, let me 'splain this to you."

As they walked her across the site, Lucas could see a caravan of cars suddenly burst up the streets leading to the hill, all of the vehicles running their flashers.

"Exactly when did you call them?" he asked Chase.

"Two minutes ago," she said. "When I got here." She pointed to a tombstone. "That's pretty beaten down, don't you think, Bob? It looks like somebody was sitting there for quite a while."

"Using the tombstone like an easy chair," Bob said.

"Maybe sat there all night. Saw the Secret Service guys going into the hospital. Shot over their heads. He's a cold motherfucker."

"It's that Linc guy," Chase said. "Lucas, we gotta run him down."

"He's next," Lucas said.

THE FEDS SWARMED THE PLACE, agents in white environment suits pulling up grass and swabbing tombstones, looking for DNA, bagging the diminutive .223 shell. Another two guys, in full suits, coveralls, booties, and gloves, removed the brick at the bottom of the shed, bagged it, and peered under the shed with a LED light as powerful as the sun.

"We got a gun," one said, laconically. "And we got a case."

Chase looked at Lucas: "If the gun still has a serial number . . ."

Lucas glanced at Bob and Rae, who simultaneously shrugged. Bob said, "I wouldn't get my hopes up, honey. This guy is not stupid. I doubt he'd go to a gun store and sign all the papers and then use the gun to shoot a kid. And then leave it behind."

"But we'll look, huh?" Chase said.

They did; and they found a serial number. Chase sat in her car on the telephone, then came jogging back: "The gun was sold to a guy named Lee Wilson. Lives near Richmond. He has a federal firearms license, but he's in North Carolina, Charlotte, right now. Says he has been for three days. With witnesses—he's at a wedding. We've got some people from the Charlotte office on the way to interview him."

LUCAS SAID, "This changes everything. Listen, the guy who got caught with a rifle in the parking garage—you still have him in the federal lockup?"

"Sure."

"Is he cooperating?"

"Not really. If he . . . thought he might even catch a tiny break, he might talk," Chase said. "Like the letter, the content of it, he'll talk about that, because we all agree it was sent anonymously. He won't talk about much else."

"I'd like to see him. Right now. Can we get his PD over there?"

"If I push," Chase said. "Why do you need to talk to him?"

"I need to clarify my thinking. My thinking has been kind of clogged up on this. I haven't been doing anything your feds couldn't have done and probably better. I gotta get outside your box if I'm going to help."

"You go talk to him—I'll set it up. I'm going to stay here and I'll monitor what happens with this Lee guy, the gun dealer."

"Good. And listen, what I'm going to say to him . . . we'll need a confidentiality agreement from the public defender. Is that possible?"

"Depends. If you let what you say be used in his defense, he'd probably sign one, maybe with some time limitations."

"We want it timed to a court defense or a plea agreement, whichever comes first," Lucas said. "He can use what I say in a trial or a plea. Not before then."

"We can ask. But exactly what are you up to?"

"You really don't want to know."

"I was afraid of that."

FROM THE SCHOOL TO ALEXANDRIA was twenty minutes in traffic. They were sitting at a traffic light, a minute away from the federal building, when Chase called to say that the would-be shooter, William Walton, had been conferring with his attorney when she called, and both were available at the federal lockup.

"They're skeptical. We're drafting an agreement but the Brick says he's not signing anything until he hears what you have to say about it."

"Brick?"

"The attorney, the PD. His name is Brett Abelman. We call him the Brick because . . . he's like that. Former cop in Newark. He's good."

ABELMAN WAS A TALL, dark-haired, broad-shouldered man with a heavy brow ridge and a nose that had been broken more than once. He was not happy to see Lucas—and he told Bob and Rae that they'd have to wait outside the interview room. An assistant federal attorney was with him and she had an improvised confidentiality statement in her hand, ready to be signed.

Abelman was gruff. "What could you ask that hasn't already been asked? Why should I let you speak to Mr. Walton?"

"Basically because what I'm going to ask him . . . actually, I'm going to tell him something he doesn't know and that you don't know, and I'm going to ask him what he thinks about it," Lucas said. "You might be able to use it in your defense. I don't see how any answer he gives could be used by the prosecution."

"If you're fucking with me, Marshal . . ."

"I'm not. I'm trying to catch the guy who shot this kid," Lucas said. "We know it wasn't Walton."

"All right." He turned to the assistant federal attorney and said, "Give me the paper, Denise. If this is a trick, you'll all be sorry. I promise you."

"I don't even know what it's about, except that I've got a ranking FBI agent breathing down my neck," the woman said.

She gave Abelman the paper and the use of the back of her briefcase as a tabletop to sign it on.

"Let's go," Abelman said. "I keep saying . . . if this is a stunt . . ."

"Yeah, I know, you'll have us all gelded," Lucas said. To the assistant DA, he said, "It'd be best if this were me and Mr. Abelman and Mr. Walton."

"I'm a very curious lawyer," she said.

"You'll have to be curious about something else," Lucas said. "This is just the three of us."

WALTON WAS BROUGHT into an interview room where he sat across a table from Abelman and Lucas. He was a short, thin man with lank brown hair, a round face, and a spade beard that tried to disguise a receding chin, but failed. His eyes and nose were red, as though he'd been crying, or possibly was allergic to the lockup.

Abelman had already told him that Lucas was coming. Abelman said to Lucas, "So ask."

Lucas said to Walton, "I can reveal some details about the case that might help your defense. Specifically, might defeat any suggestion that you were part of a larger plot to kill a senator's child. That might be important."

Walton stirred in his chair, said nothing, glanced at Abelman. Abelman said, "Huh. Keep talking."

"I have a preliminary question, though," Lucas said. "This isn't what I'm here for, but if you could answer it, I'd be willing to tell a courtroom that you cooperated on this point."

"What's the question?" Abelman asked.

Lucas looked at Walton. "Do you know or have you ever heard of a gun dealer named Lee Wilson?"

Abelman said, "Whoa," but Walton put up a hand and said, "I can answer that question."

Abelman: "You sure?"

Walton nodded and looked back at Lucas. "Yeah, I'm sure. To answer your question, no, I never heard of him. Never bought anything from him. That's the honest to God truth."

Lucas nodded. "Thanks. Now, this is what I really want your opinion on. What if I were to tell you that 1919 is a joke, set up by some hackers who were trying to troll the local neo-Nazis?"

Walton stared at him for a long moment, his face slowly going redder than it already was and then he said, softly, "What?"

Abelman said, "You're telling us that . . ."

Walton half rose from his chair, eyes on Lucas, and he shouted, "What?" Spittle flew across the space between them. "It's a joke? It's a joke?" He looked at Abelman. "Is he fucking with me?"

"I don't think so . . ."

"A teenager put it together, that's why the site's so crude," Lucas said.

"What about the letter? You all got the letter? The letter says . . ."

"I know what the letter says," Lucas said. "The letter is bullshit. Somebody was trolling you—or maybe the letter writer really thinks 1919 is real, but believe me, there's nothing there. Nobody wants anyone to shoot any kids. It's a joke. It's a fraud."

"What about me?" Walton brayed. "Do I look like a fuckin' joke?"

"Easy," said Abelman.

"Don't tell me *easy*, you fuckin' kike."

Lucas ignored the slur. "I think you're a victim of one, a joke . . ."

"Can't be! Can't be!" Walton shouted. "I'm going to prison because some goddamn nerd decided to have a little fun? Can't be! You're lying to me, you piece of shit."

A guard came in the back door and they all turned their heads, and he said, "We could hear some shouting outside. Everything okay here?"

"Do I look like I'm okay?" Walton shouted at him. "Get me out of here."

The guard came up to take him by the arm and Walton shouted at Lucas, "You lying motherfucker . . . I know you're lying . . ."

"Easy," Abelman said.

"Fuck you, Jew. You fuck. You can't . . ."

The guard took him out and the door closed.

"NICE GUY," LUCAS SAID, when he was gone. They could still hear him shouting, through the steel door.

Abelman said, "I'd like to meet one innocent nice guy in here, but so far, I haven't. I was hoping I'd get something out of this, but I don't see what it could be."

"I would think if you could argue that there was no big plot, it was nothing but a deranged man who snapped and so on . . . the court might give him some kind of a break."

"If he hadn't been targeting a senator's kid, maybe. But he was. He's going away for a long time," Abelman said. "They got movies of him setting up the rifle. Movies like in a movie theater. I got nothing. I asked an ADA if we could talk and you know what she said?"

Lucas shook his head.

"She said, 'No.' Usually, they put the 'no' in a complete sentence, which makes you think there's some wiggle room. Something between an adjective and a verb. Not this time. It was 'No,' and she said it with a smile and I could see her fang teeth. They're gonna nail him to the wall and there's nothing I can do about it."

LUCAS PICKED UP BOB and Rae and they went out the door, talking about next moves, when Chase called and said, "I'm told you're all done. You get what you wanted?"

"Yes. I did," Lucas said. "What happened with the gun dealer?"

"He's got a shop outside of Richmond and the building owner has a key and the code to the alarm system. He's got an unlocked file with his sales receipts in it and the building owner is going to let us in with this guy's permission. He said he thought he remembered the sale of the gun. He thinks he sold it to a woman."

"That'd be a little unusual. Woman shooter."

"Yes. Anyway, I'm on the way there, to the shop. We could meet there."

"Got nothing else to do," Lucas said. "See you there."

SEVENTEEN

Wilson's Outdoors was located between a pharmacy and a sandwich shop in a low-rent strip mall outside the town of Glen Allen, an hour-and-a-half drive south of Alexandria on I-95, and a few miles north of Richmond.

On the way down, Bob and Rae listened to Lucas's account of his interview with William Walton, then amused each other by speculating on what Lucas might possibly have gotten out of the interview.

"Actually, we do know what he got," Bob said, as they closed in on Richmond. "He got a guy really, really pissed off at him. So when the guy gets out of prison, lo, these many years in the future, he'll probably buy another gun and go to Minneapolis and shoot Davenport."

"Damn hard time finding me in Minneapolis," Lucas said. "I live in Saint Paul."

"Well, pardon me for fuckin' breathing," Bob said.

"Did you really get something from him?" Rae asked.

"Yes. I'm actually pleased with myself. I'm like a genius."

"We all say that," Rae said. She turned to Bob. "Don't we? You were saying that last night."

"No, I said he was a penis, not a genius."

Rae snapped her fingers. "That's right. Penis, not genius."

THEY ARRIVED AT THE STRIP mall and Rae said, "That's a federal Ford pulling in there, or I've gone blind, one or the other." She pointed to a dark blue Ford Excursion, and Lucas, who was driving, turned that way, and Rae pointed again and said, "Gun shop."

The gun shop was dark, a narrow space, two barred windows with a barred door between them, and a "Closed" sign in the window. They parked and got out as the Ford pulled to a curb. Two suited men got out, followed by Chase, from the backseat, talking, as ever, into her cell phone.

Lucas, Bob, and Rae walked over, and Chase said, "You got here quick. The mall owner's on his way over."

Five minutes later, a tall bearded-and-turbaned Sikh showed up, carrying a wad of keys. He introduced himself as Mandeep Kaur. "I hated to hear what Lee had to say, that the gun might have come from here," he said.

"Lee's a good man and this has upset him. I know he tries to weed undesirables from his clientele."

"How would he go about doing that?" Chase asked.

"He interviews them, if he has any doubts," Kaur said, as he found a key and unlocked the front door. "He says he can pick up on it, if a potential buyer has mental problems. Maybe he looks for anger? Pushes them, to see if he can get them riled up."

They stepped inside the shop to the sound of a beeping alarm. Kaur flipped on the lights, found another key, walked a half dozen steps down the main entry aisle, then stepped between two racks of camo shirts to the side wall, used the key to open a steel box mounted next to a showcase, and punched in a code that killed the alarm.

"Lee's office is in the back."

He led the way around a showcase full of pistols to a door that led to the back of the store, then into a small side room that held a desk and a dozen hip-high black filing cabinets.

"He's old school, there should be some three-ring binders . . ."

They found four fat three-ring binders, two with sales documents listed by the buyer's name, and two listed by serial numbers on the gun. They found the sale in the second numbers binder, near the end of the file.

"Rachel Stokes," Chase said. "Sale was last December. It's all here, address, she lives in a place called The

Plains." She looked up, her glasses sliding down her nose. "I'm cranking the SWAT again."

"We'll lead off," Lucas said. He tipped his head at Bob and Rae: "This is what we do."

"Reconnaissance only, until I get the SWAT team there," Chase said.

Lucas said, "Of course" and she gave them the address. Rae poked it into an iPhone app that said they were an hour and a half away from the address, back up I-95. They jogged to the truck, Chase shouting behind them, "Wait for me, wait for me." She spent a minute talking to the two agents she'd arrived with and then all four of them were in the truck and rolling.

Rae said, "Oh-boy oh-boy oh-boy oh-boyo. Gotta drive fast, Lucas. Faster, faster, if we want to be first."

THEY DROVE UP I-95 with lights and siren and ignored a shortcut on state highways to stay on I-95 as long as possible, until they cut cross-country through the town of Manassas to I-66, out I-66 and off at the small town of The Plains and then back out in the country, down a narrow blacktopped road. As they went along, Jane Chase was on the phone, gathering information about the target house: "Stokes, not much on her," she reported. "No criminal record. Nothing— not even a traffic ticket."

"Fake name?" Rae wondered.

"Lot of docs on her," Chase said. "Driver's licenses going back fifteen years . . ."

"She bought that gun," Lucas said. "She might be laying low, but she bought that gun."

AND THEY GOT there first.

As they cruised the target, Rae said, "Tough-looking place."

Bob: "Nothing moving."

Chase: "Car in the back."

Lucas: "If we stop down by the next house, we could circle around and come in through those trees." The next house down had a large woodlot littered with rusted farm machinery, extending along the road toward the target. "Get within fifty yards anyway."

Chase: "The SWAT squad is mobilizing and on the way."

Bob: "*I'm* mobilizing."

Rae: "We're mo-bile, ag-ile, and hos-tile."

Chase: "We should wait for the SWAT."

Lucas: "Let's go around and take a look before it gets dark. That can't hurt."

"Yeah, bullshit, it *can* hurt," Bob said. "However, I fully support the idea."

THE NEXT HOUSE down the road was like the Leaning Tower of The Plains, tall, narrow, paint-peeling clapboard, and leaning, with a dent in the roof line that promised big trouble, sooner rather than later.

Lucas pulled the truck into the driveway and continued to the end of the gravel, so they had the leaning tower between them and the target house. As they rolled to a stop, Rae said, "You know what this house smells like? Like tomato soup and peanut butter."

"You got it," Bob said.

"Why tomato soup and peanut butter?" Jane Chase asked.

Lucas pulled the latch on the Tahoe's door and turned to her: "Because if you go into a Burger King, you can collect enough packets of ketchup to make tomato soup. Peanut butter because it gets you the most calories for a buck. And sometimes, you can get it free from the government."

AS THEY GOT out, a white man came to the screen door wearing a formerly white T-shirt, gray sweatpants, and flip-flops. He was tall, radically thin, and unshaven. A dog moved up beside him, a pit bull, to look them over; the two of them collectively smelled like tomato soup with a whiff of dog shit from the yard. The dog looked better fed than the man. "He'p you?"

Lucas held up his badge. "We're U.S. Marshals. We're interested in the house up the road. Miz Stokes, is it?"

"Something's wrong, ain't there?"

Lucas frowned: "Wrong how?"

"Rachel's always walking up and down the road, looking at stuff, every day, rain or shine. Haven't seen her in the best part of a week. Randy's car been sitting there for a week, hasn't moved. We was gonna call the cops to check, but . . . we didn't. Us'n and the cops . . . don't get along."

Rae said, "Oh, boy."

Lucas: "Who's Randy?"

"Her brother."

A black woman came up behind the man, put her arm around his waist and said, "Rachel's nice. Randy's not. He don't like black folks."

Rae: "He's not a shooter, is he?"

The woman asked, with a hint of skepticism, "You a marshal, too, black lady?"

Rae said, "Yes, me'n these two guys are marshals, this white lady is FBI."

The man said, "Randy's sure enough a shooter. That's all he does, besides drink."

"How about Rachel?" Chase asked. "We have her down for buying a gun, a rifle."

The man said, "I don't think she'd know which end of a gun is which. She probably bought it for Randy. Randy has some felonies. You know. Dope, mostly. Ran over somebody once, when he was drinking. He can't buy his own guns. But he's a shooter: give him half a chance, he'll talk your ear off about it."

Lucas asked, "If we walk up through those trees . . . how close can we get to the house?"

The man scratched his head, but the woman said, "If you go back there . . ." She pointed. "If you go back there and along that bob-wire fence, you come up behind that garage and they couldn't see you from the house. If you stay on this side of the fence, you gonna have to walk through some blackberries, but there's a hole in the fence, you go through that, and you can walk around them. Then the fence ends, but toward the garage."

Bob said to Rae, "Load up," and the two of them turned toward the truck.

Chase said to the couple in the doorway, "If we walk over there, you're not going to call them and warn them, are you?"

The woman said, "We got no phone anymore."

BOB, RAE, AND LUCAS pulled on bulletproof vests, and Bob and Rae got their rifles and a lot of ammunition. Lucas was good with his Walther. Lucas said to Chase, quietly, "You stay with the truck: you're like the headquarters. Talk with the SWAT and call the local cops, whoever they are—maybe the sheriff, out here, you know, whoever, and tell them that we have an operation going on. We don't want some patrol cop spotting us and thinking we're Arab terrorists and taking a shot before he finds out who we are."

"I think I'd rather go."

"You've already been shot once and we don't have a vest for you. Soon as we know what the situation is, we'll call you. In the meantime, get on the phone."

She relented and climbed in the truck, and the couple came out to watch as Lucas, Bob, and Rae walked down the line of the driveway, past a crumpled outbuilding that Bob said had once been a chicken coop, and down the fence line. They went through the hole in the fence before they got to an expansive blackberry patch, and, as the woman said, when they broke out of the cover of the woods, they had a detached garage between themselves and the house.

They took turns peeking at the house and the car parked beside it. When Lucas peeked, he turned to the other two and said, "You see that door? It's open."

Bob and Rae took turns peeking again, and Rae said, "You're right. There's no screen, and there're bugs out here. I think we got us a problem."

Lucas said, "Okay. Bob, you go around the other side of the garage, Rae, you stay here. I'm going to walk up to the door like I'm the mailman . . ." He was wearing a sport coat over the vest and he turned the lapels inward, buttoned up the coat to cover it.

"You look like a preacher," Rae said. "Except for the Walther."

"If I get in trouble, hose the place," Lucas said.

"This is where I say, 'Maybe we should wait for the SWAT team,'" Bob said.

Lucas: "Really?"

"Oh, fuck no. You go, we hose. If there's serious trouble, get down on your belly real quick."

"And get to that door real quick," Rae said. "They can't have seen us yet. If you get to the door in one second, they won't have time to react, if they're in there at all."

————

WHEN THEY WERE SET, Lucas said, "I'm going," and he walked fast to the back door, the Walther held down along his leg. There was a one-step back stoop outside the door, and Lucas stepped up and pushed the door with one finger of his free hand and shouted, "Hello?"

Then he smelled them.

RAE SHOUTED, "Lucas. Lucas."

"Somebody's dead," Lucas shouted back.

"Wait there," Bob shouted.

He waited and Bob and Rae jogged across the yard, and Rae sniffed and said, "Oh, yeah." She and Bob led the way through the door, their rifles up and tracking.

The light inside was dim, because all the blinds and curtains were closed, and when Bob stepped into the kitchen with Rae at his shoulder, Lucas said, "Stop," and reached past Rae's hip to grope for, and find, a light switch. He flipped it on and a dark shape on the floor became a body.

"Clear it, or wait for SWAT?" Bob asked.

"I think we wait for crime scene," Lucas said. "There's nobody here. Not alive. I'd feel them."

"So . . ."

"Keep your muzzles up, I'm going to walk past you . . ." Lucas brought the Walther up to chest height, stepped carefully past the body and peeked into what he thought was a living room. He saw another shape on the floor. Groped for lights again, found the switch and flicked it on. "Got another one in here . . . Let's back out."

"Stink would gag a maggot," Rae said.

"Of which I'm sure we have some," Bob said. "These people been dead a while."

"You guys cover the doors, just in case," Lucas said. Out in the yard, he called Chase: "We entered the house. We've got two dead on the floor, we didn't look in any rooms except the kitchen and the living room. There could be more. They've been dead for a while. Maybe a week. If the SWAT team is coming, they can clear the house, but I don't think there's anyone inside, not alive. We need a crime scene unit and some local cops to control the road."

"Locals are on the way, I'm coming with the car," she said. "SWAT will be here in fifteen minutes or so. I'm coming."

IN AN HOUR, there were thirty people on the scene, mostly local cops and FBI. The two victims were tentatively identified as Randy Stokes and his sister Rachel Stokes, from a wallet in the man's pocket and a wallet from a woman's purse that had been sitting on a sideboard.

One gun was found in the house, an old Smith and Wesson .357, but no long guns. They did find a box of .223 shells scattered on the floor, so guns were apparently missing.

Then came the preliminary paperwork: statements about the discovery and the processing of the scene, that sucked up the rest of the morning and early afternoon, and done in the back of one of the SWAT trucks.

"What's happening with this Linc guy, the guy that Cop mentioned on Gibson's tape?" Lucas asked Chase. "We know he was lining up to shoot someone."

She was shaking her head.

"I checked while I was waiting in your truck," she said. "We've been working it hard, but so far, we've come up empty. I mean, there are several dozen possibilities nationwide, six in Maryland and Virginia. We've checked all of the local people out, but didn't get much. Like, two of them are dead—these were old guys, going way back. Two guys are still around, but one of them is black, so he's not a good possibility, even if we could find him, which we haven't. The other one was convicted of embezzlement and did fifteen months in a state prison, but, you know, a white-collar crime, no violence involved. Now he works for a private custodial service in Petersburg, Virginia. He works nights, nine at night to six in the morning, and his work crew agrees that he was there all night when the kid was shot. People who know him say he's got no politics at all. His probation officer agrees with that. Given where he lives, it seems unlikely that he'd be hanging around White Fist. We're still looking at him, but . . ."

"He's not the right Linc."

"We're pretty sure he's not," she said. "We're starting to throw a wider net, but so far . . . nothing."

"What about these Stokeses? We need to interview everyone who knew these two, see if Linc turns up."

"Already underway," she said. She had a smear of grease under her nose, Vicks, because the odor in the house made her gag. "We're not seeing anything yet."

"Okay. Look, we're gonna take off." Lucas nodded at the army of cops surrounding and infiltrating the house. "You've got more than enough people here. Goddamnit, I thought we had something solid."

"We do—this will lead to something," Chase said. "Where are you going?"

"Out to look around," Lucas said.

"Looking for Linc?"

"Or whatever we can find."

"Lucas . . . the kid who was killed . . . I didn't like your face back there, at the cemetery. If you find Linc, we need to put him on trial and make an example of him."

"Sure."

"We don't need him pushed into a confrontation and shot," she said.

"Sure."

"We don't need him executed."

"You got it, boss lady," Lucas said. He tried a smile.

"You've got a mean smile sometimes," Jane Chase said.

EIGHTEEN

Bob drove while Lucas worked his phone, heading north to Maryland and Charles Lang, who might or might not be a Nazi, but did know names. He was home, he said, mourning for Gibson. They arrived at three o'clock, after a quick stop at a Burger King for fat and carbohydrates.

"If I was the king of Burger King, I'd make the French fries taste like McDonald's French fries," Rae said, as they left the Burger King parking lot. "I mean, how hard can it be?"

"Harder than you'd think," Bob said. "I read someplace, probably not the *New York Times*, that McDonald's fries used to be cooked in beef fat, but they can't do that anymore, so what they came up with was a bunch of chemicals that they put in regular cooking oil so it smells like beef fat. Burger King would have to figure out what the chemicals are."

"Your mind is a fucking garbage dump," Rae said.

Lucas just ate. Truth be told, the repartee was annoying him, but he didn't want to pull rank to shut them up. They were Bob and Rae, his friends. Rae picked up on his attitude.

"What are you thinking about, big guy?"

"Linc."

"That gonna do any good? Thinking about it?"

"What else we got? You oughta try it," Lucas snapped. Then, "Sorry."

The repartee stopped and they drove mostly without talking to Lang's house.

WHEN THEY PULLED into Lang's driveway, the man himself walked out on the front porch to meet them. "I can't talk about Stephen without weeping and It's embarrassing," he said. He actually had a black mourning armband pinned to his jacket sleeve, and Lucas wondered if it might not have once had a swastika on it. "His family is asking about when they can get the body . . ."

"That'll be up to the medical examiner and the FBI," Lucas told him. "I suspect it'll be a few more days. They gotta do chemistry."

"I'm trying to stay in touch, but there are so many bureaucrats, and nobody wants to tell you anything."

Lang ushered them through the house to his office, slumped behind his desk, and asked, "How can I help?"

"We're looking for a man named Linc, who Stephen saw at White Fist," Lucas said. "I don't know if it's L-i-n-c or L-i-n-k, but I've been assuming it's short for 'Lincoln.' He may be a shooter for one of your alt-right groups, and he's probably way out there. Have you seen the name?"

Lang sighed and said, "I've been fumbling my way through Stephen's database." He patted a laptop sitting on his desk. "I don't know my way around, but I could do a search. I don't know that name myself. If it's L-i-n-k, it could be a nickname . . ."

"Well, let's look," Rae said.

LANG WAS RIGHT ABOUT FUMBLING: he poked tentatively at the laptop's keys, but after a couple of minutes, he threw up his hands and said, "There's no Linc, Link, or Lincoln in this computer, and this is everything we have. I mean, not in the computer, but up in a cloud somewhere, but it looks at the cloud, too, and there's no sequence of those letters. Anywhere."

Lucas said, "Damnit."

"Ask the ANM," Lang said. "They organize politically, so they've got lists. Probably the best lists that exist. A lot of their members would be considered alt-right."

"There's a problem with that," Lucas said. He told Lang that John Oxford had cut himself off from ANM.

Lang said, "Look. He may have taken himself out, but he knows names. A lot of ANM, from what little I know about it, involves face-to-face relationships, and Old John will still know those names. He hasn't erased his memory. He could find a way to get to one of them, and put out the word, and have somebody call you."

"Worth a try, I guess," Lucas said. He wasn't sure that it was, but he didn't have much else.

Bob said, "Why don't we go jack up Toby Boone's brother? Collect a few names there, jack up some more people."

"Threaten them," Rae said. "Make them sweat."

Lucas was staring at Bob, who asked, "What?"

Lucas scratched his nose, said, "You were almost onto something there, Bob—you just got it exactly backwards."

"Way to go," Rae said to Bob.

OUT IN THE DRIVEWAY, away from Lang, Lucas called Jane Chase. "I need you to send me the names and addresses of the White Fist members you found, but we only want the names of the married ones, or the ones living with a woman. And preferably those with kids."

"What are you going to do?" she asked.

"Investigate," Lucas said.

He explained, and Bob, standing behind him, listening in, said, "Holy cow—a ray of hope. That could work."

Chase said, "I'll get on it. And we've got something

here. There might have been a shootout or something, because we've got a smudge of blood on the front door that couldn't have come from the victims. We're going to get DNA on a third person. Everybody here thinks he's probably the killer. And if he was here to get the rifle . . ."

"Excellent," Lucas said. "You push the DNA. We'll talk to the women."

WHILE THEY WAITED for Chase to come through, Lucas called John Oxford and told him what they wanted, and Lucas added the part about Oxford still knowing names, without mentioning that Lang had suggested it. He also tried a little flattery, about the strength of Oxford's organizing. The flattery didn't work. Oxford was notably cranky, but finally said, "I'll make some calls, but I can't tell you that anything will happen. I am fuckin' well out of it now, thanks to you, fuckhead."

"Yeah, well, if you save a little kid's life, I'll send you a fuckin' sticky gold star for your fuckin' diary," Lucas said.

"That went well," Rae said, when Lucas rang off.

"Not gonna get us anywhere," Lucas said. "We need that list from Jane."

CHASE CAME BACK in half an hour, downloading a list of names and addresses to Lucas's iPad. "Not as many as I'd hoped—most of the members are singles."

She'd gotten seven names. Two of them were in Frederick, where Toby Boone's shop was located, and not far apart. Three more were in the general Frederick neighborhood, so they decided to start there.

Frederick was a forty-minute drive, traffic beginning to build in the late afternoon. The two targets, Mark Sutton and Jack Byrd, lived three blocks apart in an older neighborhood of painted brick and red-brick apartment and retail buildings, some of them shuttered, some looking over cracked sidewalks to vacant lots.

They took Sutton first. As they pulled up outside Sutton's apartment, Lucas said, "You guys know what to do . . ."

"Isolate, isolate, isolate . . ." Rae muttered.

TWO FBI AGENTS HAD SPOKEN to Sutton the day before: he'd been reluctant, but not aggressive. He lived on the second floor of the building, up narrow wooden stairs that knocked and groaned as they climbed, the building smelling of damp rotted plaster and flaking wallpaper.

They found Sutton's apartment door, with a bell. Bob rang, and Lucas stood well back. They heard footfalls inside, and a moment later the door popped open, and a short stocky man in jeans, a Levi's snap-button shirt, and white socks opened the door and looked out and asked, "Police?"

"U.S. Marshals," Rae said, holding up her ID. "Mr. Sutton, we need to talk to you. Can we come in?" And, she added, "This is not what you think. We'll only need to talk. We're not here to arrest anyone."

The man glanced back over his shoulder, and then said, "Ahm, uh, my wife's not dressed." He turned his head and called, "Amy? Are you okay if some marshals come in?"

A woman shouted something back—"One second"—and ten seconds later called, "I'm okay. They can come in."

Both Bob and Rae had their hands on their pistols as they edged through the door. The apartment had a living room with a broken-down velvet-covered couch that looked across a shaky wooden coffee table at a new wide-screen television; there were two ashtrays on the coffee table full of cigarette butts. A half dozen plastic toys were lying against one wall—the FBI agents had said there were two children at home, both toddlers.

Bob and Rae pointed Sutton at the couch, and the three of them went that way, Bob saying, "Listen, we're sorry to barge in on you like this, I know you spoke to FBI agents yesterday, and we thank you for that . . ."

Lucas trailed, and as Sutton sat down, he glanced at Lucas, then did a second take, frowned and asked, "Are you the boss here?"

Lucas smiled and shook his head. "No, I'm with the Marshal's Service Inspector General. I tag along on se-lected interviews and evaluate, mmm, the behavior of our marshals."

"Really? That's weird."

"Gotta agree with you on that, brother," Bob said.

He snorted once, turned to Lucas and said, "No offense."

"Do the interview," Lucas said. "We gotta keep moving."

A SMALL KITCHENETTE sat off the living room and a woman appeared in a doorway from the back of the apartment, stepping into the kitchenette. She looked at her husband and Bob and Rae, talking on the couch, and then at Lucas.

She was thin, with bones in her face, and a prominent nose; blondish hair swept back, not in a ponytail, but cut short, held in place with hair butter, and showing the tracks of a heavy comb. She was wearing jeans with a white blouse. Lucas thought she looked Appalachian, though if he were asked to define that, he couldn't: she just looked like Depression-era photographs.

Lucas smiled at her and said, "I smell baby formula," and she said, "We've got two."

"So do I," Lucas said. "At least we're out of the formula stage. Out of Huggies. Now they poop in regular underpants."

"Oh, God, I'm really looking forward to that," the woman said, with a quiet laugh. "If I could sell poop, I'd be a rich woman now."

Lucas said, "I'm Lucas."

She said, "Amy. How do you do? And what's going on?"

"I do all right, I guess . . ." He told her the story about being with the inspector general's office and evaluating the behavior of Bob and Rae, then grimaced and said, "They've got a tough problem. They're looking for a guy named Linc, who's involved with Toby Boone's group. They're working hard, but they're not getting anywhere."

"Toby got raided yesterday," the woman said. "Were you there?"

"No, I don't go on raids. I'm more of a desk guy, except when I'm doing something like this," Lucas lied. "This Linc guy, we've heard that he'd set up to shoot some children. We think he already killed one kid."

"I heard about that. He shot the wrong kid, that's what they're saying on CNN."

"He did, and he's going to shoot again. We think he's . . . unbalanced. Bob and Rae are trying to locate him, they thought your husband might have some idea of who he is. Linc and Toby Boone are friends. And he's friends with a guy named Cop."

"He, uh, Mark, doesn't talk to marshals much. He's not much for police in any way, shape, or form."

"I understand he's had his problems with the law." Lucas glanced at the couch, where Bob, Ray, and Sutton were deep in discussion, then leaned toward Amy Sutton and said, quietly, with a grin, "We've been talking to as many of the White Fist people as we can find, and, well . . . most of them don't have a pretty young wife and babies to come home to. They're real dead-enders . . . kind of . . . strange guys. Rather have a gun than a woman. In my observation."

She nodded. "There are some unusual men around Toby. He sort of pulls them in. Me'n Mark . . . I'm trying to get him away from all that. We're hoping he can find a job in trucking. He used to be a loader, but he'd like to be a driver. Get that white-line fever."

They talked about that for a moment and she said full-time drivers could make more than fifty thousand a year, and Lucas said he heard that it could be even more than that. Then, "Where are the kids?"

"Put them back in the bedroom. I call it their playroom."

"They're quiet," Lucas said. "One of each or . . ."

"One of each, "she said. "C'mon, let's take a peek. They *are* pretty quiet. Maybe too quiet."

They walked down a short hall to a bedroom door, and Amy opened it quietly, and they both peeked. The kids, a boy maybe three and a girl maybe two, were piling up stuffed animals into a pyramid, intent upon the process.

Amy nodded and pulled the door shut and whispered, "Don't know what they're doing, but they're working at it."

"So damn cute at that age," Lucas said. "I've got an older girl, we just got her through the teenage years, and let me tell you, that can be a trial."

They tiptoed back to the kitchen and Lucas took a business card from his pocket and said, "If you have a chance to talk with Mark about this later, I mean, you know, this Linc guy, if it turns out we can save a child's life . . . give me a ring. I won't tell anyone where the tip came from. Not even other cops. But we're pretty desperate."

She nodded, didn't say anything, but took the card and stuck it in her back jeans pocket. Lucas asked, "You guys lived here long. Settled in?"

"We move around a bit . . . I'd like to get a permanent place before we put the kids in school so they don't have to change much . . ."

They chatted for a while, about schools, and then Bob and Rae stood up, and Bob shook hands with Sutton and said, "Listen, if anything occurs to you, man, call us. You've got my card. I mean, we're talking about children."

"Yeah, sure," Sutton said. There was an undertone in his voice of "fuck you and the horse you rode in on."

Out in the hallway, before the door was closed, Bob asked Lucas, "How'd I do?"

"I liked the handshake at the end," Lucas said, for the sake of the Suttons. "I thought that was very sensitive."

IN THE STREET, Rae asked, "How'd it go?"

"Pretty well, I think. I feel a little sleazy, though," Lucas said. He looked up at a second-story window and saw a drape move. "Let's keep moving. Six more. How was Sutton?"

"About a level-six asshole," Bob said. "Wouldn't talk to Rae. Rae'd ask a question, he'd answer to me."

"He tried to look down my blouse, though," Rae said. "You gotta give him that."

"Everybody tries to look down your blouse," Bob said. "You oughta put up a sign that says, 'Dollar a look.'"

"That's all really wonderful," Lucas said. "Keep moving."

"Don't pretend you haven't looked," Bob said.

"Keep moving."

OF THE SEVEN NAMES ON CHASE'S LIST, nobody answered the door at two of the houses.

Lucas thought he'd done well with Sutton, and of the next five houses, they found people at home at three. Bob and Rae isolated the husband, while Lucas tried to chat up the wife. That worked with two of the three, but the third wife might have been meaner than her husband and essentially told Lucas to fuck off. She said, with bared teeth, as she dropped Lucas's card in the kitchen wastebasket, "You've certainly given me something to think about." She had a glass sitting on the kitchen shelf with stamp-sized Nazi flags mounted on toothpicks, for what purpose Lucas had no idea.

They didn't get to the last house. They were on their way when Lucas took a call from an unknown number and the woman on the other end said, "I'm supposed to tell you, Leroy Nathaniel Carter. I don't know why. I'm supposed to say, look at the initials."

Her voice sounded hollow, and Lucas could hear chatter in the background, as though she were calling from a big-box store, like a Walmart, or Costco.

"Who, uh . . ."

"Wasn't supposed to say no more."

Click.

Rae was driving, Lucas in the front passenger seat, and Rae asked, "Was that . . ."

"A name. Leroy Nathaniel Carter. LNC. Linc."

"That's better than a poke in the eye with a sharp stick," Bob said from the backseat.

"Which one was calling, do you think?" Rae asked.

"I don't think it was any of them. Whoever it was, she had somebody else call me, so I wouldn't recognize a voice." He got on the phone to Chase, gave her the name. She came back in five minutes, said, "Got an address from a parole officer. He's just done six years for aggravated assault. He's been out for three months. We should get the SWAT team back."

"Give me the address," Lucas said. "No point getting in an uproar before we know if he's home."

"If he's home . . ."

"Jane, give me the fuckin' address."

"Lucas, the guy, his record, he was some kind of gang enforcer, and crazy. He is not somebody to take lightly."

"We won't. Give me the address."

CHAPTER

NINETEEN

Leroy Nathaniel Carter lived in a town house complex on the western outskirts of Baltimore, forty minutes east of Frederick, with his girlfriend, an employee of the U.S. Department of Health and Human Services.

They made it before dark, but not much before. To Lucas's midwestern eye, the town houses looked brutal: cheaply built, all pale green, six or seven individual houses stuck together in a row, with three clumps on each block, facing three other clumps on the other side of the street, all identical, block after block. The designers might have hoped to give the place a little humanity, and less of a barracks feel, by curving the streets, but that hadn't worked.

The navigation app took them to the right street, but house numbers were hard to see in the increasingly dim light. When they thought they had the right one,

Bob fished the Maglite out of his gear bag and shined it on the front of the place, caught the numbers. "This is it."

There were lights on, and they drove around the block, saw more lights in the back. Lucas called Chase and asked if they could enter without a warrant.

"We've got a warrant—went after one as soon as you called. I'm about halfway up there. Do you have your iPad?"

"Yeah, sure."

"I'm going to transmit a copy of the warrant to you, for the home of a Carol Lou Lacey. She's the girlfriend. You'll have it in one minute. Or, you could wait until I get there."

"I think we want to move," Lucas said. "I don't want to hover outside the house too long and I don't want to move away to where we can't see it. What's the basis for the warrant?"

"Paroled felon believed to be in possession of a firearm. It's a no-knock because of the weapon angle."

"Send it."

"I did. You should have it."

Lucas had turned on the iPad as they were talking. He checked his mail, found a PDF of the warrant, sworn by Chase before a federal judge. Bob: "That's the coolest thing I've seen in weeks."

Rae asked, "How're we going to do this?"

Bob and Rae were trained in violent felon apprehension; that was much of what they did. They'd take the front door, they decided, while Lucas watched the back.

Bob would kick the door and he and Rae should be on top of the occupants before they could resist.

In theory anyway.

THEY DECIDED THAT BOB would go with his handgun, Rae with her M4 carbine, and Lucas would take Bob's M4 around to the back. They moved to a park three blocks away, and armored up. Bob and Rae would wear helmets and U.S. Marshal jackets with reflective lettering, in addition to vests. Lucas would wear a Marshal jacket over his vest.

A cyclist rode by, did a circle, came back and peered at them: "What's happening?"

"A law enforcement issue," Rae said. "Be best if you went on your way."

"Do you have warrants?" the man asked, still circling. He was wearing black cycling shorts, a black cycling shirt with Italian words on the chest, and a black helmet that looked like half of a football.

"You a lawyer?" Bob asked, as he pulled on his jacket.

"I'm a concerned citizen," the man said.

"Go home and call your congressman," Lucas said. "We'd hate to have to bust you for interfering with the arrest of a violent felon."

"What if I took your picture with my iPhone?"

"That would be annoying, but not illegal," Lucas said.

The cyclist rolled in a circle, like he was thinking

about it, and then Rae jacked a shell into the chamber of her M4, a lethal ratcheting sound, and the cyclist said, "Okay," and rode off, away from the target house.

"Why are bicycle riders so much more annoying than motorcycle guys?" Bob asked.

"I don't know, I drive a Porsche," Lucas said.

"Well la-dee-fuckin'-da," Rae said. "Listen, guys, I'm getting my rush on. Let's go."

THEY DROPPED LUCAS on the block opposite the target, where he would wait in the street until he saw the Tahoe pull up in front of the target. Then he'd run through the yard to the back door of the target house. Like Rae, he could feel the adrenaline; and God help him, he liked it.

The Tahoe disappeared around the corner and, fifteen seconds later, he saw it pull up outside the target. He jogged through the side yard of the house behind the target, to the back door, and he heard the front door go down and Bob and Rae shouting. The back door looked cheap, like the house, and he kicked it at the lock, once, twice, and the door splintered and broke open and he was inside looking at a man and a woman sitting at a kitchen table looking at the muzzles of the guns held by Bob and Rae, then they turned and looked at Lucas, and Bob said, "Leroy Nathaniel Carter, you're under arrest on suspicion of possession of a firearm as a felon."

The woman screamed, "Get out of my house!"

Then Carter was on his feet, a huge man in jeans and a T-shirt, muscles bulging in his arms and chest, red-faced, and he shouted, "Fuckin' cops. I hate you fuckin' . . . "

And he lurched toward Bob with the woman right behind him.

Bob said, "Back, back . . ."

"Go ahead and shoot, motherfucker, go ahead and shoot me . . ."

"Stepping right," Rae said to Bob, and Bob switched his handgun to his left hand and the woman shouted, "Get that nigger out of my house . . ."

Carter lurched forward another step. He was huge, most of it muscle, some of it fat, but he was slow. Bob had finished third in the heavyweight division of the NCAA wrestling tournament, losing on points only to the eventual champion, and while not as big as Carter, he was very fast and very well trained. Bob stepped into Carter and hit him in the solar plexus with his right fist, a sound like a meat axe going into a side of beef, and Carter bounced backwards and opened his mouth as if to object, but then turned white and sank to his knees and then toppled onto the floor, holding his chest.

The woman, Lacey, bent as if to help him, but then made as if to slap Bob on the face, which wouldn't have bothered him. But she wasn't slapping: she raked him with knife-like fingernails, cutting his forehead open, and Bob bumped back, blood streaming from his forehead below his hairline, and then she turned on Lucas with her nails, which were an inch long and filed to silver points and swung her hands to slash him . . .

Lucas had at least a foot of reach on her. The punch started at shoulder height, snapped out to her chin, caught her perfectly, one of the better punches Lucas had thrown in his life, and the woman flew backwards and landed on top of Carter, rolled off and lay on the floor, one leg twitching, no other sign of life.

"Hope I didn't kill her," Lucas said; but he wasn't hoping all that hard.

"I was kind of hoping you did," Rae said. "Cuff 'em. Bob, you okay?"

"Sliced the shit out of me," Bob said. Blood was trickling down into his eyes, and he wiped it with the back of a hand, but he put the cuffs on Carter and the woman, who still wasn't moving, but was breathing.

"We need an ambulance," Lucas said. "She might have a broken jaw."

RAE CALLED 9-1-1, and an ambulance and a couple of local cop cars were dispatched; Lucas called Chase, who was still ten minutes out. "Any sign of a gun?"

"Haven't looked," Lucas said.

"You've got a warrant."

THEY HAD GUNS.

There were four AR-15–style black rifles, two 9mm semi-auto handguns, a .357 Magnum revolver, a twelve-gauge shotgun with cut-down stock and barrel that made it illegal, and, most interesting, a bolt-action CZ 527 American in .223, mounted with a Sig Sauer scope. The CZ and scope would make a decent light sniper combination.

The ambulance showed up—Lacey's eyes were open, but she couldn't close her mouth, and wasn't clearly responsive to questions. An EMT thought her jaw might be broken, and that she might be concussed, and they took her away.

Carter had gotten off the floor, and was sitting on a kitchen chair, stunned, but not so stunned that he hadn't immediately asked for a lawyer. Lucas, looking through the bedroom, found a copy of the letter: not an early version, but apparently a much-copied one, and the original had not been quite centered on the photocopy machine.

Chase arrived, looked at the letter, and said, "Same letter, different copy. The goddamned thing is everywhere."

They were standing in the living room, and she turned and looked at Carter sitting in the kitchen chair: "You think he shot the kid?"

"I dunno," Bob said. His forehead had been patched up by the EMT, who suggested that he might wish to go to an emergency room for stitches. "I can tell you only one thing about that: the ammo in the apartment is not the same as it was in the rifle we recovered. There aren't any partial boxes of it, nothing of that brand. So . . ."

"He has the attitude and we've got that recording," Lucas said. "We get a lawyer on him, maybe he'll have something to say."

Chase nodded: "We'll have a better idea by morning. We'll seal up the house, get a crime scene crew over here. Bob, go get your stitches."

BOB GOT HIS STITCHES, with Lucas and Rae waiting in the hospital with him, like nervous parents. The stitches were done by a young physician's assistant, who told Bob that she was so good at it, he wouldn't have scars, as long as he didn't mess with the cuts. She put a big bandage on his forehead that made him look as though he'd had a lobotomy, and sent them on their way.

At the Watergate, they got more burgers. Rae asked, "What do you think about Sutton?"

"I don't know," Lucas said. "He's at least a candidate. But, I don't know. I guess we'll find out in the morning. I'm going to watch some football, then go to bed, and sleep in. This was a long day."

"Hate those letters floating around," Bob said. "They all make that same argument—that if you kill a senator's kid, the next senator might listen to you when you want a vote changed. It makes a weird kind of sense, if you're nuts."

"Carter was a felon with five rifles and a sawed-off shotgun, plus a couple of pistolas," Rae said. "You want nuts, there it is."

LUCAS WATCHED SOME FOOTBALL, went to bed, and was actually up and moving when Chase called the next morning.

"Guess what?"

"From your tone, I guess he wasn't the guy," Lucas said.

"Two steps forward, one step back," Chase said. "We have a connection, just not Sutton. Remember when I said we had blood on the door of Rachel Stokes's house that probably didn't come from her or her brother? Like somebody else had been shot?"

"I remember."

"Well, the science guys got a match—DNA from the blood on the door matches DNA from the cheek-piece on the rifle we found under the cemetery shack. Whoever killed the Stokeses also shot the kid; the killer must've gone to the house specifically to get the gun, and then killed the Stokeses to eliminate witnesses."

"How does that eliminate Sutton? You couldn't have done DNA . . . Oh. Wait. You already had it. Sutton was typed when he was convicted of that ag assault charge."

"Yup. We'll re-do him, but I think he's out of it."

"Well, at least we got him on a gun charge and re-sisting arrest," Lucas said. "That'll put him away for a while."

Long silence.

Lucas repeated, "That'll put him away for a while."

"About that . . ."

"Ah, shit."

"Look, we're really worried about these alt-right groups and all the guns. Turns out Sutton and Lacey are involved in three or four of them. They can give us some real insight into their operations and the membership. Lacey has a federal job that she's scared to death she's about to lose, and *will* lose, if we charge her with assaulting a federal officer. We think, you know, if we don't charge them . . . they could be really useful in this alternate modality."

Lucas: "You said, '*alternate modality*.' I mean, Jesus, Bob nearly got his fuckin' head cut off. You at least ought to use real words."

"Well, you know. I'm a fed," Chase said. "Sometimes I can't help myself."

"Sometimes that excuse wears a little thin."

"Suck it up, Lucas. Listen. I know you tend to sleep in," Chase said. "Are you up and around?"

"Yes. I'm getting dressed."

"I'm about a mile away. Meet me in the restaurant in ten minutes."

LUCAS'S BRAIN USUALLY wasn't fully working for an hour or so after he got up, especially when he got up early; Chase, on the other hand, was a lark, bright and cheerful at the crack of dawn, every hair in place, looking good in a raspberry jacket, dark blouse with navy slacks and matching shoes and a purse designed to hold a .40 caliber handgun, which she'd begun carrying when she found out that it impressed other federal suits.

Lucas was drinking a Diet Coke with pancakes when she arrived. She was one of those women that waitresses seemed commanded by, and as she slid into the booth opposite Lucas, one rushed over to get her order of a cup of coffee and toast, plain, no butter.

"We need to talk about the letters," she said. "Actually, let me restate that. *I* need to talk about the letters. You need to listen."

"You find something on them?"

"Yes. Letters. And words and sentences and paragraphs. We've had our analysts looking at them."

"You've got analysts for everything, don't you?"

"Yes. Now, be quiet," Chase said. "Nobody we've arrested or looked at, with two or possibly three exceptions, could have written those letters. And, the letters are all absolutely identical in content and by that I mean, the original text, type fonts, spacing. For instance, the writer always puts two spaces after a period, which means he probably learned to type on a typewriter, rather than a keyboard. There are at least three iterations. We have one copy-machine version that is perfectly straight on the page, one copy-machine version that is crooked, and one copy-machine version that has a smudge on a word at the bottom of the page, as if maybe somebody got a bit of spit on it, or maybe was reading it while eating breakfast and got some milk on it, or maybe . . ."

"I get the idea," Lucas said. "All copied, but different."

"That's right. What we don't have, is an original copy. The analysts have questioned why we would have all these different copies if they came from the same secondary source. The primary source, the writer of the letter, could have made as many copies as he wished, by pushing a button on his laser printer. We think there's one person behind the letter, but they're spreading out in chain-letter fashion. A person gets one, copies it, and sends it along to friends or group members who might want to read it and perhaps act on it."

"And what are we doing about that? By 'we,' I mean you, the FBI."

"What we're doing is pressing the people we've arrested for names of people who might have sent these letters to them. We're hoping to find more letters, and by cross-indexing names, get up the pyramid to the original sender."

"Can you identify a printer if you get an original?"

"Yes. Color laser printers—this is a color laser printer, by the way—actually have tiny dots, invisible to the naked eye, sprayed on the paper that will identify exactly what printer printed the letter, and even when it was done."

"You gotta be shittin' me."

"Nope. That's not a secret, but not a lot of people know about it. We would like to keep it that way. If we can find an original letter, we can match to the printer."

"You said with two or three exceptions, none of the

people we know about wrote the letter. How do you know that?"

"Because we've taken samples of all their writing styles and word patterns. All the little stuff—word choice, vocab, spellings, and so on. With three exceptions, none of the people we've looked at could have written the letter, because they're all nearly functionally illiterate. The person who wrote the letter is literate, trained in writing to some degree, probably a college graduate. The exceptions are Stephen Gibson, Charlie Lang, and John Oxford from ANM."

"I don't think ANM," Lucas said. "Could be, but my gut says they're not involved. They're very different, but they're not psychotic."

"Stephen Gibson has a color laser printer. I would expect Charlie Lang does, too. If we could find an original printed copy of the letter, we could either pin it to one of those machines, or clear them," Chase said.

"The copies aren't clear enough to see the dot-codes?"

"No. These codes are tiny. You literally can't see them with the naked eye, and neither can copiers."

"So I'm looking for letters."

"You're looking for specific letters—printed letters, not copied letters."

"Even then," Lucas said. "It might not be the shooter. It could be somebody who stumbled over the 1919 site and decided to send out some letters, to get somebody else to shoot."

"Could be," Chase said. "But it's what we got right now."

They both stopped talking for a moment, as the waitress delivered Chase's coffee and two slices of dry toast, sliced diagonally and carefully arranged on the plate.

When she was gone, Lucas took his cell phone out of his pocket and said, "Let me make a call."

"You mean . . . right now?"

"When better?"

LUCAS CALLED RICHARD GREENE, of the Greene Mountain Boys, who picked up on the third ring. "Marshal Davenport—we had nothing to do with that shooting, believe me."

"I hope not. I'm calling about something different. I've been told you know everything on the alt-right. A number of people in these alt-right groups have gotten letters suggesting that the meaning of the 1919 group was to encourage somebody to shoot a kid, so that could be used as a leverage to change votes in Congress. We need letters. We need you to ask about them. Carefully. With people you trust."

"Yeah, I heard about Stephen Gibson. He must've touched a hot wire."

"We're all over that. If you could reach out . . . you don't have to tell anyone why you want to know, just provide us the names. You were talking about getting brownie points with the feds, should you need them. This would get you some. Or many."

"I understand. Listen, let me think about it for a while. I'll call you if I get something."

CHASE SAID, when Lucas was off the phone and had explained about Greene, "He seemed eager to get those brownie points. I wonder what he did, or he's planning, that he needs them?"

"Not my problem," Lucas said. "It's yours. Say, you gonna eat all that toast?"

CHAPTER

TWENTY

Saturday morning.

Lucas caught Bob and Rae coming back from their morning workout, told them to go look at the Washington Monument. "I already saw it. It's that big white pointy thing, like a monument to a famous Anglo's sexual fantasies," Rae said. "If you don't need us, I'm going to the National Gallery. Call when you need me."

Bob had an old friend with the Marshals Service, stationed in Arlington. He said he'd call the guy, set up a lunch. "You won't need us before lunch?"

"I don't see anything coming," Lucas said. "I think you're safe for now. Take the Caddy if you want."

"Nah, I'm gonna try to figure out the Metro . . ."

LUCAS WENT BACK TO HIS ROOM, called Weather, talked for half an hour, then watched a couple of TV broadcasts, went online and tried to figure out the relative importance of the various DC news outlets, and finally sat and thought though a variety of possible moves.

At eleven, he left the hotel and walked north on a narrow leafy residential street to Pennsylvania Avenue, then left until Pennsylvania intersected with M Street, and west on M to a nearly unmarked red-brick building with a brass plate next to the door. The plate read, "Steaks and Spirits, LLC," as though it might be a law firm.

Lucas looked at his watch: 11:35, five minutes late. He'd be amazed if he wasn't the first to arrive.

Inside the door, a tall man in a nubby sport coat, worn with a black T-shirt and jeans, asked, "Do we have a reservation?"

"We do," Lucas said. "Smith and Jones."

"Um, which Smith and Jones?"

"Tall blond guy, short white-haired guy."

"Of course. They arrived a few minutes ago. This way."

So Lucas was amazed: he wasn't the first to arrive, but the last. He followed the maître d' through a maze of high-backed leather booths filled with serious-looking men and women in expensive clothes, speaking in hushed voices, and finally through a polished mahogany door into a tiny private room just large enough to seat six people.

Senators Henderson and Smalls were looking over menu folders when he came in, and Smalls said, "Ah, the late Lucas Davenport."

"Sorry. It's an interesting walk. I stopped to look into a bookstore window."

"Got to have your priorities," Henderson said. "My priority is not to walk in Washington, DC."

"That's why you're such a weak sister," Smalls said. "I run three miles every morning after my yoga."

"While you're out running, I'm working for the American people," Henderson said, as he reached for the bread basket. "I'm thinking the oysters."

"Oysters respect no political party," Smalls agreed. "I'm thinking a dozen, or maybe a dozen and a half. The caloric content is negligible."

"The mignonette is terrific here, though it has a tendency to make me fart," Henderson said. "Fortunately, I'm only dealing with underlings this afternoon."

"Then fart away," Smalls said. "Lucas?"

"I'm going for the buffalo burger with red onions and deli mustard," Lucas said.

Smalls: "Prole."

THE WAITER CAME AND WENT, wine for the senators, a Diet Coke for Lucas, though the Coke raised an eyebrow. "They have any wine you want, but he'll probably have to send out for the Diet Coke," Henderson said. "Now. Where are we? Are we done with the shooting?"

"Maybe," Lucas said. "Not only will I not promise that we are, I'm thinking it's about fifty-fifty."

Smalls: "Shit. That's not acceptable. What are we

supposed to do, sit on our thumbs until some other kid gets shot?"

Lucas told them about the letter and how it had turned into a chain letter. "It's all over the place, the FBI is doing some kind of analysis thing."

"The FBI is always analyzing their asses off. In the meantime, these NRA lunatics . . ."

"Hey. Lay off the NRA bullshit," Smalls said.

"Yeah, I know, I looked at your donations," Henderson said.

Smalls waved him off and said, "My sources at the FBI are a little confused by all the action. Lucas: start at the beginning and tell us everything that happened, in detail."

Lucas did that, stopping for chit-chat when the food arrived, then resuming and leaving out only the identification of Audrey Coil as the creator of the 1919 website. Smalls didn't know about that and Henderson wanted it held privately for as long as possible—forever, if possible.

When Lucas finished, the two senators, both lawyers, cross-examined him as they pushed oysters into their faces, and then Henderson said, "I think you're wrong about the fifty-fifty. I think it's more like seventy-thirty in favor of another shooting. It seems like every time you turned over a rock, you found another nutcase with a copy of that letter."

Lucas had told them about Richard Greene and the Greene Mountain Boys, and said, "If Greene comes through with a batch of letters, it's possible that we'll be able to trace them back to the original sender. Or the FBI will."

"And if my cocker spaniel went puck-puck-puck, he'd be a fuckin' chicken," Smalls said.

"I'll keep pushing," Lucas said.

"Do more than push," Smalls said, rapping his knuckles on the tabletop. "Do whatever you need to. *Anything you need to.* Anything. Stop this shit."

Lucas glanced at Henderson, who seemed to hesitate for a moment, then gave a quick nod.

LUCAS LEFT STEAKS AND SPIRITS and took his time walking back to the Watergate. Across the street from the hotel, he thought, "They said *anything.*"

He'd thought of something, that morning, and inside, he told the concierge, "I need an electronics store. The cheaper, the better."

There was nothing close by, and he wound up taking a cab to the store, which turned out to be little more than a hallway with a rack of crappy cell phones on the wall. He bought one, and the Pakistani owner took five minutes to explain about the SIM card and the available minutes. He asked no questions and Lucas got out of the store without ever mentioning his name or anything else about why he wanted the phone. But then, he was in Washington. Halfway back to the hotel, Greene called: "I had to make up some crazy excuses, but I can tell you who has three of these letters and they've agreed to turn them in."

"Give me the names," Lucas said. "They'll be interviewed by FBI agents."

"You won't give my people any trouble?"

"I can't promise anything—but *receiving* letters isn't any kind of crime I can think of, and I can promise you that I'll ask the FBI to take it very easy, that these are cooperating witnesses."

Greene asked, "Okay. Let me give you some names."

Lucas took down the three names. He called Chase from the hotel, gave her the names, asked that the feds take it easy: "They're volunteers, even if they are nutcase assholes."

"I'll pass the word," Chase said. "Thank you."

Lucas lay on the bed, the curtains pulled to dim the room, sighed and began making phone calls with his newly purchased and totally anonymous burner phone. "Yes, I don't want to give you my name. I'm an FBI agent and I have a piece of information that I think it's important for people to know. The FBI has figured out who created that 1919 website and it's a pretty amazing surprise . . ."

BOB CALLED AT TWO O'CLOCK, but Lucas had nothing for him. "Why don't we get dinner together? Go out to someplace nice?" Lucas asked. He now had nothing to do but wait.

"I'm good with that," Bob said. "Seems like things are winding down. Or maybe winding up, but I'm not sure what we're needed for."

"I'll call Rae," Lucas said.

Rae was good with dinner.

CHASE CALLED AT FOUR O'CLOCK, excited and exasperated: "We've got big trouble."

"Who was shot?"

"Nobody. But all the local TV stations, plus the *Post*, the *Times*, and the *Wall Street Journal* are calling, asking if it's true that Audrey Coil set up 1919 as a gag."

"Ah, shit."

"It gets worse: they've got that other kid's name, Blake Winston. I called the Winston house and talked to Mrs. Winston, and as I was talking, she said a TV truck was pulling into their driveway."

"Ah, shit."

"We're not going to be able to contain it," Chase said. "You might want to hide out, because I suspect Senator Smalls will be coming your way."

"Ah, shit."

"Stop saying that. Say something intelligent."

"I'm going home," Lucas said.

"You can't!" Chase said. "We collected those letters, interviewed the recipients, and we might be starting to unravel things."

"You got an original?"

"No, but we got enough copies now that we've

started asking people to name possible sources. There can't be too many of them for what we think is the second generation of copies. When we cross-index the names, there's a good chance we'll get to the first generation, and that guy—or guys—should give us a lead to the original writer."

"Good luck with that," Lucas said. "I'm going to get in bed and pull the covers over my head. Smalls is gonna pee on my shoes."

SMALLS DID THAT.

"One question," he said when he called, two minutes after the beginning of *The Situation Room with Wolf Blitzer*, "Did you know about Audrey Coil?"

"Maybe."

"Did you tell Elmer?" Smalls asked.

"Maybe."

"You motherfuckers, you covered this up to protect Roberta Coil."

"Actually, I did it to protect Audrey Coil. She could be in serious legal trouble, if somebody wants to give it to her—and she's a kid. She's seventeen."

"She oughta be in jail, along with her mother for the cover-up," Smalls said.

"Jesus, Porter, this whole thing was about a cover-up. You were there at the creation."

"Things could be interpreted differently," Smalls said. "But there's no point in getting into all of that. What's happening with the shooter?"

Lucas told him about the FBI analysts and the letters.

Smalls said, "Listen, Lucas, I'm pissed about the Coil thing, but that's politics. I'm pissed but not surprised. I'm still counting on you to close this thing out."

"I'm working on it," Lucas said. "That hasn't changed."

"Is there anything I can do to help?"

"In fact, there is. Could you get me a reservation at Steaks and Spirits? Seven o'clock tonight?"

"I meant something *easy*," Smalls grumbled. Then, "I'll make a call."

LUCAS WENT TO DINNER with Bob and Rae, who marveled at the restaurant, at the lack of bad music that made it possible to actually talk, and further, that Lucas was paying for it out of his own pocket. Like Henderson and Smalls, they ordered a dozen oysters each, followed by steaks and spirits.

"Now that I'm sitting here in my shabby-chic dress because I can't afford anything actually chic, tell me what the occasion is," Rae said.

"Goodbye dinner, see you next time," Lucas said. "The fact is, the FBI is taking over. There's nothing more for us to do."

"Yeah, I sort of figured that out," Bob said, and Rae nodded.

Lucas said, "I called Russell, he's fixed your travel back to New Orleans at nine o'clock tomorrow. Got to be out at National by seven, what with all the guns and stuff."

"Probably won't see you tomorrow, then," Bob said.

"Probably not."

Rae: "You got anything good coming up?"

"No, not really. I'd like something simple: a straight-up cannibal on the run, maybe a child rapist. Somebody we could corner and feel good about shooting," Lucas said. "This political shit is giving me a rash."

Rae ran a hand over her close-cropped hair, then said, "I have to tell you, I get all excited when you call. So does Bob. We know it's going to be something good. Don't hesitate to call us again."

Bob said to Rae, "You know what? Let's get back home and hit the computers. Dig around. Find something we can do, all three of us. Let's not forget, there's a whole world of scum out there. Wastes of good skin. Douchebags."

"Asswipes," Lucas added.

"Miscreants," Rae said. The two men looked at each other, grinned and shook their heads. "What? So I got a vocabulary, unlike some people?"

"If you find somebody to chase, try to find him in an interesting place," Lucas said. "New York, Miami, New Orleans. The scuzzier the better. I don't want any Denvers or Seattles or Portlands. No place where you might wound a hipster by accident."

"What if it's not a him? What if it's a her?" Rae asked.

"Even better," Lucas said. "I haven't shot a female miscreant in a while."

"You did punch one out, though," Rae observed. "Nice punch, too. I was impressed."

LUCAS GOT BACK to his room at ten o'clock, after a final nightcap with Bob and Rae in the hotel bar. He went to an all-news station on the TV, and when a new program came on at ten, found himself looking at Audrey Coil, sitting teary-eyed and badly lit in a lounge chair with a brown teddy bear in her lap, being interviewed by a woman with a non-DC haircut and consoling expression. Lucas suspected she might be a talking head from E!

Coil was confessing: "It started out as a joke . . ."

Lucas said to the television, "All right, I don't believe the fuckin' teddy bear."

Rae called: "You looking at the television?"

"Audrey Coil. Yeah. I was wondering about the teddy bear."

"What teddy bear?"

"In her lap."

"You must be watching a different station. On mine, she's standing outside by her daddy's Porsche Cayenne. She must not have a lawyer: a lawyer would never allow her to admit this. Not live, on TV."

"She's live? What channel?"

Lucas turned to the channel, where a woman who resembled a sleek white-tipped shark was pressing a microphone into Audrey's face. Still tearful, no bear.

The shark: "You're saying that it was the temptation of television that did it."

"Yes. Yes. It's like you're not alive if you can't be on television. Television is validating. This is something we have to talk about, I'll be talking about it on my blog, with my girls."

"What about the young boy who got shot?" the shark asked.

Audrey's face went cold: "I had nothing to do with that. That was some crazy man."

"But . . ."

"I don't know that man. He's obscure."

Lucas thought, *Jesus.*

A THIRD CHANNEL: "Listen to me, please. Everybody makes mistakes, I'm only seventeen. I was simply messing around. Then, when it came out, I got invited to be on television. What was I supposed to do?"

ANOTHER CHANNEL, a man in a dark suit and a two-hundred-dollar haircut and an indoor tan that left white circles around his eye sockets, interviewing another dark-suited man with a red necktie. They were standing in what Lucas recognized as the driveway to the Winston house.

Red necktie said, "The Winstons feel that Blake is far too young to expose himself to this kind of questioning. He had nothing to do with the creation of the 1919 website and has pledged to cooperate with authorities in any way he can."

"But he does the video for the Coil website," said fake-tan guy.

"Yes, of course. But he knew nothing about Audrey Coil's other activities. Alleged activities. Actually, all you have to do is look at the website to know that Blake Winston wasn't involved—he's a very effective young filmmaker and a skillful creator of websites for his school friends. The 1919 website is primitive, to say the least. Nothing that Blake Winston would create. Or that any other youngster familiar with the creation of online sites, would create."

Blah blah blah.

THEN A CUT, to an FBI briefing room, and the words, "Recorded earlier."

Jane Chase stepped up to a podium looking tired, harassed, hair slightly mussed, but in an attractive way, as if, Lucas suspected, she'd spent some time looking in a mirror, mussing.

Another caption came up, that read, "FBI Agent Jane L. Chase" and then, when that blinked off, a new caption, "Agent in charge of 1919 probe."

Chase nodded wearily at a group of reporters and said, "I'm sorry for the delay. I can't promise you anything, of course, and I can't really provide details at the moment, but I can tell you that we've made significant progress today in tracking down the person who shot young Jamie Wagner at the Stillwater School. Significant progress . . ."

And a moment later, "I'm aware of the allegations being made about Senator Coil's daughter Audrey. Senator Coil is on an airplane on the way back from Jerusalem, where she was part of a U.S. Senate delegation discussing American military support for Israel. We haven't at this point been able to reach either of the Coils, but we have agents on their way to Tifton, Georgia, to interview Audrey Coil . . ."

Lucas nodded. Chase looked good. She looked even better when she said to the pack of newsies, "I'm sorry, but I'm tired and these lights are hot. If you don't mind . . ."

She peeled off her jacket to reveal a handgun in a shoulder holster, a hard metallic presence next to her fine-boned face. She paused, then, to let everybody get a good look at the gun, then pointed at a reporter and said, "Yes?"

Lucas recognized the reporter: the same guy from the *Washington Post* who had been trolling through the Watergate and had seen him with Elmer Henderson. The reporter said, "A good source tells me that you have the rifle used to shoot James Wagner. Is that correct?"

"I can't talk directly to that, to specific items of evidence we may or may not have uncovered, but, I'll repeat that we've made significant progress today."

The reporter came back: "Does it have anything to do with a double murder in Virginia?"

An almost mischievous look flickered across Chase's face. "Again, if you didn't get it, we've made . . ."

In other words, *Yes.*

Made Lucas laugh. She was a star. And he thought, *The lights are no longer hot, babe, because LEDs don't burn, but really, who'd know that, out in the unwashed viewing audience?*

LUCAS WENT TO BED, but lay awake and thought about the 1919 shooter.

The key to the man's psychology—the DNA had proven the shooter was male, which Lucas had never doubted—was anger mixed with calculation. Anger about the people who ran the country and a calculation of how that might be fixed, by influencing the U.S. Senate.

Since the 1919 site was nothing more than a teenage fraud, and that was now public, the calculation had been completely overturned, but the anger would remain. Not only would it remain, but it would almost certainly intensify.

The shooter, the calculator, had been careful in his selection of targets, in his selection of his sniper's nest (being so far away from the target that the Secret Service and the FBI hadn't even considered it) and unlike the man arrested in the parking garage, had not even taken a look at the garage—all the cars coming and going were on a thirty-day video loop and had been checked and cleared.

His brain would be working overtime, both constraining and inflaming the anger.

There was, Lucas thought, the possibility that he'd crack, would load up a black rifle and a sack full of mags and shoot up a school or a synagogue or a government building.

It seemed, though, from the care with which the young boy was shot, that he didn't want to get caught. He wasn't a suicide-by-cop. He'd want his revenge, but he'd make a point with it.

Satisfied with his analysis, Lucas went to sleep, to wake up only once, long enough to wonder, *What if I'm wrong?*

Then, *Nah*, and he went back to sleep.

TWENTY-ONE

Saturday morning.

Dunn needed another gun, because he needed to shoot at least one more kid. The first kid was a wrong one, but that was okay; with all the publicity, the U.S. Senate knew what might be coming and all he had to do was prove it.

One more shot, but he needed that gun.

The day was warm with hazy blue skies, a good day for a road trip, cross-country to Merkin, West Virginia, and the Merkin National Gun and Knife Show. There were gun shows all over the place, but Dunn decided to move away from the Virginia-Maryland-DC area, where federal agents were apparently raiding everything in sight.

They had hit a group called White Fist, according to the *Washington Post*, and more significantly, apparently had found his rifle and his sniper's nest at the cemetery.

They might, he thought, be able to get DNA from the rifle, but since he'd never been DNA-tested, they'd have nothing to compare it to. He'd have to be careful in the future. If he got caught in a spot that would require a DNA test, he'd have to shoot his way out.

Or something—the "something" not defined. He'd have to wait for the moment, if it ever took place, but he was now looking for a carry pistol, in addition to a new rifle. The good thing about West Virginia gun shows was that no background check was required on person-to-person sales of anything.

All the gun stuff was giving him a definite tingle: he should have explored guns earlier in life.

THE MERKIN GUN show was staged in the auditorium of the local National Guard Armory, a beige concrete building that looked like an oversized Quonset hut with its hemispherical roof. The show pulled in a few hundred people, mostly big happy people, both men and women, driving pickups, on top of the fifty or so exhibitors. A friendly woman sat at a card table inside the door, selling tickets. Dunn paid his five dollars and accepted a pink plastic wristband that "will let you get in and out the whole weekend, honey, so don't go taking it off the minute you get outside, in case you need to come back for another look."

Inside the auditorium, he drifted past the tables displaying dozens of different kinds of rifles and pistols, and scopes, ammo magazines, knives, hatchets, camo shirts and pants, targets of all kinds, books about guns, self-defense, and the Second Amendment. The distinct odor of Hoppe's No. 9 bore cleaner, mixed with the scent of carnival hot dogs, hung over the auditorium.

Not an unpleasant smell, Dunn thought; like a whiff of WD-40 or the tang of road-trip gasoline.

At the first table, a group of beefy men were gathered around a Barrett .50-caliber rifle mounted on a heavy tripod, available for the bargain price of $9,999.99; on a stand behind the gun, a rack of .50-cal cartridges were mounted in a plexiglass rack, each cartridge bigger than Dunn's middle finger. He'd seen similar-looking guns in movies—*The Hurt Locker*, maybe?—but never one in real life. Not something he needed, really. He kept moving.

Looking around, two-thirds of the men at the show had beards and were overweight and out of shape, going for the Papa Hemingway vibe; most of them seemed to be wearing khaki photographer's vests. The other third were snaky-looking lightweights like himself, jeans and long-sleeved shirts, a bit of camo here and there, distant looks in their eyes. American flags on their rolled-bill hats.

At his first stop, a cafeteria-sized table covered with black rifles, with a few wooden-stocked rifles thrown in, the dealer, one of the Hemingway look-alikes, asked, "See anything you like?"

"I don't want to burn ammo for the noise of it," Dunn said. "I'm looking for precision. Out to a thousand yards or so. Starting to do that."

"Huh. What's your budget?"

Dunn shrugged: "Cash, up to a grand, maybe a little more."

"You do look like the precision type," the man said. He turned toward the back of the room and pointed: "See that POW/MIA flag? Will Gentry had a nice-looking Remington 700 Long Range last night. His table's right under the flag. Don't know if he's still got it, but that'd get you out to a thousand yards for a dollar a yard. Depending on the barrel, of course."

Dunn nodded: "Thanks."

"Tell him Bunny sent you," the man said.

GENTRY WAS ONE OF THE SKINNY KIND, blue suspicious eyes under a black ball cap, which coordinated with a black T-shirt and black jeans. The cap showed gray stars and stripes on the black background, in an American flag design, overprinted with the words, "GUN SAFETY—Rule #1: Carry One."

He nodded at Dunn: "What can I do you for, my friend?" West Virginia accent, not quite Southern, but not midwestern, either.

"I'm a beginner thousand-yard shooter. Got a piece of property where I can just about reach out that far," Dunn said. "Bunny told me you had a Remington 700 Long Range that I might like."

"I do," Gentry said. "In a seven-millimeter Remington Mag. It'll poke holes at a thousand yards all day long. Let me get it for you."

———

HE WALKED DOWN THE TABLE to a stack of gun cases that was sitting against the back wall, pulled out a solid black case, popped it open. Dunn liked fine machinery, but had never been part of the gun world. Gentry was: he lifted the rifle out of the case—snaky-looking, like the dealer, a skinny weapon with an over-long barrel. Gentry turned it in his hands, stroking it, fondling it.

A fat scope was mounted on top of the rifle.

Gentry passed it over the table and Dunn took it, hefted it, looked through the scope at an exit sign at the other end of the arena. "How many rounds been through it?"

Gentry shrugged. "Don't know, but the barrel's good. I took it out last week."

He went back to the case and pulled out a folded piece of tan paper. Unfolded, it was a target, with five seven-millimeter holes grouped in a space that could be covered with a bottle cap. "An inch and a quarter off a bench at two hundred yards," Gentry said.

"Good shooting," Dunn said. He looked through the scope some more, worked the action, stuck his thumbnail in the chamber and peered down the muzzle end of the barrel, which was clean as a surgeon's scalpel. He said, "I don't have a huge amount of money to spend here, but I do have cash."

Gentry wagged his head once: "With that scope, I need to get eleven hundred."

"Bunny thought I could probably get it for under a grand—I mean, it's used."

"Used, but perfect," Gentry said.

"Look, I know that's a fair price, with the scope, if a little high, but I don't have that kind of money with me . . ." He was lying, he had almost two thousand dollars in his pocket.

They went back and forth a bit and Gentry finally agreed to take a thousand even, with the scope, and to throw in two boxes of his own hand-loaded 7mm: "If you can't punch up a target at a thousand yards with this gun and my ammo, then you need to learn how to shoot better," Gentry said, but with a smile.

Dunn paid cash and Gentry gave him a card and packed up the gun. "Don't go shooting any DC school boys with it," Gentry said, with a quick barking laugh.

He wasn't looking at Dunn, which was good, because Dunn flinched.

Got himself together and said, "That's something else, isn't it? That whole DC thing?"

"There's some goofy motherfuckers out there, bro," Gentry said. He passed the case over the table. "Have a good time with it. Treat it right and it'll be your best friend."

ON THE WAY out, Dunn lingered at a table of hand-guns, the rifle case in his hand. The woman selling the handguns spotted him as a buyer, rather than a looker, and hurried over and asked, "What can I sell you?"

"Maybe nothing," Dunn said. "But I'm working over in Baltimore on a contractor crew, we're tearing out some old houses. Not a good neighborhood and it's getting to be almost dark before quitting time. I got a house gun, but I'm kind of looking around for a decent piece that I could actually carry in my pocket. You know, without people looking at me, knowing what's in there."

"Baltimore. Whew," the woman said, blowing air. She was wearing a bright blue T-shirt that showed a target face with a cluster of bullet holes around the ten-ring, and the words, "Yes, I do shoot like a girl." She said, "Baltimore's not a good place for an honest white man. I'll tell you what, and I'm not just selling here, I got exactly what you need. Exactly."

She had a bookcase-like rack behind her, pulled a plastic box off one of the shelves, opened it, and took out a hand-sized black pistol. "Sig 938. Shoots nines. I gotta say, it's not the most pleasant gun to shoot, you wouldn't want to go around plinking with it, but it's accurate and it'll flat kick ass. Magazines will hold six rounds and you get two mags with the gun. But here's the best part."

She walked down the table, picked up what looked like a leather triangle, and brought it back. "This here's a Sticky holster. The outside is sticky fabric, but the inside is super-slick cloth." She slipped the gun into the thin holster, and said, "Here. Put it in your jeans pocket."

Dunn did, and the gun disappeared. He took a few

steps around the table, and the gun was invisible, even with his tight jeans.

"Now," she said, "Pull the gun."

He stuck his hand in his pocket, and the gun slipped out with no felt friction at all. "Man, that's slick," he said. He looked at the gun. "How much?"

"This particular model retails for six hundred dollars new . . ."

"But it's not new . . ."

She took $475 cash. Dunn suspected that what the IRS didn't know about the transaction, wouldn't hurt anyone except the IRS.

DUNN WENT OUT TO HIS CAR, put the rifle on the floor of the backseat, out of sight, took the Sig out of its case, thumbed six rounds into one of the mags, slapped it into the pistol, put the pistol in the Sticky holster, put the holster in his pocket and used the wristband to get back into the show.

He was armed and he liked the feeling. Realistically, though, he had everything he needed. He watched some guy throwing hatchets at a wooden stump, sat in on a video about threats to gun-owners' rights, and listened to a man give a talk and show a video on low-light shooting and night-vision scopes. The particular scope he was touting sold for $4,199.99, and Dunn decided he could do without it, though the technology was interesting.

He left the show after the night-vision movie and drove over to the business district.

MERKIN, WEST VIRGINIA, was not a pretty town, or a rich one, but it was an old place, and interesting in its own way, every kind of house from colonial to ranch, red-brick buildings on the single commercial street, kids throwing footballs in side yards, girls ambling aimlessly along the sidewalks, enjoying the warm afternoon sun and the new color in the autumn leaves.

Dunn found a café, a slow-moving place with greasy, salty, good-tasting hamburgers and fries, and decent banana cream pie, and lingered further over a second cup of coffee, thinking about the rifle in the car, and a second shot. And the pressure in his pocket, the new carry gun.

Time slipped away and it was late afternoon when he started back to Warrenton. He crossed the Virginia line at twilight, on Highway 33 west of Rawley Springs, not moving especially fast on the two-lane road, when two deer bolted from the forest at the side of the road.

He hit them both, the lead deer in the hip, the second one, full on; the second deer tried to leap at the last moment and caught the top of his truck's brush guard, rolled over it and hit the windshield. Blood exploded across the glass and the deer flipped off as the truck careened into the ditch at the side of the road. Dunn, half-blinded by the blood-slicked windshield, managed to keep the truck upright and finally stopped it, a hundred feet past the point where he'd hit the deer.

He got out of the truck, dazed, sank up to his ankles in the ditch muck, climbed the bank to the blacktop surface; he could smell the wet-copper odor of blood on the truck. He was looking at his truck when another pickup came along, and pulled over. A bearded man got out and asked, "You okay? Hit that deer?"

Dunn scrubbed at his forehead and said, "Yeah. One minute ago."

"They're like rats, they're all over the place." The man looked down at the truck and said, "I got a chain, but I don't believe I could get you out of there. You're pretty much sunk down in the mud. You're gonna need a tow."

"Yeah . . ."

"Damn good thing you had a brush guard on there; doesn't look like you took much damage."

They got a squat black tow truck out of Harrisonburg and a Virginia state patrol car with it. Dunn waded back to the truck, when he saw the cop car coming, lights flashing in the growing dark, and stashed the carry gun under the front seat. He told his story to the patrolman, who gave him a quick Breathalyzer test, "It's a routine thing we gotta do," and cleared him on that. The tow truck arrived and the truck driver and Dunn began trying to figure out how best to get the truck out of the ditch, with unwanted advice from the patrolman.

When they had the tow rigged and ready to go, the patrolman said, "Let's go look at those deer."

Dunn walked him back to the spot where he'd hit the two animals. One of them, a spike buck, the second one he'd hit, was dead. They found the other one off the side of the road, a doe, looking at them, eyes unhurt, pulling herself into the trees with her front legs, her back legs dead.

"Must have broke her spine," the patrolman said. He took his pistol from its holster, moved up close. The doe stopped struggling and looked at him, then at Dunn, catching Dunn's eyes, and the patrolman shot her in the head and the violent crack made Dunn jump and deafened him for a moment.

"That's done," the patrolman said, cheerfully enough.

Dunn's truck was halfway up the wall of the ditch, and they walked back, Dunn's ears still ringing. The tow truck driver had the truck up out of the muck in another five minutes, and the driver said, "Sorry this happened, bud."

The patrolman, looking at the blood on the windshield, said, "Man, it looks like that buck exploded." He added that he'd file a report that Dunn might need for an insurance claim. The tow truck driver had a pressure tank with a washer and hosed down the windshield, took a credit card for three hundred dollars, and he and the patrolman disappeared down the road toward Harrisonburg.

Dunn got a flashlight out of his toolbox and walked

back up the road to where the buck was lying in the ditch. He shined the light farther back in the woods, saw the tawny coat of the doe, stared at it for a moment, sad, still a little stunned by what had happened, shook his head, and walked back to his truck.

At Warrenton, he went to a twenty-four-hour car wash and hosed the remaining blood off the truck. The windshield showed a short crack at the bottom edge, on the passenger side, probably caused by a hoof or possibly an antler. In Dunn's experience, the crack would grow. There were a few scrapes on the hood. That wasn't uncommon with trucks that worked construction sites, but Dunn, as a neat freak, scowled at the scratches, picked at them with a fingernail, and decided he would file an insurance claim, asking for a new paint job.

When he got back to the truck, he looked around, then got the Sig out from under the front seat in its sticky/slippery holster, and put it back in his jeans pocket.

At home, he took the rifle out of its case, and toyed with it, loading and unloading it, looking through the scope, through a window at a streetlight that must have been a half mile distant, and then at a lighted house window a block away. As he was looking at the window, a man appeared in it, from the waist up, well lit, and Dunn put the crosshairs on his ear and pulled the trigger slowly. When the trigger broke, he said, "Bam!"

———

AND HE RESUMED HIS RESEARCH into possible targets, eventually picking out a girl named Cynthia Cootes, daughter of Franklin Cootes, the junior senator from New Hampshire. Unlike the Coil situation, Cynthia Cootes hadn't moved with her father to live in Washington. Her father, in fact, lived part-time on a boat in a Washington marina, while his wife and daughter remained at home.

Her photo on the 1919 site had been taken at the National Book Festival, where her father spoke about a book he'd written on offshore sailing. A feature story first in the *Hampton Union*, and later apparently stolen (or closely replicated purely by coincidence) by the *Washington Post*, reported he annually sailed with his daughter from New Hampshire, around to the Chesapeake and up to Washington. Cynthia Cootes was shown standing on a stage with her father, holding the book.

He couldn't find a reference to her school, but he did find her home address, and when he looked it up on Google Maps, he found that it was on a semirural road outside Hampton. The bad part was that the road didn't have any immediate exit; the good part was, it was heavily wooded. He could work with it.

THE TRIP WOULD REQUIRE some travel. Dunn didn't want to fly, because that would mean declaring the gun. He checked, and found that Hampton was an eight-hour drive: manageable on a three-day weekend, even allowing time for scouting.

If he waited 'til the following weekend, he might lose some momentum, but the news stations were still hot on the story of the first shooting, so he shouldn't lose much.

A pleasurable stress soaked down into his shoulders. He'd already had an effect on the way the nation worked.

One more shot, and the founders of 1919 could go to work, if they hadn't already. He wished he could meet them; he doubted that he ever would.

HE CLICKED ON THE TELEVISION without thinking about it, almost as a reflex, since the remote was right there by his hand. He looked through the scope at a typically goofy family in a pizza ad, the whole bunch of them stuffing their faces with "Chicago-style" pizza of about ten thousand calories per serving; all the eager eaters were improbably thin.

The pizza eaters disappeared and a talking head said, "We have more breaking news on the Audrey Coil story. Coil has admitted that she invented the right-wing 1919 website as a way to get herself on television—"

Dunn blurted, "Wait!"

THE STORY STUNNED HIM IN WAYS that the collision with the deer hadn't. He clicked through three different stations catching bits and pieces of the story and then ran into his office and went out on the 'net and got the whole thing. Reading story after story, he sat frozen at the computer.

Couldn't be true.

One reporter even suggested that Audrey Coil, obviously good at media manipulation, might be doing it again. But nobody believed that. Coil hadn't just confessed, she'd been caught. The FBI was leaking details . . .

And he saw a press conference with the FBI agent in charge, a brisk young woman with a shoulder holster. A reporter asked her if the FBI had found the gun used to shoot James Wagner, the victim of the Stillwater School murder. She demurred, a firm cut to her mouth, and threw out some bureaucratic talk about making significant progress.

The same reporter asked about a double murder in Virginia, and again, the demurral, that said nothing but *Yes, we have it all* . . .

Dunn went to bed at one o'clock in the morning, long past his usual bedtime. He didn't sleep—he thought he didn't sleep—but he did get a visit from Rachel Stokes.

SHE WAS DRESSED as she was the night he killed her; she seemed to be alive, but there was a bullet hole in her forehead that gaped open like a third eye. He'd also shot her in the jaw, but that didn't keep her from talking, although the bottom half of her chin and her throat were seeping blood, the same coppery smell left by the two deer.

"You killed me for nothing," she said. "I had a good life, I was a good woman, and you killed me for nothing because you are a fool."

"I'm not a fool," he said, the dread gripping his heart and squeezing.

"You're a fool and you always were a fool. I thought I might like you and you shot me and you shot me again and you killed my brother, for nothing, for a miserable little tramp who wanted to be on TV. There was never any plan, there was never any 1919, it was all about a teenager trying to get on television."

"I'm dreaming."

"You're not dreaming. You're living this. You're wide awake, Elias. I came back with a message for you. You're bound for hell, Elias."

"I don't believe in that shit," Dunn shouted. "Go away, go away."

"You say you don't believe in it, but you do, Elias. You felt that hell-bound prickle when you sat in the graveyard, shooting that little boy. You felt that prickle in your arm hairs, that cemetery tickle/prickle. The one that tells you there *is* a hell, and that you will burn there, all for being a fool . . ."

He may have been dreaming and he may have been hallucinating; at five o'clock in the morning he put his feet on the bedroom floor, rubbed his head, and when he leaned back, and put one hand on the sheets, he found it soaked with sweat, but smelling of blood. He staggered away from the bed, into the bathroom, where he stared at himself in the mirror. His face seemed narrower than it usually did, drawn, white as paper; dry, not sweaty. He felt weak, as though he might have sweated out every drop of fluid in his body.

He went down the stairs, got a bottle of berry-flavored vitamin water from the refrigerator, gulped it down, some of it slopping down onto his T-shirt. Turned on the television, searched the news channels, but nobody was talking about Audrey Coil at five o'clock on a Sunday morning.

He turned the television off, sat down, stared at the blank screen. The feds had the gun. They had apparently found the Stokeses. If they looked at all the people who worked with Randy Stokes, they'd come to him. If they got DNA off the rifle, if they found his DNA from the accidental gunshot wound at the Stokeses' place . . . they'd get to him.

He wouldn't just be a fool to some psychological twitch called Rachel Stokes, he'd be a nationwide fool. He'd be renowned as a fool.

NOW RACHEL STOKES climbed back inside his head: "You're a fool. A fool. A foooool . . ."

He shook her off, went back to the computer, the *New York Times*, the *Washington Post*. Long stories there, Senator Coil out of touch, but they had printed versions of Audrey Coil's television interviews before she'd been apparently turned off by a family lawyer. Exterior shots of the house.

He kicked back from the computer, then leaned into it again. A Google search turned up an address, and a street view showed the same house as he'd seen on television. The satellite pinpointed it, a sprawling, single-story bricks-and-boards place with a barn in back that was larger than the house; and a bright blue swimming pool tucked out of sight in the heavily landscaped lawn.

Audrey Coil had done this to him: made him into a fool. He paced through the house, hating on it. The girl's image was a tick in his brain, with Rachel Stokes there as well, taunting him.

He put both hands over his ears, staggered back up the stairs to the bedroom, fell on the bed.

He never passed out. He couldn't. He hoped for it, some sort of darkness, oblivion. He got Rachel Stokes, with a bullet hole, sneering . . .

AT SEVEN O'CLOCK Sunday morning, back at the computer, on Google Maps, eleven hours, twenty minutes from door to door, Warrenton, Virginia, to Tifton, Georgia. He paced some more, thinking about it, but he was never in doubt.

He loaded his cabin gear into his truck—never could tell what you might need on the road—along with the new rifle and the carry pistol, ammo, three days' clothes, his dopp kit. He got gas, donuts, and coffee at a Sunoco

station, and headed out of town, down the highway to
I-95, the right turn onto the freeway and nothing ahead
but Tifton, Georgia, a little less than twelve hours away.

This was the only road to redemption, the only way
to erase the insult.

RACHEL STOKES RODE WITH HIM, in the passenger
seat, now silent, but always looming. He was afraid to
look at her, the mutilated head, the sunken eyes with
their blackening flesh around the sockets, the smell of
blood suffusing the truck.

Dunn put his head down and pushed south.

Sunday morning, coming down.

TWENTY-TWO

Sunday morning.

Rae called first: "We're at National. I wanted to give you a chance to tell us to turn around and come back."

"It's a snake-hunt now," Lucas said. He yawned, kicked off the bedsheet, scratched his chest, and put his feet on the floor. "The FBI has DNA, they've got a million leads to work. They got analysts crawling out their ass. That's not really what we do. You go on home and do some research. Find something for us."

"So last night when I was going to bed, I started thinking about Audrey Coil, and I was thinking, Wow! I wonder how that could possibly have happened, with Jane plugging leaks in the FBI like the little Dutch boy and the dike."

"Despite Jane, the FBI leaks like a sieve. That's how it happened," Lucas said.

After a deliberate silence, Rae said, "Maybe. Maybe the FBI. But you're up to something, you sneaky shit. I can tell. You're getting rid of witnesses, that being Bob and me."

"You have no faith in my integrity; you should be ashamed," Lucas said.

"I got plenty of time to be ashamed when it turns out that I'm wrong. Until then, I say you're a sneaky shit and you're up to something."

When he got off the phone, Lucas considered shaving and getting a shower, but he figured Jane Chase would be calling about the time he got in the shower, so he lay back on the bed and waited.

She called ten minutes later; twelve minutes after eight o'clock.

"You up?"

"Almost. You have something for me?"

"I've got something to do, if you guys aren't doing anything else."

"I sent Bob and Rae home," Lucas said. "They're getting on the plane now. I gotta get some tickets myself. Maybe get out of here tomorrow morning."

"One more day. Two at the most," she said. "You're my good-luck charm."

"I saw you on TV," Lucas said. "Great move there, taking off the jacket, showing the gun. You looked hot, in that eastern-establishment, women's-college way. There's gonna be a made-for-TV movie about you. Somebody's already writing it."

"Lucas?" she said, sweetly. "Fuck you."

He laughed and asked, "What do you want to do?"

"We're talking to everybody who got letters and especially a guy who got what we think is a first-generation letter. We got a list of names from him. Unfortunately, it's a long list. I'd like you to come in and chat with him. He'll be here, with his lawyer, at nine, which gives you about forty-seven minutes to get here. Wait. Forty-six."

"I can almost do that," Lucas said. "I might be a few minutes late. I need a bagel or two."

WHEN PRESSED, Lucas could clean up and get out the door in seventeen minutes, in jeans, casual shirt, and sports jacket; a suit and tie took him twenty. Twenty minutes after Chase called, he was in the Watergate restaurant, collecting two bagels with cream cheese.

The hotel had called a cab and as he was heading for the front door, bagel bag in hand, he ran into Jeff Toomes, the hotel security man and ex-cop who'd tipped him off about being followed by Stephen Gibson. "I saw Bob and Rae on their way out of here," Toomes said. "They said they were going home . . . You must be getting close on the 1919 shooter."

"Maybe close," Lucas said, edging toward the door.

Toomes shook his head. "Goddamned country is going to hell in a handbasket. When did we get to the place where we shoot children because of politics?"

"Hate to say this, but I saw it coming," Lucas said. "Maybe not this exact thing, shooting kids, but this level of craziness. The rats have finally gotten out of the woodwork."

"When some crazy guy shoots up a church, you think, okay, he was nuts, he cracked, went psycho," Toomes said. "With all these guns floating around, what do you expect? Background checks are bullshit. That guy who shot up the concert in Nevada, killed all those people? He bought all his guns legally. So that happens. But this guy, shooting a kid . . . he's not exactly your basic psycho, is he? He's a psycho, but he thought he was working for a political program."

Lucas said, "You're exactly right, Jeffrey. We might not be able to stop the undetected psychos, but if a guy's got a program and if we can figure it out, we got a chance."

"Okay. You're gonna find him, aren't you? I mean *you*, personally."

"Yeah."

"Listen, when you find him, kill the motherfucker."

Lucas didn't answer, but reached out and tapped Toomes once on the chest.

THE WEATHER HAD CHANGED OVERNIGHT, an overcast setting in from the west, with only a sliver of blue on the eastern horizon. The clouds had a meanness about them, as well: the arrival of autumn in Washington, a hint that summer was on the wane?

A wind kicked some scrap paper down the street and there was a coolness to it, a briskness, that Lucas felt through his summer jacket as he waited for the cab. A chill.

Sunday morning, coming down.

FRANCIS BACON was being treated well in a conference room at FBI headquarters. Chase's assistant met Lucas at the entrance and escorted him through a maze of hallways and elevators to the room where Bacon was sitting, a lawyer at one elbow, a dish of nuts and a can of ginger ale at the other, talking with three agents, including Chase.

Chase pointed at a chair and said to everyone, as Lucas sat down, "We're being joined by the Marshals Service. Lucas Davenport."

To Lucas, she said, "We're getting a list of everyone Mr. Bacon can think of who might conceivably have sent him the letter. Somebody well spoken, educated, uses some tech, has a computer and a laser printer . . . what else?"

"Angry," Lucas said. "Maybe, *quietly* angry. Somebody who might work hard at a real job, but thinks everybody is taking advantage of him. People who don't work. People who don't respect American ideals."

"Shoot, I don't know anybody who doesn't think that," Bacon said. He was a blue-eyed, square-faced, snub-nosed man in a plaid shirt and jeans, who reminded Lucas of an electrician who'd done work on his lake cabin. "I'm not talking about people like me. I mean, I know I'm a right-winger. But I mean like average people. Or teachers. Or lefties. They're as pissed as we are."

"This guy isn't quite like that, though," Lucas said. "He might make you a little nervous, but you don't know exactly why. Might look at you a little sideways. Might look stressed, like he can't relax. Maybe is a bachelor, but maybe divorced and angry about that. Tells you what's what, and expects you to agree with him and you kind of go along with it, because you get this feeling that you really *don't* want to piss him off."

Bacon said, "Huh." He scratched his nose, looked at his lawyer and then at Chase, and said, "Let me look at that list you've been writing down."

Chase pushed a yellow legal pad across the table, and Bacon scanned it, then asked, "You got a pen?"

Chase slid a pen across to him, and he spent a moment, working down the list. "Kinda surprises me, but there's more than one like that," Bacon said. He pushed the list over to Lucas: four names had check marks next to them.

Lucas looked at Chase. "I'll take these four."

"What do they do?" Chase asked Bacon. "Do they have jobs? What do you know about them?"

Bacon said he thought Carl Stanley and Rollie Klein had spent time in prison, Klein for robbery, he thought, and Stanley for embezzlement. He'd met both, and both were the kind described by Lucas: they seemed smart, even educated, and maybe a little crazy.

Elias Dunn and Harold Sandberg, he thought, weren't criminals, but were right-wing, hard-core, smart, and definitely educated. Dunn was an engineer, Bacon thought, but he didn't know what kind; Sandberg was a moderately unsuccessful inventor. "He makes some money from his inventions, but not too much. He thinks he's always getting cheated and he's sort of . . . out there. But he is smart, and a little crazy, and he does use computers."

One of the agents went away with the list of four names and came back ten minutes later with addresses for all four men, and printouts of the rap sheets for Klein and Stanley. Bacon was apparently right about Dunn and Sandberg—Dunn had no criminal record at all, Sandberg had been arrested for disturbing the peace during a political demonstration in New York City, but the charges had been dropped.

Klein had once been a minor official at the Port of New York and had been convicted of large-scale theft, misdirecting entire cargo containers of consumer products from Europe to warehouses operated by accomplices, then covering the misdirection with forged paperwork. Klein had claimed that he had nothing to do with the thefts, that he'd been framed by higher-ups at the port, who were cooperating with a New York organized crime family. He refused to roll over on accomplices, claiming that he didn't have any, because he didn't commit the crime. He did three years in prison and apparently had been radicalized while he was inside.

Stanley had been convicted of setting up a phony charity that collected money for the ostensible purpose of feeding homeless people in Washington. He may have fed a few, but most of the donated money he simply stole, to feed a gambling habit. He'd done eighteen months in a federal prison. He had an erratic history of political involvement, as a money-raiser and bundler for both Democratic and Republican political campaigns.

"Klein's a possibility, depending on what happened to him in prison. I don't like him much, not for shooting a kid. He was a schemer, not a hitter. No history of violence," Lucas said, scanning the rap sheets the agent had brought back. "He got out two years ago. Maybe somebody could talk to the warden, see what kind of rep he had, who his friends were."

Chase pointed at one of the other agents, and he said, "I got it."

"I don't like Stanley at all," Lucas said. "He's a hustler, and a hustler's not going to make the mistake of murdering a kid. I mean, he might kill somebody, but he'd want an explicit payoff and right now. Not something vague, not something later. Since we know who set up the website, we know he hasn't been offered a payoff."

"We've got nothing on Dunn, not much on Sandberg," Chase said.

Lucas went back to Bacon: "How'd you meet Dunn and Sandberg?"

"At lectures. You know, you get these retired generals and admirals and so on, they set up blogs and start commenting on world affairs—and they write books and give talks. A lot of them are really, really conservative. You see a lot of the same faces at these things. People ask questions, go back and forth, you get to know who some of the smart ones are. Dunn and Sandberg are smart. Sandberg's hard-core and he lets you know it. Say if a general seems weak, he'll tell him to his face. And he gets really, really angry. Dunn doesn't talk much, but . . . you get a feeling about him. He could do something. He doesn't seem angry, but he always asks the toughest questions. Sometimes, even the hard-right guys don't want to answer."

"Like what?" Lucas asked.

"Like, 'What's your program? You say all this stuff, but what's your program? What do you want to do?' Stuff like that. He wants specifics on how somebody will get things done. How they'll change the world. If the guy starts talking about raising money for candidates or lobbying or linking up websites, Dunn will shake his head and walk away."

Lucas turned to Chase. "I like that. And I like Sandberg, the angry thing."

Chase went to Bacon: "If you had to choose one, which would you pick?"

Bacon had to think it over, finally shook his head. "I don't know. Like I said, there's something about Dunn that's spooky. But Sandberg . . ."

Lucas asked Chase, "Can you get access to their IRS records?"

"Yes. I'll have to put together some paper, but I could have it this afternoon."

"Do that, then. Have your analysts look at it."

"What are you going to do?" Chase asked.

"We've got their addresses. I'll cruise them, take a look. Call me as soon as you get the IRS stuff. I want to know where they work, where their money comes from. I'd like to talk to their employers."

LUCAS CAUGHT A CAB BACK to the hotel, checked the addresses for Dunn and Sandberg. They both lived in Virginia, Sandberg close-in, Dunn farther south. He got in the Cadillac and headed out.

Sandberg lived in a semi-crappy apartment complex in Manassas, two-story red-brick buildings, not new, shaggy lawns, no particular amenities. He wasn't home: a young couple, apparently coming back from a central laundry room, toting two plastic baskets full of folded clothing, said they hadn't seen him for a couple of days. Lucas asked about his car, and the woman said that he drove a Toyota FJ Cruiser that he'd had repainted a military green. "Blue one day, green a week later. An ugly Army green," she said.

"And he hasn't been around?"

She pointed to the next door down the hall: "I live right there. The walls are about an inch thick. I'm standing in the kitchen, I can hear every word from his TV."

"Worse than that," the man said. "We heard him fart one time."

The woman: "That's true. Anyway, we think we did."

"We did," the guy said. "He also boils cabbage. You can smell it right through the walls. Which explains the farts."

They didn't know about his political affiliations: "We don't talk." They had the idea that he might have had something to do with a commercial sign manufacturer, from T-shirts they'd seen him wearing.

LUCAS WALKED AWAY, a thrill crawling up between his shoulder blades. Whoever the killer was, he hadn't expected him to be home. And he thought he knew where he might be going. Sandberg was now at the top of his personal list. He called Chase, told her to pound on the Sandberg material from the IRS. "He looks real to me," Lucas said. "I think he's a candidate."

DUNN'S HOUSE WAS IN WARRENTON, half an hour west of Manassas, Lucas tracking his way in with his nav app. The place was impeccable, the lawn perfectly green, perfectly cut, the house a perfectly efficient pale yellow cuboid with white trim. No sign of a car, but then, it was midday and Dunn might be shopping or at a park or whatever. An engineer, Bacon thought.

He rang the doorbell, got no answer, peeked through the door window and saw an interior as impeccably neat as the lawn.

The nearest house was thirty yards away, with a red minivan parked in the driveway. Lucas went that way. When he knocked, an elderly man came to the door, peered out, opened the door and asked, "Can I help you?"

An elderly woman was doing something at a dining room table at the back of the house, and called, "Who is it, Tommy?"

Lucas identified himself and the woman came to listen. They'd lived next to Dunn for seven years, said that he was quiet, standoffish but friendly enough, divorced, a civil engineer. "I guess he works all over the place," the man said. "I don't think he has a regular employer, he's freelance."

"Right now he's working on a job down in Gainesville, that new development. I saw his truck down there and I thought I saw him, too," the woman said.

"Have you see him around today?" Lucas asked.

"Not today, but we haven't been around much today, we're helping our daughter move," the man said.

The Gainesville job site would be on his way back to Washington, the woman said: "It's right off the highway, but . . . today's Sunday. There won't be anybody working."

Lucas thanked them, took a last look at the Dunn house, and headed back east toward Washington. Had Dunn skipped? Had Sandberg skipped? Maybe they were out on the river, rowing their boats. He spotted the new Gainesville development, raw dirt and idle heavy equipment sitting around, doing nothing on a cool Sunday afternoon. Then he saw a man get into a trailer . . .

What the hell, he had a minute. Lucas pulled over, made a U-turn and went back to a turnoff into the development. The trailer was battered-looking, like every construction trailer Lucas had ever seen. He knocked on the door and a man shouted, "Who is it?"

THE MAN'S NAME WAS SPENCER MONROE and he was a foreman on the job site who'd come in to look at grading plans.

"He wouldn't be working today. I got no idea what he does on weekends," Monroe said of Elias Dunn.

Monroe was a large red-faced man sitting behind a metal desk with an illegal paper spike stacked with spiked papers. A bright yellow hard hat was hung on a rack behind him. "He put in a full day on Friday. Why are you looking for him?"

"We want to talk to him about a friend of his, actually," Lucas said. "A background check for a federal job."

"That's a weird thing to do on a Sunday," Monroe said; there was a tone of skepticism in his voice.

"We normally wouldn't, but I was supposed to meet him at his house," Lucas lied. "Said it was the only time he had free. But he wasn't there."

"Huh. He's normally a reliable guy. Punctual," Monroe said. "So you're not investigating the murders?"

"What murders?"

"A guy who worked here," Monroe said. "Him and his sister were killed up by The Plains."

Lucas thought his mouth might have dropped open. "The Stokeses?"

"Yeah, Randy Stokes and his sister, she was, like, Roberta or something. You know about them?"

"Rachel," Lucas said. "I don't know exactly where I am. I've been following a navigation app. How far is The Plains from here?"

Monroe shrugged: "Right up I-60—maybe fifteen minutes."

"Then how far is it from Warrenton?"

Another shrug. "I dunno. Maybe ten, fifteen minutes." He picked up a pencil and drew a triangle on a piece of scratch paper and made points at the tips of each angle. "This is us here in Gainesville. This is The Plains, this is Warrenton."

"Did Elias Dunn know Randy Stokes?"

"Sure. I don't think they'd hang out together, they wouldn't be pals. Randy was sort of a dumbass and El isn't. But they'd run into each other. In fact, I think I seen them talking."

"Did Stokes ever talk about his shooting hobby?"

"All the time—that's about all he did talk about, other than how unfair life was. Drank like a fish, hungover every morning. I'm not the big boss here, but I kinda think Randy wasn't going to make it through to the end of this project. He was going to get his sorry butt fired for pure laziness."

LUCAS WALKED OUT to his car and called Chase.

She picked up and said, "We haven't gotten the IRS—"

"Forget it," Lucas said. "It's Elias Dunn."

CHAPTER

TWENTY-THREE

Lucas headed back to Warrenton and Dunn's house. On the way, he called Henderson, who was in his car, on his way home from church. "Quite the interesting sermon," Henderson said, without even saying hello. "The minister—junior minister, actually—spoke on the *Book of Common Prayer*, the history of it, and how it should guide individual members of different political beliefs. Quite enchanting, even if he did have his head up his ass. So, what's going on?"

"I believe I've identified the shooter . . ."

"Yes!"

". . . but I don't have him yet. Can you either loan me your plane for a flight to Macon, Georgia, or get me a first-class ticket for a flight to Macon? For tonight?"

"Can't get you the plane, my wife is in Los Angeles with some woman named Oona, trying to exhaust each other on Rodeo Drive."

"Do you care?"

"I do not. I can get you on any flight you wish, any class you want. That's because I know people. What time do you want to fly and where do you want to fly from?"

"National or Dulles, either one. Macon if possible, but I'll take Atlanta. One flight if possible, before dark."

"I'll have my assistant call you back," Henderson said. "I want you to call Porter and tell him. He's now suspicious of our relationship and you need to kiss and make up."

LUCAS CALLED PORTER SMALLS, who hadn't gone to church, and who said, "I'll look forward to the denouement. I'm looking at my vocabulary-word-of-the-day calendar, and denouement means the point in a narrative when the different pieces of the plot are pulled together and we reach the climax."

"I knew that," Lucas said.

"Well, you had all those hockey pucks hitting you in the head since childhood, so I'm always uncertain of where you stand, brains-wise," Smalls said.

"Thank you."

"You're welcome. Stay in touch. I would like to hear something before your friend Henderson does."

AT DUNN'S HOUSE, Lucas pounded on the door, got no response. The older couple in the nearest home were no longer there, so he moved to the other side of Dunn's house and a woman came to the door, peered through the tiny door window, then shouted through it, "Who are you?" and Lucas held up his ID and badge and she opened the inner door.

"Federal marshal?" She had dirt on her face, as though she'd been cleaning behind the refrigerator.

"Yes. Have you seen Mr. Dunn today?"

"What'd he do?"

"We don't know if he did anything," Lucas said. "Have you seen him?"

"Yes, I have," she said. "He was loading things into his truck early this morning and then he took off. To where, I don't know. Somebody told me once that he has a cabin in West Virginia, but I don't know that for sure. We don't talk much. I think he went over to the Bixbys' place before he left. The Bixbys are across the street in the red house."

Lucas thanked her and headed across to the Bixbys. Again, the only person home was a woman, older, with carefully set silver hair and a pale British complexion and long British nose. She also looked through the door window before opening the door, although she didn't shout through it. Lucas showed her his ID and asked about Dunn.

"My husband . . . they're not exactly friends, but they talk from time to time." Her accent was from farther south, like South Carolina. "Elias is a civil engineer and my husband is a building contractor, so they have things in common. I didn't see Elias this morning, but I heard him talking to Frank. My husband, Frank.

Elias was going on a short trip but won't be here for the trash pickup, so he asked if he could leave a bag of trash with us, if we'd take it out for him."

"That was this morning? And you still have the trash bag?"

"Yes, we do. We have a little trash and recycling corral out back. The bag is there. Do you need it?"

"Yes, I believe so. I'll know in a few minutes when some FBI people show up. Why would Mr. Dunn leave his garbage?"

"Because we have crows," the woman said. "They know all about the bags, and they'll peck right through them to get at the contents and then they spread the stuff all over the street."

"Okay. Could you show me that corral?"

THE CORRAL WAS A TEN-FOOT-WIDE square of red bricks surrounded by a five-foot-high woven fence, with a trash bag sitting by itself, in the middle of the square. Two rakes and a shovel were leaning against the fence, with an upended wheelbarrow.

"And that's Mr. Dunn's trash?"

"Yes, we haven't put ours out yet."

Lucas thanked the woman and walked into her backyard and called Chase. "Where are you?"

"We're on the way."

"Do you have a warrant?"

"Not yet. It's a Sunday, that presents certain logistical difficulties. But we'll get one."

"I have a bag of trash that Dunn took to a neighbor's house this morning. He said he was going on a trip and asked them to put it out for him."

"Excellent. We don't need a warrant for that. We'll transport that as soon as we get there. We'll be there in twelve minutes, according to my app."

THE FBI ARRIVED IN THREE FORD SUVS. Chase hopped out, looked at Dunn's house, and said, "We've got his truck make, model, and tag number. We're looking for it. The judge who handles Sunday warrants may be playing golf, but I just got a text that says somebody knows where he is, and have gone to look for him. Where's the garbage?"

Lucas showed her the garbage bag, and two minutes after that, the bag was on its way back to Washington.

The feds had the Rapid DNA technology that could provide a fast DNA result within two hours, although its findings couldn't be used in court. What it could do was confirm that a suspect was almost certainly the producer of a particular sample of DNA. Whatever was in the garbage bag could be used to match DNA from the rifle used to shoot James Wagner and from the blood at the Stokeses' house. A more scientifically advanced and court-acceptable DNA sample would be obtained from biological samples taken from the house and from Dunn personally, when they caught him.

Lucas sat with Chase in the back of one of the Fords, with two more feds in the front seats, and filled them in on the connection between Dunn and the Stokeses, and provided them with the names of the people at the job site who could confirm the connection.

"Do you think he's running?" one of the front-seat feds asked.

"I don't know why he would think we were closing in, unless he's on a DNA register somewhere," Lucas said, evading the question.

Chase said, "He isn't. We don't know his name at all, not from before today."

"But he was known to at least some of these alt-right guys," Lucas said.

"Yes."

THEY TALKED ABOUT the case in general for twenty minutes or so, everything that everybody already knew, speculated on the possibility that more shooters would come out of the woods, or that an actual 1919-type extortion would occur, inspired by Audrey Coil's website.

Chase was working her phone as they talked, trying to get the warrant moving, and then Lucas, bored, and another bored agent got out of the truck and walked around Dunn's yard and peered through his windows. The blinds were firmly down on most of them, but where they could see in, the house was almost preternaturally neat. "Too neat," the other agent said. "The guy's an obsessive-compulsive at some level."

———

WHEN THEY WALKED back to the truck, they found that Chase had gone across the street to interview Mrs. Bixby, and had apparently been invited inside. She reappeared in ten minutes and told Lucas, "Dunn lives by himself. Had a wife, they divorced a few years ago, her whereabouts are unknown, current name is unknown. No known personal friends, no visitors. Mrs. Bixby says he's smart and not bad-looking, but there's something that's always been off-putting about him. I'm going to go talk to the lady in that house . . ."

She pointed to the first house Lucas had gone to—they'd seen the woman at the door, watching them—but before Chase could go that way, her phone dinged and since she carried it in her hand like a permanent appendix, she glanced at it and said, "We got the warrant."

They headed for the house, and as they did, two more FBI trucks arrived, one with a crime scene crew. One of the agents who had arrived with Chase had a battery-powered lock rake, and they went through the front door without having to break anything.

As soon as they did, an alarm went off. Chase said, "Damnit, turn that thing off."

The agent with the lock rake said, "I can turn it off, but I don't think . . ." He found the alarm box in the kitchen, pulled out his cell phone, made a call and identified himself. "You know who I am and this is an urgent national security . . . then get me to that call center. Right now, fast as you can. Well, try . . ."

He put his hand over the microphone and said, "They're switching me to the call center that services this alarm. But I can tell you right now, we're too late. Somebody's called Dunn and told him that we're here."

"Get the number for that phone," Lucas said. "We can track the phone."

The agent nodded and a moment later, went back to the call. He identified himself again, gave Dunn's name and address, listened for a moment, then said, "Do not alert him. He's a fugitive. If you need a more official order, we can email or fax you a form . . . We'll do that."

He hung up and said to Chase, "Dunn's phone is dead. No response at all. He's probably pulled the battery, or thrown it in a river. He probably knows it can be tracked."

"That means he doesn't know this alarm has gone off."

The agent nodded. "He doesn't. The alarm center couldn't reach him."

Chase turned to the other agents inside the house. "Move the crime scene van inside the garage. We'll want to get the rest of the vehicles out of sight, in case he comes back."

The agents started moving and Chase asked Lucas, "What do you think?"

"I don't think he's coming back. He took the garbage out two days ahead of time."

"Where's he going?"

Lucas shrugged: "Maybe he's got a bolt-hole some-where. Somebody mentioned that he might have a cabin in West Virginia . . ."

CHASE GOT INVOLVED with the crime scene team in taking the house apart. They got biologics from the drain in the shower, which were bagged for the more elaborate DNA tests. Lucas was interested in the proce-dures, and at one point, Chase came back and said, "He has a whole right-wing library in his office. Lot of theo-retical stuff. Political commentaries. He seems more interested in Mussolini than in the Nazis."

Lucas didn't know what to make of that, and said so. After an hour of hanging out, he got a call from Henderson's assistant who said, "You're out of National at 3:14, arrive at Hartsfield-Jackson in Atlanta at 4:37. Couldn't get you to Macon in one flight and it was faster to send you into Atlanta and then put you in a car. You've got a car, an SUV, reserved in your name at Hertz. Drive time from Hartsfield-Jackson to Tifton is two and a half hours."

Lucas looked at his watch: almost one o'clock. It'd be tight. "I'll take it."

Lucas told Chase he was leaving. "There's nothing for me here, that you can't tell me by telephone."

"What are you going to do?"

"Poke around. Maybe go home."

"Give me one more day."

Lucas shrugged. "To do what?"

She had no answer to that.

AS SOON AS HE WAS IN HIS CAR, Lucas called Russell Forte, his supervisor with the Marshals Service, who worked out of the service headquarters in Arlington. "It's Sunday," Forte said.

"Really? I thought it was Tuesday. We think we've identified the guy who shot the kid."

"Can I put out a press release, taking credit?"

"Not yet. I need a gun."

Silence. Then, "I assumed you had one. Or maybe several."

"I need a rifle. I need it in the next hour and I need it in a case that I can ship on an airline."

"Ah, Jesus, I'm in a canoe."

"You can still canoe," Lucas said. "Make a phone call, pull some strings, get me a rifle. Couple mags to go with it. Doesn't need a scope or selective fire. I'll pick it up at headquarters in one hour. Less than an hour. Forty-five minutes. I won't have time for a lot of paperwork."

CHASE CALLED. "We got a little break. Nobody knows this but us chickens, but Senator Coil flew into National, stayed behind security and caught a flight to Atlanta. She's on her way home."

"Good. She won't be on TV, at least, not right away. Listen, in case I run into him while I'm poking around, send me any photos you've got of Dunn."

"We've got a couple, now. You'll have them in five minutes. By the way, he might know we're looking for him. About ten minutes after you left, the team found a second security system, one of those do-it-yourself things that sends video out to an internet site. They would have taken video of all of us walking around his house. If he has a computer with him, and checks the site, he'll see us."

"Why don't you take down the cameras?"

"We've done that, Lucas. But we can't even find where it's going out to, the video that's already been shot. Even if we find the security server, I doubt they'd take the site down, even if we yelled at them. I mean, they'll have hundreds of surveillance videos coming in all the time, we can't simply order them to shut down."

"Figure something out," Lucas said.

"We're trying," Chase said. "The big brains are scratching their heads. I don't know what will come of it."

"I thought *you* were a big brain."

"Well, yes, but I'm on the strategy side. This problem is tactical," she said.

"More left to the second lieutenants."

"Exactly."

LUCAS PICKED UP A CARBINE in Arlington, from a marshal who wanted to make sure he knew how to operate it and that he'd eventually get it back—Lucas had to tell him that he'd already been shot by one, which did make an impression. The case was big and awkward, but about as secure as a case could get, with an actual padlock holding it closed.

"That'll put a bullet where it's aimed, if you know how to shoot," the marshal said. "Try not to whack it around too much."

Lucas stopped at the Watergate to grab some clothes and made it back to National forty minutes before they'd close the door on his flight. Checking the gun and ammo took up half that time, even with his marshal's ID, and he made it through security and as he was jogging down to his gate, took a call from Chase.

"Where are you?"

"Jogging," Lucas said.

"You know, jogging can be dangerous in DC."

"I'm in DC and I'm jogging, but I've got a gun."

"All right. I'm calling to tell you that we got a return from Rapid DNA. Dunn's our man," Chase said. "No question. We tracked down that cabin in West Virginia, maybe a survivalist deal, the way it looks from a satellite view. We've got two SWAT teams on the way."

"Luck," Lucas said.

He was jogging under a speaker when a plane announcement was made and Chase asked, "What was that sound?"

"Bus," Lucas said. "Jesus, almost got hit. Gotta go."

He turned off his phone and the airline attendant at the gate said, "You made it. Last guy on."

———

HENDERSON HAD GOTTEN him a seat in first class. The woman in the seat next to him, who'd already begun knitting something in a color of green so dreadful that Lucas didn't want to sit next to it, said, "You must be important."

Catching his breath, as he settled into the seat, Lucas asked, "Why?"

"They told us they might have to hold the plane for you."

"I'm not that important," Lucas said. "Must've been somebody else."

She shook her head. "No, I think it was you."

TWENTY-FOUR

Dunn gassed up at an I-95 truck stop north of Savannah, where he took a few minutes to go online with the truck stop's Wi-Fi and check his security cameras.

And saw the FBI agents crawling through his house.

They'd found him.

He'd felt it coming, wasn't completely surprised. He decided that he was going in, way back when he'd first found the 1919 site, even if it cost him. He'd already begun preparing for it, when he'd pulled the battery from his cell phone that morning.

HE SAT IN THE TRUCK, watching the agents tear through his house, his mouth beginning to tremble, but he fought back tears. He wouldn't cry about it. He wouldn't exactly be martyred, since the website was a fake, but if he took out the Coil girl, at least people would see a lesson: you don't fuck with serious people.

And he fantasized about hiding out in a wilderness—that had been done, and successfully—but it was, he thought, a fantasy. He could try, but the deep state would get him.

Before he left the truck stop, he called up a map program and found a Walmart Supercenter in Fitzgerald, Georgia, a half hour northeast of Tifton. He'd stop there for the night, he thought, outside the target town, in case somebody might have anticipated him.

He'd scout the next morning, find a spot, hit the girl, and run. The truck would be a liability after he hit her, because they'd have a starting point for him. Had to think about that.

From Savannah, he picked up a few miles of I-16 going west, then cut cross-country to Fitzgerald, arriving well after dark. He went inside the Walmart, got a sandwich, ate in the truck, then crawled inside the camper back, wrapped himself in a sleeping bag and tried to sleep.

He was almost there when Rachel Stokes showed up.

"WELL, WHAT ARE YOU GOING TO DO?" she asked. She was standing outside the truck, but spoke through the side window, so he could only see her shattered face. "Everybody in the world is looking for your truck. You're a rat in a trap: they've got your face, they've got your license tag, they're going to put you in one of those supermax prisons where you'll see nothing but four white walls all day, every day, for the rest of your life."

"No, no, I'll be down in hell with you," Dunn said.

"Audrey Coil won't be here with us, because Audrey Coil will get away with it. Her mother's a senator and well connected with the deep state, they'll take care of her, the girl who chumped you, the girl who made you a fool."

"Get the fuck away from me . . ."

She cackled. "Your ass hurts, doesn't it? Shot yourself right down the ass crack. What a fool. They're going to find you with a bullet hole in your ass crack."

He resented her hilarity, but also the vulgarity of it all. A quality woman like Rachel shouldn't be using works like "ass-crack."

The fact was, he did hurt after the long drive. He wasn't bleeding, didn't think he was infected, but he hurt.

RACHEL STOKES STAYED FOR A WHILE, bobbing up and down in the side window, to taunt him, the Walmart sign in the background. Dunn never slept—he didn't think he slept—but he might have, when he thought about it, because he wasn't as exhausted as he should have been, getting up in the dark, at five o'clock in the morning. The sun wouldn't be up until after seven o'clock.

He pulled out his dopp kit, removed the razor, toothbrush, a travel-sized tube of Crest toothpaste, and a bar of motel soap, got a washcloth from his go-bag, went inside. In the otherwise empty men's room, he peed, brushed his teeth, washed his face, then quickly shaved and scrubbed his armpits without taking off his shirt. Parts of the store were still closed, but the bakery was open and he could use the sugar.

He felt better with a couple of apple fritters inside him, saw a Wi-Fi symbol on his way out. He hadn't realized that Walmarts had Wi-Fi, but they apparently did. Back in the truck, he tried to go online, but could only see the Walmart Wi-Fi sporadically. He moved the truck across the lot, closer to the store, and got a solid signal.

He spent ten minutes looking at satellite views of the Coil house, decided the best play would be to shoot from the woods across the street from the house. The woods were a couple of hundred yards across, running in a band along the road; another road ran parallel to the woods, a few hundred yards back. If he took down Coil, and whoever was with her, he should have time to make it back to the truck. From there . . . well . . .

And he took a moment to look up Tifton area schools. With a bit of research, he decided that if Audrey was going to school, as the news reports had said, it would be the Tift County High School. The Coils were Democrats and, given the various political pressures, were unlikely to be patronizing Christian schools. A public school would be the thing; and the public school's first bell was at 7:55.

HE CONSIDERED THE PROBLEM of his truck and what was undoubtedly a widespread police search for it. If he left it parked at the side of a country road, a sheriff's patrol well might run the tag. Then he'd be done.

So, forty-five minutes after he got up, he left the Walmart parking lot and headed east and north, away from Tifton.

Looking.

He thought he might have found his place twice, but both times, there was a problem. Once, too many cars; too many people. Another time, two people already outside, could have been a father and a son.

The third time, he turned up a dirt driveway with a single battered mailbox at the end of it, to find a trailer in the woods, a light on in the back—the bedroom?—and one in the kitchen. A blue Ford pickup, maybe ten years old, sat by the door. Dunn put the Sig 938 in his pocket, safety off, told himself to remember to keep his finger off the trigger—that's what he'd forgotten when he shot himself in the ass—and got out of the truck.

As he walked up to the door, a man opened it and peered out. "Who're you?" he asked. A middle-sized dog stood behind him, which wasn't ideal, but Dunn said, "Are you Clayton Delaney?"

He chose the name because the last thing he'd heard in his truck was the song, "I Remember the Day Clayton Delaney Died."

The man said, "What?"

Dunn pulled his hand from his pocket, put his finger through the trigger guard and shot the man twice in the chest. The man fell inside. The dog leaped over him, coming for Dunn, but Dunn hit the dog on the side of the shoulder and then leaped past him, into the trailer, and slammed the door.

Nobody else there, nothing but the body. The man was sure-enough dead. The place stank of nicotine and bacon and potatoes, but the keys to the truck were right there, on the kitchen counter.

Dunn looked out the door, where the dog had retreated halfway across the dirt circle that marked the driveway turn-around, and then stood, whimpering, then growling. He didn't want to shoot again, so he walked half-sideways past the dog to his truck, and moved it around behind the trailer.

He went back to the blue Ford, got inside, fired it up. Half a tank of gas, more than he'd need.

He left the trailer, with the dog standing outside, and headed south toward Tifton. A plan formulating, now. Getting the truck had been easy—you could get any number of trucks that way, he thought.

He wasn't that far from the coast. Maybe get a job on a boat headed south; get into Mexico or Venezuela or one of those places.

Maybe.

TWENTY-FIVE

Lucas had become a police detective at a time when he always kept quarters in his pocket, in case he had to make phone calls. From phone booths. After looking up people in a phone book, which hung inside the phone booth on a chain—the book was always missing a few critical Yellow Pages and almost always smelled like somebody had peed on it.

Now, there were no phone books and no booths in which to hang them, or in which you might take an emergency leak. Quarters were worth half as much as they had been.

But, he thought, a cell phone had its advantages. He got out of Hartsfield-Jackson in a Nissan Pathfinder, at five o'clock. Before he left Hertz, he used his phone to check Google for sporting goods stores in Macon and found a Bass Pro Shops store that was open until seven.

He opened his phone's navigation app, asked, and was told that with current traffic conditions, he could be there a few minutes after six. The app's voice—a woman's—sounded impatient. If he wanted to get there before the store closed, he'd have to move. And he could move, at illegal speed, because his phone also had the Waze app, which warned of speed traps and patrolling cops.

The nav app was correct, almost to the minute, as was the Waze. He spent twenty minutes in the store, and emerged with a double-extra-large camo shirt and large-size pants. On an impulse, and because he'd always wanted a pair anyway, he bought a pair of Fujinon image-stabilized marine binoculars.

He could have made it to Tifton by eight, but, after a quick search on his phone, stopped at an outlying Burger King for a no-meat Impossible Whopper, fries, and a Diet Coke. The Whopper was okay, maybe a six on a scale of one to ten, but he was burping salt all the way to Tifton.

LUCAS LANDED A SMALL SUITE at the Country Inn in Tifton, where he arrived at 8:30. After inspecting his room, he carried the rifle up the back stairs, took it out of its case and worked it, loading and unloading it: it worked smoothly and had been freshly cleaned. That done, he put it back in its case and hid it behind the bed, in case a motel employee came into his room while he was gone.

He pulled on his bulletproof vest with the yellow

"U.S. Marshal" lettering on the back, and pulled the double-extra-large camo shirt over it. It was sloppy, but workable, if he rolled up the sleeves. The pants fit fine. He folded the new clothes and set them aside.

The binoculars came in their own hard case and he took them out, inserted the batteries, put on the neck strap, fiddled with them until he understood how they worked.

Next, he set up his iPad, went on the motel Wi-Fi to Google Earth and called up a satellite view of the Coil house, which was in an exurban area northwest of town. From the satellite, the countryside around Tifton looked like a giant yellow-and-green jigsaw, the yellow being irregularly-shaped farm fields, interspersed with forest land.

The Coil house, which appeared to be long and single-storied, was on a small lake or a large pond. In addition to the pond, the Coils had a good-sized swimming pool, glowing aqua-green in the satellite image, screened from the road by the house and what in the north might have been called a woodlot.

Lucas didn't know what you'd call it in the south, but there were a lot of trees, which was both good and bad. Nobody would see him, but he might not see Dunn, either.

Had to think like Dunn. He peered down at the satellite view, thought that Dunn might be looking at the same thing. Where would he put himself? How would he kill Audrey Coil—or maybe all the Coils?

An ambush at the house seemed simplest; otherwise, how would Dunn know where she'd be? Maybe the Tifton high school? Was there a private school? Lucas didn't know, but, he thought, neither would Dunn.

Would Dunn risk a straightforward house invasion, going in with a high-capacity gun in an effort to kill everybody? He might . . . but if he did, there would be no guarantee that Audrey would even be in the house. He'd want to see her, Lucas thought.

THOUGH IT WAS DARK, he decided to have a look at the house and headed out again, across Tifton—a bigger town than he'd expected—past an ag college and around a couple of corners and then out Carpenter Road. The road was flat blacktop, with widely spaced houses set well back, usually in stands of pine trees. With a couple of turns off Carpenter, he was cruising past the Coil place, which was lit up like Christmas, with five cars in the circular driveway.

No signs of media, but two of the cars had a cop-like appearance—rode hard and put up wet, bland sedans, older.

There were woods across the road from the Coil house, and from two particular angles, a shooter could see down the opposite ends of the driveway right to the front door. The ends of the driveway were thirty-five or forty yards apart, the wooded shooting positions perhaps sixty to seventy yards apart. He drove on past for a half-mile or so, then turned around, waited a bit, and then drove past the house again. No change. Still a cop vibe from the sedans. Maybe there were cops inside the house, as bodyguards.

The woods across the road from the south end of the driveway seemed to have a piece of higher ground, a hump, that would make a better shooting platform than the lower ground on the north. Lucas made a mental note.

WHEN HE GOT back to the Country Inn, he called Weather to tell her where he was; they talked for fifteen minutes and she said, "I still don't understand why you're there by yourself. What happened to Bob and Rae?"

"I sent them home—at the time, it didn't seem like we'd need them," Lucas said. "Now . . . well, this was a last-minute thing. I'm operating on a hunch."

"You're going to talk to the local police tomorrow, right?"

"Sure. If . . . I can. I need to look at the situation. I could be embarrassing myself."

"Lucas . . ."

"I'll talk to them," he said. When they were off the phone, he added, "After I look at the situation."

HE HADN'T COMMITTED to calling the Tifton police to alert them of his presence, as Weather had demanded, because he didn't want to lie directly to her. He would eventually call the police, he believed, but not until after he'd dealt with Dunn.

If he talked to the police, and told them what he believed about Dunn's movements, they'd probably throw a cordon around the house, which Dunn would see. And the cops would probably call the feds, who'd send in even more troops. The same thing would be true if he talked to the Coils ahead of time. If all those officers and agents did everything right, and Lucas had guessed right about Dunn, they'd wind up surrounding him and maybe arresting him.

They'd make him a hero to a segment of the population.

Rae had guessed right about why Lucas had sent her, and Bob, back to Louisiana. He didn't want witnesses.

Lucas hadn't come to Tifton to arrest Dunn.

He'd come to kill him.

HE WENT TO BED EARLY, after spending more time with the Google Earth satellite views of the Coil house; by the time he was finished with them, he felt he could find his way around the timberland across from the house. He also found a place where he could leave the car, before walking into that timber. The walk would cover the best part of a mile, on the margin between a long strip of timber and an agricultural field of some kind, so he'd have to be careful not to be seen with the rifle, which would attract the police.

Dunn had different problems. Unless he was on a straightforward suicide run, which seemed unlikely for a man of his qualities, he'd want his truck nearby. The most likely place for it, Lucas thought, was a farm road that ran parallel to the road where the Coil house was located, but on the other side of the woods and perhaps four hundred yards away from either shooting position.

From the woods, he could shoot Audrey as she came out of the house, then spray the place with the rest of a magazine, then run. A long run, probably a minute and a half, but it was doable.

Of course, Dunn might still be in Virginia, or at that property in West Virginia . . .

EVEN WITH ALL THAT TO THINK ABOUT, Lucas got some sleep that night. His cell phone alarm kicked him out of bed at 4:30, and he showered, shaved, carried the rifle, his vest, and the camo down to the car at five o'clock, on a cool damp morning. He'd found a Walmart Supercenter in Tifton, checked the parking lot for Dunn's truck—didn't find it—went inside and bought some bakery and two Diet Cokes.

He was back on the road at 5:15, with more than an hour before first light, and two hours before sunrise. He found the turnoff to the place he'd leave the car, parked, got out into a heavy dew. Thought about snakes: he always thought about snakes when he was in unfamiliar territory. He'd planned to change his jeans for the camo pants, but the camo pants were commodious, so he pulled them on over his jeans. If a snake could bite through two layers, well . . . okay, he'd die. Probably of a heart attack.

When he was dressed, he took the rifle out of the case, slapped in a full mag, jacked a shell into the chamber, checked the safety, touched the butt of the Walther on his belt, and started off in the dark. There were clouds, and only occasionally a strip of moonlight, but the woods loomed to his left, dark, an impenetrable mass. To his right, he could see across an open field, with farmhouse lights a few hundred yards away. The difference in feel allowed him to keep moving, though he stumbled from time to time, catching himself, cursing under his breath. His shoes were soaked within a hundred yards.

His iPhone was tracking him, through the GPS app, and thirty-five minutes after he started away from the car, he thought he was about opposite the Coil house and turned into the woods to his left, walking into a nightmare.

He began by tangling with a barbed-wire fence at the edge of the field. He managed to clamber over it, though he ripped the shirt and probably the pants; he thought he was clear, but the binocular strap caught on the fence, twisted and yanked at his Adam's apple.

More cursing, ineffectual because it had to be so quiet. Once in the woods, the tree branches slapped him in the face, until he was forced to walk with his arms up in front of him, fending off the low-hanging branches. Inching forward, he took another half hour to travel what he thought was perhaps two hundred yards, falling twice, stumbling all the time, like an over-the-edge drunk, barely managing to keep the rifle's muzzle out of the dirt.

The GPS hadn't let him down. When he got to the edge of the woods, he found he'd overshot the Coil house, but not by much. Staying back in the trees, but with some light now, from the house, he worked back to the high point where he could see down the driveway to the front door.

Three cars were parked in the driveway—one of the cop cars was gone, as well as a Lexus SUV, probably a friend. A couple of lights still burned in the house, but it felt as though it were asleep.

He backed away, got as deep into the woods as he could, while keeping the front door in sight. He found a tree trunk, down in a swale, and sat down and leaned into it; the tree smelled of sap, of turpentine. As he settled, he could feel the night quiet settling on him, the stillness that comes just before first light.

He put the binoculars in his lap, and waited.

Very slowly, the morning's light began to seep through the trees.

DUNN FOUND HIS WAY through Tifton. He got turned around once, but as he was unable to use his cell phone's navigation apps, he was driving a route he'd sketched on a piece of paper. He was a surveyor, though, so the map was a good one, if the streets turned out to be confusing.

The truck was a rattletrap: he'd need to get another one soon. Half a tank of gas, that'd get him a couple of hundred miles. The thing smelled of ten years of bad food and frequent farting, plus a bit of wet dog. He'd never let a truck go like this one had . . .

He found the Coil house after that minute's confusion, cruised it, not slow, but right at the speed limit. He didn't need to get stopped. There were lights on, three cars in the driveway. He continued on down the road to the intersection, took the left turn, waited a few minutes, then drove back past the house. Maybe slowed a bit, to look. Took the next right.

First light had come and gone, giving way to the dawn. Still an hour or so to sunrise, but landscape and building details were beginning to crystallize across the countryside.

LUCAS SPOTTED THE RATTLETRAP pickup rolling down the road past the Coils' house. There hadn't been much traffic, and what there was, he'd scanned with the binoculars. Light was bad, and he hadn't been able to see much, but when the rattletrap went by, with weak yellow headlights that seemed to jiggle in their brackets, he caught a glimpse of an angular white face turned toward the Coils' place.

And he thought, "Wait!"

Could have been him. Could have been Dunn. He watched the truck as it continued on down the road, then took the first left—the same turn Lucas had taken when he'd cruised the house the night before. Five minutes later, he saw headlights turn from that intersection back toward the Coil house, weak yellow lights that seemed to jiggle as they came on.

If that was Dunn, and if he was intent on a house invasion, he'd pull into the driveway and hit the door.

Lucas crouched, moved closer to the road, settled into a spot where the door was *right there,* where he could cover any approach to it. The truck came on, and Lucas put the binoculars on it again. Angular white face turned toward the Coil house . . .

And he thought, "That's him."

THE ROAD WENT ALL THE WAY back to Carpenter, a half mile away, but the truck didn't. The truck turned left at the first intersection and Lucas loped back through the woods, now well lit by the growing daylight. He stopped just inside the tree line, and watched as the truck took another left, on the road that ran parallel to the woods and to the Coils' road. The fields were flat and unobstructed, and he watched as the truck slowed and then pulled onto the shoulder, perhaps a hundred yards farther down from the Coil house.

Dunn.

There was no longer a question in Lucas's mind.

If Dunn came straight across the field, to the trees,

he'd be a hundred and twenty yards away from Lucas's spot. Lucas stepped carefully farther back into the woods, then turned and jogged through the trees to the point where he thought Dunn would enter them. After a moment, he slowed, and turned back toward the fence line that marked the edge of the field and looked toward the truck.

A man had gotten out and was crossing the roadside ditch into the field. Lucas put the binoculars on him, now in good light. Dunn's face was crisp: pale, harsh, alert. He was carrying a rifle.

Lucas pulled back into the woods, began moving toward Dunn's probable entry point. The other man was still three hundred yards away, Lucas only fifty or so from his ambush spot. He took it more slowly. If Dunn spotted him, there'd be a gunfight, which he really didn't need, having been on the losing end of one of those only six months earlier.

In three minutes, he was set up behind an old, gnarled pine tree, looking out at the fence line. He could see Dunn coming—the other man was jogging now, the rifle carried in both hands, out in front of him. He was dressed all in gray. Work clothes, Lucas thought. He looked again with the binoculars: a clear image, chest to head.

THE TREE LINE was farther away than Dunn had expected and he was out in the open longer than he'd hoped to be, feeling conspicuous, endangered. He'd found a reasonable spot for the truck, a pulloff over a culvert, that didn't appear to be much used. He broke into a jog as he came to the fence, and thought, "Remember the fence." It'd slow him on the way out. He crossed the fence with no trouble, moved a couple feet into the trees, and looked at his watch.

Ten after seven. Sun was about to come over the horizon and the fair-weather clouds glowed pink overhead.

He took another step and a man's voice, clear, baritone, said, "Dunn! Stop there!"

Dunn thought, "Shit!" and brought up the muzzle of his rifle, pulled the trigger. Nothing happened. He paused, then flipped the safety and tried again.

He never felt the impact from the incoming bullets. He simply dropped.

LUCAS WAITED UNTIL DUNN crossed the fence. This could play out a couple of ways, but would work best if Dunn fired a shot or two. Dunn looked up, as though admiring the pink clouds and Lucas put his rifle's sights on Dunn's chest, thirty yards away, and said, "Dunn! Stop there!"

Dunn brought up the muzzle of his rifle, pointing off to Lucas's left, appeared to squeeze the trigger, but nothing happened. Lucas, in a tiny corner of his mind, thought, "Safety," and Dunn apparently picked up the thought, flipped the safety and fired three rapid shots into the brush, well to Lucas's left.

Lucas fired two quick shots into Dunn's chest and Dunn sank to his knees and then fell over backwards, the rifle dropping to his side.

Lucas's rifle had thrown two expended shells off to his right. He could see them, little pieces of gold on the forest floor. He picked them up, moved them to a different tree closer to Dunn's line of fire. Then he pulled off his camo shirt, exposing the bulletproof marshal's vest, quickly checked Dunn. He was dead, two coin-sized blood spots in the center of his chest.

That done, he moved quickly but carefully through the trees until he could see down the driveway to the Coil house. Two men were standing behind the cars in the driveway, both with rifles, scanning the trees.

Lucas shouted, "U.S. Marshal! U.S. Marshal! Got a man down. Coming out with my hands up. U.S. Marshal!"

One of the men shouted, "Come ahead. Hands in air."

Lucas put the rifle down, walked out of the woods with his hands up, his badge case in one hand.

He was halfway up the driveway when Roberta Coil stuck her head out the door and blurted, "Davenport. What are you doing here?"

TWENTY-SIX

The ramifications of the Tifton shooting trailed out over months.

Most immediately, Roberta Coil vacillated between gratitude and condemnation. She was pleased that a threat to her daughter and possibly herself had been eliminated, but angry that Lucas hadn't called in a battalion of FBI agents once he'd detected the problem. Audrey Coil didn't have much to say about that, and her mother kept her firmly, if only temporarily, away from anything that looked like a camera or a reporter.

THEN THERE WAS the usual bureaucratic chaos—a clusterfuck, in the unofficial nomenclature—involving the Tift County Sheriff's Department, the FBI, and two separate investigators from the Marshals Service's Office of Professional Responsibility (one each from Internal Affairs and Discipline Management) concerned by the fact that Lucas had been involved in three shootings in the space of six months—one of them being Lucas's own wounding in a Los Angeles firefight.

Lucas was interviewed by the Marshals Service investigators the day after the shooting, although their conclusions weren't released for more than a month. One of the men called Lucas to say that the investigation had concluded that the two fatal criminal shootings had been righteous. As for Lucas's wounding, they recommended that he undergo retraining in "cover and concealment," which wasn't going to happen if Lucas could avoid it.

"Yeah, probably wouldn't help," one of the investigators told him. "What you did was stupid and there ain't no fixing that."

"Thank you," Lucas said.

SENATOR ELMER HENDERSON called three times, the first time the day after the shooting. "I've got Porter here in the office with me. Well done, my boy."

"I hope the Office of Professional Responsibility agrees with you."

"They will. We've had a number of colleagues calling over there, emphasizing the need for fair treatment of hardworking, risk-taking marshals. They've effectively signaled back that they get the point. You might even get a medal."

"I'd like a medal," Lucas said. "I could wear it to parties."

———

TWO DAYS AFTER DUNN was killed, when Lucas was nearly finished with the bureaucracy, Rae called and asked, "I was right, wasn't I?"

Lucas: "I'm sorry?"

"Don't play dumb, Lucas. You wanted us out of the way. You didn't want witnesses."

"You've got an overactive imagination, is what I think," Lucas said. "How's Bob?"

"Bob's just fine."

"You find a case we can work?" Lucas asked.

"Jesus, Lucas. The Dunn thing? That was damned cold. Damned cold."

"Okay . . . I don't know what to tell you. Except . . . yeah, you were right."

"Good. I wanted to hear you say it. And yeah, we've got a case. Did you hear about the Coast Guardsmen getting murdered down in Fort Lauderdale?"

"Something about it. Like a couple of months ago?"

"That's the case. I'm going to email you the file. The FBI is stuck in a ditch, as usual, the locals all deny that it was in their jurisdiction . . ."

"Send me the file," Lucas said. "Lauderdale in the winter. I can see that."

AUDREY COIL WAS NEVER charged with any crime, as two separate U.S. Attorney's Offices concluded that nothing she'd done had constituted a crime. She hadn't recommended the shooting of anyone, all she'd done was post some photos and neo-Nazi articles on the same page. The articles were protected by the constitutional provisions guarding freedom of speech and of the press, and there was nothing illegal about taking photos of people in public places and posting them.

There were mutterings in the press about fixing what appeared to be a hole in federal laws, but that quickly went away when the press realized they'd be shooting themselves in the foot.

A LAWYER FOR THE PARENTS of James Wagner, the boy killed by Dunn, announced plans to sue Audrey Coil, but nothing happened with that, because Audrey had no assets of her own. They did sue Dunn's estate and eventually got most of it, amounting to over a million dollars even after the attorney's fees. Part of the money was used to create a bronze statue of their son, which was erected in the schoolyard, showing him about to shoot a basketball. The rest of it was donated to a local animal shelter, as both mother and son had volunteered at the shelter and were committed to animal rescue.

HENDERSON CALLED A SECOND time and asked, "Can you believe it?"

"Can I believe what?"

"Audrey Coil. You don't know?"

"Oh, Jesus, she didn't—"

"No, no. She didn't get shot. Listen, I won't tell you about it, you got to see it to believe it. I'm sending you an email with a YouTube link. I'm sending it . . . now. Watch it."

Mystified, Lucas opened his email and clicked on a link. A video came up, with a freeze-frame on Audrey Coil's face, which was carefully made up to look like a Leonardo da Vinci Madonna. Her hair was covered by a white shawl, like the Virgin Mary might have worn, and a voice-over said, "Audrey Coil, by Blake Winston."

The freeze frame began to move, and then pulled back, and Audrey Coil was shown walking barefoot along a dirt path with a half dozen other women, all wearing white shawls over their hair and long white gowns that might have been sewn from bedsheets. Music: a woman and choir began singing "Down to the River to Pray" as the women walked slowly down a bank to the edge of a narrow, slow-moving river. A black preacher waited by the water's edge, and as the chorus of music swelled, the women were taken one at a time and dipped in the river, newly baptized.

When the baptisms were over, the camera tracked back to Audrey Coil, who began, "I know there's no way that I can make full recompense . . ."

Lucas was struck dumb and stayed that way for a while, walking around in his living room, running his hands through his hair.

———

JANE CHASE CALLED LUCAS a couple of weeks after he got home.

"It took me a while, but I put it all together," she said.

"Put what together?" Lucas asked.

"What you did," she said. "I wondered right from the beginning why you wanted to interview William Christopher Walton, or Bill-Boy as we now call him, at the federal lockup. I had a quiet off-the-record chat with Brett Abelman, Bill-Boy's attorney, and he told me what you did during the interview. You poked at Bill-Boy to see what would happen. He blew up and that's what you wanted to see."

"Why do you call him Bill-Boy?"

"Apparently, many years ago there was a TV series called *The Waltons* and one of the main characters was called John-Boy—but you're trying to move me away from the question of why you got Bill-Boy to blow up."

"Jane . . ."

"I thought, now why did he do that? The answer is, because you thought Dunn would react the same way. He'd be enraged and he'd go after Audrey Coil. You used a teenaged girl as a tethered goat to attract Dunn to the place where you could kill him. But how could you set up Audrey Coil? Well, you didn't know who Dunn was, so she'd have to be exposed as the creator of the website—Dunn would have to be told that the whole site was a fake. You could only reach him through the media. I talked to the media outlets that got the original tips on Audrey, and guess what? Gasp! The phone that the calls came from was a burner."

"Everybody's got one of those. Except me," Lucas said. He'd thrown the burner in the Potomac.

"And then I asked myself, why would Davenport, who'd just exposed Dunn as the killer, not even hang around to see if we could bag him right there in the Washington area? Why would he race to the Marshals Service headquarters and get a *fucking high-powered rifle* and fly out to Atlanta and then drive to Tifton before we'd even finished processing the house? Why would he lie to me about being out jogging when he was probably at National getting ready to fly?"

"I wasn't lying. Actually, I was jogging to the gate. I was a little late," Lucas said.

"The real answer to that question was," Jane Chase said, "Davenport didn't want a bunch of agents converging on Tifton and interfering with his killing of Dunn. Davenport didn't want Dunn arrested, he wanted him dead."

"Did you ever see the boy who was killed?" Lucas asked. "Or his mother? Or were they gone by the time you came down the hill, to school?"

After a moment of silence, she said, "They'd already moved the body . . ."

"You didn't see him. Didn't see his face, didn't see his mother weeping over his body. So don't give me any bullshit lectures about Dunn. Dunn got what he needed to get."

"It was murder."

"No, it was a killing," Lucas said. "But not murder. I called out to him, he fired first, and I shot back. I gave him a chance to quit and he didn't take it."

"We've only got your word for that," Jane Chase said.

"And everybody agrees my word is just fine," Lucas said. "Have you talked with Henderson or Smalls?"

"Yes. They told me to shut up and sit down. That absolutely infuriates me. I'm an attorney and a highly capable FBI agent and they told me to shut up. Big Senate bulls and I'm this cute little girl FBI agent who has to be told not to get her panties in a twist . . ."

"Jane, this is not about a patriarchal problem. Did you talk to Roberta Coil?"

More silence, then, "Yes, I did."

"What'd she say?"

"She told me to shut up and sit down."

"Maybe you should do that."

More silence, and then, *click*, and she was gone.

IT TOOK A WHILE, but both Cop (Rusty Wannamaker) and Toby Boone were convicted of different murder charges in the killing of Stephen Gibson. Wannamaker agreed to plead guilty to first-degree murder and to roll on Boone to avoid a federal trial that could have resulted in the death penalty. For his cooperation, he got life without the possibility of parole. Boone's case was more difficult, even though Wannamaker rolled on him, and he wound up pleading to conspiracy to commit murder with a negotiated fifteen-year sentence, to avoid a trial on first-degree murder.

OLD JOHN OXFORD of the American National Militia called in October.

"I see you killed the killer," he said.

"And?"

"He got what was coming to him. I wanted to let you know that after you talked to David Aline, we had some members keeping an eye on him—he knew about it in advance, we weren't spying. And sure enough, they picked up some FBI attention. I don't know exactly how you identified him and I'm not very interested in finding out. What happened, though, is that it created a change in our whole organization."

"Do tell."

"Yes. We're going to follow the model of the Irish Sinn Féin party. Do you know about them?

Lucas said, "I can Wiki it."

"They were closely tied to the IRA, but they were a legal aboveground party, while the IRA stayed underground. We're going to create an aboveground, open party and begin aboveground advocacy, while we also continue with the underground movement. Since you somehow figured out David, he and his cell will be joining me and my cell in the over-ground group."

"I have to tell you, John, I don't think you'll get a warm reception. People may cut up the government, but basically, they like it. They support it. And you essentially want to get rid of it. Try getting rid of Social Security and Medicare and you'll get your heads handed to you."

"Watch," Oxford said. "We've got too many idiots in high office, spending money that we don't have. The new culture is exposing them. Americans can only accept so much cynicism before they rebel."

"You might be right in the long run, but we live in the short run," Lucas said. "Right now, it's all very bleak. Frankly, I don't think you're the group to change that."

"Sorry to hear it," Oxford said. "When you were here, I thought I detected a bit of sympathy for the ANM. We thought you might be interested in involving yourself."

"I'm not political, John. I work with politicians, because that's the way the cards got cut, in my life anyway," Lucas said. "But I'm not political. I just don't think that way."

"Everything's political . . ."

"No. I don't believe that."

"Then what are you going to do, Davenport?" Oxford asked. "Sit on your hands as the country disintegrates?"

"I'm going to hunt," Lucas said. "That's what I do, John. I hunt."

HENDERSON CALLED A THIRD time and said, "God help me, you're the only guy I can talk to. If Porter heard about this, he'd soil his Depends." Then he broke into a near-obscene cackle.

"Jesus, Elmer, that sounds really bad, whatever it is you're gonna say."

"Roberta Coil comes up for reelection in two years and from the outside, it looks grim."

"I thought it was worse than that: I thought she was doomed."

"Over in that direction, for sure. But! But! The Republicans down there line up to take shots at various political offices, and the Ag Commissioner has been guaranteed a shot at her seat. Name of Eric Gabriel. He's already got some TV spots out there, paid for with dark money, of course, light shining on his head, and they call him the Angel Gabriel."

Another cackle.

"Go ahead and tell me. I'm pre-disgusted."

"A good ol' boy down there snuck out of the Gwinnett County courthouse with a sealed juvenile court record that involves the Angel. Turns out, when Mr. Gabriel was seventeen, he got caught diddling ten-year-old twin sisters."

"Ah, God," Lucas said.

"We're gonna unload that particular document about, mmm, three weeks before the election. Give it some time to settle in with the voters. Bob is going back to the Senate for another six years."

"Everything about that is disgusting," Lucas said.

"Hey. That's where we're at," Henderson said.

———

LUCAS TOLD WEATHER about Henderson's call and she said, "We really need to keep Coil in the Senate."

"No liberal disgust?"

"Well, Roberta Coil didn't do anything."

"C'mon, Weather."

"C'mon yourself," she said.

"How come everybody in politics is a snake?" Lucas asked.

"It's like your friend Elmer said—that's where we're at." She shook her head and asked, "How's the Coast Guard file coming?"

"Interesting," Lucas said. They were in the living room and he picked up a fat manila folder full of computer printouts that had been sitting on a coffee table.

"You look happy," she said.

"Well, they've got some bad boys running around in Lauderdale. *Bad* boys."

An off-duty Coast Guardsman is fishing with his family when some suspicious behavior from a nearby boat catches his eye. It's a snazzy craft, zipping along in front of him until it slows to pick up a surfaced diver . . . a diver who was apparently alone, in the middle of the ocean. None of it makes sense and his hunch is proved right when all three Guardsmen who come to investigate are shot and killed. The case is automatically the FBI's turf. But when the FBI's investigation stalls out, they must call in Lucas Davenport. And when his case turns lethal, Davenport will need to bring in every asset he can claim, including the notorious Virgil Flowers.

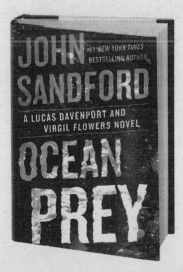

CHAPTER

ONE

Five years earlier, the high school guidance counselor sat Barney Hall down and said, "Barney, you're bright enough, but you're not college material. Not yet." He was looking over Hall's standard test scores and other accumulated records from thirteen years in the Lower Cape May Regional School District. "You're not mature for your age. If you hadn't been sent to detention once a week, you wouldn't have done any studying at all."

Hall was a cheerful, good-looking, middle-sized kid with broad shoulders and bright white teeth, who must have said a hundred times in his life, "Watch this—and hey, hold my beer, willya?"

He had a girlfriend named Sue, who he'd known since fourth grade, who was happy to hold his beer, most of the time, and then apply the bandages afterwards. Hall worked after school and all summers as a mechanic in his dad's yacht salvage yard, or junkyard, depending on who was doing the talking.

"I'm trying to do better, sir," he told the counselor.

"Don't bullshit me, son. Would I be correct in believing that you were drinking beer at Toby Jones's wedding last weekend and got drunk and fell off the dock and damn near drowned?"

"I'm a good swimmer, sir. There was no danger."

"That's not the point, Barney. Anyway, if you want to do anything in life, you need to get serious, and right quick. Knowing you, looking at these records, I'm thinking your best course would be the military. The military would give you responsibility from day one. If you don't come through, they'll slap your ass in the brig. You need that discipline. Mind, I'm not saying the Marine Corps. You're way too smart for that."

"I wasn't thinking college, not right away," Hall said. "I've been talking with Sue, and . . . how about the Coast Guard, sir? There're some Coasties that hang out at my dad's place and I like listening to them talk. I've been on the water and working on boats all my life."

The counselor poked a finger at him: "That's the smartest thing I ever heard you say, Barney. You do a few years in the Coast Guard, get yourself some rank and responsibility and they'll even send you to college when you're ready. God help me, you could wind up an officer."

"Whoa. That'd be awesome, sir."

"And do me a favor, son. Get rid of that T-shirt." The T-shirt featured a basketball-sized, full-color image of a bantam rooster, with the legend, "Everything's bigger in Texas."

Hall looked down at the T-shirt. "It's just a chicken, sir."

"It's a cock," the counselor said. "You know it and I know it. I don't want to see it in this school again."

HALL MARRIED SUE in the June after high school graduation, joined the Coast Guard at the end of a glorious summer, and after boot camp and advanced training, was stationed in Fort Lauderdale.

Sue Hall went to Broward College, became a registered nurse, and started working on a bachelor's degree in nursing. Hall found the boatyards of Marina Mile to be the most amazing places he'd ever been. When Sue got pregnant with their first one, he got off-duty work rebuilding diesel engines in one of the Marina Mile engine shops. The extra work would get them child-care money so Sue could finish her BS degree.

At night, they'd drink PBR under palm trees in their trailer park, until Sue got pregnant, when they switched to ginger ale, and she'd say, "Barnes, we're gonna do good in life. I can feel it coming on."

The owner of the engine shop had a pile of old boats out back, which he couldn't sell, and Hall kept looking at a 1999 Boston Whaler Outrage 260 which had been stripped of the twin outboards and had a hole in the hull, and now sat derelict atop a tandem trailer with two flat tires on each side, overgrown with weeds. After some talk, the owner agreed to give Hall the boat along with two badly abused, but salvageable, Merc 225s and the trailer—all Hall had to do was work five additional unpaid hours a week, in the evenings and on weekends, on top of his regular weekend shift, for two years, and the boat was his.

Plus, he could use the shop and its tools to rehab the trailer and the Mercs and do whatever fiberglass work the boat needed. The boat was solid, except for the hole, which could be fixed.

THAT'S THE ENTIRE backstory as to why Hall, Sue, and their first boy, Lance, almost a one-year-old, were trolling down the debris line on the outer reef south of Pompano Beach, Florida, looking for dorado—mahimahi—when Hall spotted something unusual happening with a snazzy-looking Mako center-console a half-mile ahead of them. He said, "Sue, hand me the glasses."

The Mako had two white outboards hanging off the back, which Hall recognized as big 350s, giving the boat seven hundred horses with which to get across the ocean.

"What's out there, Barnes?" Sue asked. She was a rangy young woman, would have been a cowgirl in Texas, sunburnt, fighter-pilot blue eyes, her rose-blonde hair frizzy from saltwater.

"Something strange going on, babe. I've been watching him, 'cause that's a sharp boat. All of a sudden it slowed down and stopped and it looks like it picked up a diver in the middle of the ocean. I mean, who was already in the middle of the ocean before they got there. Went right to him."

"You don't see that every day," Sue said.

Hall was still on the glasses. "He's, uh, looks like they've got some lift bags coming over the side . . . in the middle of the ocean."

"Maybe picking up some bugs?" She was referring to spiny lobsters.

"From a guy they left in the middle of the ocean?"

Sue said, with a sudden urgency, "Barnes, I've got a bad feeling about this. Let's turn around. Bring the boat back north."

"Yeah." That seemed like a good idea.

Hall turned the boat in a wide fisherman's semi-circle and headed back north, but kept watching the Mako through the glasses. He was careful to be standing behind the center console when he used the binoculars, because he'd learned early in his Coast Guard training that if you saw somebody whose arms, head and chest formed an equal-lateral triangle, they were looking at you through binoculars—and every few minutes, one of the men on the Mako would check them out with binoculars.

Twenty minutes after it stopped, the sleek-looking craft lurched forward and headed south. Hall got his cell phone, called into the watch officer at the Coast Guard station at Fort Lauderdale.

"Sir, this is Barney Hall. I'm south of Pompano

Beach in my own boat, but I saw something strange out here. There's a black-and-white Mako 284 heading toward Port Everglades. We saw him picking up something from the middle of the ocean. He was running fast, then stopped, and there was a diver waiting for him right there in the water. There were no other boats around, no dive flag. They were using lift bags . . ."

"Can you stay with him, Hall?"

"No sir, not entirely, he's running fast. I can keep him in sight until he makes the turn. I'll be a mile back of him by then."

"He looked suspicious?"

"Yes, he did, sir. If I was on duty, I'd stop him, for sure."

"We'll do that, then. We'll have somebody waiting for him inside."

HALL TOLD SUE to put on her life jacket and bring in the fishing lines; the baby was already wrapped in a fat orange PFD. He turned the boat and they tracked the Mako until it made the turn into the Port Everglades cut. Hall got back on his phone and called the watch officer and said, "It's Hall, sir, he's making the turn."

"We're on it, Hall. Good job."

THE MAKO WAS ambushed by a Coast Guard RIB— rigid inflatable boat—which had orange inflatable tubes wrapped around a hard-shell hull. The Petty Officer

Second Class who was running the boat got on Channel 16 and called, "Mako 284 *Chevere* this is the United States Coast Guard coming up behind to make a courtesy inspection. Cut your speed to five knots and hold your course. We'll board you from the starboard side."

Coast Guard inspection boats were usually larger RIBs with pilot houses; the boat that had been scrambled to intercept the Mako was smaller, three men aboard, no pilot house. The Coast Guard boat pulled up behind the Mako and the petty officer in the bow saw two men waiting in the stern—bulky guys, dressed like sport fishermen, bright-colored shirts and shorts, sunglasses and billed hats.

Then, as they were a few feet off, ready to board, one of the men on the stern of the Mako lifted up a heavy long-nosed black rifle with a red-dot sight. With a motion that was practiced and almost graceful, he shot the two Coast Guardsmen in the bow, and then twice shot the PO2 who was running the boat. The four shots together took no more than two seconds. The gun barked rather than banged, a flat noise because of the suppressor on the barrel; the gunshots were loud, but not especially audible over the sound of the boat engines.

The PO2 had killed the boat's speed for the boarding and when he saw the rifle come up he reached forward to hit the accelerator, but a bullet took him in the throat and then another in the chest, and the slugs turned him away and he fell into the bottom of the boat, dying, blood spreading around him on the wet floor, a purple flood. The Coast Guard boat turned into a slow circle across the wide port and the Mako accelerated away.

AS THE MAKO left, Hall, Sue, and the baby nosed through the cut in their rehabbed Whaler and saw the Coast Guard boat turning away from it.

Hall watched for a moment, then said, "There's something wrong, Sue."

"Get over there," Sue said. "That Mako's running like a thief in the night. I'll get the gun." They kept a .38 Special in a waterproof can down an equipment hatch.

Hall pushed the boat as hard as he could, but they were a full minute away from the Coast Guard RIB. He couldn't see anybody aboard as he approached. He slipped his cell phone out of his pocket, but when he got alongside, he saw the three bodies in the bottom of the boat. He dropped the cell phone, grabbed the VHF, and screamed, "Mayday, Mayday, Mayday, Port Everglades, three Coast Guards shot in boat chasing black-and-white Mako . . ."

The Coast Guard came back instantly: "Mayday caller identify yourself!"

"This is Coast Guard Petty Officer Two Barney Hall. We have three men shot inside the Port Everglades entrance. They look bad, man, they look really bad."

Then the watch officer: "Hall, can you help them? We're on the way, but you gotta do what you can . . ."

"My wife's a nurse, I'm putting her on board, sir. Should I go with her or go after the Mako?"

There were several seconds of silence—Sue had handed him the .38, and was already clambering into the Coast Guard boat with the baby and their first aid kit—and then the officer came back: "Your call, Hall. Chopper's coming, but it'll be a few minutes."

Hall looked down at his wife who had checked one man quickly and then moved to the bow. She'd done two years in emergency rooms and she knew what she was seeing; she looked back at him and shook her head and Hall shouted into the radio, "I'm going after the sonsofbitches, sir."

HE DROPPED THE hammer on the Whaler. The Mako was most of a half-mile ahead of him, moving fast down the Intracoastal Waterway, and there was no way Hall would have caught the other boat if the Mako hadn't swerved to a pier, where three men jumped off. One ran to a parked SUV, opened it, and backed it to the edge of the pier. Two others ran what looked like black buckets to the white SUV. A fourth man was still on the boat, carrying more black buckets to the bow. They were in a frantic hurry: radios automatically monitored channel 16, so they'd heard Hall's Mayday and the Coast Guard's response.

After moving more buckets to the bow of the boat, the fourth man hoisted a five-gallon gas can out of a hatch on the Mako's stern and began spraying the boat with gasoline and then, as Hall roared toward them, stepped off the boat, lit what looked like a piece of newspaper and threw it toward the Mako. The boat exploded in flame.

The three men who'd been loading the black buckets into the SUV jumped into the car and the fourth man ran up to the back door and yanked it open. Hall had the .38 in his hand—he was close enough to feel the heat from the flames—and fired three wild shots at the car, no hope of hitting anything because the careening Whaler was pounding the deck against his feet, making any kind of an accurate shot almost impossible.

And impossibly, one of his shots hit the fourth man in the head.

The man dropped flat on the concrete pier, stone-cold dead. The driver of the car jumped out, grabbed the man by his shirt, looked at him, dropped him, looked for a moment at Hall, his face unreadable behind dark glasses, then leaped back into the car and spun it out of sight.

The Mako was burning like a torch.

The watch officer was shouting, "Hall, Hall where are you?"

"Look for the fire, sir; I'm south of the cut where the fire's at."

FOR HIS ACTIONS, Hall was given the Coast Guard Medal. Other than the man killed by Hall, none of the men on the Mako or in the car were caught or even identified. The dead man was a minor hoodlum from Miami Beach, who the feds called a "known associate," though he appeared to be an associate of every piece of scum on the Beach, which was a lot of scum.

The Mako's Florida registration was real enough; the owner wasn't. The fire, which sank the boat, wiped out fingerprints and DNA. The SUV was never identified or found. No gun was found on the sunken boat or in the area around it.

Hall was presented the medal by the rear admiral who commanded the Coast Guard's District Seven. When the admiral asked him his plans, Hall said, "My hitch is almost up, sir. I'm going to college at FIU. If I go full-time, I'll be out in three years. Then I might be back, if I can get into OCS. I really like what we do."

The admiral patted him on the shoulder with some affection. "You'll get in. With your history, I can guarantee it. Get a degree in something useful."

"I'm thinking crime science," Hall said.

"That'll work," the admiral said.

"Sir, if you don't mind. I do have a question."

"Go ahead."

"Nobody's been caught for killing our guys," Hall said. "Where's the FBI?"

"I asked that exact same question a couple of weeks ago, but I wasn't as polite as you are," the admiral said. "I asked, 'Where the fuck is the FBI?' The answer was, 'Nowhere,' and you can quote me on that."

CHAPTER

TWO

Virgil Flowers left the courtroom and caught an elevator going down. He turned as the doors began to close and a dark-haired hatchet-faced woman in an old blue floral dress, carrying an antique white woven handbag, standing outside in the hallway, looked straight into his eyes and held them. She was only a foot or two from the elevator doors, but made no effort to step inside.

When the elevator doors closed, a woman next to Virgil said, "Well, that was weird. I thought she was going to shoot you."

"Couldn't get a gun in the courthouse," Virgil said. A couple of people behind him laughed, more nervously than heartily.

Virgil worked his way down to the Hennepin Government Center's basement cafeteria, where he spotted Lucas Davenport sitting at a table to one side, legs crossed, reading a free newspaper. Davenport saw him at the same time and waved. He'd walked to the courthouse from the federal building.

Virgil went over and shook hands and asked, "You eat?"

"Not yet. I wasn't sure when you'd get out." Davenport was a tall man, but thin, weathered, and athletic, dark hair shot with gray and crystalline blue eyes; he was fifty-two, and looked his age. He was wearing a blue woolen suit jacket, a white dress shirt, black woolen slacks and cap-toed dress shoes; a light cashmere coat was draped over the back of his chair. He might have been a prosperous attorney, but he wasn't.

"What's that?" Virgil asked, nodding at a two-inch thick brown file envelope sitting by Davenport's right hand.

"Maybe a case," Lucas said. "I'm thinking about it." He stuck a hand in a jacket pocket, pulled out a twenty-dollar bill and handed it to Virgil. "Get me cheeseburger, fries, and a Diet Coke."

"What, I'm a waitress now?"

"I'm saving the table," Lucas said. "Or would you rather eat standing up?"

Virgil came back a few minutes later with a tray, scraped out a chair, put the food down, and said in a quiet voice, "There's a woman sitting behind me . . . don't look right away, be casual about it. She's wearing an old blue dress with flowers and has a white handbag sitting on the table."

He sat down and Lucas looked casually past his

shoulder and checked the woman. He turned back to Virgil and picked up his cheeseburger and asked, "Who is she?"

"She's the wife of the guy I testified against. He's going to prison for ten years or so."

"What'd he do?"

"Robbed credit unions. One every three or four months, down in southern Minnesota and northern Iowa. I caught him a couple of months ago, in Blue Earth. He was the family's sole support."

"She does look mean. I'd be worried, if I were you," Lucas said. "Did you get mustard?"

"Only ketchup. I don't think she's armed, but . . ." Virgil picked up a piece of silverware and waggled it at Lucas. " . . . I'd rather not have a fork stuck in my eye."

"Not to worry. If she rushes you, I'll put three Hydra-Shoks through her bellybutton."

"Thank you, I'd appreciate it," Virgil said. Davenport got up, went to the cafeteria line, and came back with three packages of mustard. Through a forkful of hot macaroni and cheese, Virgil said, "Frankie says hello."

"How are the twins?"

"Loud. Very loud. Relentless," Virgil said. The twins, one of each, were two months old. "Frankie would need about six tits to keep them happy—don't ever tell her I said that. My mother's down there with them. I get two hours of sleep a night."

"I thought you were keeping your mother away?"

"That would be like keeping gravity away," Virgil said. "Not gonna happen. She still staring at me?"

"Still staring," Lucas said, watching Virgil's stalker from the corner of his eye.

"I can feel her eyes burning a hole in the back of my neck," Virgil said.

Lucas asked, "What happened with your novel?"

Virgil had been writing wildlife magazine articles for years, but since the previous winter had been working on a thriller novel. Lucas was one of the few people who knew about it. Virgil said, "Didn't fly. Not good enough."

"You gonna give up?"

"No. I've got this agent in New York. She told me that I could make a living at it, but I didn't know what I was doing yet. She gave me some ideas, and I'm starting over."

"You can do it," Lucas said. "I'll be bragging to people that I know you."

Virgil was as tall as Lucas, but with blond hair worn too long for an agent of the Minnesota Department of Criminal Apprehension. He was wearing his court clothes, a gray suit, white shirt and blue necktie, an ensemble unsettled by his cowboy boots, though the snakeskin was well-polished. He poked his fork at the brown file envelope next to Lucas's hand. "What's the case?"

"Three Coast Guardsmen got shot to death a few months ago, down in Fort Lauderdale," Lucas said. "Broad daylight. Nothing's happened on that. Nothing."

"I remember reading about it."

"The FBI has been investigating, but haven't been getting anywhere," Lucas said. "The thought was floated by a U.S. Senator from Florida that maybe the Marshals Service could take a look."

"Was the senator one of your political godfathers?"

"No, but people talk," Lucas said. "He called me directly."

"So when he suggested the Marshals Service might take a look, he meant you. Personally," Virgil said.

"Yes. That didn't go over real well—it implied that the FBI wasn't getting anywhere," Lucas said.

"Which they weren't."

"True, but the implication was resented. The FBI has a lot more clout in the Justice Department than the Marshals Service and they've been peeing on our shoes. Actually, my shoes," Lucas said. "The longer the case stretches out with no progress, the more pressure . . . Uh, the woman with the handbag got up, she's . . ." Virgil pulled his head down. " . . . going to the cafeteria line."

"Check what she orders. I've seen a woman get burned bad by a slice of hot pizza. Red hot, stuck to her face, couldn't get it off," Virgil said, resisting the urge to look at the woman. "Anyway, you're tangled up in a bureaucratic feud. What are you going to do?"

"I've been reading the files," Lucas said. "They keep coming, but they never have much in them. Lots of paperwork. The feeling is, we're dealing with drug smugglers and the drug is most likely heroin, and it may be coming in from Colombia, but nobody knows for sure."

"That's it? That's all they got?"

"The Coast Guard says that a freighter probably dumped a bunch of heroin in water-tight containers on a reef off Lauderdale. It was being recovered by a diver from a fishing boat, and when the Coast Guard tried to stop the boat, three Coast Guardsmen got shot and killed and the boat was burned to get rid of biologic evidence. A Coast Guardsman killed one of the smugglers, but the rest got away. The Coast Guard has been watching the general area of the dump, but they haven't seen any more recovery efforts. Maybe it's all gone. Then again, the Broward County sheriff has picked up rumors that it's still sitting out there."

"Has anybody been looking for the stuff? Navy divers?" Virgil asked.

"Yeah, that's mentioned in the files, but the search area is large, the water is really deep for divers and the visibility isn't all that good," Lucas said. "They had one of those remote-control submarines looking for a while, but didn't find anything."

"Then how are the smugglers finding it?"

"They've probably got precise GPS coordinates that'll put them right on top of the containers," Lucas said. "The Coast Guard thinks the containers may have some kind of proximity device—push a button on a transceiver and it sends out a locator beep. That's what they tell me, anyway."

"Huh. What do you think you could do? You're not

a diver, you don't know shit about submarines or GPS. If the feds . . ."

Lucas said, "Your friend bought two slices of pizza."

Virgil: "When I went by there, the pizza was so hot the cheese was bubbling . . . What's she doing now?"

"Staring at you. Carrying the pizza to her table . . . Okay, she's sitting down. She's eating the pizza. Still staring."

"It's creeping me out," Virgil said.

"It's creeping me out and I'm not even you," Lucas said.

Virgil wrenched the conversation back to the heroin dump. "What could you do down in Lauderdale? Other than get out of Minnesota in November?"

"What could I do? That's what I've been thinking about," Lucas said. "The FBI doesn't do confrontation. We need some confrontation to shake things up. Push people around. Deal some get-out-of-jail cards in return for information. Street-cop stuff. Find out who gets upset."

"You're gonna do it?"

"I dunno. Those meatheads at the FBI . . ." Lucas stroked his chin with a thumb and forefinger, staring past Virgil, not at the woman, but at the blank wall to one side. Virgil let him stare, uninterrupted. Then, abruptly, Lucas looked back at Virgil and said, "Yeah. I'm gonna do it."

move. . . . As readers follow Davenport in his pursuit, Sandford uses quick pacing and sharp dialogue to keep the plot moving. Multiple twists and turns are thrown in for good measure, all leading up to a Sandford-esque ending." —*The Real Book Spy*

"Sandford's power of storytelling shines through the pages." —*Mystery Tribune*

"An exciting tale full of warped characters, clever plot twists, and vengeful violence. Sandford is in fine form, smoothly adding touches of dark humor and masterfully building the tension, chapter by chapter." —*Lansing State Journal*

"If *Golden Prey* doesn't make you an instant fan of the series, you may not have a pulse. . . . Sandford changes the narrative points of view frequently, keeping things moving at breakneck speed and providing enough action for at least a couple of books, [yet] leaving the reader wanting more, more, more." —Bookreporter.com

JOHN SANDFORD

"If you haven't read Sandford yet, you have been missing one of the great summer-read novelists of all time."
—Stephen King

For a complete list of titles and to sign up for our newsletter, please visit prh.com/JohnSandford